MUSIC FROM ANOTHER WORLD

Also by Robin Talley

Lies We Tell Ourselves
What We Left Behind
As I Descended
Our Own Private Universe
Pulp

ROBIN TALLEY

MUSIC FROM ANOTHER WORLD

inkyard
press

ISBN-13: 978-1-335-14677-9

Music from Another World

This edition published by arrangement with Harlequin Books S.A.

For questions and comments about the quality of this book, please contact us at CustomerService@Harlequin.com.

Inkyard Press
22 Adelaide St. West, 40th Floor
Toronto, Ontario M5H 4E3, Canada
www.InkyardPress.com

Printed in U.S.A.

MUSIC FROM ANOTHER WORLD

SUMMER, 1977

Wednesday, June 1, 1977

Introducing the California Pen Pal Project

Dear girls,

Welcome to our first annual California pen pal project! Over the next five months, this project will foster exciting new friendships and strengthen the faith of the incoming junior girls at New Way Christian Academy and Holy Angels Catholic School.

At the bottom of this letter are the names of one girl from each school. To earn credit for this assignment, you must write at least two letters each month to your assigned pen pal and complete a final report by the end of first term in November.

You should answer at least one of the following questions in each letter, and include summaries of your pen pal's responses in your final report.

Pen Pal Questions
1. Describe yourself using three adjectives.
2. Who are the members of your family?
3. What are your favorite hobbies?

4. What is your favorite television program?
5. How do you plan to maintain your strong Christian morality this summer despite the temptations of modern society?
6. What is your favorite Bible story, and why?
7. Do you have any interesting activities planned for this summer?
8. What is it like living in your part of California?
9. What is your favorite subject in school, and why?
10. How can you and your new pen pal support each other in your spiritual challenges as you transition into your final years of high school and the new lives that await you after graduation?

Pen pal pairing:
—Tammy Larson (New Way Christian Academy, Ocean Valley, CA)
—Sharon Hawkins (Holy Angels Catholic School, San Francisco, CA)

Tuesday, June 7, 1977

Dear Harvey,

I hope it's okay for me to call you Harvey. In school, when they taught us to write letters, they said adults should always be addressed as "Mr." or "Mrs.," but from what I've read in the newspaper, you don't seem much like the adults I know. I'd feel wrong calling you "Mr. Milk."

Besides, it's not as if I'm ever going to send you this letter. I've never kept a diary before, but things have been getting harder lately, and tonight might be the hardest night of all. I need someone I can talk to. Even if you can't answer back.

Plus, I told Aunt Mandy I couldn't join the prayer circle because I had too much homework. Tomorrow's the last day of school, so I don't have any homework, but she doesn't know that. If I keep writing in this notebook, maybe she'll think homework is really what I'm doing.

I guess I <u>could</u> write to my new "pen pal" instead. That might count as homework. It would be closer than writing a fake letter to a famous San Francisco homosexual, anyway, but I can't handle the thought of writing to some stranger right now.

Technically <u>you're</u> a stranger, too, Harvey, but you don't feel like one. That's why I wanted to write to you, instead of "Dear Diary" or something.

It's ironic, though, that my pen pal lives in San Francisco, too. I wonder if she's ever met you. How big is the city, anyway? I read a magazine article that said gay people could hold hands walking down the street there, and no one minds. Is that true?

Ugh. The prayer circle's starting over. Brett and Carolyn are leading the Lord's Prayer again. It's probably the only prayer they know.

We've been cooped up in the church basement for five hours now—my whole family, plus the youth group, plus a bunch of the other Protect Our Children volunteers. Along with Aunt Mandy and Uncle Russell, of course. The results from Miami should come in any minute.

You probably already know this—wait, who am I kidding? Of course you know, Harvey—but there was a vote today in Florida. They were voting on homosexuality, so our church, New Way Baptist, was heavily involved, even though we're on the opposite side of the country. Everyone in our youth group was required to volunteer. I worked in the office Aunt Mandy and Uncle Russell set up in their den, answering phones and putting together mailings and counting donations to the New Way Protect Our Children Fund. We had bake sales and car washes to raise money to send to Anita Bryant, too.

You know all about Anita Bryant, obviously. You're probably just as scared of her as I am. Although, come to think of it, whenever I see you in the newspaper, you look the opposite of afraid. In pictures, you're always smiling.

Don't you get anxious, having everyone know? I'm terrified all the time, and no one even knows about me yet. I hope they never find out.

Maybe I should pray for <u>that</u>. Ha.

Okay, the Lord's Prayer is over and now Uncle Russell's making everyone silently call on God to save the good Christians of Florida from sin. I hope I can keep writing without getting in trouble.

<u>Ugh</u>, look at them all, showing off how devout they are. The only two people in this room who aren't clasping their hands in front of them and moving their lips dramatically are me and Aunt Mandy, but that's because I'm a grievous sinner—obviously—and Aunt Mandy keeps peeking out from her shut eyes at the phone next to her.

I'm not sure how much you can concentrate on God when you're solely focused on being ready to snatch up the receiver the second it starts to shake. Maybe she'll grab it so hard, it'll crush to a pulp in her fist like one of Anita Bryant's fucking Florida oranges.

I wonder what <u>you're</u> doing tonight, Harvey. Probably waiting by your phone, too. Only you're in San Francisco, and if you're praying, you're praying for the opposite of what Aunt Mandy and everyone else in our church basement is praying for.

It seems pointless to pray now, though. The votes have already been cast, so we're just waiting to hear the results. There's a reporter from my aunt and uncle's favorite radio station in L.A. sitting at the back of the room, ready to interview Uncle Russell once we know what happened. Even though we basically already do.

My mom showed up at church tonight with a box of balloons from the supermarket, but Aunt Mandy wouldn't let anyone touch them until the announcement, so at the moment the box is sitting in the closet under a stack of old communion trays. The second that phone starts to ring, though,

I just bet Aunt Mandy's going to haul out that box and make us all start blowing up those crappy balloons.

I wonder if you've heard of my aunt. She wants you to. She knows exactly who <u>you</u> are, of course—you're her enemy.

Which makes me your enemy, too, I guess. I'm not eighteen, and it's not as if I could've voted in an election in Miami even if I were, but I've still spent the past two months folding up comic books about the destruction of Sodom to mail out to churches in Florida.

I'm a soldier for Christ. That's what Aunt Mandy calls me, anyway. And since I do everything she says, she must be right.

Writing to you instead of praying with the others is the closest I've ever come to rebelling. That's how much of a coward I am, Harvey.

I wish I had the nerve to tell my aunt to go shove it. That's what I'd <u>really</u> pray for—the nerve, I mean. If I thought prayer ever helped anything.

Shit, the phone's ringing. More later.

Tammy

Dear Diary,

I've never seen anything like what I saw tonight. Or felt anything like it, either.

I need to write about what happened. It's almost midnight and I don't know if I can fit this all in one entry before I fall asleep, but I've got to get down as much as I can.

It all started when my brother didn't come home.

He said he'd be back from work in time to watch the network news with us. Instead it was just me and Mom watching static creep in from the edges of the screen as the reporter in Miami adjusted his wide, striped tie. I waited one minute, then two, to see if he'd correct himself—maybe he'd made a mistake, or someone had given him the wrong information—but he kept droning on about Anita Bryant winning by a landslide as more and more of his face got scrambled.

The sound came through strong as ever, though, and his story never changed. The vote was two to one against homosexuality. Anita Bryant and her cronies had done what they'd sworn to do. The gay rights ordinance in Miami was getting repealed.

"Sharon, see if you can get the rabbit ears to work," Mom said, but she wasn't looking at the screen. Her eyes were fixed on the clock.

I climbed to my feet and fiddled with the antenna. By the time
the static cleared, Anita Bryant herself was on the screen. She was
standing on a stage in some hotel ballroom, talking proudly about
how the "normal majority" had won and the militant homosexuals
had lost. She was wearing at least fifty pounds' worth of lipstick and
eye shadow, and I wanted to throw a glass of orange juice straight
at her painted-on face.

Anita Bryant's the person my brother hates most in the world,
and since my brother's the person I love most in the world, I hate
Anita Bryant, too.

She's got this inexplicable obsession with gay people. I don't really understand why some men want to be with other men, either,
but I also don't understand why she seems to spend so much time
thinking about it. There are probably a lot more homosexuals here
in San Francisco than there are in Florida, but it's not as if they
bother anyone. I'd never even met a homosexual until I found out
my brother was gay.

I'm the only one who knows that about him, though. I'm the only
one who can. If Mom ever found out... I don't want to think about
what she'd do.

"I shouldn't stay up much later, I'm afraid." Mom's eyes were
still on the clock. "Neither should you. Have you already done your
homework?"

"Tomorrow's the last day." I messed with the rabbit ears some
more until the static was mostly gone. "No homework tonight. All
I have to do from now until September is write to that new pen pal
the school gave me down in Orange County."

"Oh, that's right. I suppose after nine months of teaching, my
brain's gotten as foggy as those seventh-graders'. Well, all the same,
we have to be at school on time." Mom bounced her foot on the
lumpy carpet. The Miami report was over, and now the network

anchor was talking about Queen Elizabeth. "Your brother's never been this late before."

I wished Mom wouldn't talk about Peter. I was already worried enough about him without having to worry about how worried <u>she</u> was.

The Miami vote was all he'd talked about for the past week, whenever Mom wasn't around to hear us. His shift at Javier's Groceries had ended more than an hour ago. Mom had called the store to check on him, but no one answered. I'd snuck into the kitchen when Mom wasn't paying attention and tried calling the pay phone at the back of Javi's, the one next to the walk-in cooler that no one but Peter and I ever use, but no one picked up that line, either.

"Should I call Kevin?" I asked. Kevin's my boyfriend, and he goes to Javi's for a Coke almost every night after he gets off work. "I can find out if he saw Peter."

"No, no. I'm sure your brother's fine. Besides, it's too late for phone calls." Mom stood up and switched off the TV, stretching her arms over her head. She was trying to pretend things were normal, but I'd learned how to see through <u>that</u> act by the second grade. "Up to bed with both of us."

I followed her silently up the stairs, but I couldn't imagine going to sleep.

Peter may not talk to Mom about everything, but it isn't like him to stay out late without telling <u>me</u>.

If he'd heard about the vote, he would've been upset. Maybe he heard the news on the radio and was too depressed to come home. If he was at the store, though, why hadn't he answered when we called?

I paced across my bedroom. Forward, backward, and again. Then a third time.

My brother and I used to share this room, and it still feels too big for just me. My twin bed is shoved up against one wall, with my dresser across from it. There isn't much in between except a desk I never use and a laundry basket that's always overflowing, because Mom says I'm old enough to do my own laundry, but I always forget.

My walls have posters tacked on them, but they're old posters I barely notice anymore—Fonzie and Charlie's Angels and the Jackson 5. I should take them down, but I don't know what I'd put up instead. When I was younger, it was easier to know what I liked. Lately, I keep changing my mind about everything.

I waited until I heard Mom come out of the bathroom, her footsteps fading down the hall, before I cracked open my door. Peter's room is right next to mine, but his door was firmly shut—no hint of light shining around the cracks. I checked to make sure Mom was definitely gone before I twisted the knob.

The tiny lamp perched on his windowsill was dark. The room's only illumination was a pale yellow stream coming from the streetlight in the alley, filtered through the old yarwood tree that bumps up against our house. The echo of light crept across Peter's floor as the wind shifted the branches.

His bed took up three quarters of the floor space. Peter's room is so tiny we used to use it as a storage closet, until one afternoon when I was in third grade and he was in fourth, and I came home from Girl Scouts to find his half of our shared room empty. He'd hauled all the musty old boxes of baby clothes that had filled the storage room up to our tiny attic, then hung his 49ers pennant on the wall and jammed his bed in across from the window.

Mom tried to argue with him about it, but she didn't try very hard. That night when I got up to get a glass of water, I overheard her on the downstairs phone, telling Dad to come visit.

"Peter needs a man in his life," she was saying in a low, shaky voice.

Her words sounded strange then, and they seem utterly absurd now. Peter needed a lot of things as a kid—we both did—but our dad wasn't one of them. He never did come visit after her call, but he sent his check on time for once.

I turned around in the tight space, then shut Peter's door and perched on the corner of his bed, my eyes adjusting to the dim light. The pit that had formed in my stomach when the anchor first announced the vote results was growing.

I couldn't just sit there, waiting. I couldn't shake the fear that Peter had done something dangerous after he heard the news. He's never been great at being careful.

We're opposites in a lot of ways, my brother and me. When our dad's parents took us to Disneyland, I stuck to Dumbo and Peter Pan, but Peter went on the Matterhorn Bobsleds so many times, he threw up in the bushes outside It's a Small World. If that had happened to me I'd have hidden under a palm tree and refused to show my face for the rest of the day, but Peter just got in line for the roller coaster all over again.

He's never seemed to care if he stands out. I asked him once if it bothered him when the boys teased him at school, and he just shrugged and pointed to all the Xs on the calendar hanging on his wall. He crosses off every day, he told me, counting down until he gets out of high school and can start his real life.

I wish I knew when _my_ real life would start. There's never been a single place where I really fit. I try to act as if I do, of course, but it always feels like exactly that—_acting_. Even with my friends.

It's that way with Kevin sometimes, too. We've been together long enough now that being with him is easier than being with anyone else—well, except my brother—but sometimes, I can't help noticing that the way Kevin thinks seems so different from the way _I_ do. As if we might as well be living on two different planets. I told Peter that once, and said it was because Kevin lived on Planet Pretentious.

I sat on Peter's bed, wringing my hands, trying to think. Mom was probably already out cold. When I get anxious I can't sleep, but when Mom's worried, she does nothing <u>but</u> sleep.

It wasn't as if she'd have agreed to let me go out looking for Peter regardless. Our neighborhood is friendly and quiet—relatively—but it's still the city, and it's dangerous for a girl to be out at night. Last year a bum grabbed my butt when I was walking past the old firehouse on Brazil Avenue in my school kilt, and that was in the middle of the day.

The wind picked up, the yarwood leaves brushing Peter's window. A twig got stuck in the frame. I reached across the narrow space, unlatched the window, and pushed it up, snaking an arm out to dislodge the branch. It was chilly outside, and I shivered in my thin blouse.

I wondered if Peter had ever thought about climbing out this window and into the yarwood tree. If my room had a window on this side of the house, would I have thought about it?

I glanced down at the alley two stories below. It was probably full of rats and garbage and who knew what else.

Still, though...

The twig tapped against the windowpane again.

I stood up. My heart was already pounding, but I didn't give myself time to worry. No matter what happened, I couldn't just <u>sit</u> there, waiting.

I grabbed a sweatshirt off Peter's bed, pulled it over my head, and hoisted myself onto the windowsill without looking down. My hands jittered as I stretched out to press the tips of my fingers against the branches, testing their weight.

Peter and I used to climb the trees in Golden Gate Park when we were kids. I didn't break my neck back then. There was no reason to think I would tonight.

Maybe if I told myself that enough times, I'd start to believe it.

The third branch I checked seemed strong enough to support my weight, and I didn't pause, not even to take a breath, before I swung out the window.

The momentum carried me too far. I was going to fall—I was certain of it—but then I swung back the other way and wrapped both arms around the branch as tightly as I could. My dangling legs felt like sodden weights threatening to pull me down, but I kicked forward blindly until I made contact with the trunk.

There was no turning back now.

I forced myself to look down, to study the angles of the branches below me. There was a thick one just below my right foot.

I inched the toe of my sneaker toward it, sending up silent, fervent prayers without taking my eyes off the branch. God must've heard me, because the next thing I knew the branch was solid beneath my shoe.

I told myself I wasn't afraid.

I wasn't. I couldn't let myself be.

I lowered myself branch by branch, trying to take deep, steady breaths, but I was starting to panic. Only when my sneakers finally met asphalt did I genuinely think I might be capable of this.

When I looked up, the tree towered over me. I couldn't believe I'd climbed down that thing on my own. Finding my brother before something else went wrong couldn't possibly be harder than <u>that</u>.

I headed quickly for the store, sticking to the darkest parts of the alley so our neighbors wouldn't see me. There was no sign of anyone outside, but the alley air smelled distinctly like pee, and there were enough broken beer bottles and cigarette butts that it was clear people <u>did</u> go there sometimes. Which people, I didn't want to know. I tugged the sleeves of Peter's sweatshirt down over my hands and moved fast, trying not to peer too deeply into the shadows I passed along the way.

When I reached the store it was dark, and the grate was pulled down and locked securely. Javi owns the store and his wife, Rosa, helps him run it, but there was no sign of either of them. Peter's beat-up old car was out front, but it was empty.

I peered through the store window, but it was impossible to tell if anyone was inside. I knocked on the grate, feeling ridiculous. "Peter? Are you there?"

No answer.

I stepped back, trying to think. The store had a back door, but all the shops and restaurants on this block were connected. I'd have to go all the way to the next street over and behind the commercial strip, along the narrow row of Dumpsters. I was lucky I hadn't spotted any rats yet tonight, but God only knew what was crawling around back there.

Besides...it was deserted in this part of town at night. At least back by our house, someone would probably hear me if I screamed.

My hands had just started to shake all over again when I heard the hissing.

I whipped around. That had definitely sounded like a person, but I didn't see anyone. Maybe I'd imagined it.

Another muffled hiss came, closer than the first.

I should run. I knew I should run, but my feet were frozen to the sidewalk, my limbs shut down by panic.

Then the hissing turned to laughter, and I almost cried in relief. I knew that laugh. "What the heck, Peter?"

I clenched my hands into fists as my brother stepped out from the shadows with a grin on his face. I shoved him hard in the shoulder, and he reached up to block my hand before I could push him again.

"Lay off." He chuckled. "It's not my fault you're such a 'fraidy cat."

"Oh, thanks." I crossed my arms over my chest. "That's what I get for sneaking out to find you in the middle of the night?"

"You snuck out?" Peter raised his eyebrows. "I'm impressed. This isn't the middle of the night, though—it's barely nine. Our boring neighborhood shuts down early."

"Well, you were supposed to come straight home as soon as you closed up. What are you doing out here by yourself? Did you...did you hear about Miami?"

Peter nodded slowly. "It was on the radio. I already knew it would happen, though."

"What do you mean, you already knew?"

"It was obvious." He shrugged, then stepped in front of the store and slid down with his back against the grate until he was sitting in a patch of darkness on the sidewalk. "Anita won by a landslide. It was the only thing that was ever going to happen."

"How'd you know?" I lowered myself next to him.

"As soon as she got them to hold that vote, it was done." He ran his free hand over his curly dark hair. "She got tired of singing about orange juice on TV and heard there was a law that gave gay people permission to exist, so she rallied all the other Stepford wives into an army, and now we're all screwed. There was no chance the straight people would've voted any other way."

I flinched, the way I always did when someone cursed. Usually Peter teased me about that, too, but not tonight. "Well, I'm straight, and I would've."

He didn't answer. It wasn't like him to be this quiet.

"Are you...?" I didn't know what to say. "You know...sad?"

"No." Peter gazed at a car turning at the end of the block. One of its headlights was busted out, and the other drew a faint, slow circle across the empty street. "I'm not sad."

"Oh. Okay." For the first time in our lives, I had no idea what to say to my brother. I knew he was lying, but I couldn't think of a single way to make him feel any better. "Well, let's go home."

"Mom'll come down. She always does when I get home." Peter kept refusing to meet my eyes. "She'll see you, and she'll ground you for sneaking out."

"Maybe not," I said, but he was probably right. Mom would be delighted to see that Peter was safe, but I'd be in trouble for sure. She says she doesn't play favorites, but somehow I'm always the one she decides is wrong. Plus, she still does Peter's laundry.

"Either way—" he pulled a pack of cigarettes out of his pocket "—I'm not going home."

"What, you want to sit here in the dark all night?"

"No. I want..." He trailed off, one hand holding tight to the cigarette pack, the other scrunching into his curly dark hair. He's done that since we were kids. On the day he started fifth grade, when he told me how Gary Knopp had shouted "Sissy!" at him on the way into the cafeteria, he squeezed his hair so tight, strands broke off in his fist. Any time he's overwhelmed, any time he wants to disappear, my brother scrunches up his hair. "I just want this to be over."

"Well, it is. Miami's thousands of miles away. They won't be talking about it on the news after tomorrow."

He exhaled heavily, as if I was the stupidest person he'd ever encountered. "Shar. This isn't over. Anita Bryant and her cronies aren't going to stop while they're winning."

"It's only one city."

"So far." Peter tightened his fingers in his hair and let out another long breath. "I've got to get out of this shitty neighborhood."

"Well...you'll graduate next year, and in college you can—"

"Screw college." He tugged on his hair again. It had to be hurting him. "I'm talking about right now. Tonight."

"What do you mean?" I was getting nervous. "You're not talking about...running away from home or something?"

"I just want to not be <u>here</u>." He swept his arm out toward the darkened street. "Our fucking Catholic neighborhood. Our fucking Catholic <u>school</u>."

"Did...something else happen today? Besides Miami, I mean?"

He didn't answer.

Peter gets beat up less often than he used to, but Gary Knopp and his friends still corner him outside the library every now and then. They don't know he's gay, but they know he's skinny, and that he doesn't have many friends, and that he's obsessed with movies but thinks basketball is boring, and that's enough. He doesn't talk about it much, but I always worry one day he'll come home with a broken bone, or worse.

"You could tell Mom," I offered. "She could speak to Father Murphy and maybe—"

"I <u>can't</u> talk to Mom. How many times do I have to tell you—"

"Okay, okay, I'm sorry." I didn't try to argue any more. Peter might be Mom's favorite child now, but we've both heard the stories about what happens to Catholic kids whose parents find out they're gay. If Mom kicked him out, he'd have nowhere to go.

"So what do you want to do?" I asked.

"Get out of here." He nodded again, quickly. He was serious, which meant I couldn't stop him. I've never been able to make my brother do anything he didn't want to do, even before he got to be a full foot taller than me. "Come on, the car's right here."

He got to his feet, holding out a hand to help me up. I didn't take it. "Come where, exactly?"

"Please, Sis. I don't ask for much, but...I'm not ready to do this by myself."

My heart started to thud again, but it was an entirely different kind of thudding than I got from climbing down the tree. He used to call me Sis all the time when we were kids, but now he only used it when something was important. "Do what?"

"I need to go where there are people who'll get it." Peter jingled his keys and bounced nervously from foot to foot. He wasn't scrunching his hair anymore, though. "Castro Street."

Shoot—it's late. If I don't go to sleep I'll be useless at school. I'll tell you the rest of what happened tomorrow.

Yours,
Sharon

Tuesday, June 7, 1977

Dear Harvey,

Sorry to write you twice in one night. I didn't plan it this way. When I wrote that first entry, I was just killing time until we got the results, but now I'm shaking so hard I have to focus on something if I don't want to lose it.

They're blowing up the fucking balloons, Harvey.

Everyone's whooping and cheering and running over to that reporter, begging him to put them on the radio. I told them I have a paper due tomorrow, so I have to keep writing. Three of my teachers are here right now, celebrating with the others, but no one's noticed I'm lying.

I'm stupid for being so upset. I knew this would probably happen.

You knew, too, right, Harvey? You expected this.

Anita Bryant on television, crowing as if she just saved humanity from the Communists all by herself. My aunt, calling all the reporters she knows, so happy she's crying.

I thought Miami was far away. I thought if this happened, at least then it would be over and life could go back to normal. Everyone could finally stop talking about the "homosexual menace." I wouldn't need to spend every day walking on eggshells, using all my concentration not to give myself away. I—

Ugh, ugh, <u>ugh</u>. Sorry, I had to stop writing, but now I'm back. My mother brought over that Stanford guy again, the one she has this fantasy about me getting pinned to, and I had to play nice.

Mom's been getting worse now that my sister's pregnant. That little bump under her frilly apron right next to that shiny gold ring on her finger reminded my parents yet again that I'm sixteen and don't have a boyfriend. Clearly, I'm going to shrivel up into a useless, flat-stomached prune if I don't have a pin on my lapel next week and a diamond on my finger within approximately five seconds of graduation, and—

Ugh, ugh, <u>ugh</u>. Now Stanford guy is trying to make eye contact. I've got to keep writing. I can't look at him. Can't look at Mom. And for <u>sure</u> I can't look at Aunt Mandy.

Okay, here's what I'll do instead. I'll tell you about the mailers we sent out to Florida for all of last month. <u>That</u> will keep my pencil moving since I've got plenty to say about <u>those</u>.

Most of our mailings have three pieces tucked inside. They start with a letter from Aunt Mandy and Uncle Russell (except, let's be honest, Aunt Mandy wrote the whole thing—Uncle Russell is only the one who signs them because his name has the word "Reverend" in front of it). The letter's all about how gays are evil, and how if they aren't going to molest your kids, then at the very least they're going to turn them gay, and that's why you should recruit everyone you've ever met to vote against gay rights.

(Along with most subtleties, the irony of using the word "recruit" this way is completely lost on Aunt Mandy.)

The second piece is a set of pledge forms. That's for when

you go door to door, or host parties at your house, or flag people down outside the grocery store, or whatever. The more people you can get to pledge to vote yes on repeal, the faster you get into Heaven.

The third piece is the comic book. We're supposed to call a "tract," because calling it a "comic book" makes it sound funny and this is deadly serious business, but whatever you want to call it, it's very clearly a comic strip some guy drew. It's all about how gay people are going to Hell and it's the responsibility of good Christians to tell them so. There's one panel that shows a lesbian who's trying to get a straight girl to sleep with her, but the straight girl's a good Christian, so she rejects her and runs away. The gist of it is that the world is going to Hell because some gay people aren't afraid to be gay anymore.

It's all so ridiculous, Harvey. I'm not sure I even believe in Hell. I don't believe in God, so I guess there's no point buying in to the rest of it.

Wow—I just wrote those words. Here, in a church. With my whole family and everyone else I know sitting a few feet away. I'm covering the paper with my arm, of course, but I'm still shaking so hard.

I'm terrified, Harvey. It's not that I'm scared about someone finding these letters to you...although if that happened, it would be the end of my life as I know it. More than that, though, I'm afraid they'll see what's inside my head.

I think Aunt Mandy already has. You probably think I'm joking, but I'm not. She can see right through people.

But I bet she couldn't see through you. How could she? You don't hide anything. You are who you are, and you don't care if other people don't like it.

I don't know how you do that, Harvey.

I've read every article I could get my hands on about you. Well, I read anything I can find about homosexuals, but I love it when they quote you most of all. You're always talking about how everyone deserves to have hope. I've never heard anyone say that before.

Do you have a volunteer campaign office full of people working <u>against</u> Anita Bryant? Do you and your friends put together mailings, too?

Maybe I can pretend that's what I'm doing next time I'm folding up the letters from my aunt. Maybe that way I can keep going without feeling like I'm about to puke.

Sometimes I can't believe you're real, Harvey. You're like something out of a fairy tale. A gay man, reviled by most of society, managing to rise above. When everyone I know hates your guts.

I despise living in Orange County, Harvey. <u>So much</u>. If Aunt Mandy knew I was writing to you, she'd probably tie me to a chair and bring in my whole family to pray the gay out of me.

Fuck, I'm about to cry. Maybe if I hide this notebook and go blow up some balloons that'll keep my tear ducts occupied.

More later.

Peace,
Tammy

Dear Diary,

Well, it's still Tuesday night—technically Wednesday morning, I guess—but I can't sleep, so here I am, writing again. As long as I'm awake, I might as well tell you what happened tonight after my brother and I left our neighborhood.

We parked on Liberty Street, a few blocks from Castro. It was dark out, but the streets up there were far from deserted. Our neighborhood might as well have been a million miles away instead of a twenty-minute drive.

"Is something going on?" I tugged my sleeves down over my hands as Peter and I climbed out of the car. The sidewalk was crowded with people, most of them youngish men, talking and moving fast. Everyone was heading north, and as we got closer to Castro, we could hear shouting ahead. Car horns kept honking, too. In the din, I couldn't understand what all the voices were saying. "I mean, besides this Miami vote?"

"Nah, I bet this is all Anita." Peter stretched up onto his toes, the leather in his boots flexing as he tried to see up to the next block. The area around Castro Street used to be just another Irish-Catholic neighborhood, but according to the news, it's been completely taken over by gay people. The nuns at school are always saying the city's on the brink of moral ruin, and it all starts with Castro Street.

"How do you know?" I asked, but I got my answer before my brother could say any more.

"GAY RIGHTS NOW!" A guy in a flannel shirt jogged past us, pumping his fist and shouting. Another guy next to him joined in.

Neither of the guys looked much older than Peter and me, and one of them had kind of long hair. I wondered if they were both gay, or if one of them was only there to support his friend, the way I was there to support Peter.

Then I saw the cardboard sign the shorter-haired guy was holding. The thick black letters were crooked and haphazard, as though he'd just made the sign minutes before with a marker he'd found lying in a drawer. It said WE ARE YOUR CHILDREN.

Peter tugged my sleeve, silently motioning for us to follow them. I sped up to a trot, turning the words over in my head.

We are your children. Of all the things to write on a sign, he picked that.

The year before last, down by the St. Francis Hotel, a man knocked a gun out of a woman's hand when she was trying to shoot the president. When the newspapers printed that the big hero who'd stopped the assassination attempt was gay, his parents disowned him. He sued the papers for ruining his life.

Did the people here seriously think someone like Anita Bryant would do anything differently from that man's parents if one of <u>her</u> kids turned out to be gay?

"Come on, Shar." Peter tugged my sleeve again. He was actually <u>smiling</u>. I hadn't thought there was any chance I'd see my brother smile tonight. "We don't want to miss it."

"Miss what?"

"Whatever it is!"

He started moving faster, into the crowd of men. A bunch of them were carrying signs now.

I followed, my heart pounding. I'd thought we were only coming to look around. I didn't know something would be <u>happening</u> here, much less something involving signs and running and chanting.

It reminded me of the peace protests, when the hippies were on TV every night singing about the war. Our teachers always warned us to stay away from demonstrations, because you never knew when rocks or bullets would start flying. I've never heard of gay people protesting, though.

I only found out about Peter the summer before last. He'd gone away to some wilderness camp in Nevada, a present from our dad's parents, who have this tendency to go radio-silent for months at a time, then pop up to insist on paying for things we weren't planning on buying in the first place. Peter came back from that camp smiling bigger than I'd ever seen him smile, but he wouldn't say why. I pestered him about it for weeks, until one night when Mom was at a church meeting and he finally said he'd tell me. We hid in my room under a blanket fort the way we used to in kindergarten, and he quietly said that over the summer, he'd fallen in love.

I didn't see how that was possible. As far as I knew, "falling in love" wasn't any different from the made-up stories we learned in nursery school about Cinderella and Sleeping Beauty.

Our mom and dad certainly never fell in love. Or if they did, it didn't do them any good.

Besides, Kevin's camp was all boys. Had he gotten a crush on a counselor's sister or something?

Finally, his smile wavering a little, Peter told me he was in love with a boy named Curtis. He said he hoped I could accept that.

Well, to be honest, I couldn't.

I'd known homosexuals existed. You can't live in San Francisco without knowing that. But it had never occurred to me my own <u>brother</u> could be one of them.

The brother I'd shared a room with for nine years. The brother who'd taught me how to roller-skate and cheat at Candyland. Who made fart noises at the dinner table and hugged me when Dad forgot to send a birthday card.

I didn't speak to Peter for a week. He'd begged me not to say anything to Mom, but I kept thinking I ought to tell <u>someone</u>. At school, they'd told us homosexuality was a curse, so I thought maybe Mom or Father Murphy could help him be normal again.

In the end, I didn't say anything. I wanted to help Peter, but I was scared of hurting him, too. The longer I thought about it, the more confused I got about how to tell the difference.

Then one day, I came home from school and found him at the kitchen table, still in his St. John's blazer. He was bent over a sheet of paper, so intent on what he was writing that he hadn't heard me come in. He had a smile on his face, a wide, open grin that made his eyes light up as his pen flew across the page. I couldn't remember ever seeing my brother look that happy.

Then I noticed the envelope on the table next to him. It was addressed to Curtis. Peter was writing to the boy from camp.

I'd always thought being gay was wrong, when I thought about it at all. But if this Curtis boy could make my brother smile that way... well, I didn't see how that could be a <u>bad</u> thing, whether or not it matched up with what my teachers said.

"Okay," I'd said. He looked up with wide eyes to see me standing there. "I'll keep your secret. You know, about the, um...that. And... I think I might be able to get used to the idea."

His eyes crinkled at the corners. "Thanks, sister dear. I wasn't exactly asking for your permission, but it's nice of you to say so all the same."

He got up from the table, crossed the kitchen, and gave me a hug. Even though we aren't the kind of family that hugs much.

Tonight, though, I couldn't make sense of what was happening. Having a homosexual brother was one thing, but being <u>surrounded</u> by homosexuals in the middle of the street was something else. I'd thought gay people usually didn't want anyone to know they were gay, but the men around me didn't look as if they were hiding anything. Weren't they worried about who might see them carrying these signs? And why were so many of them even <u>there</u>?

"Why are they protesting something that happened in Miami?" I asked. "How many thousands of miles away <u>is</u> that?"

"Doesn't matter." Peter kept swiveling his head around, as though he was trying to see everything at once. The chants were getting louder, and he had to raise his voice so I could hear him. "It's only a matter of time before it happens here."

"Wait, you mean Anita Bryant's coming to <u>California</u>?"

"Probably. She and her friends aren't going to stop now that they've won."

"You think so? Oh, my gosh." When I turned to him, though, instead of looking worried, my brother was laughing. At me.

I groaned. "What's so funny?"

"You always sound about nine years old when you say that. '<u>Oh, my gosh</u>.'" He did a high-pitched trill on the words.

"Shut up. That's not what I sound like at <u>all</u>."

"Hey, do you hear that?" Peter cocked his head.

The crowd was getting louder, the sounds of the protest drifting over the stores and houses in front of us. Whistles, and shouts, and a faint rhythmic sound that might've been drumming poured in from the next block.

"How many people are up there?" I asked.

"Hundreds?" Peter shrugged. "Thousands?"

<u>Thousands?</u> Of <u>gay</u> people?

He practically dragged me past the restaurants and bars that lined the block. People were spilling out onto the sidewalk, thickening the crowd around us even more. The street was full of honking horns. Drivers leaned out the windows, shouting for everyone to stop clogging the street.

We turned another corner, past an intersection jammed with traffic, and suddenly we were in the middle of a sea of people like nothing I'd ever seen. A wall of fast-moving bodies, all marching north, a fierce energy thrumming through the group.

Before I understood what was happening, Peter and I were swept up in it. We didn't have a choice—it was march or be trampled.

My brother had already started shouting along with everybody else. "TWO, FOUR, SIX, EIGHT! SEPARATE THE CHURCH AND STATE!"

"FUCK YOU, ANITA!" a man shouted up ahead. Others shouted in agreement, a few of them banging on drums that hung around their necks. One of the men held up a sign with painted letters that read SAVE OUR HUMAN RIGHTS. Behind him, a cop on a motorcycle was trying to cut into the crowd, but the marchers kept going while the cop just watched, revving his engine. A few of the men glanced warily at the officer. As far as I know it's still illegal to be gay, but he didn't seem to be arresting anyone.

A lot of the men in the crowd had long hair, and some of them were wearing earrings or leather jackets. I didn't see anyone who looked quite as young as Peter and me, but there were a few who didn't look <u>that</u> much older. College students, maybe.

It was dizzying. Everywhere I turned, there were more men, and when I twisted around to look behind us, I even saw a couple of girls. Lesbians, maybe, but I didn't know how to tell. The news reporters only ever talk about gay men, but the girls I saw in the crowd tonight were chanting along with everyone else. Most of them had short hair, and two of them were riding along the edges of the crowd on motorcycles, gunning their engines even louder than the cops. I would've thought the sight of a girl on a motorcycle would be strange, but it was actually kind of cool.

"GAY RIGHTS ARE HUMAN RIGHTS!" the girls chanted along with the rest of the crowd. "GAY RIGHTS ARE HUMAN RIGHTS!"

When I glanced back at my brother, his eyes were alight, his smile wide. I wondered how it felt to be surrounded by people like him. Even for me, it was exhilarating. There were so many of us gathered, it felt like we could do anything. And the chanting crowd, the anger in the air... It was cool to be so surrounded by all that energy. All that ferocity and strength.

"It's him!" Peter was grinning, jumping up on his toes to look over the crowd. "It's Harvey!"

I strained to see until the guy in front of me stepped aside and I could glimpse the cluster of men at the front of the march. One man, taller than the others, was carrying a bullhorn, and as the crowd parted, he turned around.

Peter was right—I recognized him right away. Harvey Milk. His picture's always in the newspaper about something or other.

"CIVIL RIGHTS OR CIVIL WAR!" Mr. Milk called into his bullhorn.

The crowd picked up the chant immediately. "GAY RIGHTS NOW!"

When I glanced at my brother again, he was absolutely beaming.

An hour earlier, he'd been sitting alone in the shadows outside a darkened grocery store. Now he was surrounded by people, grinning wider than he ever had.

I've never fit. Not at school. Not at church. Not anywhere, really.

But my brother fit here. Maybe I did, too.

The charge in the air, the power in all these voices... Maybe I'd finally found my place.

Up ahead, Mr. Milk changed the chant and this time, I joined in.

"WE'VE GOT THE POWER TO...FIGHT BACK!" I shouted, my voice ringing out into the crowd. "WE'VE GOT THE POWER TO... FIGHT BACK!"

An engine revved behind me, and I twisted around. A motorcycle zoomed past us with two girls sharing the seat. The girl in back had her arms wrapped around the other one's waist. I couldn't tell if it was because she was afraid of falling off or because they were lesbians. I guess it could've been both.

The chant changed again. "ANITA! YOU LIAR! WE'LL SET YOUR HAIR ON FIRE!"

Anita Bryant's been on TV since I was a kid, selling orange juice and tissues and macaroni and cheese, singing and smiling and filling up the otherwise-silent living room while Mom and Peter and I sat on the couch waiting for M*A*S*H to come back on.

But now, her followers want to hurt my brother. They want to hurt those girls on the motorcycle, too, and Mr. Milk with his bullhorn, and all the people here chanting with us.

And I want to hurt them back.

"CIVIL RIGHTS OR CIVIL WAR! GAY RIGHTS NOW!"

I pumped my fist with Peter and the others, shutting my eyes and relishing the motion.

We marched for hours, past City Hall and up to Nob Hill. We wound up at Union Square, miles north of where we'd left Peter's car, surrounded by thousands of people, all of us chanting on long after our voices had started to give out. Mr. Milk gave a speech about seizing our power and standing up to Anita and all the people like her, and even though it was the middle of the night, I felt more awake than I could ever remember feeling.

We had to make it home before Mom noticed we were gone, so with the chants echoing in our ears, Peter and I walked down to Market and hitched a ride back to the car. Mom was asleep when we slunk in—there was no movement from behind her door, anyway—and Peter and I crept straight to our rooms, our clothes smelling of smoke and exhaust and all the other smells you bring home from downtown in the middle of the night.

It's strange. I never noticed how quiet it is here. There's the occasional siren from a faraway street, some birds chirping, the sound of that tree scraping against Peter's window through the wall.

Still, I can almost hear my heart beating. And I can hear the shouts ringing in my ears, too.

I don't want to fall asleep. I'm scared I'll forget this feeling, and I want to remember it forever.

Yours,
Sharon

Wednesday, June 8, 1977

Dear Harvey,

Have you ever tried blowing up a dozen balloons in a row?

It's terrible. I don't think there's any breath left in my body.

Either way, I'm home now. It's the middle of the night, but I can't sleep. Whenever I close my eyes I'm back in that fucking basement, blowing up balloons with the rest of the youth group while our parents sit on the couches behind us drinking Dixie cups full of grape juice from the communion stash. My cousin Eddie and the other little kids kept trying to grab the balloons out of our hands so they'd fly around the room making fart noises.

Through it all, Uncle Russell was praying at the top of his lungs while Aunt Mandy called more reporters. She sounded so happy, I'm surprised she wasn't fucking <u>floating</u>.

There are few things that terrify me more than my aunt being happy, Harvey.

I was sitting on that floor, feeling like my head was trapped in a vise, when it occurred to me. Maybe it was the lack of oxygen from blowing up all those balloons, but the thought popped into my head and now I can't shake it:

Why am <u>I</u> the one who has to be so terrified all the time?

Why do I sit around worrying about whether someone will figure out my secret, while everybody else gets to have a fucking party because Anita fucking Bryant convinced a bunch of people thousands of miles away that she's right and I'm going to Hell?

You probably figured this out years ago, but to me, sitting there on that basement floor, it was a brand-new, mind-blowing idea:

This is fucking BULLSHIT.

Look. I'm not saying I want to skywrite the words "I'm queer!!!!!" outside the house when my parents wake up tomorrow or anything. They'd just haul me straight to Uncle Russell, and if he couldn't fix me, it'd be electroshock therapy time.

And it's not as if running away is an option. There's nowhere to go. Sure, I've had fantasies about getting an apartment in L.A., but I'd need money for that, and I don't know how I'd ever get a job. All I can do is recite Bible verses, and they don't pay you to do that unless you're Uncle Russell.

But tonight, sitting there on that basement floor, I wasn't thinking about running away. I was thinking about Patti Smith.

Do you know her music, Harvey? I've never heard her playing on the radio here, but maybe it's different in San Francisco.

I had no idea who Patti even was before last Easter. I was at a slumber party with the girls from the youth group, and we snuck downstairs to watch Saturday Night Live. We aren't supposed to watch that show, since our parents say it's sinful. We didn't see what was so sinful about it, but it was funny. Then, halfway through the episode, Patti Smith came on with her band, and when I saw her, my heart stopped.

Patti Smith looks... I don't know how to describe it. She

almost looks like a man—she was wearing a shirt and tie, even—and she sounds like a man, too. Her voice is low and gravelly, and the first words she sang were…well, I can't write them down, but they were the bravest words I've ever heard anyone say.

All I wanted was to be Patti Smith. She's obviously never been scared of anyone. There's this <u>anger</u> in her voice, this <u>soul</u>, that's like nothing I've ever heard.

I never knew I could be <u>angry</u>. I've always been too busy being scared. I've been keeping this inside so long it feels like I'm about to burst open and leave nothing but a puddle on the carpet where I used to be.

But that's bullshit, too.

My aunt and uncle and Anita Bryant and all the rest of them—they <u>want</u> people like me to be scared.

Well, I'm through giving them what they want. Tomorrow, I'm going to the record store and buying every Patti Smith album they have.

I'm getting out of this place, Harvey. Even if I only manage to do it in my head.

Peace,
Tammy

Dear Diary,

I should've known today would be terrible.

I'm writing this in study hall. I barely managed three hours of sleep last night, but it's the last day of school, so classes are a joke. Mom always says teachers run out of energy the first week of May.

I still have to keep up with my friends, though, and I didn't realize how tricky that would be without sleep.

"Guess where I went last night?" I asked Rhonda on our way out of English as we wound through a hall full of kilted, giggly girls.

"You'll never believe where I went," she said, instead of guessing. We cut through a contingent of freshmen and looped across the small chapel to the bathroom, the one hardly anyone goes to. It's the best place to talk without the whole school hearing your every word. "After we closed, Craig took me to this dive bar down on Naples. I thought I'd get chlamydia just from walking in the door, but it turned out he knew all the guys there, and they were great. They bought me drinks all night and I got so wasted."

By the time she was finished telling me all that, I was in a stall, halfway through peeing. I always have to charge to the bathroom after English or I'll burst.

"That sounds fun," I called through the stall door. Rhonda and I used to hang out all the time, but now that she's going out with her boss, I only see her at school.

"It was, but I still feel kind of drunk. That's okay, though. No one will notice on the last day of school."

I stepped out of the stall and went over to wash my hands. The bathroom door swung open. Rhonda and I both went silent, but it was only Diane and Jennifer. They'd been in English with us, too.

"Did you say you're still drunk from last night?" Diane asked Rhonda as she pulled a cigarette and a matchbook out of her purse.

"Yeah. Craig and I stayed out until really late."

"You and Craig." Diane laughed. "Do your parents still not know?"

"Hell no. They'd only ground me for the rest of my life."

"They need to relax." Diane struck the match over the sink. "He's not _that_ much older than you."

"I know! My dad's seven years older than my mom. Craig's only five years older than me, but you know they'd never listen if I pointed that out. They're total hypocrites."

"Our parents think it's still the fifties or something," Jennifer called from over the door of the stall I'd just come out of. "We're all supposed to stay virgins 'til our wedding nights."

Diane and Rhonda laughed. I laughed, too, a second too late, but I don't think anyone noticed. _I'm_ a virgin, and as far as I know so are all my friends, but things are changing faster than they used to.

"What our parents don't know won't hurt them." Rhonda fluffed her hair. She'd asked the hairdresser for bouncy Farrah Fawcett-Majors curls, but she'd wound up looking more like Janet from Three's Company. "They can think I'm a virgin when Craig's walking me down the aisle if they want."

We all laughed again, but I can't picture Rhonda marrying Craig. Or really, I can't picture Craig marrying Rhonda. Whenever I see

them together at the pizza place where they work, he's always trying to look down her shirt. If there's any truth to the lectures Sister Catherine gives us, that's not how men act around girls they
want to marry.

Besides, are we really supposed to be thinking about marriage
already? We're sophomores in high school. I can't imagine getting
married ever.

"So what did you do last night?" Rhonda asked me. "Were you
out with Kevin?"

"No. I..." I shut my mouth. I'd been about to tell her all about
going to Castro Street and the march and seeing Harvey Milk...and
then I remembered Peter.

I couldn't tell anyone where I'd been, even Rhonda.

"I just watched the news with my mom," I said instead. "Did you
hear about this vote in Florida? It sounds as if it's a really big deal."

Rhonda had already turned to the mirror and started touching
up her lipstick. "What about Florida?"

"You mean about homosexuality?" Jennifer called over the sound
of the toilet flushing.

I blushed, which was ridiculous, since I was the one who'd
brought this up. But I blush very, very easily. Rhonda knows that—
everyone does—so hopefully she didn't read much into it.

"What about homosexuality?" Diane asked.

Rhonda laughed. "Leave it to Sharon and Mrs. Hawkins to watch
a report about homosexuality in Florida the night before the last
day of school. Hey, you got another one of those?"

Diane rolled her eyes, but she held out her pack of cigarettes to
Rhonda.

"You know how Anita Bryant's on the news all the time lately?"
Jennifer came out of the stall, and I slid over to make room for her

at the sink. "She got them to pass a new law in Miami because homosexuals were trying to get teaching jobs."

"Anita Bryant? Really?" Rhonda laughed and tried to sing Anita Bryant's jingle from the orange juice commercials, the one about the Florida sunshine tree.

"Now let's talk about homosexual-i-ty!" Diane sang back to the same tune, making us all laugh.

"Oh, man, do you remember when she came back and sang on Miss America when we were kids?" Jennifer shook her head. "It's not fair she only came in third."

"We weren't even born when that happened," I said. Rhonda and Diane were still singing jingles, but I kept talking anyway. "Look, Miami had a law that said it was illegal to discriminate against gay people, but Anita Bryant got them to vote to overturn it. So now it'll be legal to discriminate again."

Rhonda and Diane stopped singing, and now all three of them were looking at me. Rhonda put her lipstick back in her purse and tilted her head. "What do you mean, 'discriminate'?"

"You know." I tried to remember what Peter had said. "It'll be legal now if someone wants to kick a gay person out of his apartment, or fire him from his job."

"That wasn't legal before?" Jennifer turned back to the mirror. "Is it legal here?"

"I..." I didn't know.

"I don't think it's right for people to be that way." Diane blew smoke out at the ceiling and started fishing around in her purse. "They know what the Bible says. Besides, it's disgusting."

"Can you imagine?" Rhonda started laughing again. "If you met one of those guys? He'd probably have on more makeup than you did!"

Jennifer and Diane laughed, too.

"My dad says gay guys all have pet poodles, and they wear high heels everywhere," Diane said. "And when they drink they stick their pinky finger out to the side."

"Hey, um..." I started to interrupt them, but I didn't know what to say. How could I tell them to stop making fun of gay guys when I couldn't say my own brother was gay?

And how did I never notice until today that my friends were just as boring and conventional as our stuck-in-the-fifties parents?

That was when the bell rang, and the door opened again.

"Do I smell smoke?" The voice was my mom's. She's the only teacher at our school who does that—calls out a warning before she comes in. It gives you enough time to put away whatever you were doing so she doesn't have to officially catch you.

(My mom is everyone's favorite teacher.)

Diane and Rhonda dropped their cigarettes and stamped them out with their saddle shoes. It meant they couldn't move their feet once my mom came through the door, but she pretended not to notice.

"Hello, girls." Mom looked at each of us, her eyes widening a little when she saw me before her face slipped back into her usual unaffected-teacher expression. If she was exhausted after worrying about Peter all night, she didn't give any sign of it. "The bell rang. Why aren't you in class?"

"We're sorry, Mrs. Hawkins." Rhonda bobbed into a tiny curtsy, which looked especially ridiculous since she couldn't move her feet.

"Well, get a move on." Mom glanced at me, but looked away just as fast. "You don't want Sister Catherine to catch you out here."

"Thank you, Mrs. Hawkins," the others chorused as Mom stepped outside.

We moved fast after that, Diane and Rhonda flushing their cigarette butts before we headed to study hall. It took me almost the whole period to write this down, but there are ten minutes left in the period so I guess I might as well get this pen pal letter out of the way now. More later.

Yours,
Sharon

Wednesday, June 8, 1977

Dear Tammy,

I guess I'm your new pen pal. Hi, it's nice to meet you. I'm sorry we're about to be juniors in high school and we're stuck doing a project more appropriate for eight-year-olds.

Here's my first answer from the question list:

Describe yourself in three adjectives.

Today? I'd say tired, overwhelmed, and ready for school to be over.

But if I'm supposed to be making a big statement, I guess I'd go with confused, lonely, and out of place. (Is out of place an adjective? Maybe it is if I put in hyphens? Out-of-place, then.)

I guess that's it for now. Sorry I couldn't come up with a better answer. I'll try to be more interesting next time.

Yours truly,
Sharon Hawkins

Thursday, June 16, 1977

Dear Sharon,

Your letter made me laugh. I totally agree, this is a ridiculous project, but I guess we're stuck with it.

Here are my three adjectives: Tall (or, well, tall-ish). Blond. And overwhelmed, the same as you. I'm glad this school year's over, too.

Sorry if that doesn't give you much to write about in your report. I'll try to do better in my next letter.

Yours truly,
Tammy Larson

P.S. This isn't in the list of questions, but I was wondering—have you ever listened to Patti Smith? I just got her album <u>Horses</u> and I'm obsessed. No one I know listens to that kind of music, but I thought things might be different in San Francisco.

Wednesday, June 22, 1977

Dear Tammy,

No, I don't think I've heard of Patti Smith. What kind of music does she play?

Here's my answer to the next question:

Who are the members of your family?

It's just me, my mom, and my brother. My mom's a teacher at my school, and my brother, Peter, is one year older than me. I have a father, too, but he left when I was a baby and I haven't seen him much since.

What's your family like?

Yours truly,
Sharon Hawkins

Wednesday, June 29, 1977

Dear Sharon,

I'm really sorry about your dad.

My family will take longer to explain, since there are a lot of us.

First, there's my parents. They met in Ohio. My dad had gone out to buy some toothpaste and my mom was working at the drugstore. When he went up to the register to pay, he thought my mom was pretty and asked for her number. My dad was a big shot then, a college football player, and Mom says it was as if a famous movie star had asked her on a date. She was still in high school, taking care of her little sister since their parents had died a few years before, and she and my dad got married right after she graduated. He got a job with a development company in Ocean Valley, so they all moved out here, including my mom's sister—my Aunt Mandy—since she was just a kid herself then.

Not long after that, my oldest sister, Laura, was born. She's twenty-one now, and she's married with a baby. Now she's pregnant again. My next-oldest sister, Barbara, is nineteen and just got married in the spring, and guess what—she just told us she's pregnant, too.

No one ever asks me when I'm getting pregnant, which I guess is a good thing. Once I made a joke about that at a barbecue and got grounded for a week. (Er...please don't mention that in your report for the teachers.)

My little sister, Elizabeth, is fourteen, and my bratty brother, Ricky, is a year younger. Look up "spoiled rotten" in a dictionary, and odds are, it'll have a picture of Ricky right next to it.

In case you couldn't tell, my parents really wanted a boy.

Anyway, sorry for the long letter. I'll try to keep my next answer more concise.

Yours truly,
Tammy Larson

P.S. Was it awkward for me to say I'm sorry about your dad, since we don't really know each other? If it was, then I'm sorry, again. Sorry for saying sorry, I mean.

Saturday, July 2, 1977

Dear Diary,

I'm not sure how to talk about what happened tonight. It wasn't at all what I expected. I went back and reread what I wrote last time, about the night Peter and I went to that march, and... I just don't know what to think now.

Maybe it will make sense after I write it all out. That's why I've got this diary, anyway. Ever since I was a kid, there have always been things that only make sense once I write them down and read them over later.

We went to Castro Street again tonight, but it wasn't anything like before.

"Tell me again why _you_ wanted to come here?" Peter kept giving me curious looks as he parked the car. It's an old junker with a mismatched paint job, and it's got more dents in the bumper than I have fingers on either hand, but it's all Peter can afford, and it's our only way to get around the city if we don't want to wait ages for the bus.

"I want to... I don't know." I shrugged and glanced in the rearview mirror. I should've worn lipstick. When we'd come up for the march I didn't have any makeup on, but now it was Saturday night and I didn't want to look like some little schoolgirl. "Get involved. Do something about gay rights."

"Do what, exactly?"

"That's what we're here to figure out." I swung open the door, trying to act bolder than I felt.

"Since when are you into gay rights, anyway?" Peter climbed out after me.

"I... I don't know." I blushed. The night of the march, I thought I'd finally found somewhere I belonged. I'd been wanting to come back for weeks, but I didn't have the nerve to tell him that. "It's no big deal."

"Relax." He tugged on the sleeve of my T-shirt. "I'm glad you had this idea. I've been wanting to come back."

"Oh. Okay, then good. So, um...do you think that march we went to actually changed anything?"

"Nope," Peter said. We climbed past pizzerias and coffee shops and stoned hippies on our way to Castro. "The Miami law's still overturned. Anita and the fundamentalists are still claiming it as a victory."

"The other night the news said other gay rights laws will probably get overturned now, too." I sighed. "The way you expected."

"Yeah. Sometimes I wish I weren't quite so smart."

I elbowed him. "They wouldn't really do it here, would they?"

"They will if they can."

"It would never pass. There must have been thousands of people out marching that night."

"Sure, but there are millions of people in California, and gay people only make up a tiny fraction. If there were a statewide campaign, even if we all voted no, Orange County alone would probably have enough fundamentalist assholes to pass it. That whole place is basically one gigantic fundamentalist asshole."

"Right." I didn't mention that Orange County was also where my new pen pal was from. Tammy Larson of Ocean Valley, located smack in the middle of the land of sunshine and hatred. It's kind of strange, since Tammy seems nice from her letters—the last one was fun to read, all about her big family—but if she knew I had a gay brother, she'd probably report it straight to one of her teachers. Then her school would call <u>my</u> school, and Peter's secret would be out for the whole world to know.

It's too bad. I could see us being friends if things were different.

"Look." Peter nudged me, angling his chin up ahead. We had a few blocks to go, but there were already two men in front of us, walking with their arms slung around each other's shoulders.

"Come on, Shar." Peter sped up.

"I'm coming. I'm coming."

By the time we'd made it two more blocks, we'd seen at least a dozen other men, and when we reached Castro Street itself, the crowd swelled. Tall men, short men, white men, Black men, Latino men, young men, slightly less young men—the sidewalks were teeming with them, and the one thing they all seemed to have in common was the way they touched each other. Right out in the open, where anyone could see.

Some of these men must've been the same ones who'd marched with us, but the mood on the street tonight was the opposite of what it had been then. Tonight felt relaxed, simple, fun. Not at all angry.

Plus, it really did seem to be all men. Almost. I did spot one girl hovering in a doorway, talking to a man in a flannel shirt. She looked like she was in her twenties, and she was wearing a leather jacket and dark glasses, even though the sun had already set. She had shoulder-length, jagged blond hair, and she was much, much cooler than I could ever hope to be.

I shrank a little in my boring gray T-shirt and tugged my two thick braids back over my shoulders. Maybe I didn't fit on Castro Street after all.

"Hey, that's the place we saw on the news." Peter pointed to a liquor store across the street. "Remember? On Gay Freedom Day?"

"Right." Last week Mom, Peter, and I had all sat together and watched silently as the local news started its Gay Freedom Day report. Apparently, this year's parade had been the biggest one yet. Mom made us change the channel before the report was over, since Gay Freedom Day reports always show pictures of naked men running around.

"It would be cool to go to that someday, but..." Peter shook his head. "It's always on the news."

"That's true." I tried to hide my relief. I don't want my brother anywhere near Gay Freedom Day. If someone saw him on TV, they might try to hurt him for real. Someone worse than Gary Knopp.

"Hey, are you two registered to vote?"

I jumped, startled to hear how close the new voice was, but Peter turned and grinned. Behind us was a guy holding a clipboard and a folder. He looked a little older than us, and he was dark-skinned, with a puffy Afro. He was wearing a red flannel shirt unbuttoned over a tight white T-shirt, Levi's, and hiking boots.

"I'm afraid we're underage," Peter told the guy in a stage whisper.

He laughed. "That's all right. Want to sign up for our volunteer list? We need all the help we can get. There are ways kids can help, too." He smiled at me, and I blushed again. I'm shorter than Peter, but did I look _that_ much younger? I knew I shouldn't have worn my hair in braids. "Have you heard about Harvey's campaign?"

Peter nodded. "He's running for supervisor again?"

"He is, and he could win it this time, but only if we can turn out enough voters."

"What do you need volunteers to do, exactly?" I asked. "Are you having more marches? We came to the one after the Miami vote."

The guy tilted his head and smiled me. "Yeah, and we need people to canvass, too. Do you two live in the city?"

Peter grimaced. "Yeah. With our mom, in the Excelsior."

The guy grimaced, too, then laughed. "District Eight? My condolences. Is it really all conservative Irish-Catholic down there?"

"Just about."

"And I mean, we are Irish-Catholic," I added, "but we aren't—"

"Conservative. I get it." The guy smiled knowingly. "That just means we need to get you registered as soon as you're legal so you can change your district from the inside out."

Peter nodded vigorously. "My name's Peter, by the way. This is my sister, Sharon." At least he didn't call me his kid sister, the way he used to in junior high.

"Leonard. Nice to meet you both." From the way he shook our hands, I was starting to wonder if Leonard was a politician himself.

He showed Peter a flyer, and I scanned the sidewalks around us. The girl in the leather jacket was gone. All I could see in any direction were men. I shifted, conscious of exactly how much I stuck out on Castro Street.

"Can I get you to sign up?" Leonard held out his folder with a volunteer form on top. I took it from him, but when I glanced down, I hesitated.

The very first line asked for a phone number. What if someone called our house, and Mom answered?

Peter was peering down at the form, too. He met my gaze and frowned slightly.

"Oh, and by the way, Sharon..." Leonard didn't seem to notice our uncertainty. He took back the folder and flipped through a few pages, pulling out a mimeographed sheet of paper. "I promised a friend of mine I'd hang this up in the Elephant Walk, but you can check it out first if you want. I know they're always looking for more women to join them."

The mimeographed text was hard to read, but I made out the words "Women's Bookstore" and an address on the opposite side of the park. The logo at the top read VALENCIA STREET BOOKS.

A whole bookstore, just for women? Did they have a rule about not letting men inside or something?

Maybe that was where all the girls I saw the other night were. Maybe Castro Street was just for gay men when they weren't having marches, and the lesbians hung out in this bookstore.

But if that were true, I wouldn't fit there, either.

A man in a cowboy hat strode toward us, waving to Leonard. I tucked the flyer inside the folder and gave it back. The man asked Leonard for a light, and while they were talking, I told Peter I was ready to go home.

"We just got here." He furrowed his eyebrows. "Why don't you go check out that bookstore? It's only a few blocks away, and there'd be other girls. I could meet you there later and drive you home."

"That's okay. You stay, though. I'll get the bus."

"Are you sure?"

He was trying to argue with me, but he wasn't trying very hard. I'm sure he'd rather have been on his own, anyway. He and Curtis stopped writing to each other last year, and he probably wanted to make new gay friends.

"Yeah. I'm sure."

"Okay, well, don't get home too late. You know how Mom gets."

"All right."

I dragged my feet as I walked away. I was annoyed with myself for not doing what I came out to do, and I wasn't in any hurry to get home and have to lie to Mom about where I'd been.

I gazed into the windows of stores and bars as I headed south. Everywhere I looked, there were more men. Most of them were smiling.

I could see why. Here, they had a place where they could all be together, without worrying about what anyone else thought.

There was a phone booth outside a drugstore, and I slowed down. I thought about calling Kevin and having him come pick me up, but he was working tonight.

That's when a poster taped to the glass booth wall caught my eye. It was handwritten on top of being mimeographed, so the words were barely legible, but the photo in the middle was clear. A girl was wearing a leather miniskirt with a man's shirt and tie. Her hair was slicked back and she was leering at the camera, half-smiling, as though she had a secret she couldn't wait to tell everyone. Dotted around the edges of the poster were more photos, showing men with long hair, sunglasses, and zippered jackets, smoking cigarettes and flipping off the camera.

It took me a minute to decipher the text below the photo:

THE PRUDES! With CREEPS IN TOYLAND and DAMNED REVERENDS. Saturday, July 2. $3. No age limit, kiddies!

The address was on Valencia Street.

I glanced back over my shoulder. Peter was nowhere in sight, but the crowd of men on Castro Street had only gotten deeper. Everyone was milling around, going in and out of restaurants and bars, talking and laughing.

I turned back to the poster. That girl, in the center. There was something about the way she sneered at the camera. I could've stood there staring at her for the rest of the night.

Or... I could go to the show. It was only a few blocks over.

It was a ridiculous idea. Except, the longer I stood there, the less ridiculous it seemed.

I could just walk over and check it out. I didn't have to go inside.

I pulled the rubber bands off the bottoms of my braids and combed out my long hair with my fingers as I walked. When I'd made it two blocks east, I realized I hadn't seen any obviously gay guys in a while. There were more girls on the street now, too, and soon I spotted a straight couple coming out of a corner store, laughing as they tried to hold hands and juggle an armful of brown paper bags at the same time. I guess I'd left the gay area of the city behind.

Before long, I found the address from the poster. There was a line outside the door of the club—if <u>club</u> is the right word for an old industrial building with blacked-out windows and run-down bars on either side.

Before I could lose my nerve, I slid in the back of the line. A pair of girls in purple lipstick, short skirts, and stiletto boots were waiting in front of me. I felt underdressed in my T-shirt and jeans, but at least I didn't have my little-girl hair anymore.

No one seemed to notice how I looked, though. In fact, no one glanced at me twice, not even the bouncer who took my three dollars and silently jammed his thumb toward the loud music spilling out from the dark, humid hallway behind him.

"I can't believe this city finally has a punk scene!" a guy shouted as I followed the short-skirted girls inside.

So <u>that's</u> what this was. A punk show. All I knew about this kind of music was that there was a punk band named the Sex Pistols. A guy at St. John's got suspended for two weeks because he wore a T-shirt with their name on it under his uniform, and the gym teacher saw him changing out of it in the locker room. Peter said they were a band in England, and that people liked them because they cursed a lot.

I doubted the Sex Pistols were in this grimy club tonight, but maybe there'd be other bands who cursed a lot. That idea was surprisingly appealing.

By the time I'd made it halfway down the narrow hall, music was already pumping out from the main room up ahead. I couldn't make out any of the words well enough to tell if the band was cursing, but I did know it was completely different from any music I'd ever heard. The radio stations I listened to played Donna Summer or the Bee Gees or KC and the Sunshine Band—disco love songs, mostly. But the music tonight wasn't anything like disco. It might as well have been piped in from outer space.

There were no smooth, Donna Summer-style voices. In fact, no one was <u>singing</u> at all—just yelling. And whatever they were yelling about, it wasn't love.

It didn't flow, either, the way I always thought music was supposed to. Instead, as I stepped out of the hall and into the big, dark room, the music shrieked and banged and pounded. There was no way to dance to it—not in the way I knew how to dance, at least. The most you could do was shake in tune to all the pounding.

But best of all, this music was <u>angry</u>.

There was a tall, skinny guy in leather pants and spiky black hair bent over the microphone on the little stage at the end of the room, his words incomprehensible under the feedback and squealing guitars and nonstop drumming. Still, the anger came through loud and clear.

It was there in the crowd, too. Everyone I saw—girls in tight jeans and boots, men in wrinkled T-shirts with safety pins stuck through their sleeves, all of them jumping up and down and waving their hands over their heads as the music thumped—they all had that same ferocity on their faces.

It was the same energy I'd felt the night of the march. The sounds and smells and sensations of the club crawled inside my veins, exactly the way the chants had from the crowd that night.

I stepped into the thickest part of the crowd, until I was out of the path of people still pouring in through the door. I shut my eyes, my body thrumming as the fury in the music filled me up.

It felt good to let myself get mad. My shoulders started moving first, and before I'd realized I was doing it, I was shaking along to the music along with everyone else.

"He-e-y-y-y," a winking voice drawled from the stage. At the sound of decipherable words, I opened my eyes. The guys in front of me were bent over a joint, and through the momentary gap in the crowd, I got a good look at the band.

The guy with the spiky hair had picked up a guitar, and a girl had stepped to the front. She had dark hair and wore a trench coat over a short, tight black dress, with bright red lipstick and platform heels, and she was squeezing the microphone so tightly I was afraid she'd crush it.

"SHIT!" the guy in front of me bellowed to his friend, straightening up and waving the joint over his head. "It's that chick you like! It's Midge fucking Spelling!"

The drummer started pounding out a new, sharp rhythm, and a moment later the girl onstage—Midge fucking Spelling, I guess—shut her eyes and growled into the microphone. I couldn't make out her words, but I knew exactly who she was. The girl from the poster.

She stepped backward, tilting her head up so her hair fell loose behind her, her eyes still shut tight. Her dress stretched and shifted and clung to her skin as she lifted the microphone to her lips and shouted at the ceiling. "WOOOO!"

A hundred voices shouted "WOOOO!" back.

"That's right, Midge!" the guy in front of me called, sloshing his drink all over his T-shirt. "Shake it, baby!"

Midge ignored him. I could only make out a few syllables from all her growling—the most frequently used one seemed to be "fuck"—but the lyrics clearly didn't matter as much as the volume and the noise and the <u>life</u> in this room.

The unquestioned rebellion. The complete lack of giving a shit.

Midge didn't look as if she was "shaking it" to me. What she was doing was bigger than that. As long as she was up on that stage, growling into the mic, the rest of us were at her mercy. No one had the option of standing still.

I shut my eyes again and lost track of how long my body rocked to the music. It was easy, almost too easy, to shut off my brain while Midge Spelling was on the stage.

At some point her growls faded out, and when I opened my eyes again, there was a blond girl in a leather jacket in front of me. Her eyes were locked on my face.

I blinked and dropped my head, startled, but when I looked up again, she hadn't moved. She looked familiar, and after another minute I realized she was the girl I'd seen on Castro Street earlier that night. Her look was understated compared to Midge's—she wasn't wearing any makeup at all, and she had on ancient Converse sneakers instead of platform heels—but she fit in perfectly, with her Ramones T-shirt and a leather collar tied below the knee of her ripped jeans. I didn't remember her wearing that on Castro Street.

The girl leaned forward to shout in my ear. I couldn't understand her at first, and I shook my head, so she shouted it again. "DID I SEE YOU ON CASTRO WITH LEONARD TONIGHT?"

I nodded and waved, since shouting over the music seemed impossible.

"I'M EVELYN," the girl shouted. "WANT TO GET A DRINK?"

Half of me wanted to stay where I was, thrumming to the music, but the bar was on the far side of the room, and it looked slightly less jammed with people. Plus, I didn't mind the idea of getting away from the guy in front of me, since his grip on his joint was so loose I was surprised it hadn't already fallen onto my shoe. I nodded again.

The noise near the bar was slightly less deafening than the rest of the club. Evelyn left me standing against a wall and came back a minute later with two glasses.

"I don't usually see women from the Castro at these shows." She still had to lean in and raise her voice so I could understand her, but at least we didn't have to shout.

"I've never been to one of these shows before," I told her, "but I saw the poster and thought I'd check it out."

"Cool. What do you think so far?"

I glanced back toward the stage. Midge was dancing wildly while the band behind her banged on their instruments. The spiky-haired guy had stepped forward to join her at the edge of the stage, jangling his guitar and pounding his head wildly in time with Midge's movements. As if they were dancing together, but in the most inharmonious way possible. "I like the band."

"Yeah, Midge is great." Evelyn pulled a pack of cigarettes out of her pocket and held it out to me. I shook my head, and she popped one into her mouth. "We were supposed to hang out after their set, but it looks like she's already gone the way of Johnny. Once those two are sharing space, the rest of the world turns invisible."

On stage, Midge and the spiky-haired guitar player were rapidly closing the distance between them. She looped the microphone cord around his neck, still growling lyrics I couldn't make out.

I started to tell Evelyn that was how it was with Kevin and me, too, but I stopped when I realized that wasn't quite true.

"How do you know her?" I asked instead.

"Just from being around the scene." Evelyn pulled the cigarette out of her mouth and released a puff of smoke. "She's incredible onstage, isn't she? I'm more into the Dils when it comes to their actual music, though. Don't tell her I said that, okay?"

I couldn't imagine ever speaking to Midge Spelling. "Sure thing."

"So, what brought you to the Castro?"

Evelyn looked really interested in hearing my answer, and it suddenly occurred to me that she might be gay. In fact...maybe she thought I was gay.

Oh, my gosh.

"I'm straight," I blurted.

Evelyn stared at me for a long moment. Then she burst out laughing. "Good for you. Me, too, so good for us, I mean."

"Oh, um, I mean—" I felt so stupid. Blood rushed to my cheeks as I desperately fumbled to erase the past ten seconds. "Oh, my gosh. Oh, gosh. I'm so sorry. I didn't mean...it isn't as if I thought— Oh, shoot."

"It's all right." Evelyn was still laughing. "Thank you for sharing. How old are you, anyway?"

"Uh..." Should I lie? There was probably no point. Braids or no braids, I'd given myself away. "Still in high school?"

She laughed, not seeming surprised at all. "So you're what, sixteen?"

"Er... I will be soon. Really soon."

"Uh-huh. What's your name?"

I'd told her I was straight before I told her my name? Could this night get any more embarrassing? "Sharon."

"Okay, you're Sharon, you're fifteen, and you're straight. Wow, we already know each other so well." Evelyn's grin was friendly, though. Behind us, the sound of the instruments onstage had been replaced by a roar of cheers and shouts from the crowd. The Prudes' set must have ended. "To get back to my question, what brought you to the Castro?"

"My brother, um, well, he's..." I cut myself off when I realized I probably shouldn't tell this stranger about Peter.

"Don't worry, I get it." She grinned. "Wow. When I was fifteen, I was spending my Saturday nights in a field tipping cows. Listen, Sharon, if you ever get back up into this part of town, you should come by Valencia Street Books. We want to reach out to more young women here in the city. Especially women your age who might not have a safe space where they can go. It's a couple of blocks up, and we have volunteer meetings every week."

"Oh, yeah. I think I've heard of it."

"Eee-vieeee." The growling voice was so familiar, I knew it was Midge Spelling before I turned my head. Her arm was around that guitar player's—Johnny's—shoulders, and they were both covered in sweat. Johnny had tied Midge's trench coat around his waist, leaving her in just her black lace corset dress. Her shoulders and most of her chest were bare. "We're gonna be in the back for a while if you want to come."

"Cool, I will." Evelyn took another puff on her cigarette. "This is Sharon."

"Hey," I said. I couldn't stop staring at Midge. Wasn't she cold?

"Hey." Midge peered down. In her heels, she towered a good six inches over me. "I saw you from the stage."

"You did?" My heart pounded in my chest.

"Yeah. When you walked in you looked like a deer stuck in the headlights." She laughed, but it was a friendly laugh, like Evelyn's.

"That sounds about right," I said, and now all three of them were laughing.

I can't believe Midge Spelling laughed at something I said. I can't believe I even existed in the same space as Midge Spelling.

"It was fun watching you dance once you got into it, though," she went on. It must've been another joke, but before I could laugh she'd already turned back to Johnny. "See you around."

They walked off with their arms wrapped around each other's waists.

"I'd better go." Evelyn lifted her chin toward the stage, where another band was setting up. Two of the guys were pointing drumsticks at each other and shouting words I couldn't make out. "You watching the next set?"

"Um. I should probably head out."

"Cool. Anyway, come by the store if you can."

"Cool." I nodded. Suddenly that sounded worth considering. "I will, thanks."

And as I turned my back, pushed my way through the thrumming crowd and walked out into the nighttime chill, there was a buzz of pleasant, unfamiliar hope thrumming under my skin, too.

Yours,
Sharon

Sunday, July 3, 1977

Dear Harvey,

I HAVE PROOF.

Ha! I always knew my aunt and uncle were hypocrites, but now I have <u>physical evidence</u>.

Since the Miami vote, I've been trying to keep my head down. I got that Patti Smith album, <u>Horses</u>. I bought a couple of other punk albums while I was at it, but none of them can beat Patti. I listen to <u>Horses</u> every night before bed with my headphones plastered over my ears.

During the day, though, I can't escape the noise of Aunt Mandy crowing about her victory. She and my uncle have been all over the news, and seeing herself on TV and hearing her own voice on the radio will always put a mammoth fucking skip in my aunt's step.

At church this morning, half the service was about how wonderful she and Uncle Russell are, the way it's been every week since the vote. One of the board members, Mr. Murdoch, got up and gave a speech about how lucky we are to have the two of them as our spiritual leaders. Then they took up yet another special offering for the New Way Protect Our Children Fund.

I sat there in the pew and watched as my parents and everyone else wrote out checks. The envelopes were stacked so high in the offering plates, it reminded me of those wobbly block towers my brother used to build in kindergarten. I don't know about you, Harvey, but for me, the most satisfying part of building those towers was knocking them to smithereens afterward.

After church, all I wanted was to go home and lie on my bed and write to you, but my aunt and uncle were hosting a pre-Fourth of July barbecue, so dozens of us wound up stuffed onto their back porch. It was more of the same—everyone talking about how amazing they are, and how they're single-handedly saving the country from sin, and how Anita Bryant must be thrilled to have such talented partners on the West Coast. I was close to puking by the end, so I told my mom I was going to the "office" in my aunt and uncle's den to see if there was any work that needed to be done.

There wasn't much. The phone was quiet, since it was a Sunday afternoon, and we'd just sent out a big mailing, so there were no envelopes to stuff. The offering plates were sitting on the bed, though, the envelopes already spilling out of their tower into a messy pile, so I sat down and started ripping them open and stacking up the checks for Aunt Mandy to take to the bank on Tuesday.

Every week we get envelopes in the mail with the same kind of checks. A lot of people want to make sure everyone knows they hate the gays, so they show it with their wallets. That's a lot easier than doing the actual grunt work.

So there I was, sitting on the bed, ripping open envelopes and sorting the checks into piles—tall stacks for the $25s and $50s and $100s, a smaller one for $200s and $250s, and a tiny one for $300s and over—but I needed paper clips, so I opened the desk drawer and fished around.

Well, Harvey, guess what I just <u>happened</u> to find?

An old check register for the New Way Protect Our Children Fund. With all the money Aunt Mandy and Uncle Russell have spent out of those generous donations.

You'd think they'd be spending it on stamps for the mailings, or advertisements, or getting brochures printed. You'd be wrong.

Harvey, that check register was absolutely <u>full</u> of payments to places that have nothing to do with anybody's children.

One check was made out to a <u>hairdresser</u>. Two were to a golf pro shop, and most of the others were to some radio station in L.A.

I looked up the station in the phone book, and it isn't one where the campaign is supposed to be advertising—but it <u>is</u> the station that reporter came from the night of the Miami vote.

It's also the station my aunt and uncle have spent the past three years begging to give them an hour-long show so they can, and I quote, "spread the Gospel to the ungodly."

Aunt Mandy and Uncle Russell are <u>stealing people's money</u>, Harvey. It was all right there in that fucking check register.

Once I figured out what it meant, I wasn't even all that surprised. This is <u>completely</u> the kind of thing they'd do.

They don't really give a shit about gay people. I never heard either of them say a single word about "militant homosexuality" until Anita Bryant came along. All they care about is how many people know their names. Now they've learned they can bring in cash if they preach about how important it is to protect all us poor innocent kids from the evil gays.

So I took it. I put that fucking check register right in my

purse, Harvey. Then I found the paper clips, closed the drawer, and went right back to sorting those checks as though nothing had changed, except I was doing it all with a shit-eating grin on my face.

My aunt and uncle will probably never notice it's gone. The dates on the register were from a few months ago, so I doubt they're using it anymore. They must think they're beyond the laws of earth and man that they can just leave something like that lying around and not have it come back to bite them in the end.

You know what's funny, Harvey—I used to think every word they said was true. When I was a little kid, I'd sit there in the pew on Sundays listening to my uncle preach about how our culture was a hotbed of sin. I'd cry on my way home from church, I was so scared of going to Hell and seeing the devil up close.

Then, when I was six, one of my sister's friends told me the truth about Santa Claus—how it was all a story our parents made up to get us to behave. I didn't believe her, so she showed me in the dictionary where it said Santa was a "mythical figure." By then I was old enough to know that if the dictionary said it, it was true—which meant everyone had lied to me my whole life, even my mom.

Back then, I'd trusted my mom.

That's when I first got suspicious about God. As far as I could tell, the way adults talked about God wasn't all that different from the way they talked about Santa. Every week in Sunday school, it was always the same: you had to be good, because God was watching.

For years, every time I thought about that—and I thought about it every Sunday, and during Bible classes at school, too—I felt horribly guilty. I was sure someone would be able to tell and I'd get in trouble, so I started being extra careful. I did everything exactly the way I was supposed to. I followed along with every word of every hymn. I never passed notes in church, even when my friends were doing it. I never ate dessert during Lent, even on my birthday when my mom said it was okay to make an exception.

But I always thought Aunt Mandy knew I was hiding something. The way she looked at me made me nervous, even then. She and Uncle Russell didn't have any children yet, and I suspected she didn't like kids much. She'd refused to let any of us into her living room since my sister once finger-painted her drapes, and that was before I was born.

Then, in fourth grade, we had to make a diorama for Science about an animal that was mentioned in the Bible, and I went over to my aunt and uncle's house to look up antelopes in their encyclopedias. Back then, our house was down the street from theirs, and we were allowed to go over without calling first. No one answered when I knocked, but since everyone in our neighborhood left their doors unlocked, I'd gone into my uncle's office and found the encyclopedias. I took some notes, and I was packing up my stuff to head home when I realized I needed to use the bathroom.

I should've just waited until I got back to my house. If I'd only held my fucking pee and gone out the side door…

But I didn't. I walked down the hall to the bathroom, past the spare bedroom at the back of the house. I heard some strange squeaking noises coming from behind the door, and I got scared. As far as I knew, Uncle Russell was at church, and Aunt Mandy was out shopping.

I don't know what made me push that door open. Did I think there was a burglar? Did I think the house was haunted?

Either way, what good did I think it would do if I walked in? It doesn't matter now, I guess.

I pushed open the door and stood there, blinking. The room was dark, the shades drawn, the overhead light off. The squeaking went on for another second, then stopped.

I don't know how long I stood there before I understood what I was looking at. I know I peed my pants, though. Then Aunt Mandy and the man on the bed with her—he was actually closer to a boy than a man, not that much older than I am now, but back then, he seemed like a grown-up—disentangled themselves and pulled their clothes back on. Aunt Mandy stalked up to me, standing so tall and lifting her chin so high it was clear I was the one who was in trouble.

It's only because I've replayed this moment in my head so many times that I remember how disheveled she looked. Her pantyhose were on the floor by the bed, her hair was matted and sticking up in the back, and her blouse was half-unbuttoned.

And me? I was standing there in wet green corduroys, shaking so hard I couldn't move or speak. I could only wait for her to tell me what to do, the way I always did.

"No one will believe you if you tell," she said, without the slightest hint of a waver in her voice. "And if you do, I'll make sure your parents find out exactly what kind of child you really are."

I couldn't move. It had never occurred to me to tell anyone else about what I'd seen. I didn't even understand what I had seen.

"I know you're not a good girl, Tammy." Aunt Mandy's eyes were locked on my face. It hurt to look back, so I flicked my eyes to the man behind her. He was getting dressed, and I realized then that I'd seen his naked butt before. <u>Ew</u>.

Aunt Mandy grabbed my chin and jerked it upward until I had no choice but to meet her gaze. I froze.

"I know your heart," she said, "and God knows it, too. We know all your little secrets."

I unfroze and sucked in a breath. She knew? <u>How?</u>

See, now I know Aunt Mandy isn't superhuman, for all that she'd used the word "we." As if she was God and the queen and some two-timing preacher's wife from Ohio all at the same time.

Then, though, I was nine, and I was scared, and I'd just seen a guy's naked butt in the middle of the afternoon. I believed her when she said she knew all my secrets.

It wasn't just some guy, either. I know that now, too. It took me until the next Sunday at church before I placed him—he was George Tinley. His father was a board member, one of the church's cofounders who'd worked with Aunt Mandy on the school-board elections years before. George went to UCLA, but he came back to town during his school breaks. After I caught them, though, he stopped coming around, and before long, his parents moved to Nevada.

I have no idea when George and my aunt first started sleeping together—whether it went on for months or years, or whether it was only that one afternoon. But knowing wouldn't erase the memory of pissing myself, or the sight of my aunt's legs around his waist.

Sorry if that was too graphic, Harvey. My heart's pounding writing all this down. I haven't thought about it, not this clearly, for years. I've been trying <u>not</u> to think about it.

I should've realized then what a fucking hypocrite she was.

All I could think about was what she'd said, about knowing all my secrets.

I believed her, Harvey. For years. Part of me still does.

She <u>can't</u> know the whole truth—I've kept this secret so well, for so long, it's all I think about most of the time—but I can't shake the feeling that in some bizarre, impossible way, she does. Sometimes I'll talk myself out of it, but then I'll catch her giving me a cold, dark look across the sanctuary, and a shiver will run through me as it all comes back.

She was right, too. No one would've believed me if I'd told.

Besides, who would I tell? My mother? Aunt Mandy's big sister, the one who took care of her after their parents died? The one who brought her out to California, then watched without bothering to get involved as her 18-year-old sister married the 33-year-old Reverend Russell Dale and slowly took over the entire family?

For all I know, my cousin Eddie isn't actually Uncle Russell's kid. He was born not that long after I caught my aunt with George. Maybe my aunt's been lying to everyone for even longer than me.

Or maybe she really is the Old Testament God in earthly form, and she'll rain down her punishments on anyone who doesn't do her bidding.

Which do you think is more likely, Harvey?

The check register's still in my purse. Maybe I'll keep it there for good. I bring my purse everywhere, so I won't have to worry about anyone finding it.

Maybe I'll start carrying this diary in there, too. That way I'll know my secrets are always safe.

From now on, whenever I'm listening to someone talk about how my aunt is God's gift to humanity, I can reach in my purse, feel that fucking check register with my fingers, and remember I have solid evidence that she's anything but.

It doesn't matter what she thinks of me. It doesn't matter what <u>anyone</u> thinks. I've wasted so much time being scared of her, Harvey. She's the one who should be afraid of <u>me</u>.

Peace,
Tammy

Dear Tammy,

I hope you had a good Fourth of July. Do you have a summer job? I've been babysitting for a few families in the neighborhood. There's one on our block that has eight kids, and I spent the Fourth with them. They have a five-year-old named Jack who's terrified of blue fireworks, but not any other color, so every time a blue one came, I covered his eyes with my hands. We were both laughing by the end.

I really liked reading about your big family in your last letter. Mine is so small, I forget sometimes that it's not that way for everyone. It must be nice having all those sisters and aunts and uncles around.

Here's my answer to the next question on the list:

<u>What are your favorite hobbies?</u>

I play softball in my church league. Or I did, up until last year, when our coach moved to Michigan and our team disbanded.

Also, I don't know if this counts as a hobby, but have you ever listened to punk music? Last weekend I went to a punk show for the first time and I <u>loved</u> it. Have you ever felt as if you didn't belong? I do, a lot of the time—well, most of the time—but that night the music was so intense, it was as if I didn't have to worry about any of it anymore.

I haven't told my friends. They mostly listen to Peter Frampton and Ted Nugent. But I wondered if maybe things were different in southern California.

Yours truly,
Sharon Hawkins

P.S. Sorry, I know I just asked you questions that aren't on the official list for the pen pal project. It's okay if you don't have time to answer. ~~Going to that show the other night reminded me of how lonely I get sometimes. You know what, never mind, this probably sounds stupid.~~

Wednesday, July 13, 1977

Dear Sharon,

Are you kidding me?

You like punk? I don't know anyone who listens to punk!

When you said you didn't know Patti Smith, I assumed that meant you weren't a fan, but this changes everything.

What bands did you see? Tell me every detail! I've never been to a show—punk bands don't come to Orange County—but I want to see one so bad.

I only have a few albums so far, the ones the guy at the record store said were good, but after Patti, my favorites are the Ramones and the Dictators. Have you heard the Dictators' version of "I Got You Babe"? It's so funny. I like Cher—her show's my favorite one on TV—but some of her music is kind of cheesy.

If you ever got to see Patti live, I think I might literally die. Her Horses album changed my life. Or maybe it's in the process of changing it right now. I'm still a work in progress. ~~Just knowing Patti exists makes me feel a little less strange sometimes.~~

Wow, I wonder what the odds are that we got matched up as pen pals when we seem to be the only two people either of us knows who likes punk. (Why don't your friends listen to it, though? I thought it'd be huge in San Francisco.)

Anyway, speaking of works in progress, my main hobby is art. I make collages. My art teacher says collages aren't real art, so I can't turn them in for credit, which I guess makes it a hobby. It's fun, though. Messing around with pencils and glue and magazines is a great way to tune out whenever I start worrying too much.

I don't know if I have any other hobbies, unless you count volunteering with my church. Everything around here is kind of about church, one way or another. You're Catholic, right? My uncle started New Way Baptist, the biggest church in our part of Orange County. People come from towns all around here every week to hear him preach and to sign up for whatever campaign my aunt's working on. I work on the campaigns, too, sometimes with my youth group and sometimes on my own. For the past few months, I've been stuffing a lot of envelopes in my aunt and uncle's den.

Sorry, this turned into another long letter! I promise I'll try to keep it short next time.

Yours truly,
Tammy

P.S. I forgot you asked about having a summer job. I just started training as a lifeguard at the country-club pool. I got incredibly sunburned on my first day and now I have to sit under an umbrella, which is embarrassing.

Also, I saw where you crossed something out in your last letter. Don't worry, I didn't try to read it. I looked back and saw that I crossed something out here, too, but I wanted to say that if there's anything you want to tell me, you can. We're never going to meet and we don't know any of the same people, so we could talk about stuff we might not want to tell other people. If you wanted to, I mean.

Dear Tammy,

How did Patti Smith change your life? Does your life need changing? It seems really cool already.

The day after I got your letter I got paid from one of my babysitting jobs, so I went straight to the record store and bought that Patti Smith album, <u>Horses</u>. I don't know that much about punk yet, but I want to go to more shows. I think there's a bigger club in North Beach, and I can take the bus there. If I ever find out Patti Smith is coming, I'll write and tell you first thing.

Her album—wow, you weren't kidding. Just looking at the picture on the cover was kind of shocking. I've never seen a girl who looked like her. I had to hide it from my mom before I'd even played it.

But the songs—<u>wow</u> all over again. Her words are almost poetry, only it's really creepy poetry.

I've listened to the whole album all the way through I don't know how many times, but I always hear words I didn't catch before. Plus, her voice <u>sounds</u> strange, too. Almost like a man's.

It's as though Patti Smith lives in a different world, and it's a scary world, but it's also <u>real</u> in a way that this world isn't. Do you know what I mean? It's as if everyone else is so busy being fake all the time, but Patti Smith's actually being honest, and it's the first time anyone ever has been. She isn't trying to pretend the world's perfect and happy and shiny all the time.

Do you ever think there might be this huge worldwide conspiracy to convince us that our lives will be perfect if we just do what we're supposed to do? I don't know if this happens at your school, but here we get lectures about how important it is to tuck in your shirt to honor the Lord, and at dances, the teachers walk around with balloons that they slide in between couples while they're dancing to make sure they "leave space for the holy ghost." Once, in fifth grade, my friend Rhonda got her hand slapped with a ruler because a teacher heard her say "dang it" at recess.

The way they all seem to see it, if we follow the rules—don't drink or smoke or have sex until we're married, don't wear skirts that show our knees, always go to church on Sundays—we'll be rewarded with a house and a dog and a husband and children and a picket fence and all the other things we're supposed to want. Except I don't know if that _is_ what I want. I'm allergic to dogs, for one thing. Plus, I'm sure my mother wanted all those things when <u>she</u> was my age, but she followed all the rules and my dad left anyway. What's the point?

Wow. Okay, I'm sorry. I know you said we could be honest in these letters, but I'm still tempted to cross out some of what I just wrote.

It's only that...it was kind of nice, putting all that down. I have a diary, but that's mostly for writing about what I've been doing lately. This feels different.

So I'll leave it. I should probably ask you not to put it in your report, but you don't seem like someone who'd tell your teachers on me.

Shoot, it's getting late and I haven't even looked at the question list. Oh—favorite TV show. This one's easy, because it's the same as yours—Sonny & Cher. Or, well, I can't stand Sonny, but Cher is hilarious. Even if her music is basically the opposite of Patti Smith's.

My boyfriend says Sonny and Cher represent middle America's response to the hippie movement. I haven't told him I've started listening to punk yet, but he'll probably have an opinion on that, too. He wants to be a psychiatrist, but he can't afford med school, so he's majoring in business at SF State.

Yikes, sorry, I'd better stop and go to bed or this will be our longest letter yet!

Yours truly,
Sharon

Wednesday, July 27, 1977

Dear Sharon,

I really enjoy getting these letters from you. It's interesting hearing about your life in San Francisco. I never would've thought teachers there would slap kids with rulers. Maybe your city isn't as different from here as I thought.

Also, I liked what you said—about picket fences and all that. I know exactly what you mean. Exactly.

My school sounds a lot more similar to yours than I expected. Plus, it's kind of hilarious that we're both into Cher <u>and</u> punk music.

Would it be okay if I asked you another question that isn't on the list? I want to know what it's like having a boyfriend. I've never had a real one, I've only gone to parties and stuff with guys. My sister says the best thing about having a boyfriend is that you don't have to worry about whether anyone will ask you to dances, but I hope she was joking.

Yours truly,
Tammy

Dear Diary,

I think my brother's mad at me.

We were leaving church this morning, and it was gorgeous out. The fog had burned away while we were inside, and I peeled off my cardigan and slung it over my purse. I was wearing a new tunic dress, a yellow one with cap sleeves, and Mom frowned down at my bare arms.

I tried to come up with a strategy in case she ordered me to put my cardigan back on. I could tell her we were outside, and that I'd bought the dress myself, with my own money. Or that I was almost sixteen and what I wore was my decision, and besides, there was nothing inappropriate about wearing a cap-sleeve dress outside, even on the church steps.

But before Mom could comment on my arms, Mrs. Upton started talking about local politics.

"It's these strange supervisor elections they're having now," Mrs. Upton said, fanning herself with a bulletin. She was my Sunday school teacher when I was in fourth-through-sixth grades, and somehow she looks twenty years older now than she did then. And she looked awfully old then. "<u>District</u> elections. I can't keep track of the candidates anymore."

"That police officer from our neighborhood is running," Mom told her in the same voice she uses with students who are particularly slow at algebra. "The one who saved the family during that awful fire—Mr. White. He says he'll clean up the city."

"Oh, good. <u>Someone</u> needs to clear out all that revolting nonsense." Mrs. Upton tilted her head meaningfully, and Mom tilted hers back in agreement.

I glanced around for Peter so we could roll our eyes. He'd been right behind us on the steps, but suddenly there was no sign of him. Mom and Mrs. Upton kept walking, still talking about politics, but I hung back, and a minute later I got a glimpse of my brother's jacket behind a column off to the far side of the steps.

"What are you doing?" I asked when I reached him. He was alone in the narrow space between the column and a stained-glass window, his shoulders hunched.

"Nothing." He glanced my way and sagged back against the column. "Just needed to get away."

"I know what you mean. I can't stand Mrs. Upton, either."

"It's not Mrs. Upton. It's Mom." He peered around the column, then added in a whisper, "I can't believe she wants to vote for Dan White."

"I've never heard of that guy. Aren't there a ton of people running?"

"Yeah, but he's the only one promising to get rid of <u>social deviants</u>." Peter said the last two words in a high-pitched whisper. "He'd carpet-bomb the Castro if he could."

"Wait, what?"

He shook his head. "It doesn't matter. Can you believe what Mom said? About 'cleaning up the city'?"

"What about it?"

"Come on, you know that's code for getting rid of all those 'disgusting homosexuals' up in Eureka Valley."

"How do you know? She could have meant anything. Most of the city is literally just dirty."

"It doesn't mean just anything. It never does." Peter rolled his eyes. At me, though, not Mom or Mrs. Upton. "But you don't get it, because it isn't about you."

I sucked in a breath. "I'm sorry."

"You never even wanted to go back there with me after that one time. I asked you to come stuff envelopes for Harvey, but all you ever want to do is listen to those bands with the stupid names."

That hurt, but he wasn't wrong. Twice he'd invited me to join him at Harvey Milk's camera shop to put together mailings with the other campaign volunteers, but I'd said no. I didn't like being the only girl around a bunch of gay men.

But I hated the way Peter was looking at me. As if I'd failed him.

"I already knew Mom thought that way." He tilted his head back, talking to the sky now instead of me. "It just sucks that she's supporting this jackass."

"Yeah."

"I've got to go." He pushed off the wall and turned his back to me. "Tell Mom I'm over at a friend's for lunch."

"Where are you really going?"

"It doesn't matter."

He left, stalking up the street in his church suit, heading north. Toward the bus stop.

I could've chased after him. Instead I went back to catch up with Mom, said goodbye to Mrs. Upton, and walked the rest of the way home, nodding along while Mom told me not to take off my cardigan until we'd left church grounds next time.

When we got home, I came straight upstairs to my room and got my diary out from under my pillow. I thought if I wrote this down I'd be able to sort it all out in my head, but I don't feel any better now than I did when my brother first walked away from me.

Yours,
Sharon

Dear Harvey,

I am <u>so mad</u> right now. I can barely write, I'm shaking so hard.

Aunt Mandy called a special youth group meeting for tonight. I didn't think anything of it at first. We have a lot of meetings, and if they're called in the middle of the week it's usually because someone needs us to urgently plan a bake sale, and I get put in charge of making six different kinds of pie.

We met in our living room—we always meet at my house when Aunt Mandy doesn't want to bother opening up the church—only to discover that the <u>real</u> reason she wanted us to meet was to plan a pep rally for the first day of school. Not for a sports team, though. No, no, she wants us to hold a pep rally about gay rights. Except she called it a pep rally about "militant homosexuality," and she tried to act as if it was all <u>our</u> idea.

"It's important that we hear from you young people," she said, after she passed around the same bowl of stale popcorn we have at every youth group meeting, "in a public demonstration of your support for the sanctity of the Christian family. Particularly now, when that man is threatening to take over the government up in San Francisco. You're the ones most affected by the threat these deviants pose, and it's important to show the world where you stand. Channel 7 already said they'll cover it."

Typical Aunt Mandy. My stomach started shrinking as soon as she started talking about you, Harvey, and all the other "<u>deviants</u>," and it only got worse when she mentioned the TV station. Obviously, Aunt Mandy would call her friends in the press about the youth group's event before she said anything to us youth.

Channel 7 is her new favorite, ever since that radio reporter went on the air and called our church "a minor player in Anita Bryant's army." My aunt doesn't take being called "minor" sitting down—she called in a favor and got him fired a week later.

It's so obvious this is all a vanity project for her. How am I the only one who sees it?

My mother, who was sitting next to her on the couch tonight, kept bobbing her head approvingly, as though every word Aunt Mandy said came straight from the Bible itself. Mom's her big sister, but she does whatever Aunt Mandy tells her, as if she has no mind of her own.

Have I told you the story of how she started our school, Harvey? I researched it all for a project during the big celebration for New Way Christian's tenth anniversary. I found a ton of stories about it in old newspapers, so I guess the adults around here must remember how it happened, but no one talks about it now.

It started when my aunt had only just graduated from the local public high school herself. She and my uncle got married that summer, and soon afterward she organized a church committee to protest the school district she'd gone to for its "progressive" methods, like teaching evolution and sex ed. She talked to the newspaper about how a couple members of the school board belonged to the ACLU, and her committee ran an ad campaign that kept them from getting reelected. Apparently that wasn't enough for her, though, because two years later, she opened her very own private school right next to the brand-new New Way Baptist Church, of which her husband just <u>happened</u> to be the pastor. The school and the church both just <u>happened</u> to be funded by generous donors from Aunt Mandy's committee, with help from the Ocean View Development Company, whose newest junior partner just <u>happened</u> to be Aunt Mandy's brother-in-law.

(He also just happens to be my father. There's always been a whole lot of incestuousness with money around here.)

The first student to enroll at New Way Christian School was my oldest sister, Laura. She was in first grade then. Aunt Mandy's committee never stopped working, though. Now my mom's the committee chair, so her whole life is spent at my aunt's beck and call.

I swear, Harvey, my mother used to think for herself. She was even kind of fun, once upon a time. With so many kids in our family, she used to schedule "special days" with each of us where we could go out with just her. On mine, we always went horseback riding on the trail near the golf course. We'd talk for hours out under the trees. It never occurred to me back then that things would ever be different.

God, I was such a stupid kid.

For the first part of tonight's meeting, while Aunt Mandy droned on about how important our fucking pep rally was going to be, I kept my eyes on my lap. Until my aunt said the words I'd been dreading. "Tammy, as vice president of the youth group, I'd like you to take on a leadership role in planning this event. Brett's very busy with his senior year starting."

At that moment, Brett, the president of our youth group, was sitting on the couch opposite me. He and the three guys next to him had walked in reeking of pot five minutes after the meeting started. Ever since, all four of them had been drifting off with vacant half smiles on their faces.

Sure, Brett was obviously <u>way</u> too busy to organize the homosexuality festivities.

There were a lot of things I wanted to say to my aunt. I wanted to tell her to shut up, first of all. I wanted to tell her that no, I didn't have time to plan an anti-Harvey Milk pep rally, either, and by the way, I knew the truth behind all her lies.

I wanted to tell her I wasn't scared of her anymore. I wanted to stop being meek, secretive little Tammy Larson and turn into Patti Smith, fearless and angry and bold.

I wanted to shout, "FUCK YOU AND YOUR FUCK-ING RALLY, AUNT MANDY!" and storm out of my parents' house forever.

And then my aunt smiled at me.

Aunt Mandy's smile is terrifying, Harvey. She does it surprisingly often, but there's never any light in her eyes.

Tonight her eyes were hard as steel, and when I looked at her, she tilted her head to the side—only a fraction of an inch, but it tightened the distance between us, somehow.

Suddenly I was nine years old again, realizing all at once that my aunt could see right past the good girl who does as she's told, straight to the screwed-up lesbian who hasn't believed in God since kindergarten.

I forgot everything I'd dreamed of saying. All I wanted was for her to stop looking at me.

"Okay," I mumbled. "Yeah."

"Lovely!" Aunt Mandy beamed, but that steely look never left her eyes. "We'll show America that the young people in this state are better than what the press would have them believe. They've got everyone thinking those deviants up in San Francisco stand for us all, when the truth is, we've got far more decent people than we do, ah…"

For once, she seemed lost for words. Probably because she'd already used "deviants" twice.

"Junkies, Mrs. Dale?" Carolyn suggested. She was sitting on the floor across from me.

"Certainly," Aunt Mandy said, but she pursed her lips. She'd wanted to say something else altogether.

"Ma'am?" Carolyn leaned forward in her seat. "Is it true that the reason the freaks are drawn to San Francisco is because it sits on the biggest earthquake fault line in the world?"

Aunt Mandy smiled a little. "Did you hear that at school?"

Carolyn nodded.

"Well, the important thing for you to understand is that this is all part of God's plan." My aunt's smile smoothed out, turning fake-warm. "He's testing us. He's sent his enemies, but he sent Anita Bryant, too. Soon, the avowed homosexuals and their fellow sinners will see God's plan in action, and the Christians will rise again."

Every word she said made me shrink deeper into myself.

Finally, Aunt Mandy stood up to lead us in a prayer. She asked God to give us the strength to save our generation from the heathen elements and secular culture and unclean music and all the rest. Finally, just when I was sure I couldn't take one more second of this shit without tearing my hair out of my skull, it was over.

Now I have a pep rally to plan. So I can shout with all my

so-called friends about the evil dirty secular heathens. People like me.

I've had so many dreams about San Francisco, Harvey. I went to the library and read a travel guide to Northern California, but it didn't say anything about gay people. I found some articles about you in the <u>San Francisco Chronicle</u>, though. You keep saying the world will get better.

It's never seemed that way to me.

Is my aunt right about San Francisco? Is it a whole city full of sinners? Are there enough to elect someone like you?

I'm trying to have hope, Harvey, like you said. Even when it's hard. But in the meantime, I'm hoping I'll have one of those San Francisco dreams tonight.

Peace,
Tammy

Dear Tammy,

I've been trying to figure out how to answer your question about having a boyfriend. It's a way more interesting question than any of the ones on the official pen pal list!

Here's a story that might help answer it. One night a few months back, we were watching TV with my brother and my friend Rhonda, and out of nowhere Kevin—that's my boyfriend—asked, "Hey, do you all believe in God?"

Now, we're all Catholic, and we take Religion every year at school, so the rest of us were kind of surprised he asked, but Kevin's into thinking about that kind of thing.

Rhonda said of course she believed in God, but she hated going to confession because Father Murphy smelled so bad she couldn't focus on her sins. Peter thought about it for a few minutes and shrugged and said yeah, he believed, but I could tell from the way he said it that he wasn't completely sure.

Then Kevin half smiled at me, and I half smiled back, and we both nodded. We didn't need to say anything more. I believe in God, for sure, but his question was too complicated to answer with a straight yes or no.

Kevin must've known what I was thinking, because he didn't ask again. We've been together long enough that we don't have to say everything out loud.

So I asked what <u>he</u> believed, and he started talking about an essay he'd read about Friedrich Nietzsche and Carl Jung. Rhonda and Peter stopped paying attention, but I listened to every word. Kevin never answered the question either, not directly, but I understood what he meant.

Everything's just simpler when I'm with him. I don't have to worry about whether I'm doing what I'm supposed to be doing, or what anyone else thinks. I don't get frustrated or feel out of place. Being around Kevin is, well...easy.

Also, he's cute. Plus, your sister's kind of right—it <u>is</u> nice not having to worry about getting asked to dances.

Huh. That was fun to write. I don't know about you, Tammy, but this pen pal assignment isn't turning out the way I expected.

And I guess we're still doing the official questions, too, so:

<u>How do you plan to maintain your strong Christian morality this summer despite the temptations of modern society?</u>

This is a ridiculous question. Also, there are only a few weeks of summer left. I've probably already given in to the temptations of modern society by my teachers' standards. I don't think they'd approve of me going to punk shows on the weekends, or making out with Kevin in his car after he gets off work on Tuesday nights.

Since none of that will help you with your report, you can use this instead: I plan to pray every day and go to confession every week to help me focus on my faith and resist temptation and blah, blah, blah—oh, my gosh I'm boring <u>myself</u>. I can't imagine how much I'm boring you.

Also, oh, my gosh again—I just realized what I wrote up there about God. Wow. It's a good thing we already said we'd keep these letters between us, but this is a big deal, so could you please promise again you won't tell <u>anyone</u> what I said, even your parents? Adults never understand this kind of thing.

Yours truly,
Sharon

P.S. I just read this letter over again, and...could you please write back soon and promise me you won't tell anyone? I'm going to mail this now, because I really do trust you, but... I don't know. I worry about a lot of things lately.

Friday, August 5, 1977

Dear Harvey,

There's something I've started thinking about. It's probably ridiculous, but after I got Sharon's letter today, I'm thinking about it more than ever.

I don't have long to decide, either. She sounded worried, so I want to write back to her today. If I drive to the post office my letter will get in the mail tonight, but it'll still take two days to get to San Francisco.

Obviously I'm not going to tell anyone what she wrote, but I like that she trusted me enough to write it. Sharon seems to trust me with things she wouldn't tell a lot of people. I want to trust her, too.

That's dangerous, though—trusting someone. Especially someone I've never met.

I want to send her the collage I'm working on. She's the one person who might understand it. I don't know if anyone would get what I'm trying to say, but that's okay. Art isn't supposed to be literal.

And I... I want to tell her, Harvey.

She lives in San Francisco, and it's obvious she isn't afraid to rebel. She's so different from everyone I know.

I think she might be okay with me being…you know.

There have even been times when I wondered if <u>she</u> could be like us. If I could get to San Francisco somehow…

Anyway, it doesn't matter. I can't get lost in some pointless fantasy. Besides, she has a boyfriend.

I just want to tell someone, Harvey. <u>So much</u>. I don't think I even realized it until this pen pal thing started, but suddenly it's as if I'm <u>desperate</u> for someone to know who I really am. I'm spending every day now getting ready for this goddamn pep rally, and the truth's ready to burst out of me.

<u>Could</u> I tell her? Could I write her a letter and actually put in the words "I'm gay"?

God, just writing that to <u>you</u> was terrifying.

What if I tell her and she never wants to write to me again? Or worse—<u>way</u> worse—what if she tells someone?

Her mom's a teacher. What if she tells <u>her</u>? Or what if she leaves my letter out on a table and her mom or her brother sees it?

Did you ever feel this way? I never thought I could tell <u>anyone</u>, Harvey.

I want to be proud of who I am, the way you are, but <u>how</u>? How do you make yourself feel something when everyone around you believes the exact opposite?

This is the kind of secret people like me take to their graves. If my family knew, my life would be over. Maybe literally.

I'm sorry, Harvey. I can't tell her. I know I'm letting you down, but I don't have your courage.

Tammy

Friday, August 5, 1977

Dear Sharon,

I can't write much tonight, I'm sorry. There's a big event coming up on our first day of school and I'm sort of running it, so I have to work on it all weekend.

But since you sounded so worried, I wanted to write back tonight and promise I won't tell anyone what you said. Believe me, I understand about keeping things private. Way better than I can say.

Could we…sorry, I know this sounds dorky, but could we make a pledge or something? I have to mail out pledge forms for my aunt's campaigns, where people promise to vote a certain way, and I thought maybe we could both make a pledge to trust each other. I promise not to reveal anything you don't want me to. I'll start hiding your letters, too, so you won't have to worry about anyone in my family finding them. I'm good at hiding things.

Then we can write to each other about whatever we want. There are some things I definitely can't tell any adults, or my friends at school either. But I have this feeling that I can tell you just about anything.

Sometimes, writing to you is like working on a collage. I forget to worry about what I'm saying and I just…create.

I worry that one day I'll be so busy drawing or writing or laying out a new piece that I'll slip up and forget to watch what I say. It gets hard to keep track of what I'm <u>supposed</u> to be thinking about. As if I'm constantly on stage, and I know I'm playing a role, but sometimes I forget which one.

Shoot, my sister's banging on my door. She said she'd help me with the flyers. I promise I'll write more next time!

Yours truly,
Tammy

P.S. Can I steal your answer for the question about how I'll resist temptation? It was a good answer. That's what I'll do, too. Except for going to confession, obviously.

P.P.S. My sister keeps yelling at me to hurry up, but I kind of want to keep writing anyway to annoy her.

P.P.P.S. ~~Shit~~ Shoot, she's out for blood. Write back when you can!

Monday, August 8, 1977

Dear Tammy,

Thanks. For promising not to tell anyone, and also for that pledge idea. I promise not to tell anyone anything you don't want me to, and I'll hide your letters, too. Not that it matters much in my house, since my mom never comes inside my room and my brother's never home anymore, but all the same.

I got your letter this afternoon, and I couldn't stop thinking about it. I went out tonight, to the same club on Valencia Street where I saw my first punk show, and I kept thinking about your letters while the bands were playing—about how you said we could write to each other about whatever we want. I kept thinking of things I wanted to tell you. The show itself, for one thing. It isn't fair that you like this kind of music as much as I do but you've never gotten to see a show.

Now that I'm back home, normally I'd write in my diary about what happened, but I thought this time I'd put it in a letter to you instead. I hope you don't mind, this might be longer than usual, but here goes...

My birthday's tomorrow. I'll be sixteen years old, but I feel about nine. I've always done what people tell me—my mom, the nuns at school, the priests at church—as though I'm not capable of thinking for myself. They see me as a little kid who needs other people to do everything for me. They don't know me at all.

I guess that's part of why I went out alone again tonight. To prove to myself that I could.

I got to the club early, and for the first hour, everything was exactly the way I wanted it. I was in the middle of the crowd, my body thrumming to the music, not paying attention to anyone else. I was dancing with my eyes shut, in my own world, enjoying the anger that pulsed through the music and the air.

Then the pain came, and everything turned upside down.

At first, all I knew was that something had slammed into my back, jamming me right between the shoulder blades and knocking the breath out of my chest. I stumbled forward, and my face crashed into the back of the tall girl in front of me. She stumbled, her high heels wobbling, and turned to scowl at me from under a thick layer of jet-black mascara.

"I'M SORRY!" I whipped up my hands, shouting so she'd hear me over the pounding music. My nose was throbbing and I was seconds away from keeling over.

"FUCK YOU!" a guy shouted behind us. It had to be the same one who'd shoved me. I steadied myself and craned my neck around to scowl at him, but he wasn't looking at me. He'd turned to the side, and he was pulling back his fist, snarling at a shorter guy who was wearing a dog collar and snarling right back at him. I dodged fast to avoid getting an elbow in the face.

"Shit!" The tall girl grabbed my wrist. "This way!"

I followed her into the crowd, my heart thudding. I've seen fights before, but never this close.

The music from the stage never faltered even as the crowd surged, some people moving toward the fight and some running away. The tall girl let go of my wrist after a minute, but I kept fol-

lowing her and her friends until there was enough distance between us and the fight. I sagged against a wall that smelled of old
beer and something worse, trying to catch my breath.

"You okay?" The tall girl leaned down with her mouth set into
a thin, worried line. She reminded me of a younger version of my
mom, if my mom wore liquid eyeliner and fishnet gloves. "Fuck,
did he hit you?"

"I'm fine." The band's music kept thumping away, and all I wanted
was to get lost in it all over again. The point of coming to shows is
not having to think, but between almost getting knocked down and
your letter running through my head, tonight was turning out to
be unlike any other show I'd ever been to. "Sorry I bumped you."

"All right, if you're sure..." The tall girl nodded, not looking especially sure herself, and went back to her friends.

I nodded at her retreating back—and that was when I noticed
Midge Spelling standing a few feet away.

Have I told you about Midge? She's the singer for the Prudes, the
first band I ever saw live. You should check to see if your store has
any of their records. Their music's just okay, but Midge is amazing. I've seen her perform a couple of times now, and she's got— I
don't know if it's what my English teacher calls "stage presence" or
something more, but she's <u>amazing</u> when she sings. It's impossible
to look anywhere in the room but at her.

I met her once, weeks ago, but I figured she wouldn't remember me. So it was a total shock when she walked right up to where I
was standing against that beer-smelling wall and asked, "You got
a light?"

She was wearing a fitted denim jacket over an even more fitted
blue, green, and yellow striped dress with a red belt. She had red
tights on, too, and matching red lipstick. I don't know how I hadn't
spotted her in the crowd before.

"Sorry. No."

"S'okay." Midge motioned wordlessly toward a guy across from us. He smiled, leaned over, and lit the cigarette dangling from her lips. I expected her to start talking to him, or at least walk away from this gross wall, but she turned back to me instead.

My face was getting warm. Having her stare right at me was unsettling. As though she could tell everything about me, just by looking. "I met you that one time, right?" she asked.

"Yeah." I figured she wouldn't remember my name, so I added, "I'm Sharon."

She blew smoke at the ceiling. "Cool. I'm Midge."

"I know." All of a sudden, I was babbling. "I saw you. With your band. You were incredible."

"Thanks." Midge smiled, but it was a mature, unbothered smile. As opposed to the goofy grin that was probably on <u>my</u> face. "The guys are great."

"Yeah, they are." I tried to think of something to say about the three men who'd clanged out the music behind Midge on the stage, but all I could remember was her crooning into the microphone. "Have you ever thought about going solo?"

She laughed. "You ever seen a girl punk singer without a band behind her?"

"No." Now I felt stupid for asking.

"Relax, it's cool. You ever listen to the Runaways? They're an all-girl rock band. Their stuff's rad."

I shook my head. Midge was somehow managing to make me feel both completely out of place and like I was the coolest person in the club at the same time. "I'll look for their record."

"Do it." Midge lifted her chin toward a guy who'd just come in. He waved her over, and she glanced back at me. The briefest, most dismissive glance I've ever seen. "Hey, so, later."

"Later," I said. To her back, because she was already walking away.

I don't know, Tammy. I've never seen a punk band whose music had anything close to the power of Patti Smith's, but the energy at these shows is incredible all the same. Almost like a high.

Sometimes. Then there are nights like this. When I almost get my nose broken and embarrass myself in front of girls who are infinitely cooler than I can ever hope to be.

When I got home, it was late. I thought Mom would be in bed and Peter would be out when I came in the front door, but no. They were sitting on the couch together, watching a rerun of one of those Love Boat movies and passing a box of Lorna Doone cookies back and forth.

They didn't notice me coming in. Two of the passengers on the show were about to make out, and Mom and Peter were both leaning forward, staring intently at the screen.

"Hi," I said.

They glanced up. "Hi, sweetie," Mom said, pulling another cookie out of the box.

"Hey, Shar." Peter pointed to something on the screen and elbowed Mom. She laughed.

"Well, I guess I'll go upstairs," I said, though they hadn't asked. "I should write to my pen pal."

Peter half waved, but Mom didn't seem to notice I'd said anything. She was reaching for another cookie.

This is embarrassing to say, but...sometimes I'm not even sure I fit in my own family. My brother seems to like me, most of the time, but my mom... I don't know how much she wanted to have me in the first place. She always used to talk about how hard it was having two babies at the same time. Maybe she would've been happier if it had just been her and Peter all along.

Sorry to suddenly get morose. Lately I've just been feeling kind of... I don't know. Lost, or something.

Yours truly,
Sharon

P.S. Right, another question. My favorite Bible story is, um... Jonah and the whale. I used to love going whale watching. I always imagined jumping off the boat and hanging out inside a whale for a few days. I don't think I realized how much that would have sucked.

P.P.S. I laughed when I saw you crossed out "Shit" in your last letter. You don't need to cross out curse words. I can handle them. How about we make another pledge? Let's not cross anything out, or go back and reread our letters before we send them anymore. Let's just write what we want to write and not worry about it. All I do is worry most of the time, and it would be nice to have a break, you know? I'm going to start by not rereading this letter, even though I probably wrote a lot of embarrassing stuff.

Friday, August 12, 1977

Dear Sharon,

Thanks for that letter. It was fun reading about the show
you went to. That's the kind of thing you usually put in your
diary? My diary isn't nearly as interesting.

I wish I could come to a show with you someday. I'm sorry
you almost wound up in the middle of some guys having a
fight, though! I was scared for you just reading it.

And I love your idea about not crossing things out or going
back to reread our letters before we send them. There's basically no one I'm totally up front with that way, so it'll be a
whole new experience for me.

Anyway, sorry, I know this letter's coming in a strangely
shaped package. I made something, and...well, there's no one
I can show it to here. My friends probably wouldn't understand it, and my family <u>definitely</u> wouldn't. I thought you
might, though. I'm nervous sending it to you, since I don't
usually show my art to anyone, but you did something different in your last letter to me, too, so...like you said, here goes.

This is my newest collage. I just finished it. I've been spending almost all my time lately working on that event I told

you about, and it's helped to have something else to do that I actually enjoy.

It probably still needs work. The background isn't quite right, so I might redo it after I've gotten more practice cross-hatching. The ocean turned out okay, especially the waves, but the bridge doesn't look the way I wanted it to. It's a photo of the Golden Gate Bridge I found in a magazine. You know that obviously. It's just that there's nothing down here like the Golden Gate.

I can't wait to hear what you think!

Yours truly,
Tammy

P.S. Happy belated birthday! I didn't mean for this to be a birthday present, but if you want, maybe it could be.

FALL, 1977

Dear Diary,

It's strange to be writing here again. I just looked at my last entry, and it was from way back in July—that time Peter got upset because Mom said she was voting for Dan White. I've been writing to Tammy more and more since then, so I haven't needed to use this diary as much. It's odd mailing those letters off, because I can't read back over what I've written the way I always did with my diary, but I love reading the letters she writes back.

I've told her about all the shows I've gone to in the past couple of weeks. Describing them to her is almost more fun than the shows themselves.

And last week I told her something I've never told anyone, about the time freshman year when Rhonda and I tried smoking pot for the first time in the church bathroom, and convinced ourselves we were about to get sucked into the toilet. I've never had the nerve to tell Peter that story—he'd laugh at me for days. But Tammy just wrote back that she doesn't like to smoke, either, because once her sister went to pet a neighbor's dog while she was high. It ran away, and she tried to chase it and wound up tripping and breaking her wrist.

She tells me things she doesn't tell other people, too. A few weeks ago she even sent me a collage she made.

When I opened the package it looked fragile, and I was so careful unwrapping all the tissue paper Tammy had wrapped around it, I spent a full five minutes to get the collage free. Then another ten minutes studying every inch of it.

I wouldn't even have called it a collage. When I think about collages, I think about my kindergarten art projects, when the teachers would set out bottles of Elmer's glue and piles of ripped construction paper and tell us to do whatever we wanted as long as we didn't put glue in anyone's hair. What Tammy made is nothing like my sticky childhood creations. This isn't a kid's craft project—it's <u>art</u>.

I wrote back right away to tell Tammy exactly how awesome I thought it was. When she replied, she seemed almost embarrassed, and she kept saying it wasn't a big deal that she'd sent it to me, but... I kind of think it was.

I owe her a letter tonight. We write more often now than we did at first, and there's a lot I want to tell her.

I need to write this diary entry first, though, because I have to write about what's going on with Peter. It hurts to keep a secret from Tammy, since I'm totally honest with her about everything else, but I don't have a choice.

It started when Kevin came over for dinner tonight. Mom was cooking when he arrived, so I brought him up to my room to see the collage. He hadn't been over since I got it.

"Wow, that's amazing." Kevin took a step back, studying it. I'd dug out an old frame that used to hold my sixth-grade softball-team photo and, after several tries, I'd managed to slide Tammy's collage in without having to bend the cardboard backing. I'd torn down my old posters and hung her collage right in the middle of my bedroom wall. "Who made it?"

"My pen pal down in Orange County. I told you about her, remember?"

"Oh, right. She must be a good pen pal to be sending you her artwork."

"Yeah, she's awesome, actually."

Kevin tilted his head, his eyes running over the lines of the collage. I shifted my weight from foot to foot as it occurred to me that Tammy might not have wanted me to show her work to anyone. She already said she couldn't show it to any of <u>her</u> friends. But it was too late to do anything about that now.

The collage is intricate—layers on top of layers on top of layers. The bottom layer is part drawing, part photo. Tammy drew the ocean in black ink with thick, dark waves crashing onto a rocky beach. The water dominates the entire image, and there's a black-and-white newsprint cutout of the Golden Gate Bridge perched on top. Somehow, Tammy made the photo look as though it blends almost seamlessly into the drawing, but she also angled it unnaturally high, so that the bridge looks impossible to reach. Behind the dark water there's a tiny hint of a horizon, but nothing more.

Pasted in among the waves are uneven, mismatched letters, blue and green and black, cut out on stark white square-shaped backgrounds. They look as if they've been cut from magazine pages, and they're the only parts of the collage that have any color at all. NOTHING STOPS THE OCEAN, BABY, the disjointed letters spell out across the top of the collage, and at the bottom another line says, NOTHING STOPS THE TIDE.

No two letters in either line are the same size or type. The colors are similar, but there are slight variations in the shades that somehow complement each other perfectly. I can only imagine how many magazines Tammy must've gone through to find exactly the right mismatched letters.

The first time I looked at her collage, I studied those letters for so long I didn't even notice the eyes, but once I did they were all I could see. They're fixed carefully all over the entire collage, tucked away, so small they don't draw your attention until you know they're there. Tiny eyes from tiny black-and-white images, cut so precisely there isn't a sliver of space around them.

Like the letters, the eyes are different, too. Beady eyes, bright eyes, wrinkled eyes, round eyes, angled eyes, cartoon eyes—there are dozens of them, maybe <u>hundreds</u>, buried in the waves.

I've had it on my wall for weeks now, and every time I walk into my room, I stare at it. I can't decide if it's creepy or brilliant. Maybe it's both.

Kevin traced his finger over the letters. I wondered if he'd noticed the eyes yet. "I love the poem."

"Poem?"

"Yeah, see?" He pointed to the word "ocean," but the cutout letters didn't look any more poetic to me than they had before. "It's about the inevitability of the human condition."

"Ah...right."

"Mom sent me up here to make sure you two weren't in your room." Peter's voice behind us made me jump, but Kevin was already smiling when he turned around. He's always liked Peter. "Guess now I can either go lie to her and have you owe me, or tell the truth and get into Heaven."

"As if Heaven would be any fun without Kevin and me." I stuck out my lower lip.

Peter rolled his eyes. "Dinner's ready."

We followed him downstairs, where Mom was spooning out chicken salad. Hardly a fancy meal, but at this point Kevin's been over for dinner enough times that Mom doesn't bother bringing out the china. He's still super polite with her, though, and by the time we'd made it through dinner he'd managed to compliment the same-old, same-old chicken salad half a dozen times.

"Delicious, as always, Mrs. Hawkins," he said, after he swallowed the last bite of his second helping. "Thank you again."

"It's always nice to have extra teenage boys around to finish off my leftovers." Mom smiled at him.

Peter stood up and started clearing the plates, even though Kevin was still dabbing his mouth with a napkin. "What time do I need to be home tonight, Mom?"

"You're going out?" She frowned. "It's a school night."

"Don't remind me." Peter groaned as he reached for the empty chicken salad bowl. Tomorrow's our first day back and I don't know who's dreading it more, him or Mom. She usually takes on a part-time job in the summers, and this year she worked nights shelving books at the library over on Portola. She's been going to bed as soon as she gets home and sleeping in until ten in the morning, but starting tomorrow, we'll all need to be at school at 8:00 a.m. again. "I'm meeting some friends to study for the SATs."

It was such an obvious lie that Kevin immediately had to muffle his laughter, but Mom only smiled. "In that case, make sure you're home by nine."

"It might take a little longer. We're meeting at Dave's, and he lives all the way up past Market."

"Ten, then. Not a minute later."

"Thanks, Mom. You're the best." Peter bent down and kissed her on the forehead. She went on smiling that same indulgent smile.

"Hey, if Peter's going out, can Kevin and I go see a movie?" It was worth a try.

"Oh, yeah, I want to see that one about the killer whale," Kevin added. "You saw the poster, right? It's like Jaws, but with, you know, a whale."

Mom smiled at Kevin again, but her expression was more strained now, and she turned to me before she shook her head. "You need your sleep. Besides, those horror movies are all trash."

Peter hurried into the kitchen with a stack of plates. At least he didn't stick his tongue out at me. I jumped up, reached for the glasses, and hurried to carry them in after him.

"Hey." I set the glasses by the sink and dropped my voice. "What was that about? You haven't talked to Dave since eighth grade."

"I'm going to the camera store." Peter rolled his eyes. "Leonard and Dean and a bunch of the guys are meeting up."

"Who's Dean?"

"Just a guy. The election's getting closer and we've got flyers to fold. I'd invite you, but Mom already said you couldn't go out, and it's not as if you'd want to, anyway."

"I..." I didn't know what to say. I <u>did</u> want to go out with my brother, and I liked the idea of helping Harvey Milk get elected. He's in the newspaper all the time now, always talking about standing up to special interests and big corporations.

I hated the way I stuck out on Castro Street, though.

Maybe I could work on another campaign or something. For one of the candidates here in our district running against Dan White.

"Don't worry about it." Peter turned off the faucet. He didn't meet my eyes. "By the way, where'd you get that piece of artwork? The one you were showing Kevin?"

Having my brother see Tammy's collage didn't bother me the same way it did when Kevin was examining it earlier. "My pen pal made it. Tammy."

"Really? Wow. She seems cooler than I thought. Anyway, I—"

"Do you two need any help?" Kevin was in the doorway all of a sudden, smiling.

"Nah, we've got it." Peter turned back to the sink without flinching at the interruption. I'm sure my smile was strained, though.

It's always gone without saying that Kevin couldn't know about Peter. I don't know what he'd think if he did. We've never talked about homosexuality.

But keeping it secret from Tammy is harder. Over the last few weeks, I've started thinking of her as a real friend. Plus, we made that whole promise to be honest, and here I am, holding back something <u>huge</u>.

I <u>can</u> guess how she'd react. She lives in Orange County. Her family <u>founded</u> a church. It's safe to assume she's not a fan of gay people.

Being honest is great and all, but that's a risk I can't take. Tammy may seem cool, but my brother's the one who's always been there for me. I need to be there for him, too.

And I need to figure out a better way to do that than I have so far.

Yours,
Sharon

Tuesday, September 6, 1977

Dear Harvey,

I don't know how I'm even going to write about today without vomiting all over this notebook.

I don't know how much more I can take.

The fucking pep rally was this afternoon. I'd spent weeks "planning" it, which mostly meant mimeographing flyers and filling out permission forms and baking cookies for all the reporters Aunt Mandy invited (I <u>knew</u> there'd be baking involved somehow). By the time the rally started, I was relieved, since at least it meant I was done.

I was stupid. I should've known the actual rally would be <u>much</u> worse than the work before it.

Uncle Russell did most of the talking, as usual, in his booming preacher voice. "God's word in the Book of Revelation tells us militant homosexuals are the harbingers of the end days! It's on all us Christian patriots to show the world where we stand, or join the sinners in Hellfire!" Et cetera.

(The junior high kids giggled when he said "Hellfire." We're supposed to say "H-E-double-hockey-sticks.")

It was the chanting that did me in, though.

It was <u>HORRIBLE</u>, Harvey.

They made us all do it. A hundred voices, echoing in unison through the gym. If I'd stayed quiet, they'd have seen and wondered why, so I had to chant with everybody else. I couldn't even dig my nails into my palms, because Carolyn was sitting right beside me and she'd have noticed for sure.

TV cameras were pointed right at us the whole time, too, so now all of California has seen me yelling "Schools aren't for sinners!" and "Christians have rights!" and "Adam and Eve, not Adam and Steve!" and acting as if I meant every word.

Harvey, I—

I'll come back in a minute.

Okay. I'm back. I just threw up.

Sorry. I know it's gross. Everything's gross right now.

At the end of the chanting, Uncle Russell made us all join hands. "Please, Lord, deliver us from evil," he said, "and protect our children from those who'd tempt them to the devil's harmful path."

Everyone except me said, "Amen."

Do none of them ever think about what they're saying?

I'm a child. They're the ones harming me.

That was when I started crying. Next to me, Carolyn was crying, too, but she was whispering prayers at the same time, and she probably thought I was crying out of passion for Jesus. That only made me cry harder.

And then—and Harvey, I don't know if she'd planned this all along, or if she decided to do it right in that moment, but I guess it doesn't matter—Aunt Mandy looked up at the bleachers, right at me. And she said, "Now we call on your youth group vice president, Tammy Larson, to offer up her own prayer on behalf of California's children."

I froze. I couldn't move at all, Harvey. Until Carolyn

pushed my shoulder from behind, and before I knew what was happening, I was standing up.

I climbed down from the bleachers. All I could see was the blinding lights from the cameras pointed in my face. I don't know how I made it down those steps and out into the middle of the gym floor, but all of a sudden Uncle Russell was sticking his microphone in my face. Then he fucking <u>winked</u> at me.

I turned around to face the crowd. I wiped my eyes and held up the microphone, and I said...

I don't remember. It was impossible to hear myself over the buzzing in my ears. I tried to remember Uncle Russell's prayer, and I said something like "Lord, forgive us our sins and use us, your children, as instruments of righteousness. In your holy name, amen."

I don't know if I was supposed to end the prayer or not, but I couldn't take another second of that shit.

Harvey... I wanted to rip the skin off my face and fling it in my aunt and uncle's faces. I wanted to scream and scream and scream until there was nothing left inside me but air.

Somehow I must've managed to keep all of that in, because no one seemed to think anything was unusual. The whole crowd chimed "Amen" when I was done. Uncle Russell lifted his arms, and everyone started clapping and stomping their feet and shouting, as if this was the most fun they'd ever had.

At first I thought they were all just celebrating the fact that we'd gotten to miss sixth period. Then two sophomore guys in the bleachers near me started chanting, in perfect rhythm to all those stomping feet. "KILL A QUEER FOR CHRIST! KILL A QUEER FOR CHRIST!"

Other people heard it, too, and they started chanting along. Soon our whole section of bleachers had joined in. Uncle Russell and Aunt Mandy and the teachers must've heard—they were only a few feet from us—but none of them said anything.

As I watched Carolyn chanting along with the others, I remembered something. God, I can't believe I ever forgot.

It was years ago—fifth grade, I think. A bunch of us had gone to a sleepover at Carolyn's house for her birthday, and we got to talking about what it would be like to kiss a boy. Annette said she'd done it once at her cousin's wedding, and she'd practiced on her hand first. Then all of a sudden, we were all practicing on our hands. I didn't want to do it—I didn't know I was gay yet, but I knew I wasn't the same as everybody else, and I was scared someone would be able to tell. But I did it anyway, since it would've looked suspicious if I was the only one who <u>didn't</u>.

Then, out of nowhere, Carolyn dared Annette and Kathy to kiss each <u>other</u>. They refused, of course, and we all started laughing and talking about how gross it would be for a girl to kiss another girl. Everyone was making gagging noises. I laughed, but I felt sick to my stomach the whole time.

Then Carolyn, who'd been making gagging noises, too, said, "How do we know for sure, though, until someone tries it?" At first we laughed some more, but <u>she</u> didn't, so everyone got quiet. Then Carolyn leaned over and kissed Annette, full on the lips.

It was the first time I'd ever seen something like that. The last, too.

When they broke apart, I swallowed. The whole room was so quiet, they probably heard me.

Then Carolyn started laughing and making more grossed-out noises, and a second later Annette started doing the same thing. Soon everyone was squealing. I joined in, saying fervent "<u>Ewwww!</u>"'s along with the others.

I still don't know why Carolyn did that.

Now, here we were. Here <u>she</u> was, chanting about killing queers.

My aunt and uncle can preach as much as they want about saving people from sin. What those kids in the bleachers were chanting—<u>that's</u> what this is about.

They don't want you to win your election, Harvey, but it's not as if this is all going to be over if you lose.

They want you gone. You, and everybody else like you.

They want us to go away. One way or another.

I don't know… Maybe that <u>would</u> be a lot easier.

At the beginning of the rally, Aunt Mandy said Anita Bryant's win in Miami was only the first step. More cities and states will start banning gay rights, she said (only she called it "standing up for Christian families"), and before long, it'll be illegal for teachers to keep their jobs unless they oppose gay rights, too (only she called <u>that</u> "keeping children in our schools safe from supporters of perversion"). She said that would put a stop to Gay Freedom Day (which she called "that annual travesty up in San Francisco") and keep homosexuals from "getting ideas" about running for office again.

I don't know what scares her more—the idea that you exist, Harvey, or the idea that someday you might not be the only gay person with power.

I'm so glad I didn't tell Sharon the truth. I can't believe I ever <u>considered</u> it. There's too much at stake. She tells me so much about what she's doing and what she's thinking, but there's no way I can do the same.

I need to be more careful. I should stick to writing about music. We have more of those stupid pen pal questions to answer before the project ends in November, so I can write about those, too.

Except I don't know how I'm going to make it to November, Harvey. I want to crawl into a hole and never come out again.

I thought I could stand up to their bullshit, but I failed. I'm not as strong as I thought.

I've got to keep my head down. Muddle through, however I can.

Maybe I can even get a boyfriend. If I could find a guy who doesn't want to make out much, or...

Fuck, who do I think I'm kidding?

I can't write any more. I'm about to lose it. I'll go hide this diary along with all the other evidence of all my sins, put on <u>Horses</u>, and do whatever it takes not to have to think about any of this anymore.

Tammy

Wednesday, September 14, 1977

Dear Sharon,

Sorry it took me longer than usual to write back. I've been really busy since school started.

I'm behind on answering questions for the report, so here's the next one:

<u>What is your favorite subject in school, and why?</u>

Art, I guess. It was always my favorite when I was younger. The art teacher I had in junior high was great. He's the one who taught me how to do shading and perspective. Which is good, since my current art teacher is also the girls' gym teacher and wouldn't know perspective if it was a tennis ball flying at her face.

Sorry. I guess that answer got kind of dark.

Have you listened to the new Iggy Pop album yet? I got it yesterday. It has a couple of good songs, but I'm not sure about the rest. The guy at the record store said it isn't selling because no one's been buying anything but Elvis records for the past month. Is it bad that I never cared about Elvis, even when he was alive?

Now I feel guilty for writing that. My mom cried for a week after he died. I don't know what I'd do if Patti Smith died. Sorry, I don't know what's wrong with me lately. I'd better go.

Yours truly,
Tammy

Saturday, September 17, 1977

Dear Tammy,

I know what you mean. I've been busy since school started, too. There's a big election coming up here in November and my brother's volunteering in another district, and I've started helping with a campaign in our neighborhood, too. There's a guy running who my brother <u>really</u> doesn't want to win, so I've been putting up signs for one of the other candidates. I don't know much about her except that she's a real-estate agent and she's not Dan White.

I haven't heard much Iggy Pop. He's friends with David Bowie, right? My brother doesn't listen to punk, but he loves David Bowie.

The last time I was at the record store I bought a bunch of singles. Some of them aren't great, but a few are cool. Nothing on Patti Smith's level, but two are by other bands with girl lead singers. One's called the Avengers—have you heard of them? They're from San Francisco.

My favorite single was by this British band called X-Ray Spex. It's this strange song about how everyone looks down on girls, but it's also about...bondage? I don't know exactly what bondage <u>is</u>, but the song is called "Oh Bondage Up Yours!" and you should definitely get it. As far as I can tell it's about society, and how we're all supposed to act a certain way and how society can't own us if we all break free. I want to know what you think of it.

Can I tell you one of my favorite things about punk? It's that all the songs are about being angry. I used to think songs had to be about love, until I found punk. There are way too many love songs already, what with pop and disco and Elvis. Most of the time I don't understand what people are even <u>talking</u> about when they talk about love, let alone when they're singing about it.

Oh, and my favorite subject is English. I want to be an English teacher, but not at a Catholic school. All we read here is Chaucer and Shakespeare and Blake. The teachers probably think if they let us read anything close to this century we'll turn into hippies. At the public school they at least get to read Mark Twain.

Since you can't say most of that in your report, please just say I love to read.

Write back when you can.

Yours truly,
Sharon

P.S. Is everything all right? Your last letter made me wonder. If there's anything going on, you can tell me. Don't forget our pledge.

Saturday, September 24, 1977

Dear Sharon,

Yeah, I'm fine. Sorry, there's just been a lot going on.

I asked the guy at the record store today if they had anything by the Avengers or the Prudes, but he said no. I've seen him there a bunch of times—there's only one decent record store in town, so I go there a lot, and he's usually there in the afternoons—and today he was wearing a shirt that said Eat the Rich with a skull on it next to a picture of a knife and fork, which is a gutsy shirt to wear in Orange County. He asked where I'd heard about the Prudes and the Avengers, and I said my friend had seen the Prudes live in San Francisco—and Sharon, I have to tell you, this guy was impressed. I could tell he was trying to hide it, but he'd never heard of them.

It's funny… I couldn't care less whether anyone at school thinks of me, but I like the idea that <u>this</u> guy thinks I'm cool.

They did have that single by X-Ray Spex, so he played it for me over the store's speakers. We got some annoyed looks from people in the disco section, but the song doesn't have any curse words, so they need to relax. It's weird, sure, but

no weirder than Patti Smith singing about humping a parking meter.

Did you ever find that Iggy Pop record? What did you
think?

Yours truly,
Tammy

Wednesday, November 9, 1977

Dear Diary,

In History today I was minding my own business, writing a letter to Tammy.

It's getting harder now to figure out what to say in those. All she ever wants to talk about anymore is music. It's not that I don't want to talk about music—sometimes, talking to Tammy about shows is more fun than actually going to shows—but for a while we were writing to each other about real things, personal things, and I don't know why we stopped. I must've said something wrong.

Our reports are due soon, but we've already finished all the stupid questions we were supposed to answer. I hope we'll keep writing after the project is over. We've already written way more than the ten letters we were supposed to.

I wish we could meet in person. I wish I knew what she looks like.

But I'm getting distracted. I sat down to write about what happened in History.

Yesterday was the election. I watched the results come in with Mom and Peter last night, and it was as if our whole city had changed in an instant. I wanted to write to Tammy about all of it, but this was all I'd managed to get down:

Dear Tammy,

I'm exhausted. I'm sitting in History class and the teacher's droning on about Charlemagne again. I stayed up way too late watching the news, and now I can't stop thinking about—

"What's this, Sharon?" Sister Catherine's voice was way too sharp and way too close. I slammed my hand down over my notebook, but it was too late. "Taking notes, I see? You can read them aloud to the class. Up front, please."

I fought the urge to roll my eyes. "Yes, Sister."

There was a time when my face would've burned as I walked to the front of the classroom, but this was too ridiculous to get embarrassed over. If I'd had to read the letter I wrote Tammy a couple of weeks ago, the one where I told her about going parking with Kevin after a movie, and how all of a sudden he opened his glove compartment and showed me he had a box of condoms in there, and how I felt so awkward I pretended to have a coughing fit and asked him to drive me home, that would've been another story.

Rhonda and Jennifer grinned as I reached the front of the room, happy to have Sister Catherine's lecture interrupted. Rhonda checked to make sure Sister wasn't watching, then winked at me as I smoothed out the page.

"'I'm exhausted,'" I read. "'I'm sitting in History...'"

When I got to the part about Sister Catherine "droning on," she interrupted me with a crisp "That's enough, Sharon."

"Thank you, Sister."

I snapped the notebook shut, but before I made it halfway back to my seat her voice cut in again. "Perhaps you ought to take over today's lesson for me, since you clearly have a much more interesting perspective on history to share with us."

I met her eyes, but quickly looked back down again. We're supposed to be especially respectful of the nuns on the faculty. "I'm very sorry, Sister."

"Oh, no, don't apologize. Go ahead and deliver your lecture, please. Here, I'll take a seat."

She sat down in my empty chair, making a big show of spreading out her habit and clasping her hands across my desk. A couple of girls laughed. I probably should've begged for forgiveness then and there, but I was too tired and frustrated to think clearly.

"All we ever talk about is ancient history." I dared to raise my eyes again. "Why does it always have to be about Charlemagne or Christopher Columbus or Henry the Eighth? There was a historic election yesterday, right here in San Francisco. Can't we talk about that?"

"I doubt a historian would argue local politics are as important to the foundations of our world as Christopher Columbus discovering this country." Sister Catherine raised one eyebrow. "More to the point—"

I interrupted her. That's probably what sealed my fate. I knew what would happen, even while I was saying the words, but I said them, anyway. "We just elected the city's first gay supervisor, but now they're trying to pass a law that says gay people aren't allowed to teach in schools, and—"

"That's enough, Sharon." Sister Catherine rose from my chair.

Oh, crap. My heart sped up as she slowly stood and turned her back on me.

"What about the rest of you?" She made her voice deceptively casual, but no one was fooled. "Do you prefer your classmate's version of history to mine?"

"No, Sister," the other girls, even Rhonda, said as one, their eyes trained carefully on their desks. No one was laughing now.

"If you'd like to discuss current events, that's fine." When Sister Catherine turned back to me, I knew that look on her face. In elementary school, if a teacher wore that expression, it was right before someone got whacked with a ruler. "There was indeed an election in this city yesterday, but Sharon is wrong when she says we elected that man."

I didn't dare speak, but the way she said "that man" made my blood boil. Sister Catherine didn't know the first thing about Harvey. She hadn't been there for that march.

"Our district has a new supervisor of its own." Sister Catherine lifted her head, a soft smile spreading across her face. "His name is Dan White, and he's a good Catholic. The man your classmate is talking about represents a different part of this city. A dangerous part. It's up to all of us to stand behind our Christian leaders and hold firm against sin."

I swallowed.

Sister Catherine looked at the clock over the blackboard. "We have twenty minutes left in class. Sharon, you will spend them kneeling before the Blessed Virgin and considering what sort of life you're choosing for yourself. When the period ends, I'll speak with your mother."

My legs wobbled as I stooped next to the statue of Mary. At least this wasn't a ruler lashing—the teachers don't usually do those once your age is in double digits—but I could feel everyone's eyes on me, and Sister Catherine's last sentence was hanging in my mind.

When Mom heard, how much would she piece together? Peter's been hanging out in the Castro every weekend and sometimes during the week, too, but Mom thinks he's been putting in extra hours at Javi's store.

She won't figure out the truth, will she? Just because I talked about Harvey Milk, and that new initiative on gay teachers?

I didn't even mean to bring up the teacher initiative, but it was in the newspaper this morning, and it's scary. It's called Proposition 6, and if it passes, gay people will be banned from working in public schools. If a straight teacher so much as <u>supports</u> gay people, they could get fired, too.

If someone found out about Peter, what would happen to Mom?

And what about me? Would this new law mean I couldn't get a teaching job someday?

A state senator from Orange County got thousands of people to sign a petition to put the proposition on the ballot next year, so I guess that'll be the next big election. The anchors talked about it on TV during the election night coverage. They showed footage from Orange County. A hundred kids were in a school gym chanting "KILL A QUEER FOR CHRIST!"

Sometimes it's hard to remember we live in the same state as those people.

My bare knees dug into the tile, but Sister Catherine was bound to be watching me, so I focused my gaze on Mary. She was standing on a flimsy little wooden table, her head bowed, her hands clasped in front of her. I don't know if Mary had any brothers, much less any gay ones, but either way, I doubt she'd have gone around spouting off in class without thinking about how easily word could get back to her mom about them.

When the bell rang, I kept my eyes on Mary as the other girls quietly gathered their books and shuffled out the door behind me. Rhonda pretended to drop her pencil, bent down on her way out, and whispered, "Meet you in the bathroom?" before she straightened back up. I gave her a tiny nod.

"You can go, Sharon," Sister Catherine called dismissively from the far side of the room. She was wiping down the chalkboard. "I'll speak to your mother soon."

"Thank you, Sister." My knees were stiff as I climbed to my feet.

She looked at me expectantly, as though waiting for me to apologize, but I just picked up my books and strode through the door.

She was the one who was wrong. Why should I be sorry?

I found my friends in the bathroom. Rhonda and Jennifer had apparently just finished telling Diane what had happened—Diane has Physics that period—because she was laughing, and she said, "She seriously talked about gay stuff to a Sister?" as I stepped through the door.

"Hey," I said.

"Hey." Diane grinned at me. "Do you have a death wish or what?"

"No. I..." I wished I could be having this conversation with Tammy. Whether or not she approved of gay people, she'd understand why I'd stood up to Sister Catherine. She's as sick of adults acting like they know so much more about everything as I am. "It is historic that Harvey got elected. I don't see why we can't talk about it."

"Harvey?" Jennifer laughed. "You mean the homosexual on the news?"

"He's more than that." I sighed. "He has a whole platform to help the city. Gay people don't just sit around being gay, you know."

"Yeah, they lie down for that." Rhonda laughed, too.

"Unless they do it standing up," Jennifer said, and then all three of them were laughing.

"I heard gay girls do this thing where one of them's the girl and one's the man," Diane whispered, giggling.

"Oh, my God, that's disgusting," Rhonda said, but she was grinning. She didn't look disgusted at all.

They turned around, as if they expected me to join in the fake-disgust parade, but I had no idea what to say. And in the end I didn't have to say anything, because just then the door swung open behind us, and my mom came straight in without her usual warning.

"Girls," she said shortly. The others must've figured out the situation fast, because they all slunk out of the bathroom without so much as glancing back at me.

"Mom..." I swallowed. "I can explain."

"No, you cannot." Mom crossed her arms. There were dark circles under her eyes. "You are <u>never</u> to speak that way to a teacher again. To a <u>Sister!</u>"

"I know. I'm sorry."

"What's gotten into you?" She stared down at me. We're the same height now, but her heels made her a couple of inches taller than me in my saddle shoes. "You know that wasn't an appropriate topic to bring up in school."

"Why shouldn't we talk about an election in History class?"

"You know very well it's not about the election. It's about that man in District Five." Mom wrinkled her nose.

"What, are we supposed to pretend he doesn't exist?" I wanted to add "because he's gay?" at the end, but I stopped myself. I couldn't use the word "gay" in front of my mom, not with Peter's secret hanging in the air between us.

Still, it felt wrong holding back. Wasn't this exactly what I was trying to argue against?

"You're <u>supposed</u> to be respectful of your teachers. Your mother, too, for that matter." Mom uncrossed her arms, her eyes narrowing. "You're grounded until further notice. You'll leave the house for school, church, and babysitting. Nothing more."

I wanted to argue. Instead I nodded heavily.

"And you'll apologize to Sister Catherine. Right now."

"But—"

"No 'buts.' We're walking straight to her classroom and so you can apologize."

"What? Mom, come on, she's probably teaching another class by now."

"Then you'll apologize in front of them. That's the price you pay."

Mom wasn't kidding. When we reached Sister Catherine's room, a group of freshmen girls was sitting in the desks my friends and I had vacated. They all watched as I dropped my eyes and told Sister Catherine I was very, very sorry.

I tried to sound sincere, because I did <u>not</u> want my mother to make me do this again, but when I lifted my gaze and saw the cold smile on Sister Catherine's face, I nearly took it all back.

I <u>wasn't</u> sorry.

Harvey Milk won the election. A gay man will sit on the San Francisco Board of Supervisors. But here in my neighborhood, everyone's acting as if it doesn't even matter.

I'm starting to see what Peter meant about getting out of this place.

Yours,
Sharon

Dear Harvey,

Oh, my God. Oh, my <u>God</u>.

You won! You <u>won</u>!!!

Did you ever think it would happen? Seriously, <u>did</u> you?

You're a city supervisor now. Or you will be soon—the newspaper didn't explain that part. It just said "avowed homosexual Harvey Milk," who was the "leader of a large constituency of homosexuals in San Francisco," had been elected. Then it quoted three different pastors saying it was a sign of the rapture coming.

I haven't seen my aunt since the results came in, but I bet she's mad the paper didn't call <u>her</u> for a comment. I wonder which she's madder about—that, or you winning in the first place.

I… I'd given up, Harvey. It was too hard. I was trying to tell myself it couldn't be <u>that</u> tough to be straight, given how many people do it.

But if someone like you can do something like this… everything's upside down all of a sudden.

I wish there was someone I could talk to about this, but

the idea of telling my friends is a disgusting joke. But I have to see them tonight, regardless.

There's a stupid party and I have to go. If I <u>don't,</u> they'll know something's wrong, and they'll start a rumor. Rumors spread faster than the clap around here. I need to go put on some lip gloss and get ready to blend in.

I should write to Sharon first, though. This will be the last letter, since our reports are due next week. I'd keep writing to her if I could, but stopping is safest. I hate having to lie to her so much.

Besides, writing to her makes my imagination spiral out of control.

There have been times—okay, there've been a <u>lot</u> of times—when I get fixated on this silly fantasy. It's embarrassing to write about even here, but, well, it involves me going to San Francisco, and Sharon realizing she's gay (despite the fact that she has a boyfriend—like I said, silly fantasy), and us living happily ever after.

It's absurd. I don't even know what it <u>means</u> for two girls to live happily ever after. I'm not sure it's actually possible.

Besides, it's not as if I can just up and go to San Francisco. I don't have any money, or anywhere to live, or any way to get a job. Plus, in outside my stupid fantasy world I don't even know if I can trust Sharon, let alone run away with her.

I've got to be careful. Back in the summer I wrote whatever I wanted to write, but I've pulled back since that stupid fucking pep rally. It would be so easy to slip up when all I want to do is tell her <u>everything</u>.

I'm so sick of pretending, Harvey.

Peace,
Tammy

Wednesday, November 9, 1977

Dear Sharon,

I can't believe it, but we've answered all the questions and now our reports are due, so I guess this will be my last letter. It feels strange to be sitting here at my desk writing to you for the very last time.

This pen pal project turned out to be a lot more fun than I ever expected. Hearing about your life in San Francisco has been fun. And I can't believe we both listen to punk.

If I ever hear about Patti Smith performing in San Francisco, I'll think of you and cross my fingers that you're there. Maybe you could think of me, too.

Sorry this is so short, but I have to leave soon. I hope you have a good rest of your junior year.

Yours truly,
Tammy

P.S. I really am going to miss writing to you. I already do. More than I can say.

Dear Tammy,

Hi! Sorry, it's actually your turn to write next. Maybe you already sent something and our letters will cross in the mail. I tried to write to you today in school, but my teacher took the paper before I could finish. Now it's after midnight and I can't sleep, so I thought I'd try again.

I don't know if you heard, but we had an election in San Francisco, and it was a big one. I keep thinking about how fast the world is changing. Do you know what I mean? I know, I know—things are always changing. When we were kids there was all of that stuff with the war, and the president resigning, and those protests were always on TV. Now things are supposed to be calmer, except it doesn't feel that way. Especially when I'm listening to Patti or the Avengers or X-Ray Spex. It's as if we're on the cusp of some new change. Something earth-shattering.

I know we're getting ready to be done with this project, and our reports are due and everything, but...if you wanted to, we could keep writing to each other, anyway. You're probably busy with school and church and everything else, but if you have time, I think it would be fun. Writing to you has become the highlight of my week, and getting your letters back is even better. I love knowing I can tell you what I'm thinking.

Anyway, if you don't want to, that's okay. I'll miss you, though.

Yours truly,
Sharon

Thursday, November 10, 1977

Dear Harvey,
OH, MY GOD. OH, MY GOD. YOU'RE NOT GOING TO BELIEVE THIS.

Harvey, I—oh, my God. I—I—

Wait. No. I've got to back up. It's two in the morning, but if I don't write this all down I'll probably never sleep again. I've got to tell you what happened, and I can't leave anything out.

The party was on the golf course, as usual. We have these every few weeks in the fall, since the club pools are closed and our parents go out a lot in the evenings.

Normally the guys will bring a keg, but this time they couldn't get one, and we had to bring bottles from our parents' liquor cabinets. We're all pros at that maneuver by now, and my own parents don't even keep the den cabinet locked. I've been watching my sisters swipe drinks since I was a kid.

All the juniors and seniors from youth group were there, and a few sophomores, too. As usual, we waited until the course was closed and the maintenance staff had gone, then we snuck in under the fence and sat along the shore of the water hazard, passing the bottles around. It was hard to taste much after the first few swallows, but no one cared. At first we all joked around together, but by the time we'd finished off the smaller bottles, people started pairing up and drifting off into the trees along the northern edge of the course.

I'd been sitting next to Carolyn all night, but neither of us had talked much. We've been part of the same group of semifriends since we were kids, but I couldn't have told you the last time we were alone together before tonight.

As the others started leaving, Carolyn and I slid down the grass and rolled up our jeans so we could dip our toes in the water. During the day the hazard's only a murky little pond, but tonight the moon was full and right overhead, and the water was a sheet of black rippling glass. We stretched out and watched in silence as more and more people disappeared into the trees, until we were the only two left.

For the first few minutes, I almost forgot she was there. I was lying on my back, staring up the sky, smiling to myself about Harvey's victory and wondering what would happen if I shut my eyes. Would I fall asleep right there by the water? Would I wake up when the sun started rising over the branches? What would happen if I stayed in that spot with my eyes closed forever, alone in the dark with nothing overhead but the stars, no sound but the water lapping gently at my ankles?

At some point my eyes must've fallen shut, because I remember everything was black when I heard her voice. It sounded soft and far away.

"Things have been strange lately," she murmured.

I opened my eyes. Carolyn was propped up on one elbow, leaning over me, only inches away. I was so surprised I almost jumped back up again, but I forced a laugh. "What things?"

"You know." She shrugged without moving away. "This whole school year. Ever since that pep rally. It was so awkward, wasn't it?"

This was a dangerous conversation. I kept my face blank. "Awkward, how?"

"You know. I could tell you thought so. Your face was so red when your aunt called you up to give that prayer."

"It was?"

She nodded.

I scrambled for an innocent explanation. "I, um. I don't like getting up in front of people."

"Also, your aunt's a bitch."

That time I laughed for real. I'd never heard anyone talk that way about Aunt Mandy. "You think so, too?"

"For sure. I bet she's shitting bricks now that San Francisco elected that queer."

I didn't like hearing her call you that, Harvey, but I was still glad she'd called my aunt a bitch. "Probably."

"Do you remember when we used to do that crap at sleepovers?" Carolyn hadn't budged. If anything, her face might've moved closer to mine. "God, we were stupid little kids."

She laughed, but her laughter sounded forced, the way mine had before.

"Um…" I tried to laugh, too. "Yeah."

"I guess that's how desperate girls can get when there aren't any guys around." She laughed again. "I could tell you had fun watching Annette and me. You were staring with your mouth hanging open like a fish." She puckered her lips, fish-style. She looked ridiculous, but she still didn't move away. I had no idea what was happening, but I wanted to put more space between us. I was getting scared.

"I wasn't having fun." I was talking so fast now she had to know I was lying. "I made that face because I was grossed out."

"You didn't look grossed out. You looked jealous."

"What?" My heart was pounding so hard, Harvey. I don't know how I managed not to get up and run. "I wasn't jealous, that's not—"

And then, before I could say anything more, she fucking lunged at me, Harvey.

She kissed me.

A real kiss. Her lips on my lips. Her tongue in my mouth, Harvey.

There was a horrible second at first when I thought she was just being mean, and that our friends were about to jump out from behind a tree and start laughing, and my life would instantly be over.

But no one jumped out. All that happened was that she kept kissing me.

She even started kissing me harder, Harvey. She—she leaned over me, sort of pressing me back into the grass, and she put her hand on the back of my neck, and…

I was sure it had to be a dream. I'd gotten drunk and passed out, or something.

But that wasn't it at all. This was real.

I've been getting crushes on girls since before I was old enough to know what the word "crush" meant, but it was only tonight that I realized there could be another girl like me right here in Ocean Valley, California.

My thoughts in that moment were racing so fast I couldn't keep track of them, but I knew one thing for sure:

This was the best day of my life. Finally, things were getting better instead of worse.

Is that what falling in love is like, Harvey? Sorry, I know that's a cheesy question, but I saw a picture of you with your arm around a man. You're in love with him, right? Was this how you felt the first time you kissed him? As if your life would never be the same?

Because after Carolyn and I started kissing, for the first time in months, I didn't feel tired or lonely at all. I was floating in space, with the real world nowhere in sight.

I would've kept kissing her forever, but after another minute Carolyn pulled back and sort of hovered over me and whispered, "Well, I guess now we know exactly how stupid girls can get when there aren't any guys around."

I laughed, and she did, too. At first I didn't understand why she'd said that, but now I see that she was being nice. She was giving me a way to back out, if I wanted to.

I didn't want to. So I propped myself up on my elbows and put my hand on the back of her neck and kissed her again.

She kissed me back, and that was how I knew she didn't want to back out, either.

I've kissed boys before, but that was never real. <u>This</u> was.

I'm not alone anymore, Harvey.

Maybe Carolyn and I can leave here someday. We could go to L.A., or all the way to San Francisco.

We could meet other lesbians. Make friends with them. We could be <u>normal</u>, Harvey.

Up until tonight, getting Sharon's letters was all I had to look forward to, but now I've got something more. Someone <u>here</u>. Someone I can touch.

First, you got elected, Harvey, and now <u>this</u>.

God, I'm falling over at my desk, I'm so tired. I need to go to bed. I have school tomorrow…and Carolyn will be there.

It's the first time in so long that I'm not going to bed angry. Nothing could ever wipe this grin off my face.

Peace & love,
Tammy

Saturday, November 12, 1977

Dear Diary,

Um.

Something's strange. <u>Really, really</u> strange.

At first I thought it was a prank, but that doesn't make sense. There's only one explanation that <u>does</u>.

It's that the letter I got today is...real.

I went to the mailbox first this afternoon, the way I do every day I'm expecting a letter from Tammy, and I got one. I opened the envelope—it was thicker than usual, so I was hoping for a long letter, the kind she used to send—but it was...different.

The pages were wrinkled and stained, as if they'd gotten wet and then dried off. The first page was a short pen pal letter, where she said she wouldn't be writing to me again.

I was disappointed, and a little hurt. Except there were extra pages behind the letter—regular notebook paper, so I knew it wasn't another collage or anything. It looked like all the pages, the short letter and the others behind it, had been ripped out of the same notebook.

Maybe she wrote the other letter after mine, and she meant to put them in different envelopes. Except the second letter was addressed to Harvey.

Was Tammy writing to Harvey Milk? That made even less sense.

But it's what she wrote that was strangest of all.

She wrote about kissing another girl.

It was a long letter, about her kissing a girl, and being <u>really, really, really</u> happy about it.

She wrote about <u>me</u>, too. She said my letters were all she had to look forward to...until now.

I think—oh, my gosh...

I think Tammy might be gay.

If it's true, it means she's been lying to me all along. Though I guess I've been lying to her, too.

How <u>can</u> she be? Her family's so into church. She lives in Orange County. She goes to a Christian school!

Though I guess my brother goes to church and to Catholic school, too, and <u>he's</u> gay.

All this time that we've been writing to each other, I thought she was normal. It's normal to be straight, isn't it?

Maybe I've been wrong about that, too.

Oh, my gosh. I'm so freaked out right now.

Am I supposed to write back? Does she even know she sent this to me? It's addressed to Harvey.

Maybe she did send it on <u>purpose</u>. Maybe she <u>wanted</u> to freak me out, but...why? She wouldn't want me to know, not unless this really is some kind of trick.

I just don't think she'd do that.

Peter could help me figure this out. Or Kevin. Well, but I couldn't tell Kevin about Tammy, not about this...

I do want to see him, though.

Yeah. That's what I'll do.

He's working tonight, but I'll go meet him when he gets off. Then I won't have to feel this way. When I'm with Kevin, things feel normal and safe, and that's what I need right now.

Okay. I've got a plan, at least.

More later.

Yours,
Sharon

Saturday, November 12, 1977

Oh, shit, Harvey.

Wait. Let me rephrase that.

OH, SHIT, HARVEY!!!!

I can't find the last letter I wrote you.

The one about that night at the golf course and Carolyn and—

OH, SHIT, OH, SHIT, OH, SHIT!

It was here on my desk, and I went to bed because it was the middle of the night and I was drunk and I <u>left</u> it there and—

Did someone find it? Did my <u>mother</u> find it????

Okay. Okay. I have to figure this out. I can't lose it until I've figured out what happened. I need a plan. Some kind of plan.

<u>What the fuck is wrong with me????</u>

Okay, no. Breathe. Breathe. Think.

It was on the desk. What else did I do on that desk?

I wrote a letter to you before I left for the party. I tore the pages out of my notebook and put them in my purse, where I keep all the things I can't risk anyone finding.

I went through every scrap of paper in my purse, Harvey. The letter I wrote after I came <u>back</u> that night is most <u>definitely</u> not there. It isn't <u>anywhere</u>.

Okay. Okay. Thinking. Thinking. What else did I do? I wrote a letter to Sharon, a short one, right before I left. I wrote it in the same notebook as usual, and I tore it out and put it in an envelope and addressed it, and—

Wait. Shit. No. I didn't.

I was running late and I had to do my makeup. I left Sharon's letter in my notebook to deal with after I got back.

Then when I got home, I was so excited I sat straight down and turned to a new page and started writing. About Carolyn, and kissing, and everything else that was in my head. When I was done, I was so exhausted I fell straight into bed.

The next morning, I remembered the letter to Sharon, and I went over to tear it out of the notebook, and—

No, wait, no. I still felt half drunk, so I slept through my alarm and I was going to be late for school. I was trying to drink orange juice and eat a donut and get my books together all at the same time, and I spilled my juice and—

SHIT. SHIT, SHIT, SHIT, SHIT, SHIT.

Harvey. HARVEY.

I spilled my orange juice and it got all over me and I had to change my skirt. I didn't have time to clean up, but it got all over my notebook, too, and—

OH, MY FUCKING GOD. ORANGE JUICE. I KNEW THIS WAS ALL ANITA FUCKING BRYANT'S FAULT.

Harvey. I remember now.

Oh, my God.

I was in such a panic to get out the door without anyone figuring out what I'd been doing. I just tore out the pages out of the notebook without paying attention and put them in the envelope.

I remember now. It was a thick envelope, the way they

always used to be back when I wrote her longer letters. I thought that was because it was wet, but—

Oh, holy <u>fuck</u>. HOLY <u>FUCK, FUCK, FUCK</u>—

Sharon knows. She <u>knows</u>.

Fuck, fuck, fuck, fuck, fuck, what if she tells someone????

She won't. She won't, she won't, she won't.

But what if she does??????

I got a letter from her today, but it's obvious she wrote it before she got mine. She said she wanted to keep writing, but—

That's because she didn't know the truth, Harvey.

We swore we wouldn't tell anyone what we wrote, but what if she thinks she needs to save my soul, or something??

Harvey! What the fuck am I supposed to do now??

Oh, my God. Oh, my God. Oh, my God.

I'm going back to bed.

Tammy

Dear Diary,

Well...I went out with Kevin again last night.

We've been spending more time together than usual this past week, ever since I got that bizarre letter from Tammy. Mom hasn't really noticed that I've been staying out late, even on school nights. She's going to bed earlier and earlier lately. Peter's been teasing me for suddenly starting to act like the girls at school who spend all their time hanging on their boyfriends, but it's still been fun, mostly.

Last night was kind of strange, though. Kevin was off work, and I brought him with me to a show for the first time. He doesn't know much about punk—he mostly listens to Journey and the Dead—but he agreed to come up to North Beach to see the Dils and DV8 with me. I could tell he wanted to give it a chance, for my sake, but it wasn't really his scene.

"IT'S LOUD IN HERE!" he shouted at me for the third time, after we'd only been inside two minutes. From the way he kept balling up his fists in front of his shoulders, I could tell he wanted to clap his hands over his ears. He kept darting his eyes around, especially at the guy in front of us with his hair spiked straight up and the girl next to him with the leather choker and the safety pin stuck through her ear. I was wearing one of my boring schoolgirl sweaters, but I'd paired it with a new short bright blue vinyl skirt I'd bought a couple of weeks ago with my babysitting money, and that seemed to make him nervous, too. I kept catching him glancing down at it and then back up at my face, as if he wasn't sure it was me.

"JUST LISTEN!" I shouted back, but Kevin shook his head and pointed to his ear, uncomprehending.

I tried to demonstrate instead. I closed my eyes and let my body start thrumming to the music. I'd never heard DV8 before, and they weren't my favorite—the Dils were better, and their set wouldn't be until later—but the beat was as mesmerizing as ever.

As the rhythm rose inside me, I forgot all about introducing Kevin to punk. All I could focus on was how this felt.

"HEY, SHARON?" His voice was shouting into my ear. I opened my eyes reluctantly. "DO YOU KNOW THOSE GIRLS?"

"WHO?" I shouted back, but I saw them before he could point.

I recognized the first girl he was looking at instantly—Midge Spelling. It was jarring to see her in the middle of the crowd again, like she was anyone else. Midge Spelling <u>wasn't</u> like anyone else.

A lot of the girls tonight were dressed up, in thrift-store fur or brightly colored ripped tights or puffy wigs, but Midge stood out as much as always. Her hair was slicked back, with a single short lock curling over her forehead, and she had on impossibly shiny red lipstick and cat-eye liner. She was wearing a bright red trench coat, the exact same shade as her lips, buttoned all the way up to her neck but open from the waist down, with tight red pants and knee-high black leather boots underneath.

For an instant I wondered how Midge Spelling looked when she <u>wasn't</u> at a punk show, but I dismissed the thought. I'd rather not know.

She was with another girl I couldn't place at first. The girl looked understated compared to Midge, but she still fit in perfectly. She was dressed in a black leather jacket, ripped jeans with a leather collar tied under the right knee, and ancient-looking Converse sneakers, and she was looking right at me.

Right. Evelyn, the girl I'd first seen on Castro Street ages ago.

"HEY! SHARON, RIGHT?" Evelyn pushed through the crowd toward us first. Midge followed her, but she was dancing as she walked, her trench coat flapping open.

I nodded at them, because the band had launched into an ear-splitting drumroll and it was impossible to talk. Evelyn gestured for us to follow her toward the bar. I took Kevin's elbow and led him after them.

He was visibly relieved at the slightly less dramatic volume on that side. As soon as we could speak again, he offered to get drinks for all of us and waded through the sea of people toward the bartender.

Evelyn smiled at me, and I smiled back, even though smiling in a punk club seems as out of place as swimming down Market Street. Next to us, Midge kept dancing.

"Cool skirt." Evelyn had to lean in close so I could understand her. "I've been hoping you'd come by the bookstore."

"I've been really busy with school."

"Oh yeah? I thought I saw you at a show here last week." She raised her eyebrows, and I blushed. Then she laughed. "Relax, it's cool. You should come by if you get a chance, though. We're launching a big new campaign. Have you heard about Prop 6?"

"Yeah, the one banning gay teachers?"

"That's it. We're teaming up with some other groups to canvass the whole city, and other places, too, if we can, and we're raising money so we can rent buses and—"

"HERE!" Kevin shouted, thrusting out three cans of Coke. His forehead had a thin sheen of sweat, as though he'd run a marathon. The crowd around the bar had gotten thicker since Evelyn and I had been talking. "SORRY, THAT WAS ALL I COULD GET. DIDN'T THINK THEY'D CHECK ID."

Evelyn took a can and smiled at him. "Thanks."

I didn't want Kevin to hear us talking about Prop 6. Ever since I got Tammy's letter, thinking about gay stuff makes me uncomfortable. And kind of lost.

Midge stopped dancing long enough to take one of the Cokes. "Thanks, man."

"Hey, Midge." Evelyn pointed toward the door. "Is that Johnny coming in?"

Midge cracked open the Coke can and glanced up. Her skinny guitar player was strolling through the door, a cigarette burning in his hand. He looked paler than last time I saw him. "Yeah. Guess I should go over."

"Make him come to you." Evelyn took a swig of Coke. "Why should women always be at the beck and call of men?"

Kevin coughed, as if he was choking on his soda. Midge chuckled and turned back to glance at Johnny by the door.

I wondered how she and Johnny acted when they were alone together. Did they always walk around with their arms wrapped around each other, the way they had the first night I'd seen them? I tried to picture it…

And then, out of nowhere, I was picturing Midge with a girl.

The image in my mind was sudden and clear. I saw Midge wrapping her arms around a girl's waist—it was the tall girl I'd seen at another club once, with the thick black mascara and the fishnet gloves—the same way she'd done with Johnny.

Then lying down, propping herself up on her elbow and kissing her, the way Tammy had written about kissing Carolyn.

"You okay?" Kevin pressed a Coke into my hand. "You look like you're feeling sick."

"I'm fine!" I said, but I must have said it kind of loudly, because all three of them turned to look at me.

"Maybe we should get going," Kevin said. Suddenly that sounded like a fantastic idea.

"Okay, well, come by the store if you can, Sharon," Evelyn said. "Tell whoever's at the register you know me. We're having volunteer sessions almost every night now."

"Cool, thanks." I twined my fingers into Kevin's and tugged him toward the door.

As we stepped outside, I lifted the can of Coke and drained it in two swallows, then tossed it into a trash can. We'd left his car a few blocks away, and it was getting cool out, so I started walking fast.

Kevin put his arm around me, and it reminded me of Midge again. I leaned in closer to him as we walked.

"What did you think of the show?" I asked.

"Well, my ears are still ringing, so it's hard to know for sure."

"It was cool though, right?"

"Sure."

He unlocked my door first, the way he always did, then went around to let himself in as I climbed into the car.

"Do you need to go straight home?" he asked as he steered us smoothly onto Broadway and pulled onto the Embarcadero. We rolled up the on-ramp, and as we climbed onto the upper level, I could see the Ferry Building rising up ahead in the dark. "Are you feeling sick?"

"Nah. I'm fine, and Mom won't notice if I'm late."

"Want to go get a burger?"

I slid across the seat, closer to him. "I'm not that hungry."

"Me, neither. How about some music? I just got the Tom Petty album."

He meant did I want to go parking. We've gone almost every time we've seen each other for the past week. "For sure, but I don't know if I'm in the mood for Tom Petty. Got any Pink Floyd?"

He grinned over at me and leaned on the accelerator. "You know it."

I laughed, and he laughed, too.

I rummaged around on the floor until I found The Dark Side of the Moon, then popped it into the tape deck. The music started up, its eerie notes filling the space between us.

Two songs later, we were pulling onto the grass on the edge of a park off King Street. Half a dozen other cars were lined up nearby, most with the windows fogged up. Somehow, guys always know exactly where to pull over.

The music was pumping through me. It was entirely different from the angry, disjointed music at the show. Pink Floyd is smoother, stranger. Nothing like the jagged rhythms that have become my automatic mental background music whenever I think about Tammy.

And I was thinking about Tammy. I'd been thinking about her ever since we left the club. I've had to fight to think about anything but Tammy ever since I read that letter.

I can't believe I'd been writing to her all that time, and I didn't know.

Did she not tell me because she thought I couldn't handle it?

Could I handle it?

The drums kicked in. Kevin leaned back, stretching his arm across my shoulders. "You sure you're all right? You seem kind of on edge."

"I'm fine."

"You're sure?"

"Uh-huh."

I turned to face him. He smiled his standard Kevin smile, warm and comfortable and real. I relaxed and smiled back easily. Any time he smiled that smile, I knew I was exactly where I was supposed to be.

His deep brown eyes were soft and warm, and I reached over to loop my hand through his. I turned up the music as high as it would go, and I kissed him.

I wanted to stop him from asking if I was all right. I wanted to stop all these thoughts whirling in my head. I wanted to stop this fear that kept churning through me with no explanation.

This was where I belonged. With my lips against Kevin's, his arms curving around my waist.

With my eyes shut, it was easy to pretend the rest of the world didn't exist. Being in that spot, with that eerie music playing and this boy running his fingers up and down my spine, was all I'd ever want.

I sank into the feeling of being close. I lost track of time as we kissed and kissed again, and suddenly the whole world was nothing but kissing and music and warmth. Deliciously uncomplicated. As though I was dreaming it all.

We kissed some more, and before long his hand was up my shirt. Usually I tried not to go much further than that, but tonight, I couldn't remember why. I wanted to keep feeling the way I did. I wanted to feel even more of it.

I climbed onto his lap, my knees straddling his hips, and he ran his hands up and down the sides of my jeans. He looked as though he was about to say something, but I kissed him before he could.

When I moved in closer, he made a noise in the back of his throat.

I took in a deep breath and ordered myself to relax and let whatever happened, happen.

And what happened was, I gave Kevin my first-ever blow job in the front seat of his Camaro.

Wow. It feels strange to write those words. It feels strange just thinking about it, now that it's over. I know it's supposed to be a big deal, and I can only imagine how Sister Catherine would react, ha, but now that I'm at home and trying to think back on what a big deal it was...

I'm mostly still thinking about Tammy. Just like before.

When Kevin and I were sitting in the car at the end of the night, listening to the last song, the words Tammy wrote popped into my head out of nowhere.

Not from the letter about Carolyn—from the one she wrote to <u>me</u>. When she said she'd miss me.

Can you miss someone you've never met?

I can. I do. I miss the <u>real</u> Tammy. The one I never got to know, because she didn't tell me the truth.

But I know why she didn't tell me. She <u>couldn't</u>.

She couldn't tell <u>anyone</u>. Just like Peter.

Now that I know about her, I could hurt her, if I wanted to. I could tell one of my teachers, and they could tell one of <u>her</u> teachers. Her family would find out.

That's when I knew I had to write back to her. I had to make sure she knew I'd never do that.

I should go volunteer at Evelyn's bookstore, too. Maybe I can help stop Prop 6 from passing. My friends might think it's gross to be gay, but I'm not like them. I need to make sure Tammy knows that.

"Are you, um...?" Kevin cleared his throat. He was staring straight ahead through the foggy windshield. "All right?"

"Yeah. I'm good. Great, actually."

He smiled at me and turned on the ignition.

Half an hour later, as he was walking me to my front door, his cheeks were pink, but for once I wasn't blushing.

"I love you," he said at the front door. It was the first time he'd ever said that. Maybe he thought he had to.

I didn't say it back. Girls don't have to say that, right? It's just something guys say.

I don't see what love has to do with sex, anyway. I don't see what it has to do with much of anything. Why do all those pop musicians write so many songs about love? Are they out of ideas? They should try listening to Patti Smith. She has plenty of ideas for songs that have nothing to do with it.

The house was dark when I let myself in. Mom's door was shut. So was Peter's, but when I peeked in, I spotted the lumpy pillows he'd left under the covers. It was obvious he was three miles north of here.

I shut his door, came back to my room, peeled off my clothes, and sat on the edge of the bed in my underwear. My head was thrumming, as though I'd never left the club.

I reached for my headphones, tracing my thumb over the <u>Horses</u> spine. I listen to it every night now, the same way Tammy does. I know every word.

Patti stared up at me from the cover of the album, her strong, constant gaze stark in black-and-white.

Her eyes are fierce. Uncompromising.

I slid the record out of its sleeve and dropped it onto the turntable, setting the needle and pulling the headphones over my ears. I slid between the sheets, my head rolling back against the pillow, my eyes falling shut. I wanted to get out this diary, write about everything that had happened, but I needed Patti first.

I shut my eyes, trying to imagine Tammy was there, listening along with me. That I was talking to her, telling her the story of to-night. I could never describe in a letter, but if I could talk to her, <u>really</u> talk, I was certain I could tell her absolutely everything. She was the only one who'd understand.

Yours,
Sharon

Saturday, November 19, 1977

Dear Sharon,

Hey…is it possible I sent you something in the mail by accident?

If you didn't get anything unusual from me, don't worry about it. There's just something I was looking for and I couldn't find it, and I thought I might've sent it to you by accident.

But if you could please write and let me know, that would be great.

Thanks.

Yours truly,
Tammy

P.S. I handed in my pen pal report last week. As far as I could tell from talking to my friends, we're the only set of pen pals who actually wrote to each other the whole time and answered all the questions. Everybody else wrote one or two letters and then made stuff up for the rest of it. Ha.

P.P.S. Please do write back soon, if you can. Please.

Tuesday, November 22, 1977

Dear Tammy,

Yes, I got your letter.

Sorry. I should've written sooner.

And...I'm sorry again, because...I read it.

I really shouldn't have. When I opened the envelope and saw all those pages, addressed to someone who wasn't me, I should've figured out what that meant. It should've been obvious you didn't mean to send it to me.

But I didn't think about any of that until much later. I could've just pretended I didn't read it—maybe that would be easier—but we made that pledge, so...

All this time, I've been trying to think of what to write to you. I've gotten used to thinking of you as a friend—a good friend—and I'd feel wrong not saying anything to my friend about this.

So I'll say that I haven't told my teachers, and I'm not going to. I never would have, anyway.

And, I'll also say...

My brother's gay. So I understand how important it is to keep this secret.

And the Harvey you were writing to—is that Harvey Milk? Do you really send letters to him, like another pen pal?

I got in trouble at school just for talking about Harvey. In our neighborhood, most people despise him.

But I saw him once. I went with Peter to Castro Street after that vote in Miami, the one where Anita Bryant had the gay rights law overturned. Harvey was leading a protest march with a bullhorn. Everyone was chanting.

I'd never seen anything like it before. Or since, either.

It was hard for me, at first, finding out you were gay. It was hard when I first found out about Peter, too. I couldn't shake the thought that you'd been lying to me all this time.

Except...I think I understand. We said we trusted each other, but you could never really trust me. Right? You can't really trust anyone.

I'm the only one who knows about my brother. Or I was, until he started going up to Castro Street. That's different, though, because his friends up there are all gay, too. He can't tell anyone else, because he doesn't know who he can trust.

Well, I'm glad he trusted me. And I know you didn't tell me on purpose, but I want you to know you can trust me, too.

There are so many things we have no control over. Things that just happen to us, like my dad leaving. We get stuck structuring our entire lives around all these things we didn't choose. It isn't fair, but no one else seems to see that.

I used to think being gay was wrong. I almost told on my brother when I first found out. I can't believe now that I ever considered that.

To be totally honest, I think part of me still thinks it's wrong. That's why I had trouble when I first read your letter.

Every adult I know has always said it's wrong, and I'm supposed to believe what adults say. My friends at school do.

But it's not as if all adults think the same way. Harvey Milk doesn't. And those people I saw in the Castro—there were <u>thousands</u> of them. They don't think it's wrong to be gay. I know what it says in the Bible, but the Bible says wives are supposed to submit to their husbands, too, and my mom did that, but my dad abandoned our whole family regardless.

I don't think we're all meant to live exactly the same way. How can we, when our lives are defined by all these accidents? Maybe being gay or straight is an accident, too.

That's why I listen to punk. It's all about being different, and how it's a good thing.

I mean, look at you and me. You happened to be born in Orange County, and I happened to be born here. I happen to be Catholic, and you happen to be Baptist. I happen to be white, and you happen to be, too.

And I happen to be straight, and you happen to be gay. If I were you, though—if I'd been born in your house, with your family—would I be gay, too? If you'd been born into my life, would you be straight?

How much of who we are is there from the beginning, and how much gets added later?

God made each of us the way we are. Why are we supposed to think being different is a bad thing?

Anyway, if you don't want to write back, that's okay. I shouldn't have read your private letter. I understand if you're mad.

But if you did write back, that would be cool. I've missed writing to you, too.

Yours truly,
Sharon

Friday, November 25, 1977

Dear Harvey,

Wow.

I… God. I don't know where to start.

I just got a letter from Sharon, and it says—it says <u>so many</u> <u>things</u>, but it says…

Harvey…her brother's gay.

Her brother, Peter. The one she writes about all the time.

<u>He's</u> gay. She's known for a while, apparently.

This is the closest I've ever come to knowing another gay person. Not counting Carolyn, or you. Since let's face it, I don't really know you, and Carolyn is…complicated.

I'd given up on ever hearing from Sharon again. To be honest, I'd given up on a lot of things.

Last night I couldn't even work up the energy to put on a record. I just lay in bed, staring at the ceiling, until the sun came up and my sister started knocking on the door. It's the day after Thanksgiving, and my mother always makes us spend hours in the kitchen packing up the leftovers and making big vats of turkey soup.

When the mail came in the afternoon, Mom sent me out

to see if there was anything from Grandma in Ohio and there it was, on the very top of the stack in the mailbox. A letter with Sharon's return address in the corner.

For a second I was so groggy from not sleeping and inhaling all those turkey fumes, I honestly thought I was imagining it. Then I grabbed the letter, ran back to my room, and ripped it open. My mom kept yelling for me to come back to the kitchen, but I ignored her until my brother started banging on my door saying Mom was going to ground me for the next five years if I didn't come back that instant. I had to hide the letter behind my bed and pretend everything was normal so Mom wouldn't notice my head was four hundred miles away.

I haven't slept since I read it. Maybe that's why my brain's looping into odd places. But…all this stuff she wrote? About the accidents that define our lives? About us switching places?

She said part of her thinks being gay is wrong, but then, part of me does, too.

There was a time when I wanted Sharon to know the truth. I was afraid she'd hate me. Now, though…

She promised not to tell anyone. Maybe I shouldn't believe her, but I do. I don't think you write the kinds of things she wrote in that letter if you hate the person you're writing to.

She might be my first real friend. Well, there's Carolyn, but ever since we kissed, she's barely looked at me. Our Sunday school teacher put us in the same group to read Bible verses and Carolyn spent the whole time sitting with her back to me, talking to Brett about whether he should go to UCLA or if USC would be better.

I don't know what's going on, Harvey. I'm so confused.

It's just…if I can be honest with Sharon, if I could be <u>truly</u> honest with someone for the first time ever…that might be the best accident that's ever happened to me.

Peace,
Tammy

Friday, November 25, 1977

Hi, Sharon.

I keep starting to write this letter, then crossing everything out and ripping up the paper.

It's late now, though, and I think I've made up my mind. This is going to be the letter I finish. I'll mail it, too.

If I don't do it right now, though—if I don't write this down, put it in an envelope, seal it, and drive the three miles to the post office so it can go in the mail tonight—I'll never have the nerve.

It's either write this now or carry these words to my grave. You already know, but I need to tell you anyway.

Here goes. This will be the first time I've ever actually told anyone.

Oh, God, oh, God, oh, God…

You obviously already figured this out, but…I'm gay.

I'm sorry. My handwriting is probably harder to read than usual. I'm just so freaked out, knowing you know.

I trust you. I do. I wanted to tell you months ago. And when I read your letter…

I think of you as a good friend, too, Sharon. Maybe my best friend.

Who am I kidding—you're definitely my best friend. I'm sorry, that's probably strange since we've never met, but I've never had a friend who really knew me before.

I always thought I'd never tell <u>anyone</u>. I'd go to bed praying that the next morning I'd miraculously wake up straight, and this was all a bad dream.

All along I knew better, though. I've liked girls ever since I was a kid. It started with…

God, this is embarrassing, but…it started with Cher.

I never missed an episode of her show. I'd sew exact replicas of whatever she'd worn that week for my Barbies. I was too old to be playing with Barbies by then, but my parents didn't notice, thank God.

I don't remember exactly when I figured out that my fixation wasn't on Cher's clothes—it was the fact that Cher was <u>in</u> those clothes. She had this one outfit where you could see her belly button, and I remember so clearly when my mom gasped and switched off the TV. I had to stop myself from lunging to turn it back on.

Your brother's so lucky. He gets to live in San Francisco, and he has you.

I could <u>never</u> tell my sisters. They'd go straight to my parents, for one thing, but also, they'd <u>hate</u> me if they knew.

I think my aunt might suspect already, though.

I've never really told you about her, but ever since Anita Bryant started her campaign, my aunt and uncle have been running a group to support her. Now they're leading the Orange County branch of the campaign to pass Proposition 6. You've heard about that, right? The initiative to ban gay teachers? Last week my sister and I stood out in front of the grocery store and got a hundred pledges to vote yes in an hour.

I hate having to lie to everyone in the middle of all this. I started a whole diary to get through it. That's what my letters to Harvey are. I always thought writing to an imaginary Harvey Milk was the closest I'd come to telling anyone, but... well, here I am now. Telling you.

Write back, please. As soon as you can. I'm nervous putting this in the mail, but also...I just enjoy getting letters from you. Especially now.

Yours truly,
Tammy

Monday, November 28, 1977

Dear Tammy,

I just got your letter, and tonight I'm going to walk down to the post office so I can put this back in the mail to you. That way you'll get it faster than if I leave it in the mailbox out front. I wish I could send it faster. Having to wait for the mail is terrible sometimes.

But you don't need to be nervous. I meant what I said before—you can trust me.

How about we both try writing to each other, the way we write in our diaries? I did that a few times during the summer, but I guess you never really could. Now that I know, though, if you wanted to write to me the same way you've been writing your letters to Harvey Milk, I'd want to read them.

I'll start. Here's what I would've written in my diary about today.

I went to the women's bookstore on Valencia Street after school. It was my first time, and I was nervous. I'd changed out of my school uniform and put on some lipstick and a leather jacket I'd just bought at a secondhand store. As soon as I stepped off the bus and walked inside, though, I could tell no one there cared how I looked.

"Hi," I said, as I stepped toward the girl at the cash register. "I'm, um, I'm looking for—"

"LOOK OUT!" a voice shrieked behind me.

I whipped around and barely managed to jump back before the dolly laden with a six-foot-high stack of boxes could careen straight into me.

"SHIT, I'M SO SORRY!" the same voice yelled as the girl behind the cash register leaped out to grab the top box before it crashed to the floor. The box below it was tottering, too, and I instinctively jumped forward and wrapped my arms around it. It was heavy, and I staggered backward, but I managed to hang on.

"I told you not to stack them so high!" the girl who'd come out from behind the register admonished. "Christ, Becky!"

"I know, I know, I know!" Becky ran out from behind the dolly and up to me. She was about my height, with pale skin, red hair, and freckles across her nose. "Are you all right? I'm so sorry!"

"She's fine." The other girl set down her box next to the cash register with a grunt, then took the box out of my hands and set it next to hers. When they were both secure, she wiped her hands off on her jeans and held one out to me to shake. She was tall and dark-skinned, with short curly hair and big hoop earrings, and she grinned at me before she rolled her eyes at Becky. "I'm Lisa. Tell Becky you're fine. You're fine, right?"

"I'm fine." I smiled back and shook Lisa's hand. Her denim jacket had at least a dozen buttons pinned on. I read SAVE THE WHALES, TRUST IN GOD—SHE WILL PROVIDE, and ABOLISH APARTHEID before I realized I was being rude and lifted my eyes back to her face. "I'm Sharon."

"Rad to meet you. Sorry my roommate almost killed you. Want a beer? It's the least we can do."

I thought she was joking until I noticed the six-pack behind the cash register. "No, thanks. I only came in to see if Evelyn was around."

Lisa didn't miss a beat. "Evie!" she shouted, without turning her head. "A woman's here to see you!"

"You sure you're okay?" Becky grabbed my elbow and looked me up and down as if checking for wounds. "I'm so sorry. The right wheel's quirky on that thing."

"The wheel is fine." Lisa waved a dismissive hand. "Becky's just trying to get out of loading-dock duty next time, but it's not gonna work."

"Sharon! You came!" Evelyn was striding toward us from a door behind the cash register. "That's great. Did you already introduce yourselves?"

"Yeah," Lisa said. "Becky nearly killed her, but Sharon saved your box of <u>Camera Obscura</u>s."

"I try to be useful," I said, hoping it sounded funny. I guess I succeeded, because Evelyn laughed. She was wearing a T-shirt and jeans, and she looked different, more relaxed, than she had when I'd seen her at the club. Her knee collar was nowhere in sight.

The bookstore was smaller than I'd expected, and except for a single narrow aisle and a nook to one side that held a paper-strewn table and a few chairs, every inch of space was crammed with book-shelves. A couple of girls with long, loose hair were studying the shelves to my right, and low voices murmured behind the door Evelyn had emerged from.

I doubted Becky was much older than me, and the others might've been in their early twenties. None of them looked like <u>real</u> adults. They were all a lot younger than my teachers.

Becky finished lifting the boxes off the dolly and steered it toward the room at the back. Evelyn stepped forward, still beaming. "I'll show you around. You want a drink?"

"Already offered." Lisa hopped up onto the counter next to the register and ripped open a box. "She said no. Whoa—did someone mean to order an entire box of Adrienne Rich?"

"We can send them back if they don't sell, but they will." Evelyn nodded confidently.

"Okay, well, I'm ordering a box of Audre Lorde on Monday, then." Lisa reached for the next box.

"Your timing is great, Sharon." Evelyn waved for me to follow her toward the table and chairs. "We've got a volunteer meeting starting in a few minutes. Want to help us fold some flyers on Prop 6?"

"Heck, yes."

I blushed as soon as I'd said it, highly conscious of how young I must've sounded, and Evelyn laughed. It was another friendly laugh, though. Everything about this place was friendly.

"I should start setting up." Evelyn reached for a jar of pens on the counter. "Could you help me bring things out from the back?"

"Sure."

I followed her into what turned out to be a tiny storeroom full of boxes and supplies. Two other girls were somehow crammed into the back, going through an inventory list, when Evelyn and I squeezed inside. At first I could barely breathe in the tight space, but soon I was carting boxes of envelopes and Xeroxed flyers and rolls of stamps out to the table. More girls had arrived, and they were gathering around it. There weren't enough chairs, so some wound up sitting on the floor, tucking their sneakered feet under them on the industrial gray carpet and sipping from bottles of beer and soda. The store had looked minuscule at first, but now that so many people were inside, it felt bigger.

Evelyn introduced me to the others as we passed out the supplies, making a big point to tell them all that I was going to help the store "connect with more young women." The way she kept saying it reminded me of how Peter loves to tell people I'm his "kid" sister, but the girls at the store were cool about it.

Lisa came out from behind the cash register and waved for me to sit beside her on the floor next to a stack of letters. I sat, grabbing a few and copying her movements as she neatly folded each page into thirds.

"Are you and Becky roommates?" I asked Lisa. Everyone else seemed to be talking in low murmurs while we worked, except Evelyn. She was still bustling around getting things organized.

"Yeah. Evie lives with us, too. And three other women, but they had to work today. We've all got other jobs, since we're not making any money from the store yet."

"You mean you don't get paid to work here?"

"Nope. We own it, as a collective. Someday we hope to turn a profit so we can put it toward some of our causes, but for now we're just trying to keep up with the rent and the light bill."

"Oh, wow. That's so cool. I thought you were all in college."

"We are." Lisa laughed. "That's why we need the extra jobs. Got to pay those tuition bills. And eat, too."

"Wow. Do you go to SF State?"

"Evie does, for grad school. Becky and I are at SFAI. Susanna over there goes to SFCM." She pointed to a Chinese girl on the other side of the table with long, black hair and a T-shirt that read THE FUTURE IS FEMALE.

By the way, Tammy, have you heard of SFCM and SFAI? They're the San Francisco Conservatory of Music and the San Francisco Art Institute.

I was surprised that there were so many feminist artists. Then I realized I shouldn't make assumptions.

"So are you all...um, feminists?" I asked, then immediately blushed. I sounded ridiculous.

Lisa laughed. "Well, it's a feminist bookstore, so I sure as Hell hope so. And to answer your next question, no, we're not all lesbians. But some of us are."

She winked. I laughed, because I could tell she wanted me to laugh, but now I was wondering exactly how many lesbians were in that store.

Another Black girl Evelyn had introduced me to, Alex, squatted down next to Lisa. "Hey, is it cool if I bring a date to your poetry reading next week?"

"Depends." Lisa grinned. "Who've you got in mind?"

"Well, since you asked..." Alex dropped down to sit on the floor, and soon the two of them were off and running, talking about friends of theirs. I relaxed, since I knew I wouldn't be called on for this conversation. Besides, I definitely wasn't cool enough to get invited to a poetry reading, with or without a date.

I couldn't believe how many girls had come to this volunteer meeting. No—not girls. Women. That's what people here seemed to say. Most of them were in jeans and T-shirts with boots or loafers, and most were wearing their hair short and loose in no particular style. No one seemed preoccupied with how they looked, or with what anyone else thought of them.

I was starting to think I might actually fit in there someday. Maybe I even already did.

When I climbed up to grab another roll of stamps off the table, Becky and Evelyn were sitting at the far end, talking about how depressing it was that Senator Briggs had gotten enough signatures in Orange County to put Prop 6 on the ballot. Which made me think of you, of course.

"It shows how crucial it is that we beat them at the ballot box," Evelyn said. "Sharon, get your friends to come here after school. We'll need all the help we can get."

"With more mailings?"

"Yeah, it's not exactly glamorous work." Evelyn swept out her hand over the pile of stamps and envelopes on the table. Behind her was a bookshelf with a Lesbian Poetry sign across the top. I wondered what makes poetry lesbian. "We'll need to start prepping for Gay Freedom Day before long, too. All the campaigns against Prop 6 are about marching."

"You think women are going to turn out for that?" Alex tilted her head skeptically from her seat on the floor. "Last time it was all gay white men as far as the eye could see."

"Yeah, but more of us have been coming every year," Lisa said. "The first year I was in the city I was the only woman in sight, but it's gotten a lot better."

Evelyn nodded fervently. "Harvey's going out of his way to invite the lesbian groups."

"Sure, because we need a man to invite us." Alex didn't look any less skeptical.

Evelyn turned my way with another vigorous nod, as if she was anxious for me to believe her. I nodded back, as though I had conversations about Gay Freedom Day and invitations from Harvey Milk all the time.

"It's the media who always forgets lesbians exist." Lisa chuckled. "If enough of us show up, they can't ignore us."

Did that mean Lisa was a lesbian? I could barely keep up.

"Anyway, we've got bigger actions planned, too," Evelyn added. "When the election gets closer, we'll start going door to door. It'll be the first statewide vote on gay rights, so donors should pony up to help."

"They'd better." Becky licked a stamp with a flourish. "Or we're shit out of luck."

Everyone laughed except me. I was still puzzling out the first part of the conversation, and wondering how many of them read lesbian poetry.

"Hey." Lisa waved at me. "You okay, Sharon? You upset Becky said 'shit'?"

I blushed. Did I come off like <u>that</u> much of a goody-goody? "Nah, it's cool. I don't give a shit about 'shit.'"

That brought up a big laugh from the group, and I relaxed a little more. They didn't need to know that was the first time I'd said the word "shit" out loud.

I'm not sure if I've ever been around people I liked as much as I was starting to like these ~~girls~~ women. I didn't have to pretend to be someone I wasn't here. They didn't know I was just some naive Irish-Catholic kid from Dan White's district, but maybe they wouldn't care if they did.

There was no tension. No expectations. They were treating me as if I was already one of them.

I want to go back to that store, Tammy. I want to do more folding and stapling. Maybe I can even knock on some doors.

That would mean more lying to Mom, though. Besides, could I seriously talk to strangers about Prop 6? What if someone slammed the door in my face? And what if I knocked on a door that turned out to belong to someone from our church—could that be dangerous for my brother?

All I know for sure is, I loved being in that place. When Evelyn finally told us we could stop for the day, the paper cuts on my knuckles barely even stung.

I only wish you could've come there with me. You would've loved every second.

Yours truly,
Sharon

Wednesday, November 30, 1977

Dear Sharon,

Wow. I want to go to that bookstore with you. I want to go <u>so much</u>.

Reading about it made me think of what you said in your other letter, about how accidents define everything. Reading about the women at that store, all I could think was how much I wish I'd been accidentally born in San Francisco. Your city's a completely different world.

Do you remember what we said back in the summer, about not going back and rereading our letters, or crossing things out? I want to start doing that again. After this horrible pep rally my aunt made me put on at school, I started reading over all my letters to you <u>really</u> carefully to make sure I didn't give anything away, and I don't want to do that anymore. I want to be straight-up honest.

Like about Carolyn. There's no one else I can talk to about her. We kissed again yesterday, for the first time since that night on the golf course. It happened in the girls' locker room before math class, but it was really quick and we both ran away afterward and I don't know what it means, and...

Actually, maybe I should tell you about Thanksgiving instead. That's simpler.

My dad's parents came out from Ohio for the weekend. That's a big deal, because they hate flying, and they hate California even more. I've only seen them a handful of times since I was born, and I'm not entirely sure they can tell me and my sisters apart, but they're obsessed with my little brother and my baby nephew.

My aunt and uncle came over to our house for Thanksgiving dinner with my little cousin Eddie, the way they do every year (my aunt hates to cook). That made things awkward. My mom's family and my dad's family have never been close, and my grandparents clearly resented Aunt Mandy and Uncle Russell being at the dinner. When my grandparents started drinking—they only drink on holidays, so they tend to get drunk fast—things got worse.

"I thought you'd have more children by now, Amanda," Grandpa said before Dad had even carved the turkey. "How old are you?"

My aunt tried to cough politely. "Now, now, we never discuss a woman's age, do we?"

"She's thirty-five," Eddie said. He was pouting, because he'd tried to read a comic book under the table and Uncle Russell had smacked him and taken it away.

"Is that so?" My grandmother sipped her wine and eyed Uncle Russell. Then she turned back to my aunt. "I always think of you as that tiny girl at Henry's wedding, but you're not so tiny now, I suppose."

"No, no, she's got that whole legion of followers," my grandfather said. "Donna sent us that article she cut out from the newspaper, remember? Something about Anita Bryant?"

"Now there's a godly woman," Grandma said. Then she

started singing, in that overwrought, trembly voiced, Anita-Bryant-on-her-Christian-music-albums way. "'Mine eyes have seen the GLO-ry of the COM-ing of the LORD…'"

Singing aside, I was enjoying watching them give Aunt Mandy a hard time, but then my mother messed it all up. "Irene, did we tell you Ricky's going to be the lead in the school Christmas pageant?"

"I'm Joseph!" my brother yelled, and of course Grandma and Grandpa immediately started cooing over him and arguing with my dad about who'd pay for them to fly out for Christmas so they could see Ricky stumble around with a stuffed donkey and some unfortunate junior-high girl dressed as Mary.

They left my aunt alone after that, but she seethed all through dinner. I've been around her when she's angry enough times that I know her fakest, most wooden smile when I see it.

Seeing her suffer really does make me happy. Maybe that makes me a terrible person, but to be honest, I'm not sure I care.

Anyway, tell me if you go back to that bookstore, please. I want to hear every detail.

Yours truly,
Tammy

Dear Tammy,

Your grandparents sound hilarious. I bet you wish they came over all the time, even if your grandmother's an Anita Bryant fan.

But… I'm sorry, Tammy. I have to admit something, and it's bad.

I'll just tell you what happened. Then you can decide what you think.

I went to the bookstore again after school today. I'd gone on Tuesday and Wednesday, too, since there was always work to do. The afternoons were quiet. I'd helped with some mailings, talked to the women there, and made it home in time for dinner.

Today was different.

"Sharon?" a voice behind me said when I was halfway through a stack of envelopes. "What are you doing?"

"Uh…" I looked up from the stamp I was licking. Evelyn was standing over me, one hand on her hip. I'd been at the store for more than an hour, working on a mailing while the others stocked books. "Volunteering?"

"Now tell me, how's the weather?" She folded her arms across her chest.

"Uh…" I glanced at the window. "It finally stopped raining, and it's actually kind of warm?"

"That's right." Evelyn tapped her watch. "It's a gorgeous December afternoon, and you're <u>inside</u> a <u>bookstore</u>?"

"So are <u>you</u>." I crossed my arms and leaned back in my chair. I'd come straight to the store from school without stopping home to change first, but I'd ditched my starched white blouse and was currently dressed in the Ramones T-shirt I'd worn under it, plus my school kilt and saddle shoes. I figured in this outfit I could get away with teasing Evelyn a little. "Is that a leather jacket you're wearing? Who said you got to lecture <u>me</u> about the weather?"

She laughed and waved for me to get up. "Come on. That mailing doesn't need to go out until Monday. We're hitting the park before the sun goes down."

I stretched my arms over my head as Lisa and Becky came out from the back room, each of them struggling to balance stacks of paperbacks. "You coming, Sharon?" Lisa called.

"Sure." I climbed to my feet and took half the books off the stack she was holding. "How long's the walk to the park from here?"

"Who said anything about walking?" Lisa set the rest of the books onto the table, reached into the pocket of her jeans, and pulled out a set of keys as I put my stack down beside hers.

"You're riding with me, right, Evie?" Becky asked.

"Yeah." Evelyn pulled on a sweatshirt. "Lisa, can you take Sharon?"

"'Course."

My mouth dropped open. Were they talking about...? "No way." Lisa grinned. "What, you've never been on a bike?"

I shook my head. I was mildly terrified, but I definitely didn't want her to know that. "Do I have to...<u>do</u> anything?"

She laughed. "Just hang on tight."

Everything happened fast. I grabbed my sweater and my school bag and by the time we got outside, Becky and Evelyn were already long gone down the block, the motorcycle engine revving in their wake.

Lisa's was humming when I climbed on behind her. The seat wasn't very long, and I tried to lean back to put space between us, which was especially awkward in a kilt, but Lisa rolled her eyes at me over her shoulder. "Scoot up, kid. Evie'll kill me if I let you fall off."

I moved forward, and Lisa reached back and wound my arms around her waist. I don't know her _that_ well yet, and being pressed up against her felt strange. But the next thing I knew, we were moving, and I understood. The bike went _fast_, and nothing was holding me in place except my arms around Lisa's rib cage. I had to hold on for dear life.

For the first block, I clutched her desperately, all of my energy focused on staying in the seat. I learned quickly that it was easier if I leaned with her on the turns, though, and as we neared the park, I managed to relax enough to watch the streets pass.

The view from the back of a bike turned out to be awesome. It was the complete opposite of walking or driving. The city moved past us in a bright, unfiltered, exhilarating blur.

When we reached the park and Lisa pulled in behind the other motorcycles, to my surprise, I was disappointed. I slid off the seat, but I was itching to climb right back on.

Lisa laughed as she climbed down after me. "It's fun, right?"

"It's incredible!"

"Get Becky to give you a ride next time. She's got the coolest bike of anyone. A present from her grandma."

She was right. Becky's motorcycle two spaces over was red, and a lot bigger and shinier than Lisa's. "Nice."

"We can teach you if you want. It'll come in handy when your boyfriend and your brother are busy. Or if you ever get tired of having men drive you around."

I sighed, wishing for the first time that I hadn't told everyone at the bookstore so much. Plus, Peter had given me a ride home the day before, and they'd all seen him pick me up. But it's not as if I can't get around the city on my own. I've been taking the bus by myself since first grade. "Maybe."

"Come on, everyone's over by the trees."

I followed Lisa's gaze. "Everyone" turned out to be a lot more people than I expected. Evelyn and Becky were there, of course, and so were Alex and a few of the other bookstore regulars, but there were men here, too. I spotted Leonard talking to a couple of other guys, and not far behind him was—of all people—my brother.

Peter hadn't seen me yet. He had his back to me, and he was smoking and talking to a guy I didn't know. He was still wearing the pressed polo shirt he wears when he's doing deliveries for Javi. With the joint dangling from his fingers, it would've been a funny image if it was anyone but my brother.

Evelyn and some of the others met us halfway to the trees. Alex was holding a softball glove, and a couple of the other women were tossing a ball back and forth under the big palm tree.

"Hey, you." Alex slung her free arm around Lisa's waist, and... wait. Now I was confused. <u>Were</u> Lisa and Alex friends? Or were they more? Do lesbians put their arms around each other platonically sometimes? "We were thinking about starting a game if we can get enough people. Either of you in?"

"Not me." Lisa wrinkled up her nose. "It's too nice out and I'm too lazy."

Alex sighed. "<u>Everyone</u> keeps saying that."

"I'll play," I offered. "I was on my church team up until last year."

Alex's eyes widened. "What position?"

"First base."

"That's perfect! We need infielders."

It was clear she did. Other than the two women tossing the ball under the trees, I didn't see anyone else who seemed to be the slightest bit interested in playing softball. We'd have to start soon, too, or the only light left would be from the lampposts that lined the park. "You might need someone on everything."

"Yeah, and not just for today." Alex laughed. "I'm in charge of recruiting women to play for the team Strangers is starting in the spring. You interested?"

"Really?" Wow. After my church shut our team down, I'd thought my softball days were over.

"Yeah." Alex beamed, her arm tight around Lisa. "It's in the early stages, but we're trying to get a schedule together, so a bunch of the bars are getting involved. There are already three men's teams, so we're trying to get at least that many women's."

"Wait, did you say bars?"

"Oh, that's right, you're underage." Alex frowned. "Well, I think it'll be all right. The managers are all cool."

I should've known—"Strangers" must be the name of a lesbian bar. I shook my head. "Thanks, but I don't think I can."

Alex groaned. "Why is everyone I ask such a downer?"

"I mean, I'll definitely play today," I added quickly. "I won't have time to be on a team, though. I'm going to be really busy with school this spring. Plus...well, I probably shouldn't join a lesbian team, since I'm not a lesbian."

Evelyn and Lisa both turned away as though they suddenly had very important patches of grass to study, but Alex nodded slowly. "The teams are open to anyone, but that's all right. Well, I'm going to try to find a few more players for today. Don't wander too far, we're starting soon."

"Hey, Sharon, isn't that your brother?" Evelyn pointed in the direction of the grass she'd been studying, which happened to be directly in front of the tree where Peter was hanging out.

"Oh. Uh, yeah."

Evelyn was looking at me curiously, and now the others were, too. I'd been hoping Peter would leave before he noticed me there—him giving me a ride home from the store was one thing, but hanging out with his new friends and my new friends in the same place at the same time was a little too awkward.

I couldn't say any of that, of course, so I took a deep breath and moved slowly in Peter's direction.

"Hey, Shar." He glanced up at me through half-lidded eyes. I wondered exactly how much he'd smoked already. "Want a hit?"

"No thanks."

"Don't worry, he isn't driving," the guy next to him offered. "I was going to give him a ride home before too long. It's nice to meet you, by the way. Pete talks about you all the time. I'm Dean."

"Hi. I'm Sharon." I eyed Dean carefully. He was very tall, and cute, with blond hair and blue eyes that reminded me of the old Ken doll I've got somewhere in the attic.

"Are you having a good semester?" he asked politely. He didn't seem to be stoned himself. I guess he was just keeping my brother company. And calling him "Pete" for some reason.

"It's all right," I said. "How about you? Are you in school?"

"Yep. First year of college."

"SF State?"

He shook his head, then shrugged, as if he was embarrassed. "Stanford?"

"Ohhh." I nodded. Dean was probably rich, then. The only kids I've ever known who went to Stanford were in the handful of rich families who go to our church. "I see."

"Sharon!" Alex shouted behind me. "We're starting in two minutes!"

Peter glanced back, looking amused. "Are you playing softball with the lesbians, Shar?"

"Hey, do you need any more players?" Dean called back to Alex. "I pitched Little League!"

Dean was totally the Little League type. I glanced at Peter and rolled my eyes—we always used to make fun of the Little League players in our neighborhood—but he didn't roll his back at me. Too stoned, probably.

"What'd you say?" Alex called back. Dean jogged over to her.

When he was gone, Peter turned back to me, his eyes looking suddenly clearer than they had a moment before. "Those are the girls who hang out at that bookstore, right? Are you friends with them now?"

"Um... I've been volunteering there. For the No on 6 campaign."

"Since when? I've been trying to get you to come work on Harvey's campaigns for months."

"Yeah... I don't know. I decided to finally do it."

"What, out of nowhere?"

"Um. It was actually because of my pen pal, Tammy. You remember her, right?"

"The artist from fundamentalist land? Sure. What's she got to do with it?"

"Well, it turns out there are some things I didn't know about her." I turned so I could watch his face when I broke the news. "Like... she's gay."

Peter's mouth dropped open, exactly as I knew it would. "You're shitting me."

I grinned. "I swear I'm not."

"She lives in <u>Orange County</u>. The most conservative place on earth."

"Yeah, and she has to work on the pro-Prop 6 campaign with her church. No one knows about her except one other girl, and me." I took a breath, realizing that last part wasn't true anymore.

Hmm.

Peter got it, too. "And now <u>me</u>."

"Um, I guess." I shrugged. "She'd be okay with that. She knows about you."

"She knows about me...how?" He raised his eyebrows.

A heavy weight landed in my stomach. "I, uh..."

Oh, shit.

I knew right away what I'd done, but I have to admit, I didn't totally understand what it meant. Not at first.

In that moment, standing there with Peter, all I could think was maybe this didn't have to be a big deal. Maybe he'd let this go.

He's my brother. All my life, he's meant more to me than anyone else in the world. I couldn't lose him.

"You <u>told</u> her?" His mouth gaped open. "You told some girl in Orange County about <u>me</u>?"

"Tammy's not just some girl. She's one of my best friends. Anyway, she's hundreds of miles from here."

Peter took a huge step back from me. "Shar. You <u>should've</u> asked me."

I swallowed again. "You're right. I'm sorry."

"And now you've told me about her, and I'm guessing you didn't ask <u>her</u> if that was okay, either."

I bit my lip. He was right.

I hadn't even realized how badly I'd screwed up until he said that, either.

I'm so sorry, Tammy. I don't blame you if you hate me. Peter already seems to.

"This is just great." He scrunched a fist in his curly hair. "How do you know she's even telling you the truth? This whole thing could be a trick."

"That doesn't make any sense. We were randomly assigned to be pen pals, so it's not as if she could've—"

"She knows where we live. Obviously. She's been writing to you for months." Peter plunged his other hand into his hair. I hadn't seen him this upset since the Miami vote. "She could write a letter to Mom. Or look us up in the phone book and call her."

"She'd never do that!"

"Okay, but even if that's true, what about her parents?"

"She'd never. She lives in terror of them finding out about <u>her</u>."

"Or so she says." His face was red. "What if she only tells one person, the way <u>you</u> did, and it gets back to us somehow? I <u>trusted</u> you, Sis!"

"I'm sorry." I was on the verge of crying. "You're right. I'm sorry."

"A lot of good that does me." He swung his leg, kicking out at a pebble in the grass. It skittered away. He jammed his foot again into the empty patch of dirt.

"I was trying to make her feel better." I shut my eyes tight. "I thought if I told her about you—"

"What, you'd score pro-gay points? This is my <u>life</u>. It's up to <u>me</u> to decide who knows!"

"I'm sorry." My tears finally broke through. "I'm sorry."

"That doesn't matter." When we were little, if I cried, my brother would stop whatever he was doing to tell me it would be okay. Now, he only shook his head. "I'm going to find Dean. You do...whatever the Hell you want. Just leave me alone."

He turned his back on me.

I waited, thinking maybe he'd turn around and give me one last look, one little hint that he didn't completely hate me. Instead he moved faster and faster away into the darkness, until I couldn't see him at all.

Soon, Alex called me over to join the softball game. I tried to play, to act as if everything was normal, but it was dark out, and in the dim light of the street lamps I couldn't think about anything except how badly I'd screwed up.

I shouldn't have told you about my brother. And I never should've told him about you.

I'm home now, lying on my bed, staring up at your collage. All of a sudden, everything's going wrong. I betrayed my brother and you. I'm barely talking to my friends at school.

Things are awkward between me and Kevin, too. There's a strain between us, and I can't pinpoint why. The space between us is filling up with all the things I don't know how to tell him.

I wish we didn't have to write letters. I want to hear how your voice sounds. I want to stay up all night talking to you. I want to ask you a question and hear what you think right away, instead of having to wait days to get your answers back. I wish we could listen to Patti Smith together, instead of me having to put on the record and pretend you're listening with me.

I'm just so sorry, Tammy. If you hate me, I guess I understand.

Yours truly,
Sharon

Monday, December 5, 1977

Dear Sharon,

Okay, well…the truth is, I kind of assumed you'd already told your brother.

He's right, though, now that I'm thinking about it. You probably should've asked first.

I can see why he wouldn't trust me. I trust <u>him</u>, the same way I trust you, but that's different. We've been writing to each other for so long and told each other so much that it feels as if we've met a hundred times already. But for your brother, it isn't that way at all.

I'm sorry you fought because of me, though. I hate that I'm messing things up for you.

And I'm sorry things are tough with you and Kevin. It's getting tough with Carolyn and me, too.

We're "together" now, I think—if you kiss every day you're a real couple, right? Because that's what we've started doing. There's a stairwell no one ever uses by the north corridor, and we go there every day after our second-period Bible class. We only have three minutes between periods, so we have to be fast, but it's exhilarating. There's never time to ask questions. Or to talk at all.

What usually happens is, she'll leave class first and glance back at me. I'll catch her eye. Then she'll turn around and walk down the hall, fast, until she disappears around the corner. I'll look around to make sure no one's paying attention—which they never are, because everyone spends the class-change time making fun of the way Mrs. Harrington draws out the name "Baal" so it sounds like she's talking about a guy's balls—and then I'll follow her.

When we get into the stairwell, we listen to make sure we don't hear footsteps, and then we start kissing. We don't stop to smile nervously, or hold hands, or do any of the other things I used to do when I'd kiss boys. We just kiss, and kiss, and we don't stop until the warning bell goes off. Then we spring apart and scramble to wipe our faces and fix our hair.

I always leave first, so I can make sure the hall is clear. Carolyn doesn't come out until after I've turned the corner. I know because when I look back, I never see her.

I don't even want to know what would happen if we got caught. It bothers me, though, that we never have time to talk. Especially when something's happened.

Like with yesterday. As we were leaving Sunday school, she was walking up ahead of me with Brett, and he asked her on a date. Just suddenly, out of nowhere. Carolyn said yes without even hesitating, and she gave him one of those nervous smiles she never gives me.

I heard the whole thing. She must've known that. But when I tried to ask her about it today in the stairwell, she started kissing me before I could finish my sentence. I kissed her back, but after a minute I pulled away, and when I asked again, she rolled her eyes and said, "Duh. Come on, you know I don't want people thinking there's something wrong with me." Then she kissed me again before I could say any more.

I've been thinking about what she said all day. Especially the "wrong with me" part. She said it as though it was obvious. As if what's happening between us is straight-up <u>wrong</u>.

That's how my aunt and everyone else here sees it. I used to think of it that way, too. Maybe I still do, sometimes.

Not everyone thinks that, though. Those women you met at the bookstore, and your brother and his friends—they don't think the way people here do.

I know it's only that Carolyn doesn't want us to get caught. I don't want that, either, of course. It's the same for your brother, and I bet it's the same way for his friend Dean at Stanford, too. Especially if his parents are paying his tuition.

So what's the answer? Who's right, and who's wrong? What are any of us supposed to do?

Sorry. I know you don't know the answers any more than I do. I just get so lost in the whole mess of it all sometimes.

Yours truly,
Tammy

Wednesday, December 7, 1977

Dear Tammy,

I have to leave for confession, so I can't write much, but I just read your letter and it made me realize something.

You said a couple of letters ago that I was your best friend. Well, I think that you're <u>my</u> best friend, too. Sorry it took me so long to figure that out.

And I wanted to say that I don't think there's anything wrong with you, or with Carolyn for that matter. Or my brother, or anyone else. I understand about wanting to keep it secret, but that's not the same thing as there being something wrong with you. That's just what you have to do to survive from one day to the next.

I'm so glad we're still writing to each other, because there's a lot I want to say to you. I want to hear everything you have to say, too.

Shoot, got to go. I'll write again tomorrow.

Yours,
Sharon

SUMMER, 1978

Dear Diary,

I haven't used this diary in months—not since I started writing every single thought in my head in my letters to Tammy. But I had to get it out again to write about tonight.

I went to a show in North Beach. I'd thought about inviting Kevin, but I decided I'd rather be alone. Now I wish I'd called him after all.

The show itself was great. This band called Crime opened, and then the Avengers came on. It was my first time seeing the Avengers live, and their singer had short, spiky bleached hair and cool makeup—big red circles of blush up high on her cheeks and dark, over-the-top eye makeup, as if she was making fun of girls who try to look like Farrah Fawcett-Majors.

The way she moved around the stage when she wasn't singing was cool, too. She gave off a very clear signal that she didn't care what anyone thought of her. She was just moving the way she wanted to move.

When the band took a break, everyone started churning toward the bar, as usual. I didn't want to get crushed, so I headed for the front door and stepped outside. It was cold out, and I hadn't brought a jacket since I always get sweaty from dancing, so I was shivering in my Clash T-shirt. It was one I'd found in the same secondhand store where I'd bought a bunch of things lately, but I'd worn it with jeans because the last couple of times I'd gone to clubs in my vinyl skirt, jerks had kept grabbing my butt.

I got so cold so fast I gave up and turned around to go back inside. That was when I spotted the poster. It was one of a dozen worn, tattered posters that had been up on that wall by the door for ages, but it jumped out to me so clearly it might as well have been outlined in neon.

It was the same poster I saw on the side of a phone booth on my way out of the Castro, almost a year ago now. The one with the picture of Midge Spelling in her leather skirt and tie.

I froze, staring at it. The poster was gray and wrinkled, with a long tear running down the side. The picture of Midge was faded, but intact. She stared straight into the camera with no trace of a smile. As if she was looking right through me.

I remember that night so clearly. The moment I first saw Midge onstage. The passion in her voice. The way she shut her eyes when she sang. The way her lips curled as she growled into the microphone. Everything about her was strong, and fierce, and beautiful, all at the same time.

Suddenly, staring down at that worn poster, all I wanted in the entire world was to go back to that night, climb up onto that stage, and kiss her.

Wait. Who?

I shut my eyes and sucked in a ragged breath. Had I imagined that thought?

No. It was real. Completely, unavoidably real.

I turned around. When I opened my eyes again, I was facing the cars and buses speeding by on the street in front of the club. I couldn't see Midge's photo, but I could feel it looming behind me.

What did this mean? What was I supposed to do?

I'm <u>not</u> gay.

I have a boyfriend. I like him. I like <u>being</u> with him. I like it a <u>lot</u>. And it's not just Kevin, either. When Peter dragged me to see <u>Star Wars</u> for the third time, I spent the whole night imagining making out with Han Solo in the Millennium Falcon when it made the jump to light speed.

I wouldn't feel that way if I was gay. Right?

Except...what if this was why I didn't understand all those songs about love?

A set of headlights swept across my eyes. I held up my arm in front of my face, blocking the light. It was the bus heading back downtown.

I didn't think anymore. I ran. When the bus slowed down at the stop by the end of the block, I jumped onto the bottom step.

I had to get out of that place. I had to get somewhere I could really think.

But thinking is all I've been doing since I got home, and I'm not any closer to understanding what happened outside that club than I was the first moment I saw that poster tonight.

Yours,
Sharon

Dear Diary,

Well, now I'm even more confused.

We lost again tonight. Anita Bryant and her people have been going from place to place, getting cities to overturn their gay rights laws. They already won in Kansas and Minnesota, and this time it was Eugene, Oregon.

There have been marches in the Castro after every vote. Peter and I were driving back from the Eugene march tonight, both of us depressed, when I asked him.

I don't know why I did it then, of all times. Maybe I was too upset to think clearly. Maybe I just couldn't stand to keep it inside one more second. Maybe both.

"So, um..." I swallowed. "Something happened."

"Yeah?" He sounded tired. Too tired for this conversation. "What?"

"Um, well..." I didn't know where to start. I was starting to realize this was probably a bad idea.

Things have been strained between Peter and me. He finally accepted my apology for telling Tammy about him, but I don't think he believed me when I said she wasn't as upset about it as he was. He was adamant that I didn't understand—that I <u>couldn't</u>.

"Are you going to tell me what it was?" he asked. A Journey song came on the radio, and he leaned down to hit Play on the tape deck. The opening notes of the <u>Ziggy Stardust</u> album tinkled out. That was always our favorite when we were kids. "I'm kind of exhausted."

"Yeah. Um." I shut my eyes and tried to focus on the music. "I... I think I might like a girl."

The car lurched.

"Asshole!" shouted a guy from the right lane.

"Oh, my gosh!" I grabbed the dashboard. "What was that?"

My brother jerked the car back into the lane. "That was me re-acting to you! What in Christ's name are you <u>doing</u>, saying that shit while I'm driving?"

"I wasn't expecting you to kill us!"

"Are you seriously telling me you're <u>gay</u>?"

"No. No! I don't know. I don't know what it means."

Peter glanced at me. For a second I thought he was going to steer the car into traffic again, but his eyes slid back to the road. "Is this why you've been hanging out with those girls at that bookstore?"

"No. I wanted to help with the Prop 6 campaign."

"Uh-huh." He didn't look at me this time.

"Look, I don't know if I really like her. I thought I did, once, but it probably didn't mean anything."

When I shut my eyes, I could see the picture of Midge perfectly, as though I was back outside the club all over again, but when I opened them, I was feeling too many things to sort them all out.

"Shar?" Peter's voice dropped as he glanced over at me. "It's okay if you're gay."

"I'm not." I shook my head, my back still turned. I was seconds from crying. "I'm with Kevin, remember?"

"Having a boyfriend doesn't make you straight. Plenty of people live totally straight lives, but they're still gay."

"Well, I'm not one of those people."

He sighed. "You're talking as if there's something wrong with being gay."

I wiped at my eyes roughly. "It isn't that."

"Okay, well. Look, I'm only saying, I don't think straight girls get crushes on other girls very often."

"Well, maybe I'm trying to start a new trend." I gave up and tangled my fingers into the ends of my curly hair, letting the tears slip down my cheeks. "Besides, I never said it was a crush. I don't know what it is. How did, um...how did you know?"

"What, that I was gay?"

I nodded.

He shrugged. "I knew by junior high. The hard part was deciding what to do about it."

"Then I can't be. I had no idea of anything back in junior high."

"I don't think it's the same for everyone. Dean didn't know until he was already in college. He had a girlfriend all through high school, then he got to Stanford and one of the guys in his dorm took him to a gay bar, and he never looked back."

"Wow. Was he happy with his high-school girlfriend?"

"I don't know. He doesn't talk much about her. Leonard had a girlfriend in high school, too, but he knew he was gay and so did she. They only pretended to be together so their parents wouldn't nag them while they both snuck out with guys."

Peter kept talking, telling me more about his friends, and I sat back to listen. These kinds of stories meant a lot more to me than they had before.

I still don't know what I'm supposed to do about all this, but it feels good to have told someone. Even though the person I want to tell is Tammy.

But first, I have to think more. A lot more. So I can figure out what it means for myself.

Yours,
Sharon

Tuesday, May 23, 1978

Dear Sharon,

You'll probably think this is corny, but…I made Carolyn a collage. I know, I know, you said I should let her make the next move and you're probably right, but I'm tired of waiting.

I'll give it to her on Saturday, at prom. I know that's even cornier, but, well, we're both going to this stupid dance with boys we don't like. We might as well have something special to remember about it years from now.

I didn't have any photos of her to use in the collage, not unless I cut up one of my old school yearbooks, so I drew the background myself. I wanted to keep it simple, so I used a regular lead pencil and sketched a picture of us the night we first kissed. I didn't draw the actual kissing part, obviously— I'm not stupid enough to put <u>that</u> down on paper—but I drew us lying by the water, with Carolyn perched on her elbow and me staring up at her. I'm mostly out of the frame, since it's really a picture of Carolyn as I remember her that night. All light and warmth in the darkness.

In the front of the drawing, I glued the words I'd cut out of my mom's old issues of <u>Life</u>: TWO OF US AGAINST THE WORLD.

On the back I wrote, "You're the only one for me."

I hope she'll like it. The drawing doesn't do her justice, though. She has red hair that she's always complaining about because it frizzes sometimes, but whenever we're close, all I can see is how <u>alive</u> her hair looks. There's no way you'd ever mistake her for anyone else.

Meanwhile, <u>my</u> hair is generically blond and flat with a part down the middle. It hangs almost to my waist because my mom refuses to let me cut it. She says long hair is feminine and boys prefer it. As if either of those are good things.

I wish I could chop my hair to my shoulders and wash it with dish soap so it puffed out, like Patti Smith's. Or even steal my dad's razor and shave it off completely. I don't know which would freak out my mom and Aunt Mandy more.

I'm dreading prom, Sharon. Tim Weiss probably plans to spend the entire night behind the gym getting stoned with the other guys instead of dancing with me. He only asked me in the first place because Carolyn convinced Brett to get him to.

Mom bought me this hideous dress. It's sea-green gingham with fat sleeves and a fatter ruffle at the bottom of the skirt. She took me to a seamstress to get the hem let out, and now it's even puffier than it was on the rack and it covers my feet completely. I'll look like a legless gingham marshmallow.

I'm so jealous that your school only lets seniors go to prom. I'm more jealous of your brother for having the nerve to just not go. Maybe next year I'll be as brave as him.

Are you excited for his graduation, though? I know you said you were nervous about him being at a different school from you for the first time, but at least he's staying with you and your mom after he starts college. Maybe it's kind of good that he can't afford to live on his own yet. I bet he's glad he'll get to see you more, too, even if he won't admit it.

Got to go—Mom wants me to put my stupid dress on so she can take a Polaroid for Grandma. I cannot WAIT for this dance to be over.

Yours,
Tammy

Friday, May 26, 1978

Dear Tammy,

Your collage for Carolyn sounds awesome. If she doesn't like it, there's definitely something wrong with her. I still have that one you sent me up on my wall, and I stare at it all the time. It's strange how captivating it is.

By the time you get this letter your prom will be over, so I hope it wasn't too unbearable. Did Tim spend the whole night smoking behind the gym? If he did, did you actually mind? I could see how you might've had more fun if he wasn't around to bother you much. At Kevin's prom, there was a group of senior guys who disappeared five minutes after they got there and didn't come back until the last song, reeking of smoke and falling all over the place. Father Murphy took them outside, and I have no idea what happened to them after that, but none of them were at graduation the next week.

You didn't mention it in your letter, maybe because you wrote it before the news came out, but you've probably heard by now that we lost another city. In Oregon this time. There was another march in the Castro. These protest marches are getting almost routine now. Getting angry and yelling about it. Shooting defiant looks at the cops. Carrying signs that say things like ANITA, THIS OBSESSION WITH US ISN'T AS CHARMING AS YOU THINK IT IS. (I made that one, but my brother carried it. He snuck it out to the car in a garbage bag in case Mom was watching.)

I wish you could come to one of these. Well, actually, I wish we didn't need to <u>have</u> any more of these, but it's not looking good. The latest polls on Prop 6 have it passing by a landslide. Our goal is just to win San Francisco—which is hardly a guarantee—and if we get anywhere else in the state, that'll be nice, too. That won't be enough to kill the initiative, though.

By this time next year, it'll probably be illegal to be a teacher if you're gay in California. Or if you just <u>support</u> gay people. Which I guess means if I want to teach, I'll have to leave the state to do it.

As for my mom…well, at least she works in a private school. Not to mention, she doesn't support gay people. Yesterday on our way in I heard her talking to Mr. Goodwin, one of the science teachers at St. John's. He said he was worried his students would feel pressured to accept homosexuality because of all the media attention Harvey's getting. Mom said, "Remind them that if they read the Bible, they'll see <u>God</u> doesn't accept it."

I hope she never finds out about Peter. Is it really possible to keep it a secret <u>forever</u>, though? Is that something you think about?

Sorry—you'd probably rather not talk about that. I'd go back and cross it out, but we said we weren't going to do that anymore, so please just ignore it.

At least today was the last day of school. Huzzah! I won't have to worry about Sister Catherine for the next three months. At graduation tomorrow I'll try to keep in mind what you said about my brother. I don't know if I believe it, but I'll take it!

Write back soon and tell me all about prom, please.

Yours,
Sharon

P.S. I forgot to mention—I saw an ad in the newspaper for a Christian radio show called <u>New Way on the Air</u>. Isn't that the name of your church? Did your aunt and uncle finally get their show, thanks to all those bribes in that check register you wrote to me about? I want to listen to it with Peter so we can make fun of it together.

Tuesday, May 30, 1978

Dear Sharon,

God, I <u>wish</u> I could go to a march in San Francisco. About anything, honestly—I'd happily go to a Save the Whales protest.

I could never travel that far on my own, though. Girls in our family aren't allowed to go anywhere unsupervised. Once my sister and two of her friends planned a ski trip, just one night in someone's uncle's cabin out by Big Bear Lake, and my parents grounded her just for asking.

So… I don't know what to say about prom.

At least it's over, and… I survived? I guess? The walls didn't collapse and crush me to death? Even though there were times when I wouldn't have minded if they had.

The grossness started before we got there. Brett's dad rented a limo, but it turns out limos aren't that big on the inside, and there were eight of us jammed in. The guys had clearly already been drinking before they picked us up. I don't know if that's why it happened or if this is how it would've gone, anyway, but we weren't halfway to school before Tim—whose lap I was half-sitting on, since there was literally nowhere else to sit—started pinching my butt.

I was so mad I wanted to scream, but I couldn't do anything

in front of everybody else. I guess he knew that, because he kept doing it even when I tried to squirm off his lap. I finally reached back and grabbed his wrist, but he only laughed.

Brett laughed, too. I'm positive he knew what was going on. Carolyn didn't notice, thank God.

When we finally got there the guys hung out in the gym with us for long enough to get our cheesy official photos taken, then disappeared. There were dozens of chaperones, but none of them seemed to notice them sneaking out to get high. Even my aunt, who was wearing about ten yards of ugly pink caftan fabric wound around her, just smiled her usual smug smile as they went by.

That was when I pulled Carolyn into the hall. I wasn't sure I'd get another chance, so I led her straight to our stairwell. I'd had to hide the collage in my dress, because my mother would only let me bring a tiny clutch big enough for lipstick and a blotting tissue. (Though I guess it could have also held a little more, because I know for a fact that at least three of the other youth group girls had the exact same clutch but somehow managed to fit condoms inside.) Fortunately, my skirt had so much extra puffy fabric no one noticed the cardboard backing of the collage taped to the underside.

"Close your eyes," I told Carolyn, so she wouldn't see me awkwardly lifting up the ruffled hem of my floor-length skirt to pull out the collage. Besides, it seemed more romantic if she didn't see the logistics at work.

Carolyn closed her eyes. She looked beautiful that night. Her dress was even puffier than mine, with baby blue lace running from the frilly collar to the frilly hem, and it had a pale pink sash that tied around her waist. It was a lot, but it suited her perfectly. Her hair was curled into soft waves that framed her face, and the deep red corsage Brett had given her was strapped to her wrist, clashing brilliantly with her strawberry-colored hair.

"Okay, you can open your eyes," I said when I had the collage out in front of her.

She blinked down at it slowly. "Oh. Wow. Is this—? Did you make this? Like a craft project?"

"Um, yeah. It's for you. I make collages sometimes. Here, turn it over."

She turned it over. Her eyes widened, and she flipped it back again without looking up at me. "Um, thanks…but I can't take this home. I don't have any way to get it out of here." She held up her own tiny clutch.

I felt stupid for not thinking of that before. "Oh. Uh, well, I taped it to my skirt to get it in here. I guess you could do that, too?"

She glanced down at her lace dress. "It won't work. They'd see."

"Okay, well…" I felt stupider with every passing second. "I guess I'll take it back home."

"You can't. It's a miracle no one noticed you had it already. We have to get rid of it."

"What do you mean? Get rid of it…how?"

"Yeah, I guess it's not as if we could put it in the trash. Anyone could see." She glanced around us. "You don't have any matches, do you?"

"Matches? No, I…why?"

"Never mind. We'll put it in my locker. It's closer than yours. Then next week we can take it out in one of our school bags."

So that's what we did. I poked my head out the door to make sure no one was in the hallway, and we crept silently away and stashed the collage in Carolyn's locker, shutting it carefully so it wouldn't clang.

There was no time left for kissing. We'd already been gone too long, so we left, the same way we always did—me first, with Carolyn following after I'd turned the corner.

When I got back to the gym, Tim was there, standing by the punch table in his burgundy tuxedo with the ruffled shirt and bow tie. He asked me to dance. My aunt was looking right at us, so I didn't have much choice. The band was playing "Stayin' Alive" and Tim was doing a ridiculous John Travolta strut, with his top button undone and his collar spread open, and I had to hobble along behind him as if this was the most fun I'd ever had in my life.

A few songs later I told him I had to get some air, thinking he'd want to stay inside and show off more dance moves (though thankfully one of the chaperones had made him fasten his top button by then). Instead, he followed me out. But this time, when he tried to grope me, I slugged him in the chest.

He staggered backward, even though I couldn't have hit him that hard. For a second he just stared at me, his eyes red and his mouth gaping open like a fish.

"Bitch," he grunted. Then he turned around and shuffled back into the gym.

I'm not going to lie, Sharon. I didn't feel bad. Even when we were in the limo on the way home and Tim was sitting as far away from me as he could get, huffing in my direction every couple of minutes, I didn't regret a single thing.

I did worry he might hold a grudge, though. When I saw him at school yesterday, I half expected him to swear at me again, but he only sneered, the same way my dad sneers at the TV when Notre Dame is losing. I only wished I had a reason to punch him all over again.

But tomorrow's the last day of school, and our youth group usually takes a break in the summers. I might be able to get away with not seeing him much until September. Punching him again isn't worth it.

Carolyn didn't say anything more about the collage, but I hope she liked it. She must've taken it home by now. We haven't had a chance to talk since prom, anyway. She had to stay after Bible class yesterday and today to talk to Mrs. Harrington about some last-minute extra-credit project.

Sometimes, when I'm with Carolyn, it feels as if my life might finally be okay. Then other times it feels like I'm about to suffocate. I only wish I knew which it was going to be in the end.

Yours,
Tammy

P.S. Yes, my aunt's stupid fucking radio show is finally happening. I don't know how I forgot to mention that. No one at church talks about anything else anymore.

Thursday, June 1, 1978

Dear Tammy,

Wow! Sorry, I'll write you a real letter tomorrow about everything you wrote in your letter, but for now I just wanted to say how awesome it is that you punched that guy! I'm sorry you had a reason to punch him, but still!

I've got to go, since I'm late to babysit (again), but I'm going to put this in the mailbox on my way just so you know you're my hero.

Yours,
Sharon

P.S. Now I'm picturing my mom's face if I told her my lesbian pen pal from Orange County was my hero, and that it was all because she punched a guy. Ha!

Friday, June 2, 1978

Dear Diary,

Wow. <u>Wow</u>. <u>WOW</u>.

I had to bring this diary out again, because...well, you'll see.

It started early this morning, with knocking. It was soft at first. So soft, I thought I was dreaming.

It took me hours to fall asleep last night. I don't know why—everything was normal enough, except I had this strange sense that something was wrong. <u>Deeply</u> wrong.

I guess I slept, though, because as I sat up this morning, fumbling for my alarm clock, an odd dream was lingering in my mind.

I was standing beside a swimming pool. It was big, the kind of pool you'd see at a park—or maybe the country club where Tammy works in the summers, come to think of it—but no one was in sight. The space was empty except for the water at my feet and a high, dark fence on every side. The wall was smooth, with no doors or gates to break it up. Only steep, sheer walls and, in the middle, the deep expanse of water, impossibly blue and shimmering.

The pool lapped silently at the concrete edges, as if the water was inviting me in, but somehow I knew—I <u>knew</u>—that if I didn't get away from that water fast, something terrible would happen.

I shook off the remnants of sleep and peered at the clock. Then I shot up in bed. I'd slept through my alarm, and I was supposed to be at the O'Sullivans' in twelve minutes. It's really bad if I'm late, since that makes Mr. O'Sullivan late to work, too. Mrs. O'Sullivan's pregnant again, and the doctor just put her on bed rest, so her husband is taking on extra shifts to make up for her lost wages. I'm watching their two kids, Penny and Chris, every weekday this summer, and some weekend days, too.

I rolled out of bed, took a thirty-second shower and stepped into my clothes with my hair still wet. I never bother with makeup on babysitting days, so I had time for a quick bowl of cereal.

Mom and Peter were already gone for the day, Peter at work and Mom running errands, so I hurried to the empty kitchen and gulped down my food while I glanced at the Chronicle spread out across the kitchen table. There was a photo of Senator Briggs at the bottom of the page, next to yet another article predicting a landslide victory for his initiative banning gay teachers. The only thing I could safely predict was that I never wanted to see another photo of Senator Briggs while I was trying to eat. My cereal was already threatening to come back up.

The O'Sullivans' house is a two-minute walk downhill from ours, and when I unlocked the front door I had exactly three minutes to get there. I stepped out into the morning fog, letting out a fat yawn and flicking my wet hair over my shoulder.

"Hi," a soft voice said.

I blinked.

There was a girl on my front stoop.

She was several inches taller than me, with long, tangled blond hair and dark circles under her wide blue eyes. Her clothes were rumpled, but her pants were the same ones Rhonda had shown me in a magazine last month, by that French designer she's obsessed with. The girl's purse looked expensive, too, and there was a map of San Francisco sticking out of its front pocket.

I'd never seen her before, not even a picture of her, but I was absolutely certain it was Tammy.

"Sharon?" There was no doubt in her voice, either.

A million words bubbled up in my throat at once, but I seemed to have forgotten how to speak. I stepped back into the foyer, waving frantically for her to come in. I was moving so fast I almost tripped, my loafers squeaking on the linoleum.

She stepped inside, her eyes shifting around, taking in everything at once. The lumpy plaid couch under the front window. The stained shag rug. The dark doorway to the kitchen with the breakfast dishes piled in the sink.

Then her gaze slid to me, and I remembered my wet hair and lack of makeup and the frayed pair of Peter's corduroy pants I'd thrown on when I couldn't find anything decent in my own laundry pile.

None of it mattered, somehow.

"I'm sorry to show up this way." She was looking right at me, but her gaze didn't linger on my disheveled hair or my lumpy 49ers sweatshirt or the zit on my chin. Her eyes were bloodshot, with the remnants of what must've been yesterday's mascara underneath, but she held my gaze, even though she looked exhausted enough to fall over at any second. "There wasn't anywhere else I could go, and— Well, um, could I...?"

"Yeah." I tried to think quickly, which wasn't easy given how hard my heart was pounding. "I have to go babysit, but you can come with me. We'll talk there."

"I don't want to impose..."

"It's okay." I didn't know what was happening, but I knew I wanted to help. In that moment, I wanted to help Tammy more than I'd ever wanted to do anything. "The O'Sullivans won't mind. You know how to take care of little kids, right?"

She smiled thinly. A very, very tired smile. "That's one of the few things I actually do know how to do."

"Good. We'll have to be fast."

I locked the door behind us and led Tammy down the block at a near-run. I didn't ask her any questions, and she didn't volunteer anything. But she wasn't carrying a suitcase, or even a backpack—only her purse. Whatever had brought her four hundred miles from home, it must've happened fast.

We reached the O'Sullivans and rang the bell. I turned to Tammy, trying to think of some kind of story we could tell them, but before I could say a word Mr. O'Sullivan swung open the door and stepped out onto the porch, his coat in his hand. Three-year-old Penny and one-year-old Chris thundered across the kitchen floor behind him after a toy truck. "Morning, Sharon. I'll be back by five."

He was already halfway down the steps when he noticed Tammy standing next to me and paused. I started to babble. "This is my friend Tammy, she's, uh—"

"I'm visiting from out of town and I offered to help Sharon today. I hope that's all right, sir. I won't need any pay, since I'm still learning how to babysit."

Mr. O'Sullivan smiled, and Tammy smiled right back at him. A completely different smile than the thin, fatigued one I'd seen thirty seconds ago on my doorstep.

Now, out of nowhere, she was bright and sunny. Even the circles under her eyes seemed to have lightened.

There was no time to figure out how she'd pulled that off. Mr. O'Sullivan was already nodding. "Fine. See you girls at five."

"SHARON!" Penny lunged through the door the second her father disappeared, throwing her arms around my calves. "Chris broked my truck!"

"Oh, no! Well, I bet I can fix it. Hey, Penny, this is my friend Tammy. Tammy, this is Penny, and that's Chris."

Tammy immediately squatted down to Penny's level. "What a cool truck!" She pointed to the bright yellow bulldozer sliding to a halt by Chris's feet. He promptly picked it up and started gnawing on it. As far as I could tell, the truck was intact. "What kind is it?"

"A bullbozer," Penny said knowledgeably. "Bullbozers push rocks. My brother eats them, 'cause his teeth are hurting, but that's okay 'cause it's not a real bullbozer, it's a pretend bullbozer."

Tammy sat on the floor beside Penny and the two of them began an in-depth discussion about trucks while I checked to see if Chris needed a diaper change. The next thing I knew, Tammy had fixed whatever problem the truck supposedly had, and Penny was sitting in her lap holding a copy of <u>Goodnight Moon</u>. Once his dry diaper was in place—Chris always pees as soon as I arrive—he toddled over, too, and Tammy lifted him up to sit beside her. Before long the three of them had read the entirety of <u>Goodnight Moon</u> five times and were starting on a sixth.

The morning passed faster than any of my summer babysitting jobs had yet. Penny and Chris adored Tammy, and she gave them her undivided attention. When it was time for lunch, I set out extra ham and cheese so she could fix herself a sandwich, but she shook her head as I was putting down the kids' plates.

"It wouldn't be right," Tammy said when I slid the bread package to her. "Anyway, I'm not hungry."

I eyed her dubiously. "When's the last time you ate?"

She shrugged, but the exhaustion was creeping back into her eyes. "I'm fine."

"Come on, you'll be doing me a favor. Mrs. O'Sullivan always says

I need to put meat on my bones. If there's extra bread gone at the end of today, she might leave me alone for a while."

Tammy smiled, but she made herself half a sandwich and gobbled it down.

I watched her while we ate, trying to reconcile the girl in front of me with the months of letters piled in the box under my bed. Tammy wasn't at all how I'd pictured her. There were the expensive clothes and the Malibu-Barbie-blondness, for one thing, but there were also the sunny smiles she could turn on in a split second. She'd seemed to change her entire personality as soon as she met the O'Sullivans. As though she was slipping into new skin.

From her letters, I'd been expecting a rebel. A girl who didn't care what anyone thought of her. The Tammy sitting here now reminded me more of the popular girls at school, the ones the nuns always chose to deliver messages to the principal's office or give tours to the new students. The girls who'd supposedly never dream of sneaking a cigarette in the bathroom or sitting in a parked car after dark with a guy.

After the kids finished lunch, I took them upstairs, read <u>Goodnight Moon</u> again, and tucked them in for nap time. When I came back down, Tammy was lying on the couch with her arm thrown over her eyes.

I stepped quietly into the kitchen and started a pot of coffee. She'd need it when she woke up. Maybe it would help me think, too.

Tammy's parents would never have let her come to San Francisco. Which meant she was here without their permission...if they knew she was here at all.

"Hey." Her voice was low behind me as I switched on the coffeemaker.

I spun around, startled. She was leaning against the counter behind me, smiling faintly. Her exhaustion made her slightly curled lips look soft and warm.

"Hey," I said. "You should take a nap, too."

"We might not get a chance to talk once the kids wake up." She stretched both arms over her head. The movement made her thin white T-shirt ride up, showing a brief flash of tanned stomach.

"We can talk tonight." I turned back to fumble with the coffee-maker. "You can come home with me after Mr. O'Sullivan gets back."

"What about your mom and your brother?"

"We don't have to keep anything from my brother. He'll want to help."

"Your whole family's into helping people, huh?"

I didn't know what to say, so I reached into the cabinet where the O'Sullivans keep their mugs.

It was strange—I'd imagined talking to Tammy in person so many times, but now that she was here, an awkward strain hovered between us. I was used to carefully thinking out what I wanted to tell her, crafting exactly the right sentences in my head before I picked up my pen, but now that we were talking, really talking, it felt like starting over from scratch.

When I turned around again, Tammy's eyes were closed.

"If you want to tell me what happened, you could." I kept my voice low, even though there was no one to hear. Mrs. O'Sullivan's bedroom was at the back of the house, and I hadn't seen her come out of it during the day yet that summer.

Tammy opened her eyes slowly. "I don't know where to start. Everything just suddenly turned to shit."

Hearing Tammy curse out loud was jarring. "What kind of, um, shit?"

"It was all my fault. God." She sighed and scrubbed her hand over her face. "I was stupid. So stupid."

I wanted to give her a hug, but I didn't know if she'd want that. She was my best friend, sort of, but technically, we'd just met. And we'd never touched at all. "It's okay. You don't have to talk about it."

"Yeah, I do." She rubbed her damp hands on her designer pants. "I've been going over it in my head nonstop. Talking about it would be a nice change."

She dropped her gaze to the linoleum floor and hopped onto the counter, tucking one of her long legs underneath her and dropping her chin into her hands. As upset as she clearly was, I still couldn't stop thinking...

Tammy's here. Right now. That's really, truly her.

"It started yesterday, in Math," she said after a long moment. "My teacher told me I had to go to the principal's office. When I got there, Carolyn was inside with her mom. My mom was there, too, with Aunt Mandy."

I sucked in a breath. "They found out about you and Carolyn?"

Tammy leaned her head back and stared up at the fluorescent lights. "I can't believe I thought we wouldn't get caught."

"What happened?"

"They..." She shut her eyes again and rubbed her forehead. "They found it."

"It? Oh—your collage?"

She nodded slowly. "They'd done a locker search. Apparently some seniors were stealing exams and they were looking for evidence, and...it doesn't matter. What matters is, they found it."

"Oh, my gosh."

"I don't think the principal spoke the whole time we were in that room." She fixed her eyes on the coffeepot. "He let Aunt Mandy do the talking. She isn't even on the school staff anymore, but they all still treat her as if she's God incarnate. She said Carolyn's mom had noticed her acting strangely the past few months, and—"

Tammy cut herself off. "I hate to bother you, but do you think I could have some of that coffee?"

"Oh, yes. Of course. I was making it for you." I hurried to get a mug, but Tammy lowered herself from the counter and beat me to it. She poured a cup, blew on the surface, and took a sip without putting in any milk or sugar first.

Was that how she always drank her coffee? I had no idea. There was so much I didn't know about her.

"The teachers found the collage in her locker." Tammy blinked twice, leaning back against the counter again and lifting her cup for another sip. "They saw the message I wrote. That was enough to make them call Carolyn into the office, and her mom, too. They thought a guy had given it to her at first, but they got the truth out of her somehow. Then they called in my mom, and my aunt. Then it was my turn."

Tammy closed her eyes. Her lower lip was trembling. I wondered if she was going to cry.

"Oh, my gosh," I said. "That's—that's not good."

Not good. What a stupid thing to say. This situation was clearly far beyond not good. I wanted to take the words back, but Tammy was already talking again.

"My aunt dangled the collage from two fingers like a smelly piece of garbage, and she said..." Tammy lifted her head and put on a fake snooty voice. "'Could you tell us what this means, Tammy? We can see plainly it's your handwriting, so don't try to deny it. There's no hiding your sin from the Lord.'"

"What did your mom say?"

"Nothing. She spent the whole time crying in the corner."

I wanted to cry myself just listening to this, but Tammy only sipped her coffee. "What happened then?"

"Well, I was trying to think up some explanation to make it sound innocent. Say it was a joke, or something. But before I could think it through Carolyn shouted, 'I didn't want to do it! She's the one who's sick!'"

"<u>What?</u>"

Tammy's lip trembled again. "She told them it was <u>me</u> who had a crush on <u>her</u>, and she <u>obviously</u> would never have felt that way, because she's a good little Christian. She gave this whole speech about how she'd been trying to save me before it got to be too late." Tammy set her coffee cup on the counter and slumped down on the linoleum floor, her long hair cascading into her face.

"They couldn't have believed that!"

"Oh, they did. Aunt Mandy would've bought it anyway—she's been waiting for me to screw up for years—but Carolyn laid it on thick, too. Said she was scared I was going to hurt her."

"What, <u>physically</u>?"

"Yeah. She told them about me punching Tim at prom, and she said last week I followed her into the stairwell and tried to— God, she made it sound as if she was lucky to escape with her life. She said I was a..." Tammy pressed her knuckles into her forehead again and winced. "An <u>unrepentant dyke</u>."

"I'm so sorry. That's <u>horrible</u>. But it's her word against yours, isn't it?"

"Well, they'd already talked to Tim before I got there, and they had the stupid collage with my handwriting on it. Carolyn told them I'd slipped it into her locker when she wasn't looking. She said she'd kept it secret because she wanted to help me without getting me in trouble. She said she'd thought that would be the <u>Christian</u> thing to do."

"Oh, my gosh, I can't believe her!"

"Yeah, well, all I could think through all those hours on the bus was how I should've seen it coming." Tammy stretched up to retrieve her coffee cup from the counter and took a slow sip. As if she wanted to make it last. "Anyway, by then Carolyn was crying, and her mom was crying, and, of course, my mom was still crying. Aunt Mandy and I were the only ones with dry eyes."

"What did they do? Suspend you?"

She shook her head. "Not on the last day of school. Besides, Aunt Mandy said the important thing wasn't that I get punished, it was that I get healed."

"What does that mean?"

"She called my dad and my uncle and told them to come to school right away." Tammy fixed her gaze on her mug and barked out a humorless laugh. "She told Carolyn and her mom to let them know if Carolyn needed any pastoral counseling to help her 'recover.' I knew when Dad and Uncle Russell got there, I'd be trapped, so I waited until Carolyn and her mother were gone, and when Aunt Mandy went over to talk to my mom, I ran."

"What, you just made a break for it?"

"They weren't looking at me, so I knew it was the only chance I'd get. Mom was bawling so loud they didn't even notice I'd slipped out the door at first."

"How did you get away?"

"That was the easy part. I just walked down the hall and went out the first exit I saw. The problem was, I hardly had anything with me. Just that." Tammy lifted her chin toward the counter, where her designer purse was tucked behind the O'Sullivans' cookie jar.

I tried to put the pieces together. The bags under her eyes. The rumpled clothes—she must've been wearing them since yesterday. "You left school and...what, came straight here?"

"Yeah. I'm sorry, I would've called, but there was no time to find a pay phone. I had to get as far away as I could before they came looking. Plus, I thought here... I don't know. I thought maybe San Francisco could be a place where I belonged. Finally."

I nodded. I understood that much. "So you took a bus?"

"Yeah. I thought about driving, since I had my car in the school parking lot, but I didn't know the way. Besides, my dad would've called the police and reported the car stolen. It's not as if I paid for it with my own money or anything. I drove to the bus station, left the car in the parking lot, and bought a ticket to L.A. Then when I got there, I switched to another bus leaving for San Francisco. By the time I got in, it was after midnight."

"After midnight, last night... Wait. How long were you sitting on my front steps?"

"Not long. First I had to figure out how to get to your house from the bus station. It turned out to be a long way."

My mouth dropped open. "You <u>walked</u> all the way across the city? In the middle of the <u>night</u>?"

"Yeah. I had some money with me, but after the bus tickets, there wasn't enough left for a taxi." Her eyelids were starting to droop again.

I shook my head. "Tammy, I—"

"I awake!" a tiny voice called. "Sharon, where are you? I awake!"

"Guess nap time's over." Tammy climbed slowly to her feet.

"What about you? Did you sleep on the bus?"

"Nah. It was my first time taking a Greyhound. I was afraid if I shut my eyes, I'd wake up with no purse at all."

"You should rest. There's a couch in the back den. I'll keep the kids upstairs."

"There's no way I'm sleeping now." Tammy took another sip of coffee. "I'm way too worried about what I'm going to do next."

I knew that feeling, too.

"Sharon!" Penny called. "Sharon, where you? SHARON!"

"Don't worry, we'll figure something out." I did my best to sound reassuring. "Is it okay if I call my brother? He'll get off work soon, and he might have some ideas about what to do."

"Sure. I'd love to meet him."

"Also…" I drew in an uncertain breath. "I probably shouldn't say this right now, but…well, I'm glad you're here. I mean, I'm so sorry about everything that happened, but it's good to finally get to meet you."

Tammy rested her temple on her fist. She wasn't smiling, but then, I wasn't, either. "Me, too."

I called the store and left a message asking for Peter to come over as soon as he got off work. Tammy got Penny up from her nap while I changed Chris's diaper again. Penny recounted the dream she'd had, which seemed to have been mostly about cheese.

The doorbell rang while the kids were finishing their snack (also mostly cheese). I'd tried to convince Tammy to eat with us, but she refused to take any more of the O'Sullivans' food, so she went to answer the door instead.

"Oh—hello, ma'am." My brother's voice, the overly polite tone he saves for new customers, drifted into the kitchen. He must've been trying to figure out who Tammy was and why she'd answered the O'Sullivans' door.

Tammy said something back to him. I couldn't make out her words, but seconds later, he was shouting in delight.

"No _way_! The one from Orange County? What are you doing _here_?"

I parked the kids on the floor with a couple of Barbies—Penny loved showing Chris how to take their clothes off and on, and Chris loved drooling on their feet—and Peter joined Tammy and me at the kitchen table. He had no compunction about eating the kids' snacks, and he gobbled down the leftover crackers while Tammy and I told him an abbreviated version of her story.

"Okay." Peter started ticking off things on his fingers, talking around a mouthful of food. "You need money, which means you need a job."

Tammy shook her head. "I need a place to stay first."

"Well, that's easy," Peter said, and I nodded. "You stay with us."

"I can't ask you to do that."

"Are you kidding?" I asked her. "What else will you do, sleep on the street?"

"We'll have to come up with a story for Mom," Peter added. "But it won't be hard. She's a softie at heart."

"Besides, you're my school-sanctioned pen pal," I reminded her. "Mom knows I've been writing to you. She's bound to think you're moral and Christian and everything."

"Hey, I know—we can tell her your parents are getting divorced." Peter leaned back in his seat, folding his hands behind his head, pleased with his own ingenuity. "Mom's always worrying that her and Dad getting divorced screwed us up, so she'll feel bad for you. All you have to do is say you didn't want to be in the middle of your parents fighting and she'll fall for it."

"That doesn't seem right." Tammy frowned.

I didn't like the idea of lying to Mom, either, but...I've been lying to her ever since I found out about Peter. Sometimes, lying is what has to be done. "We'll say you just wanted to get away for the summer. That'll give us time to figure something else out."

"In that case, I definitely have to pay my own way." Tammy nodded. "You're right. I need a job."

"That's even easier." Peter grinned. "The stock guy at Javi's quit last night. Said he was sick of sweeping floors and tossed his dirty apron on the counter right next to the bananas. Rosa looked ready to murder him. All day she's been grumbling about having to find someone new. If I tell her I've got someone, she'll be so happy, she'll probably give us both a raise."

Tammy looked uncertain. "I'd be the new...stock guy?"

"Javi and Rosa are great," I told her. "You'd be fine."

"Okay..."

"Chris!" Penny shouted in the next room. "You have to share with Penny!"

Chris immediately started wailing.

I went over to separate them while Peter leaned in to tell Tammy something I couldn't hear. She laughed.

It was strange to hear her laughing after everything that had happened. But that's who Tammy is, I guess. She's been hiding how she feels for years, and she's gotten good at it by now.

I sat down while Penny told me a detailed story about what Chris had been doing with her Barbies. Behind us, Peter and Tammy went on talking in low voices.

I was nervous about how this was all going to work, but more than that, I was happy she was here. Happier than I'd ever thought I'd be.

There's more to write about what happened after we left the O'Sullivans', a lot more, but I'm about to fall asleep on the sofa, and I think it's finally safe for me to go upstairs. More later.

Yours,
Sharon

Friday, June 2, 1978

Dear Harvey,

It's close to midnight. I'm so tired I could fall over, but I'm writing this instead, because I need something to help me stay awake until Sharon gets up here.

I'm writing from <u>your</u> city, Harvey. I didn't think it would ever happen, but I'm here. I know I'm not dreaming, because I just looked out the window and even in the dark, I can see the fog.

I've always wanted to come here, but I think it's only now hitting me how alone I am.

I miss my sisters. I miss my bratty little brother. I miss my <u>mother</u>, Harvey, and for as long as I can remember, avoiding her has been my number-two priority, after avoiding my aunt. Sharon's mom has been so kind and firm and cautious she reminds me of the good days at home, before Mom started to completely hate me.

And then there's Sharon.

She's nothing like I imagined, Harvey. In her letters she says so much. Now that I'm here with her, it's shocking how little she says out loud. Still, I can tell how hard she's thinking in every single moment. It's spread out across her face.

Like when we lied to her mother today. Sharon stayed pretty quiet—Peter and I did the talking—but every time I flicked my gaze her way, she was watching us so carefully, I could almost see a thousand different thoughts running through her head. I guess I'll need to learn how to read her face, since I can't read her words anymore.

That's not so bad, though. Looking at her face.

Her mom was thinking a lot while we talked, too. She was just as obvious.

"You ran away from home?" Mrs. Hawkins asked, after I'd finished telling her our story. The four of us were sitting around the kitchen table. Sharon's mother's hands were clasped around a glass of iced tea, and her shrewd eyes were locked on me. "Does anyone know where you are?"

I shook my head. There were tears pricking at the corners of my eyes, real tears. I was exhausted, and overwhelmed, and frustrated at having to lie. My tears added to the drama of the story I was telling, though, so I didn't try to hide them.

"What about your grandparents?" she asked. "Or family friends?"

"I don't have any other family, and my friends' parents are all friends with my parents. I couldn't talk to any of them."

Mrs. Hawkins nodded. She seemed to believe me. Only the first part had been a lie, anyway. "What did you plan to do once you reached San Francisco?"

"I'm not sure." I tried to smile, but the tears were threatening to fall. "Get a job. Find a place to live."

"For how long? Are you planning to move back home before the school year starts?"

"I..." I trailed off. "I don't know."

"You have to graduate. You can't let this ruin your future." Mrs. Hawkins sighed. "Well, summer just began, so I suppose we can discuss that later. For now, you're welcome to stay here."

"Thank you so much, ma'am. I can't tell you how much this means to me."

"It's not as though I'd have turned you out on the streets." She sighed. "All the same, I don't feel right about your family not having any idea where you are. I understand if you don't want to speak to them, but please give me your phone number. I'll call your mother so she knows you're safe."

I froze. Across the table, Sharon fidgeted, but it was Peter who jumped in.

"Her mom isn't stable." We all turned to stare, and he tapped his nose. "Drugs. That's why they're getting divorced."

I dropped my eyes to the table. We hadn't brainstormed that.

My mother's never done drugs in her life. She hates drugs, and everything else that has to do with hippies. She'd be furious if she heard this particular lie.

But then, she's already furious with me. That's why I'm here.

I kept my eyes down and lowered my voice to a whisper. "I didn't want to talk about it."

"Ohhh. Oh, ah…" Mrs. Hawkins glanced from me to Peter and then to Sharon. Sharon nodded, confirming her brother's story. "Well, I can understand your concern. Tammy, you're sure you don't have any other family? Aunts and uncles, or…"

I shook my head again without looking up.

"All right." Mrs. Hawkins sighed again. "Please give me your mother's number, anyway. I have to at least try to reach her."

I couldn't see any way out of it. "Yes, ma'am. May I borrow a pen?"

"I'll call Javi about the job," Peter said, climbing up from the table as Mrs. Hawkins passed me a pen and the back of a bill envelope to write on. I wrote down the number for our church office. It only gets answered on Sunday afternoons when Uncle Russell's secretary is there, so I can only pray Mrs. Hawkins won't try to call it then.

While Peter was on the phone, Sharon and her mom set up a foam sleeping pallet on the floor of Sharon's room. Mrs. Hawkins told Sharon to loan me pajamas and soap for the night, and said she'd pick up a toothbrush and clean underwear for me in the morning. I smiled in gratitude while, next to her, Sharon turned bright red.

Before I could ask whether Sharon felt awkward about sharing a room with me, Peter was standing in the doorway, grinning. "You got it! I told Javi and Rosa you're trustworthy and you could start right away, and they want you to come in with me for a test shift tonight. If you do all right, the job's yours."

"Tonight? Wow. Uh, that's great." Now I was the one who felt awkward. "Thanks, Peter, that's nice of you. It's only that I've, well…never worked in a grocery store before. Or, um. Any kind of store."

"You'll be fine." Sharon smiled at me. "Sweeping's easy. Just aim for the dustpan."

I forced a laugh.

"Come on, Tammy." Peter motioned for me to come with him.

"Er…" I glanced down at my rumpled pants.

"You should change first," Mrs. Hawkins said firmly. "Sharon, loan her something to wear, maybe your…no, that won't do any good, all your pants will be too short. Come with me, Tammy, I've got something that'll fit."

Mrs. Hawkins led me down the hall and started pulling things out of a closet. I turned back, hoping to catch Sharon's eye, but she and Peter were still in her room. Sharon was closing the door behind them.

I wished I could hear what they were talking about. Peter seemed glad to have me here, but I wasn't sure about Sharon. She was thinking a lot, but saying less.

I wound up wearing one of Mrs. Hawkins's sweatshirts and a pair of jeans that had once been Peter's. When I pulled my hair back, I barely recognized myself in the mirror.

Maybe I could get it cut now that I was here. Different clothes, different hair—different me.

"Looking good, Tammy." Peter smiled when he emerged from Sharon's room. "Ready?"

"I guess." I was still nervous, and more tired than ever, but I smiled back at him. "Did you tell them I don't know how to sweep?"

"Your secret's safe with me." He grinned.

We walked to the store instead of driving—people walk places here; I guess I should've known that—and it wound up being a lot less intimidating than I'd expected. Javi and Rosa were both incredibly nice, and cleaning and stocking the shelves wasn't so bad. Better than lifeguarding. No snotty kids to yell at, and no sunburn, either.

At the end of the night, Rosa offered me the job and gave me fifteen dollars out of the register. That's more per hour than what I'll get paid after this, but she said since I was new in town, she was giving me a tip on top of tonight's pay.

I had to fight not to cry again. Up until she'd handed me that fifteen dollars, what was left of my cash had been reduced to a couple of quarters tucked into the seam of my purse.

When we got home, Sharon was on the couch, watching

TV and writing in a notebook. She glanced up and gave us a half smile, but Peter just waved to her and gestured for me to follow him upstairs. When we got to the top, he whispered that Sharon didn't like to be interrupted when she was writing in her diary.

Well, Harvey, since Sharon's writing in <u>her</u> diary, I figured I'd do the same thing. I've been carrying this notebook and my aunt's old check register around in my purse for months. I thought I was being paranoid, keeping them hidden, but I guess I made the right call.

It's late now, though, and there's no sign of Sharon. I'm ready to pass out on this foam pallet any second now.

I wonder if she's writing about me. I wonder what she wants to say to her diary that she doesn't want to say out loud. I stopped writing to you, Harvey, when I started writing everything to her, but maybe now that we're in the same place, things are changing again.

I have no idea how I'm going to sleep tonight with her only a few feet away. I guess I'll have to just shut my eyes, put the pillow over my head, and try to pretend things are normal.

Except—let's be honest, Harvey. There's nothing normal about any of this.

Peace,
Tammy

Saturday, June 17, 1978

Dear Diary,

It's been more than two weeks since I last wrote here, but it feels like a million years. My last entry was the day Tammy came to San Francisco. So much has happened I haven't had a second to write since then, but I'm hiding from Tammy now, and I have the whole night. Maybe I'll understand this better after I've got it down on paper.

It started when Kevin came over for dinner tonight.

"I figured out how to do it, in the end," Tammy was saying with a grin. Kevin, Mom, and even Peter and I were bent over our spaghetti in hysterics. Tammy was telling us a story about how Rosa had taught her how to use a mop, and I don't know if it was as funny when it was happening as it was when she described it after the fact, but either way, Tammy's an excellent storyteller. It's no wonder I enjoyed her letters so much. "The mouse who was responsible for that mess is on my takedown list for life."

"Its life, or yours?" I asked.

She laughed. "Whichever ends first."

"The mouse is toast. Don't worry." Peter wiped his eyes. "The other day I had to repack five deliveries because of turds in the bags. Next time I see the tiniest flick of a brown tail, I'm grabbing Javi's cleaver."

"Language, please, Peter," Mom said, but she was laughing, too.

"Sorry, Mom."

"I think my roommate's got a switchblade." Kevin grinned at Tammy. Tonight was the first time they'd met—she's been working a ton of hours to earn as much as cash as possible, so we haven't had time to do many fun things yet—but they were already acting like old friends. "If you want to dispatch it with something stealthier."

"If you saw me with that mop today, you wouldn't make that offer." Tammy climbed to her feet and reached for Kevin's empty plate. "I'd probably wind up stabbing myself."

"Sharon, help her clear the table," Mom said. "Despite our guest's eagerness to lend a hand, I do expect my own children to wash dishes on occasion."

"Can we do the rest of the cleanup after we get back tonight?" I bent down to collect the water glasses.

Mom frowned. "Remind me where you're all going on a week-night, again?"

I took a deep breath, preparing for another lie. It's getting harder to keep up with all our stories. Fortunately, Peter jumped in. "It's summer, Mom! No school, remember? We're going over to Kevin's to watch the Giants game."

Mom didn't smile. I wonder if she suspected something was up, since neither of us have ever gone out of our way to watch baseball before, but she didn't argue. "Well, be back before it gets too late. You've got work tomorrow, all of you."

"Thanks, Mom. Love you." Peter kissed her on the cheek. Mom smiled, and I wondered how many extra lies Peter had bought us with that move.

Our actual plans had nothing to do with the Giants. Kevin had to study for a big exam for his summer course, but he was giving Peter, Sharon, and me a ride north first. Peter was going to visit his friends in the Castro, and since Tammy finally had a night off, I was taking her to the bookstore. She was nervous about meeting other lesbians for the first time, but it was an official volunteer night—we were putting together a big mailing to Fresno—and this way we could keep busy if Tammy was too anxious to talk much. Plus, it would be her first chance to work on mailings that didn't include cartoons about gay people being demons.

Tammy's quickly become part of our family routine, and Mom seems to have accepted that she isn't going back to Ocean Valley anytime soon. She's called the number Tammy gave her a bunch of times, but never gotten an answer, which backed up our story about Tammy's mother being a drug addict who can't manage to answer the phone.

It feels normal now to have Tammy there in the morning when we have breakfast, or waiting for a turn in the bathroom before work. At night, Tammy, Peter, and I watch TV together, and when Mom comes home from her library job and sees us all together in the living room, she'll say "Good night, Three Musketeers," and go upstairs with a wave.

It's fun, spending time with Tammy and Peter. When I wind up alone with her, though—that's harder. We told each other so much in our letters, but now that we're in the same place, it's as though we can't think of anything to say. Maybe we're afraid to.

Or maybe it's only me who's afraid.

On the nights when Peter goes out, I always come up with some excuse for why I need to go to bed early, while Tammy stays downstairs watching TV. I can never sleep on those nights, though. I lay awake in the dark, staring at the ceiling, until I hear Peter come in, followed by the sounds of his and Tammy's soft voices and muted laughter drifting up the steps.

When she finally comes up to bed, I pretend to be asleep, but that's getting harder. Knowing she's lying there silently on the floor beside me. Hearing the sounds of her soft, steady breathing.

"It's been great finally meeting you, Tammy," Kevin said, smiling his Kevin smile as he passed her a stack of silverware. "My girlfriend's talked about nothing all year except how cool her pen pal is, so I'm glad to see she was telling the truth."

Tammy thanked him while I turned away, blushing.

I'd given Kevin the same story we'd given Mom. I felt terrible lying to him, too, but Peter was adamant that we keep Tammy's secret—and he was probably worried Kevin might figure out the truth about him, too.

Besides, I wasn't sure how he'd take it. Kevin's nothing like Gary Knopp, but I don't have any reason to think he's more accepting of gay people than anyone else at our school. That's why I've never told him about volunteering on Prop 6. He knows I hang out at the bookstore, and he thinks that's great since he's always loved bookstores, but he'd never set foot inside any building that said "Women's" on the front door. He asked me once what kind of books a women's bookstore sold, and when I told him there were books about women's health, he started waving his hand around frantically and said, "Sorry I asked!"

I know guys don't want to think about periods and stuff, but Kevin wants to be a doctor, so it seemed kind of ridiculous. But it was also a relief knowing he wouldn't ask me about the bookstore again.

It's getting harder, keeping all my worlds separate.

"Hey, so, I wanted to say," Peter whispered, following me into the kitchen, "thanks for helping out. With making sure Tammy can stay here."

I turned around, startled. "You were the one helping us, remember?"

"Sure, it started because of your pen pal thing, but..." Peter shrugged. "I'm just saying, she's really cool. Getting to hang out with her makes work a lot more fun. She gets it, you know? She's used to hiding."

"I'm used to hiding, too," I whispered back. "I lie to Mom all the time about working on the Prop 6 campaign, and going to punk shows."

"It's not the same. I know you thought you liked that one girl that one time, but—"

"Shhhhh!" I whipped around to make sure Tammy wasn't in earshot. I'd never told her about that, and I certainly wasn't planning to now that she slept in my room.

"Look." He rolled his eyes. "Tammy and me, we're lying about who we are. It's a bigger lie than the kind you're used to, and it hurts a lot more."

It hurt to hear him say that, too, but I nodded. I knew he was right.

"Unless you've realized you're not that straight after all." His lip curled up. "Have you?"

"Don't," I muttered. Kevin was striding into the kitchen.

"Ready to go?" He zipped up his sweatshirt. Behind him, Tammy was grinning, probably over some hilarious conversation they'd just had. "I have sixty pages of econ to go over before tomorrow."

Peter and I got our jackets and Tammy pulled on a sweater Mom had loaned her. She'd insisted on wearing T-shirts for the first week she was here, because, she claimed, that was just what people wore in June, but she finally accepted the reality of northern California and started dressing in layers after she wound up walking home from work shivering night after night.

We said goodbye to Mom and went outside.

"I feel like I should put on makeup," Tammy whispered as we stepped out into the bright, chilly evening. Peter and Kevin had gone on ahead toward the car. "But I didn't bring any."

"Don't worry, none of the women at the bookstore use makeup. I wore mascara there once and felt so self-conscious I snuck into the bathroom to wipe it off."

Tammy laughed, her elbow knocking into mine. "I'm so excited to finally see this bookstore. You make it sound like paradise."

"Well, it's just a bookstore. It's the women there who make it cool."

"I believe you. That's why I'm nervous."

"Don't be." I smiled. "They're going to think you're amazing. How could they not?"

She smiled back. "Thanks, Sharon."

It feels strange to hear her say my name out loud. A good kind of strange.

The guys were standing beside Kevin's car, having some kind of argument about the Eagles. Tammy laughed at something Peter had said and tossed her new short hair. She'd used the first few dollars she'd earned to get it cut, and it doesn't even reach her shoulders anymore.

I was shocked when she first stepped out of the salon—the change was so dramatic, she might as well have been a different person than the girl who'd first shown up on my doorstep—but she was smiling such a huge smile. When I first met her she'd looked like Marcia Brady, but now she's closer to a young, blond Dorothy Hamill. Or maybe Billie Jean King.

We dropped off Peter first, a few blocks down from Castro so Kevin wouldn't realize where he was going, and a few minutes later, we were pulling up in front of the bookstore. A little thrill ran through me at the sight of it, the way it always does. The bookstore's a fascinating island in the middle of a much more boring world. Or it was, anyway, up until Tammy arrived and made the whole universe interesting and confusing all at once.

We said goodbye to Kevin. Evelyn was by the door when we arrived, talking to Lisa.

"Hey! This is my friend Tammy." I was practically bouncing on my toes, I was so excited for them all to meet.

"Hey, Tammy." Evelyn looked nearly as happy as I was. "It's cool to meet another young feminist."

Tammy beamed as she shook their hands. That was probably the first time anyone had ever called her a feminist. I'm still getting used to that word myself. "It's cool to meet you, too!"

"We're set up in the usual spot." Evelyn pointed behind her. "Sharon, can you show Tammy how everything works?"

"Definitely."

Half a dozen women were gathered around the table. I recognized them all from other volunteer nights. The table was piled high with brochures, envelopes, and sheets of paper filled with addresses, so Tammy and I took seats and grabbed stacks of our own, each of us reaching into our purses for a pen.

"Here, we have extras," Alex said, passing some over.

Lisa settled into a seat opposite us, and I watched as she and the others discreetly took in Tammy—her short hair, her sparkling green eyes, the sunniness she projects everywhere she goes. She smiled at them all, as easily as ever.

"That's a gorgeous tattoo," Tammy told Alex, pointing to her shoulder.

"Thanks." Alex was wearing a T-shirt with the sleeves rolled up, and at the crown of her light brown shoulder was a deep black double-headed ax. I'd never noticed it before, but it <u>was</u> a cool design. The ink wound in intricate coils along the handle of the ax, the dark color fading as it neared the edges.

"It's a labrys." Lisa glanced at me. "It's a lesbian symbol."

"Wo-o-oww." Tammy stretched out the <u>wow</u> so long she sounded breathless. Everyone around the table was smiling at her after that. "That's so cool."

"Thanks." Alex grinned. "A friend did it for me."

"Were you scared?"

Alex laughed. "Yeah. I figured it'd hurt, so I bit my lip while I was waiting for the needle the first time." She demonstrated, sinking her teeth into her lower lip. "That's what I do whenever something scares me. That little bit of pain reminds me I can handle more."

"<u>Did</u> the needle hurt?"

"Like Hell, but it was worth it." Alex grinned while Lisa and Tammy laughed.

"Maybe I'll get one, after I've saved up some money." Tammy rubbed her shoulder. "How much does your friend charge?"

Alex raised her eyebrows. "No offense, but...are you eighteen?"

"Er." Tammy laughed. "I was hoping your friend wouldn't ask."

Everyone at the whole table was laughing now, me included.

I can't believe how easily Tammy manages to fit in anywhere she goes. Two weeks ago, she was a pampered Orange County girl in designer clothes. This afternoon I saw her wearing a stained apron and joking around with Javi while she swept dead flies out from behind the display window. Now here she was, effortlessly talking tattoos with the lesbian feminists. She didn't seem nearly as nervous as <u>I'd</u> felt the first time I came to the bookstore.

"Are you sure you want a tattoo?" I asked her, when the laughter died down. "What if you got it and then changed your mind later?"

Lisa gave me a wry smile. "You think it might be a passing phase?"

"What?" I had no idea why, but Alex and the others were laughing harder than ever.

"Heads up, everyone, I've finally got the sign-up sheets for the bus trip to Napa," Evelyn called from the cash register where she was shuffling through a stack of envelopes. Becky stood next to her, counting out dollar bills. "It's tomorrow, and we need more people."

"Where's Napa from here?" Tammy asked.

"North." Lisa pointed. "An hour and a half away. Easy trip. We'll knock on doors, give the usual talking points."

"I have to work tomorrow," I reminded Tammy. "You do, too."

She sighed. "Shit."

"We'll have plenty more door-knocking trips, don't worry," Evelyn added. "Plus we need volunteers to travel for the debates in the fall. Harvey and Sally against Briggs and his cronies."

"That sounds so cool." Tammy licked an envelope so fast I was afraid she was going to give herself a paper cut, but she sealed it quickly and reached for another. The stack of finished mailings next to her was already high. She'd clearly had a lot more envelope-sealing practice than the rest of us. "I can't wait to see them hand Briggs his ass. He's been _my_ senator for years, and he's never had the first clue what he's talking about."

The smiles around the table faded. "_Your_ senator?" Lisa asked.

"Well, formerly. I'm from Ocean Valley, in Orange County. I was lucky to escape with my life."

Tammy laughed, but this time it was a tacked-on laugh. As if she wasn't sure if she was joking or not.

Alex leaned toward her, looking a little uncertain herself. "What brought you here, then?"

"Sharon." Tammy turned that sunny smile my way. It was the first time she'd looked at me since we set foot inside the store, and the sudden shift made me blush. "We were pen pals, so the second I got loose from my family, I came straight here. I knew she was the one person I could absolutely trust."

I was blushing so hard by the time she finished talking I'm surprised I didn't burn to a crisp, but no one was looking at me. Every single person around the table was nodding at Tammy.

Becky came over from the cash register and draped herself over the back of Tammy's chair, leaning in to look at her intently. "When did you get to the city?"

"Two weeks ago." Tammy grinned. Her hesitance from earlier was long gone—if it had ever been there—and she seemed totally unfazed by all the attention focused on her. "Now here I am, surrounded by cool women working against Briggs. Should've run away years ago."

There were more laughs around the table, but Becky didn't join in.

"That was me a while back." She slid into an empty chair next to Tammy. "Except I was running from small-town Utah. How are you holding up?"

"Not bad, thanks to Sharon and her family." Tammy smiled again. She was talking about this as though it was nothing more than a funny story. When she'd told me what happened, she was in tears. What on earth was happening? "Her mom's letting me crash, and I'm trying to save money while I figure out what to do next."

"Are you in school?" Lisa frowned.

"I was. You should've seen my school down there. The textbooks are all thirty years old, but they get new Bibles every year. And we have to wear skirts that cover our knees, but the girls bring in straight pins and roll them up when the teachers aren't looking."

Everyone laughed again, and Tammy launched into the story of the pep rally she had to organize in support of Prop 6. She made that sound funny, too, doing an imitation of her uncle's midprayer smoker's cough that was so good, even I laughed.

This story had sounded entirely different—and entirely unfunny—when she'd written about it to me months ago. Having her here,

<u>physically</u> here, was like getting to know her for the first time all over again.

By the time Evelyn disappeared into the back room and came out again with two six-packs, Tammy had already made plans to visit the SFAI darkroom with Alex so she could experiment with using photo paper in her collages, and traded running-away-from-conservative-family stories with both Becky and Lisa. When Evelyn finally shooed us all out so she could close up, Tammy and one of Lisa's housemates were in the middle of an intense debate about whether Princess Leia qualified as a feminist, given that she was a princess who got rescued by a man.

As far as I could tell, Tammy might as well have been born in this bookstore.

I said goodbye to the others, but Tammy lingered to get Alex's phone number so they could make darkroom plans. I stuffed my hands into my jacket pockets while I waited.

I shouldn't have been surprised Tammy loved being there so much. I love it there, too. But the way she made instant friends with everyone...

I guess I was jealous. For so long, I'd thought of her as <u>my</u> friend. Now it was obvious <u>everyone</u> who met her liked her just as much as me.

It had even happened with Peter. He'd thanked me for helping Tammy. As if I'd done it for him.

"Thank God we're out of there," Tammy said when the others were finally out of earshot.

I turned, astonished. She met my gaze, and there was something different in her smile. A warm, crinkled note in her eyes that hadn't been there when she smiled at the women in the bookstore.

"Oh, no, don't get me wrong." She brushed a chunk of thick blond hair out of her eyes. "Everyone was great, but that was kind of exhausting, you know? I kept thinking I had to be so <u>cool</u> all the time. I couldn't relax for a second."

I laughed, and the thick coil of tension in my chest loosened and floated off into the fog. "Come on, that wasn't hard for you. You're automatically cool."

She laughed, too. "You've got to be kidding. <u>You're</u> the one who fits in there perfectly. They treat you like part of the family."

I blushed, turning away so she wouldn't see, but she only laughed again. "You blush easily, don't you?"

"Um." I scratched my neck, blushing harder. "Yeah. Ever since I was a kid. It's so embarrassing."

"Don't be embarrassed. It's cool. You wear your heart on your sleeve. Well, some of your heart, anyway."

Now I was blushing so hard there was no point turning around. My cheeks were burning so bright they'd be impossible to miss. "I wonder which part."

"I wonder, too." She grinned again.

We caught the bus, and for once, it wasn't awkward. We talked, we laughed, and we smiled for the entire twenty-minute ride. When we got home and stepped into the dark, empty living room, though, we fell quiet, the sensation of being alone together rushing back like always.

It <u>hurts</u> to be alone with Tammy. I don't know why, and I don't know how to make it stop.

She must've felt it, too, because she went straight for the stairs. "I'm so tired all of a sudden. I'll probably fall asleep the second I lie down."

"Okay." It was obvious she didn't want to be alone with me. "I'm getting a snack. Maybe watch TV."

"Cool. See you tomorrow."

"See you."

But I didn't get a snack after she disappeared upstairs, and I didn't turn on the TV, either. Instead I grabbed a few sheets of paper out of the kitchen drawer and sat down to write this.

Since Tammy got here, I've been keeping my diary hidden on the highest shelf in my closet. That's where I'll stick these sheets of paper, too. She's been upstairs for an hour now while I've been down here writing, so it's probably safe to go up, but I'm not any clearer on what's going on between us than I was before.

Who knows? Maybe if I hope hard enough it'll all start making some kind of sense tomorrow.

Yours,
Sharon

Dear Tammy,

Oh, my gosh. Oh, my gosh. Oh, my gosh.

Sorry, I know it's odd for me to write you a letter while we're living in the same house, but I'll probably be gone by the time you get back from work (I'm meeting Kevin), so I'll leave this on your pallet. If we're lucky you'll see it as soon as you get back.

Tammy...something's wrong. Really wrong.

Half an hour ago, while Mom was out at the meeting for the church auction, I was alone—well, Peter was here, but he was upstairs getting ready to go out—and I was rummaging around in the kitchen for something to eat when the phone rang. I grabbed it off the hook and looped the cord around the door of the fridge. "Hello?"

"Hello." The woman's voice on the other end was tinny, hard to make out over the hissing sound that always hangs in the background when someone calls long-distance. I grabbed a leftover chunk of roast beef off the top shelf. "May I speak with Sharon, please?"

"This is she." I carefully balanced the plate as I swung the fridge door closed.

"Ah, wonderful." The woman paused. There was a smile in her

voice, but it sounded thin. As though she had to remind herself to do it. "I apologize for disturbing you. My name is Mrs. Dale."

I didn't recognize the name. "To what do I owe the pleasure of your call, ma'am?"

"You're very polite." Mrs. Dale chuckled. "Your mother raised you right."

"Yes, ma'am." I didn't laugh as I opened the silverware drawer and grabbed a fork. Something about Mrs. Dale's voice made me want to keep my guard up.

"Is the rest of your family at home this evening, Sharon? Or are you there alone?"

I set my plate on the counter and crossed my arms. "I'm terribly sorry, but what is this call regarding?"

"Now, Sharon, there's no need for you to be nervous with me." The woman chuckled again, and if I hadn't been nervous before, I definitely was now. "We're practically family ourselves. Your good friend Tammy is my niece."

I swallowed hard. Panic simmered in my stomach.

Mrs. Dale. Of course.

But...why would your aunt call me?

The panic rose slowly toward the base of my throat.

"I hope you're still there, Sharon." The smile in her voice was razor-sharp. "I'm only calling to make sure you're safe. Are you alone, or is anyone with you?"

Something about the way your aunt talks made it seem as if I had to answer her. Like if I didn't tell her exactly what she wanted to know, I'd be in enormous trouble. "My brother's here."

"Yes, of course, your brother." She sounded delighted at this news. "Splendid. Now, Sharon, I won't keep you. My top concern, again, is that you're careful. I do hope you'll keep in mind that you can't allow yourself to be led astray this summer while you're away from the positive influence of school. You're a bright girl with a promising future ahead of you, and it would be a shame if anything were to interfere with that. The choices you make right now could determine everything."

I stared down into the receiver. "How did you get my number?"

"I must be going, dear. Please do think about what I said, and God bless."

The receiver clicked. The hissing stopped.

Aunt Mandy hung up on me.

I dropped the phone back into its cradle, my hand shaking.

What the <u>Hell</u> was that?

I tried to replay her words in my head, to make some sense of what had happened, but it was already swimming together.

Let's talk as soon as we can. I'm scared, Tammy.

Yours,
Sharon

Dear Diary,

My hand is shaking, trying to write this down. I'm back at home, and Tammy should be, too—but she's not.

She doesn't know her aunt called. I have to tell her. Being the only one who knows is eating me up inside.

But all I can do now is wait, so I'm going to try to keep my head busy writing about the rest of tonight.

As soon as I'd left the letter on Tammy's pallet, I grabbed my jacket. Peter had already left, so I headed for the bus stop and made my way to the restaurant where Kevin works. We hadn't made plans to meet up tonight, but I couldn't stand to be alone.

I didn't know what time he'd finish his shift—they usually aren't very busy on Sunday nights, so sometimes he gets out early—but I wound up waiting more than an hour on the hood of his Camaro a couple of blocks from the restaurant. When I finally saw him, I did my best to act as if nothing was wrong.

"Sharon?" Kevin frowned as he approached, like he wasn't quite sure it was me. He was dressed in his shiny black vest and bow tie, his apron bunched in his hands.

"Hi." I slid down from the hood, smiling. It's usually easy to smile at Kevin, but not tonight. "I wanted to surprise you."

He smiled back, but his smile didn't look much easier than mine. "That's great. I'm beat, but it's good to see you."

"I thought maybe we could go somewhere."

"Sure."

He unlocked my door first, the way he always does. As I slid into the passenger seat, I took a deep breath, trying to push back all the thoughts creeping into my head.

"Where do you want to go?" he asked, a Santana tape blaring as he twisted the key in the ignition. He smelled faintly of salad dressing.

"How about the park?"

He glanced at me and nodded, smiling more easily this time.

My heart pounded, and I tried to focus on the music's soaring rhythms as we steered down the hills. Ever since I finished that letter to Tammy, I'd been trying to convince myself I wanted to see Kevin, but now I wasn't so sure. I'd almost managed not to think about that phone call during the hour I'd sat on his car, but now I couldn't <u>stop</u>.

I was terrified of what it could mean for Tammy. To be honest...I was terrified of what it could mean for me, too. Was her aunt making some kind of threat?

The guitar music pouring out of the tape player was smooth, melodic. Pretty. I tried to focus on it, but thinking about music made my mind shift into thinking about Midge Spelling. That was no good, either.

The images were fresh in my mind. The way she looked on that poster. The way Johnny had wrapped his arm around her waist, leaning into her as though they had their own private language. The way her lips curled around every sound she uttered.

Kevin pulled over beside a park a few blocks south, and I leaned over to kiss him before he'd even turned off the engine. He laughed, but he went along with it, twisting the key with one hand and sliding the other around my waist. I shut my eyes, until I realized I was still thinking about Midge.

I was kissing him, but I was thinking about kissing <u>her</u>. I was wondering—and not for the first time—whether kissing a girl would feel different from kissing a boy.

Would she be that much gentler? Would her skin feel that much smoother?

I wrenched my eyes open. Kevin was so close all I could see were his pores and his eyelashes. I'd never noticed how thick they were.

This wasn't fair. He had no idea what was happening in my head. I couldn't tell him, but I couldn't let it keep going, either. I may not know what it meant to be "in love," the way the disco singers talked about, but I knew what I had with Kevin wasn't it.

I pulled away.

"I, um." I took a long breath. I'd never imagined saying these words, but suddenly I was absolutely sure they were the right ones. "I think we should break up."

He froze, his arm still around my waist. A second later he drew back sharply. "What?"

"I'm sorry."

"You're..." He shook his head, as though he was in a fog. "<u>What?</u>"

I fumbled for my purse. "I'm sorry. I should go."

"Go <u>where</u>? What are you talking about? Things have been kind of off lately, sure, but...you show up out of the blue and say you want to come here, I thought—"

"I'm sorry, Kevin."

"Please stop saying you're sorry."

"I— Okay."

I wanted to apologize again. I wanted to say it as many times as it took until he believed me, but it was clear he wasn't going to.

I climbed out of the car, and by some miracle, I didn't start crying until I'd made it halfway down the block.

The bus stop was one street up. If I walked slowly enough, I might be able to make the tears stop before I got there.

I shut my eyes, expecting Midge to float into my mind again. The usual image of her growling into a microphone, her lips curved wide.

Instead, the face I saw Tammy's.

Tammy, laughing with the women at the bookstore. Tammy, rolling her eyes at Peter in the living room, Dallas playing on the TV screen behind us. Tammy, crying quietly in the O'Sullivans' kitchen.

Tammy, dressed in rumpled clothes on my doorstep, smiling faintly as my whole world changed to let her in.

When I got home, the house was dark. I grabbed an open box of Lorna Doones someone had left out on the kitchen counter and dragged myself up the stairs. I've been lying on my bed ever since, writing, hoping—

Wait. That was the door.

She's home. She's here.

More later.

Sharon

Dear Harvey,

It's six in the morning, but I've already been awake for an hour. Sharon's fast asleep. I know because I can hear her snoring all the way downstairs. She has a very distinctive snore, but she's a light sleeper. I snuck down here so I could write without waking her up.

Aunt Mandy's back in my life, Harvey. I can't believe I was naive enough to think I'd left it all behind. But to think she'd talk that way to <u>Sharon</u>...

I should back up. There's a lot I need to tell you.

Javi asked me to help him clean out the walk-in cooler after we closed last night, so I got home late. I was starving, and I went straight to the kitchen, but before I could open the fridge there were footsteps behind me and a hand on my elbow.

"Hey," I said softly. I knew it was Sharon before I turned around.

"Hey." She let go of my elbow, but she wasn't smiling. "You need to come upstairs."

I wanted to be pleased—I've been living here for almost three weeks, but it still feels as if I'm trespassing in Sharon's bedroom. She hasn't hidden the fact that she doesn't want to be alone with me. But from her dark look, I knew something was wrong.

"Come quick," she said. "My brother's out, but he could come home any minute, and I don't want him to hear."

By then I was getting really worried. "All right."

I followed Sharon up the stairs to her room. It was dark, with only the distant light of a street lamp from the window to see by. My sleeping pallet was rolled up on the floor beside the dresser, where I always tuck it after I get up in the morning, and there was a folded piece of notebook paper on top of it. Sharon bent down and grabbed the paper, holding it out to me.

I sat on the floor, my back against the dresser. Sharon sat on the bed across from me as I unfolded the letter and smoothed it out on my knees, tilting it so I could read it in the faint light. I was wearing a pair of jeans I'd bought at a secondhand store Sharon took me to, and the denim at the knees was almost threadbare against the crinkled paper. It was strange to read a letter from Sharon while she sat there, watching my reaction.

As I read, though, I quickly forgot how strange it was. Twice, I put down the paper and locked eyes with Sharon, silently pleading with her to tell me what she'd written wasn't true, but both times she only said, "Keep going," and folded her arms tighter across her chest. By the time I got to the end, I was trembling.

"She seriously called you," I said.

It wasn't a question, but Sharon nodded anyway. "It was bizarre. She talked as if I was incredibly important and completely beneath her at the same time."

"Yeah. She can almost hypnotize you into believing she really does have your best interests at heart." My hands shook as I refolded the paper. I blinked hard, trying to focus on what mattered here, when focusing was the last thing I wanted to do. "She didn't ask if I was here?"

Sharon shook her head, glancing toward the door as though she was afraid my aunt might be standing on the other side at this very moment. "I wouldn't have told her, anyway, but... no. How did she get my phone number? How does she know who I am?"

Now I was half-afraid Aunt Mandy was hiding outside the door. But there was only one possible answer to Sharon's question. "She must've found the letters."

She went rigid. "My letters?"

"After I sent you that diary entry by accident, I started carrying them in my purse." I shut my eyes. I knew exactly what this could mean for Sharon and Peter. Now I had to wait for her to realize it, too. "But when there got to be too many, I hid them in my sisters' old room, in the space under the top dresser drawer. No one would've found them, even if they opened the drawers. Unless they were determined to search the whole room from top to bottom."

Sharon frowned. I could see her trying to work it out. "Is that what you think happened?"

I nodded slowly. "Once they had the letters, Aunt Mandy could've gone into the school rolls to get your phone number. Or she could've just called information. She had your address already."

"How?"

"I...kept your envelopes."

I knew it was ridiculous, saving envelopes just because Sharon had touched them. But I hadn't had much to hold onto back then.

"If she found..." Sharon's face had shifted from confusion to alarm. "If she read my letters, she knows..."

"Everything about you. And your brother." There was no point holding back. She deserved to know exactly the danger I'd put them in.

"There were things in those letters I've never told anyone. Things my own family doesn't know."

I couldn't meet her eyes. "I'm so sorry, Sharon."

"I have to tell Peter." She dropped her chin to her chest. "He's going to hate me."

I squirmed. "This is my fault, not yours."

"He'd never hate you. Besides, it's not your fault, either— it's your aunt's."

"I'm so sorry." I felt sick to my stomach. "I'll talk to him."

"No, don't." She shook her head. "This is on me. I'll do it. But…why do you think your aunt called _me_?"

"Well." I swallowed. "She's trying to figure out if I'm here, and I can think of two possible reasons for that. Either she wants to convince me to come back home—which isn't likely, since then it would've been my parents who called— or she knows I have her check register."

"Oh, my gosh. I forgot all about the check register."

"It's still there." I pointed toward where I'd left my purse on the floor.

"How would she know you have it?"

"Well, I used that desk more than any other volunteer, and…" I bit my cheek. "I'm _so_ sorry, Sharon."

"It's all right."

"No, it's not. She wouldn't know anything about you, or your brother, if it weren't for me. Once she realized I'd taken that stupid thing, she probably tore apart the whole house looking for it. With the radio show finally starting, she's probably trying to make sure no one's going to find out what they did to get there. And I guess my family didn't mind my running away, or they'd have searched the house earlier, looking for evidence of where I went."

I shrugged, as though none of this bothered me, but from the crease that formed between Sharon's eyebrows, I don't think she bought it.

"What'll she do?" Sharon wrapped her arms around herself even tighter. "Come looking for you?"

"God, I hope not. Nothing you said would've made her think I was here, right?"

"No! Of course not."

"Then we're probably safe for now. It's a long trip when all she's got is a hunch." I sat back against the dresser, pinching the bridge of my nose between my fingers. I'd forgotten how exhausting it was, being terrified. "Is there any food up here?"

Sharon lifted a box of Lorna Doones. "I was starving, too."

We devoured the cookies. Sharon hunched forward on her bed at first, but after a while she climbed down to sit next to me on the floor.

She still looked worried. I reassured her again, and again after that, that I didn't think my aunt was going to show up on her doorstep, but the crease between her eyebrows never went away. I wondered if something else might be bothering her, too.

As she bent over to shake the last few cookies out of the box, I studied the outline of her face in the dim light. For months, I'd wondered what would happen if Sharon and I ever met in person. I'd built up a dozen scenarios for it in my head. Now it was reality, and it was as simple as sitting on a worn rug, talking to the girl who'd once existed for me solely in the form of ripped-out notebook pages.

"What else is wrong?" I asked her after a quiet moment, wiping a cookie crumb off my lower lip.

"What do you mean?"

"I don't know. Did you go out with Kevin tonight, like you said in the letter?"

She glanced at me, then darted her eyes back to the floor. We were sitting side by side against the dresser, and suddenly it struck me exactly how little space there was between us.

"Yeah," she said. "I... We... I guess we broke up."

My eyes widened. "What? Tonight?"

She kept her eyes on the shag carpet. "Yeah."

"God, what happened?"

She told me a story that didn't make much sense— something about going to meet him after work, going for a drive, then blurting out a breakup. It was obvious she'd left part of the story out, but I didn't ask what. If there was something she didn't want to tell me, asking wasn't going to change that.

"Do you think it's really over?" I asked.

"Yeah. All through the bus ride home, I ran over what I told him in my head, trying to figure out if there was some way I could take it back. Except...I don't know if I want to take it back. I like him, but...there's too much I'm confused about right now."

"Wow. You two were together for so long."

"Yeah. I wish..." She blinked rapidly. It was too dark to tell if she was crying. "I don't know. There's so much I don't know."

She brushed a stray hair out of her eyes. The light caught a long, curly strand, making it shimmer.

"I know what you mean." I tried not to stare. "I keep making huge mistakes because of all the stuff I don't understand."

"Like what?"

I sighed. "Remember in our letters, when we said we were going to be totally honest with each other?"

Sharon smiled. I love it when she smiles. "Of course."

"Well, I mean, obviously I wasn't really ready at first. It's so ironic now—I should've trusted you from the beginning. I trusted <u>Carolyn</u> instead, and look how that turned out."

Sharon's smile faded at the sound of Carolyn's name. "Why do you think she said what happened was your fault?"

"Because she's a psychopath?" I sighed again. "No, I think she was just scared. There were a dozen different lies we could've used to convince them we were innocent, but she didn't even want to <u>try</u>. She just wanted to keep them thinking she was a perfect Christian princess."

I'd cared so much about Carolyn once. I'd thought I did, at least. But it wasn't as if she'd ever lied to me. I'd known who she was from the beginning. I guess it was my fault all along for not seeing what was right in front of us.

"She's horrible." Sharon's voice was so thick with anger that I jerked my head up, startled. "Going after you, just to save herself. Besides, you <u>were</u> innocent. You know they never would've acted that way if you'd been kissing a <u>boy</u> in the stairwell."

My shock had faded enough for me to manage a half smile. "Good point. Honestly, getting caught has its upsides, too. I don't love that I'm fending for myself now, obviously, but at least I don't have to hide."

"Wow. I hadn't thought of it that way."

"Me, either. Not at first. But now I'm glad they know about me. I want everyone to know."

"Hey, do you think we could go back to our pledge?" She met my gaze.

I nodded, my eyes on hers. "Yes. From now on, no more hiding."

"Okay." She took a deep breath. "Good. Okay. Then I guess I should go ahead and admit…I kind of miss writing to you."

I laughed, flushing with happiness. I hoped it was too dark for her to notice. "Me, too, but I miss getting your letters back more."

"Yeah. Maybe that's what I really meant. I always imagined you in a certain way from your letters. In some ways the real you is exactly what I pictured, but you're totally different at the same time. Being around you—the real you—well, it makes me dizzy sometimes."

My smile widened. "Should I say I'm sorry, or…?"

"No, no. But I think, now that you're here, we should do something fun."

I laughed. "In sinful San Francisco? You want to prove my aunt right?"

She laughed, too. "Want to come see a punk show with me?"

"You're kidding, right?" I laughed harder. "Of course I do. I've been hoping you'd bring it up."

"Cool. We can do it the next time you have a night off and there's an all-ages show. There are always posters up near the bookstore."

"Could we go see that band you wrote about? The Prudes?"

Sharon dropped her gaze. "I don't know. They weren't that great last time I saw them."

"But you gushed so much about the lead singer. What's her name? Marge?"

"I, um. I don't remember. Hey, there's a new band I heard about, maybe we could see them instead. The Dead Kennedys."

"Ha. Great name. Bet they're from Orange County."

We kept talking. About music, at first, but other things, too. We talked about Carolyn, and about Kevin. We talked about our parents, and how we'd always felt destined to disappoint them. How we knew we were supposed to feel bad about that, but sometimes it was hard.

When we heard Peter come in, we could've gone out to see him, but we both instinctively lowered our voices instead. This night was only about the two of us.

I'm thinking a lot since I woke up this morning to the sound of Sharon's soft snores in the next bed, but I don't want to write down the rest of what I'm thinking. I don't want to have to read it later and be disappointed all over again.

But...she broke up with him, Harvey.

Something's changing. I don't know what, exactly, but I'm actually starting to have hope.

Yours,
Tammy

Monday, June 19, 1978

Dear Tammy,

I was thinking about what we said last night—how we miss writing to each other—and I realized we could start doing it again. It might be <u>kind</u> of strange to write letters to someone who literally sleeps in the same room as you, but no one else has to know we're doing it. Besides, we can keep the letters short, since we already know what we've been doing all day. But just sitting down last night and writing "Dear Tammy" again felt cooler than I'd ever imagined it would.

Ha—you just let out a big snore. Did you know you snore? Did you know I'm sitting here writing this letter a few feet away from you while you snore?

Anyway, let me know if you're up for it, and please don't tell my brother. He'd make fun of me for years.

Yours,
Sharon

Tuesday, June 20, 1978

Dear Sharon,

This is the best idea I've ever heard. Yes, let's keep writing to each other. It's perfect—we won't have to wait days for the mail to come anymore!

And for your information, you snore, too. Your snoring is kind of cute, though. I didn't know snoring <u>could</u> be cute.

I'm about to fall asleep and you're still downstairs, so I'm going to leave this on your pillow now. I'll try to keep my snoring to a minimum tonight!

Yours,
Tammy

Wednesday, June 21, 1978

Dear Tammy,

You're right, about not having to wait for the mail. I hadn't thought of that. Finding your letter on my pillow last night was awesome. I'm writing this one at work during nap time so I can give it to you to read before dinner, and that's awesome, too.

Hey, I don't know if you remember, but Gay Freedom Day is this Sunday. Lisa and Alex were talking about it again at the bookstore yesterday while you were in the back room with Evelyn. Want to go?

Uh-oh, Penny woke up early. Got to go!

Yours,
Sharon

Thursday, June 22, 1978

Dear Sharon,

You're kidding, right? Of <u>course</u> I remember. I've only been looking forward to Gay Freedom Day in San Francisco for <u>years</u>.

Do you think we'll get to see Harvey? In <u>person</u>?

It doesn't seem possible. It'd be like running into Charlton Heston or Grace Kelly. It barely seems real.

You and Peter probably went last year, too, right? God, we'd barely started writing to each other back then. Both of us were still keeping all those secrets.

Anyway, <u>yes</u>. I can't wait!

Yours,
Tammy

Friday, June 23, 1978

Dear Tammy,

Er, no, we didn't go to Gay Freedom Day last year. Things were... different then. This year, though, everything's going to be awesome. And you'll be with us!

I'm writing this in the morning before work, so I've got to go or I'll be late, but I won't get another chance since we're going out tonight. You'll like the Avengers—their lead singer's almost as good as Patti Smith. (Well, not really. But you'll still like her.)

See you soon!

Yours,
Sharon

P.S. Speaking of my brother...last night I finally told him about your aunt calling. He wasn't actually surprised. He said he'd figured your family might have read my letters and found out about him, but that they were hundreds of miles from here and either way, getting to have you come here mattered more. He isn't scared of your aunt the way I was, either—he said anyone who hates San Francisco as much as she does isn't going to risk getting her shoes dirty walking on our streets. He made it sound so obvious that I feel silly now for being worried, but then...he didn't have to hear her voice on the other end of the phone.

Friday, June 23, 1978

Dear Sharon,

It's late, and…it's possible I'm a little drunk. So, I'm sorry in advance if anything I write here is something you'd rather not hear. I'm going to try to stick with our honesty pledge and not cross anything out.

Tonight at the show, I was watching you dance, with your eyes closed and the music pounding. You were off in your own little world, a world I can only try to imagine, and I realized something.

Well, okay, I've actually known it for a while.

Sharon…I want to share that world with you.

I used to think that was how I felt about Carolyn. Back then, I didn't understand how it really felt to want to be with someone.

I understand it now.

When I was watching you tonight, I felt something I never felt with her. Something I've never felt with anyone. I didn't know I <u>could</u> feel it.

Anyway…I'm sorry. I know you're straight. You wrote it in black and white and everything. If you tell me to back away, I promise I'll never say anything about this again.

But right now...I want to be with you. More than I've ever wanted anything.

Okay. I read this over and I realized there's no way I can give this letter to you. I never would've written it at all if it hadn't been for those drinks.

We sleep in the same <u>room</u>. Besides, you're <u>straight</u>. There's no way you can feel what I'm feeling.

Reading this will only make you feel terrible. If I give you this letter it'll ruin our friendship.

Your friendship is the best thing in my life. I won't give that up. I can't.

Sorry. I guess I won't bother signing this.

I... Sharon, I...

God, I wish things could be different.

Dear Harvey,

I'm stupid. I'm so incredibly stupid, sometimes I can't believe it.

First there was that ridiculous letter I started writing to Sharon last night. At least I wised up before I actually gave it to her. God, I can't imagine how badly I almost messed everything up.

But what I did tonight might've been worse.

Javi and Rosa were out, and they left Peter and me in charge at the store. Sharon came over, too—we were planning to go out after we closed up. Until I fucked everything up.

The store was empty except for us for most of the night, and after I swept the aisles we were all hanging out by the cash register, waiting for closing time, talking about Gay Freedom Day and flipping through the <u>L.A. Times</u>. That's what gave Peter the idea.

"Hey," he said, holding out a page for me to see. "Isn't that your uncle?"

I'd seen the ad before, for my aunt and uncle's radio show, but I hadn't paid attention to the date. It turned out the premiere was tonight.

<u>Saved from the Wrath of God</u>, the top of the ad read. Below it, a few lines of smaller text were printed:

Searching for faith during sinful times? Tune in to hear the Lord's message, from the Reverend Russell Dale. Call in with prayer requests and points for theological discussion.

"Hang on." Peter looked at his watch, then looked at the ad again. "Their first show's on, live. <u>Right now</u>."

"God, I'm so glad we don't get the L.A. stations here," I said. "I don't know if I could handle hearing my aunt's voice. I'd probably break out in hives."

"Well, <u>I</u> want to hear it." Peter stuck out his lip in a fake pout. "From your stories I'm expecting a fundamentalist cartoon villain. Like the bad guy at the end of a Scooby-Doo episode who talks about how they could've gotten away with it if only it weren't for those meddling gay kids."

"I wish my aunt was that easy to get rid of," I said. "Then maybe I could've fought back instead of running away."

"What do you think she'd do if an actual gay person called her show?" Peter tapped the ad with his finger. "Would she self-immolate from fear of tainted phone lines?"

"Probably. Or she'd pretend to faint and my uncle would pretend to revive her on-air."

"You should do it," Sharon told her brother, grinning. "Use the pay phone. Tell her you're searching for faith in these sinful times."

"Oh, my God, I should." Peter's eyes got comically wide, and he turned to me. "Can I? Please? I'll tell her I'm having sinful homosexual thoughts and I need her to pray them away."

I laughed. I can't believe it now, but honestly, the idea sounded funny to me. "Sure. Just as long as I don't have to talk to her."

So that's how the three of us wound up gathered around the pay phone at the back of the store. We had to hunt to find enough dimes for the long-distance call, but we were having a blast, each of us psyching the others up.

Peter dialed the number, holding the phone out so we could all hear as it rang. I thought whoever picked up would tell us to take a hike, but when the voice answered and said, "Yes, caller, did you have a prayer request?" I got a sinking feeling in my chest.

I should've reached over and hung up right away. Instead I stood there, a rabbit in the headlights.

Peter didn't notice. "Yes, hello, ma'am," he said, using the same superpolite voice he uses when he's on deliveries and hoping for a good tip. "I was hoping you'd pray for me."

"Certainly," my aunt said. Her voice was so smooth, and my heart was pounding so hard. "Could I get your name, please, sir?"

"It's Paul, and no need to call me sir. I'm only eighteen." Peter's voice caught, as if he was embarrassed, but he was still grinning.

"All right, Paul," Aunt Mandy purred. "Where are you calling from?"

"San Francisco. It's hard, living here."

"My, you're calling from a very long way away," my aunt said, her voice stuffed with fake sympathy. I'd heard her do this countless times before. "Tell me, Paul, my child, why is San Francisco such a difficult place to live?"

I could tell Peter was on the verge of cracking. He was enjoying tricking my aunt a little too much. "I suppose it's because of all the homosexuals."

Sharon clapped a hand over her mouth to keep from laughing. Then her eyes cut to me. I don't know how I must have looked, but the smile drained off her face in an instant.

"Ah, yes, your city is known for that form of sin," my uncle said. He sounded gruff, but kind of bored, too. As though he had better things to be doing than talking to "Paul" about San Francisco's homosexual problem.

"Yes," Peter said. He was almost choking from trying so hard not to laugh. It probably added to his performance as far as my aunt and uncle were concerned. "Sometimes I get, um...<u>urges</u>."

Peter burst out laughing as soon as he finished his sentence, but somehow he managed to slam his hand over the mouthpiece in time. It worked. My aunt and uncle didn't hear.

"Oh, you poor young man," my aunt said, her voice coming through faintly now that we were even farther from the receiver. "We're very happy to pray for you. Please know that if you have faith in God, he'll protect you from the devil's temptations."

Peter took his hand off the mouthpiece and said, "Oh, good. Because the devil's been checking me out lately every time I go to the Elephant Walk, and I've got to tell you the truth, ma'am, because I know you're a woman of God—he's been looking good these days."

That's when I made my biggest mistake of the night.

Maybe I had a death wish. Maybe I just couldn't handle the tension anymore, and I had to let it out.

Maybe it really was that funny.

But when Peter fell over laughing at his own joke, not bothering to cover the mouthpiece anymore, I laughed, too.

I couldn't stop. I laughed, and laughed, and laughed.

My aunt and uncle definitely heard.

I was still laughing when I took the receiver. I meant to hang it up. Honestly, I did, but then my aunt said, louder than before, "Well, Paul, I suppose you and your friends in San Francisco think this is all very funny."

And I—God, I don't know what the Hell was wrong with me—I pulled the phone up to my mouth and said, "Yes, we think it's absolutely hilarious."

I reached up to drop the receiver back on the hook, and that's when we heard my aunt's voice again. She sounded different this time. Less smooth. More alert, as if she'd just awoken from a deep sleep. "Wait. Who was that? Where did you say you were calling fr—?"

That was the last we heard before I dropped the receiver onto the hook with a sharp clatter.

For a moment we all stood there, staring at each other. Sharon's face was white. Peter tried to ask what was going on, but I couldn't speak.

It was Sharon who suggested we go home after closing instead of going to the club after all, since tomorrow was going to be so busy with Gay Freedom Day. I nodded—I couldn't trust myself with actual words—and even Peter agreed.

We didn't talk much the rest of the night. Not that I would've known what to say, anyway.

I don't know what's going to happen now, Harvey. All I know is that I took a situation that already sucked and I made it a whole lot worse.

Yours,
Tammy

Saturday, June 24, 1978

Dear Tammy,

Hey.

I don't think I completely understand what happened when we called in to your aunt's show tonight. I could tell you were upset, and I figured you'd tell me in a letter if you wanted me to know. Only...we've been home for a while now, and you haven't given me any letters yet.

If you don't want to tell me, that's okay, but if you want to talk, you know where to find me.

Yours,
Sharon

Saturday, June 24, 1978

Dear Sharon,

You're asleep already, so I'll leave this by your bed for you to read in the morning. It's been an hour since you gave me your letter, so I'm sorry I didn't write back sooner. I didn't want to think about it, but...there's no point. It's done.

It was <u>so stupid</u> of me to pick up that phone tonight. I don't know why I did it. Maybe it was just that I was having so much <u>fun</u>. That's new for me, you know?

I'd thought it would be awful to hear my aunt's voice again, and it was, but for a second, it felt <u>good</u>, too. Hearing her right where I left her, getting totally taken in by a gay teenage boy on what was supposed to be the crowning achievement of her life. Maybe I felt so superior I genuinely thought she couldn't hurt me anymore.

I should've known no one's ever safe from Aunt Mandy. Especially not me.

She recognized my voice. She knew we were calling from San Francisco. She knows about Peter from your letters. That fake name probably gave us away as much as his real one would've.

And this means... Well. She knows I'm here, with you. She might've already suspected, but now she knows for sure.

I don't know what'll happen. I don't know what she'll do. Whatever she thinks will get her what she wants, probably.

I'm so scared, Sharon. I hate that I'm <u>still</u> so scared of her. Maybe that's the kind of thing that never goes away.

I'm so, so sorry. Things were going so well, and now I've ruined it all.

Yours,
Tammy

Sunday, June 25, 1978

Dear Tammy,

No, you haven't.

I don't have time for a real letter—I'm just writing this one fast while you're in the shower so I can leave it for you before I go downstairs—but I wanted you to know you haven't ruined everything. You couldn't, not ever.

We'll figure out this thing with your aunt. For now, it's Gay Freedom Day. It's a day to be happy. So please, try to relax and enjoy it, all right?

Yours,
Sharon

Dear Diary,

So that was my first Gay Freedom Day.

The house is dead quiet tonight. I've been lying on my bed, staring up at the ceiling for the past two hours. Peter and Tammy are both who knows where and Mom is asleep, as usual.

The afternoon was amazing at first, being in the middle of all that energy in the air. It wasn't exactly perfect—it was hard to shake all the fears that phone call with Aunt Mandy the night before had stirred up—but Tammy seemed to have taken my letter this morning to heart, because despite everything that had happened, she was so excited to be there for the parade, it was contagious. She must've said the word "wow" a hundred times before it was halfway over.

"Wow," she said again, beaming, as a dozen motorcycles revved their engines up ahead of us. Her face kept lighting up, over and over again. "Did you see that, Sharon?"

I grinned. "The motorcycles? Yeah, they were tough to miss."

"That woman had a shirt that said Dykes on Bikes." Tammy's usual sunny smile had been overtaken by an all-out Cheshire cat grin the moment we'd reached Castro Street and gotten our first glimpse of the huge flag hanging in the distance, with massive stripes in all different colors. "That's what they call themselves. They don't think it's a bad word at all!"

"They don't? Really?" I hadn't noticed the woman's shirt. How would a shirt like that even get <u>made</u>?

"Nope," Peter said from Tammy's other side, grinning just as wide as she was. "Words mean different things when different people say them."

"Wow. Okay. Oh, my gosh."

"<u>Oh, my gosh!</u>" He laughed again and flicked a braid off my shoulder. He's done that every time I've worn my hair in braids since we were little kids, and it annoys me as much now as it did then. I elbowed him back just as a drag queen in a one-piece bathing suit blew us a kiss from atop a tinsel-covered truck.

"I've wasted so much time being scared," Tammy said, reaching out to catch the imaginary kiss. "But my aunt isn't more powerful than all of this. She can't be. There are thousands of us here! This is the world now, whether she likes it or not."

"Exactly." Peter reached out, pretending to take the kiss from Tammy and slapping it onto his own cheek.

He'd somehow maneuvered us to the front row of spectators, but the crowd was impossibly tight all around us. I knew Gay Freedom Day was a big deal, but I'd never imagined this. There had to be tens of thousands of people around us, and fifty feet away a cluster of TV trucks with cameras on their roofs was taking in the scene.

Peter even heard a rumor that a gray-haired woman was walking around the crowd with a sign that read I LOVE MY GAY SON. I'm not sure how much faith I put in that rumor, though. I can't imagine any parent carrying a sign like that, here or anywhere else.

"Sharon! Tammy! Hey!" I recognized Evelyn's voice, and I waved with a smile. She was wearing dark sunglasses and a white T-shirt that said WOULD YOU WANT MICHELANGELO TEACHING YOUR

CHILDREN ART? It was also very obvious she wasn't wearing a bra under it, but then, a few minutes earlier I'd seen two women walk by with no shirts at all. "You missed an awesome show last night."

"Oh, right, sorry," I said, while Tammy's smile faded. "We were going to go after work, but...uh, something came up."

"It's cool." Evelyn grinned and waved at the marching band going by. They were playing a startlingly upbeat version of "Somewhere Over the Rainbow" while men in short red shorts and bright white knee socks twirled batons. "Next time, right?"

"Peter, Peter, Pumpkin Eater." Leonard's voice sang out from behind Evelyn. She stepped aside as Leonard and Dean maneuvered toward us through the sea of people. I was about to introduce them to Tammy, but before I could say anything Dean pushed through the crowd and plastered his face onto my brother's.

"What the—?" I lunged forward, my instincts telling me to pull Dean off before he hurt Peter, but Tammy laughed and grabbed my arms.

"Oh, my God, you two," she said, laughing. "Your kid sister's right here, man."

"Oh, shit." It was Dean who answered, drawing back from Peter in an instant. "Sorry. You okay, Sharon?"

"I'm fine," I mumbled, wishing I could turn myself invisible.

The others were still laughing, but Peter was blushing, too. My brother doesn't blush as often as I do, but when he does, he turns an even brighter shade of tomato-pink.

"Hey, were you at that meeting on Briggs a couple of weeks ago?" Evelyn asked Dean. "I thought I saw you there."

"Oh, yeah! One of your friends gave my boss a ride home on her bike. I was so jealous. I've always wanted to ride one of those."

"You mean you haven't? Oh, my God, it's amazing. You have to get somebody to give you a ride—it's such a rush."

Evelyn and Dean got into a very enthusiastic discussion of motorcycles while I ordered the blood to stop rushing to my cheeks.

"Dean's cute." Tammy waved at a float carrying a few nervous-looking politicians dressed in shirts and ties. "Well done, Peter."

"I mean, I don't know that I've <u>done</u> anything..." Peter bit his lip and glanced my way, but I kept my gaze fixed firmly on the parade. His cheeks were luminescent. "We're friends, that's all."

"Yeah, that's totally how I greet all my <u>friends</u>..." Tammy sounded as if she was going to tease him more, but then trailed off as she glanced my way, too.

I tried to steady my breathing. I was still in shock.

Did my brother go around kissing guys in public all the time? What if someone saw?

Last year a gay man was stabbed to death right in this neighborhood. It was on the news for weeks.

"Whoa, look at that float." At first I thought Peter was only trying to change the subject, but I followed his gaze past a large contingent of men marching over the cable-car tracks with NO ON BRIGGS! signs, and over to a pickup truck with eight young kids crammed in the back. A sign taped to the side read LESBIANS WANT THE RIGHT TO BE ORDINARY MOMS.

"Are those seriously kids of gay people?" Peter asked.

I shook my head. "How's that possible?"

"Anything's possible." Tammy bounced on her toes. "It's a whole new world."

I couldn't help smiling. "Is this how you pictured Gay Freedom Day?"

"Just about." Tammy beamed at a group of women marching past us. One of them was waving a hand-lettered sign that said PRESERVE ABORTION RIGHTS. Two others, dressed in flip-flops, halter tops, and cutoff shorts that barely covered their underwear, were walking with their arms around each other's waists. The words

GAYS FOREVER were scrawled across their backs in bright blue finger paint. "I never thought I'd get to see it."

I smiled at her. Tammy bumped my elbow, the backs of her knuckles brushing mine. Only for an instant, but I was already blushing all over again.

We watched in silence as the next few floats passed. The parade was nearing its end, and the crowd was getting louder and more boisterous, surging toward the end of the block.

"Is something going on up there?" Tammy stood on her tiptoes, twisting to see.

Peter must have finally detached himself from Dean, because he was coming up behind us when I turned to look. The last floats were trailing off.

"How much of this do you think people will see on the news?" I pointed to the camera on the top of the truck behind us.

Peter shook his head. "Not much. They only show the most salacious stuff."

"What I mean is, you need to start being more careful."

His eyes narrowed. "What are you talking about?"

"Well, I mean..." I cast my eyes back toward the spot where Dean had first attacked my brother's face. "And..." I nodded toward the TV camera.

Peter followed my gaze and crossed his arms over his chest. "What's your point?"

He couldn't possibly not know what I was getting at. Tammy was watching us silently, but I could tell from her wide, anxious eyes that she understood, too. "What if someone got you on film—you know, looking gay, and it wound up on the news?"

"I look gay every single day." Peter chewed on the corner of his lip and turned toward the stage set up at the far end of the block. Music was playing over the speakers, and people were moving quickly in that direction. "I don't look any more gay here than I do anyplace else."

"You know what I mean. I thought you were worried about people finding out."

"What, I'm not allowed to have a life?" Peter took a step forward, then another, following the crowd. I struggled to keep up as he weaved between bare-chested men and women with fringed haircuts. Tammy stayed close on our heels. "Maybe I like Dean. Maybe I like him a <u>lot</u>. Why shouldn't I get to show it?"

I didn't understand. I thought my brother <u>wanted</u> me to help him keep his secret. Also... "You've barely talked about this Dean guy. Suddenly you're infatuated?"

"What are you, the relationship police?"

"No, I'm only—"

A huge cheer from the crowd cut me off.

"Whoa! Is that—?" Tammy pointed to the stage, until the cheering got so loud I couldn't hear her.

A man was walking toward the microphone, so far in the distance all I could see was his white T-shirt and black armband. But the energy around us was enough to tell me who it was.

Peter fought through the crowd, clearly trying to get as far away from me as possible. I spotted Evelyn not far behind us, standing with Lisa and Alex, all of them waving their arms and shouting happily as the crowd's cheers turned deafening.

Supervisor Milk was about to speak.

"It's him!" Tammy shouted into my ear. "I can't believe it!"

I searched the crowd again until I spotted my brother. He'd somehow circled back around, and he was behind us now, near Evelyn and the others. He had his arm around Dean, and his chin was lifted high. He wasn't looking at me, and it was clear that was deliberate.

I swiveled back around to face the front as Harvey's speech began.

The crowd had quieted enough that we could hear him, his voice carrying out through the microphone and over the thousands of faces gathered, fresh cheers erupting after almost every line. His voice was powerful, but it was his words that were arresting.

He sounded so <u>happy</u>. So strong.

He talked about being gay as though it was normal—as though it was <u>fun</u>. He said everyone should be treated equally, and somehow, when <u>he</u> said it, it sounded so obvious I didn't know why everyone else didn't think exactly the same way. He talked about Anita Bryant and John Briggs, and how we all had to work together to stop Prop 6.

He was literally giving us orders in the middle of a huge party, but no one minded. His were the kind of orders we <u>wanted</u> to follow.

Mostly, though, he talked about coming out. He said <u>all</u> gay people should come out, to <u>everyone</u>. He said there could never be equality until the whole world knew how many gay people there really were.

I never thought of that before, but it makes sense. If <u>everyone</u> was out, no one would have to lie.

But it still didn't seem possible. As far as I could tell, he might as well have been describing some magical land from a fantasy story. Even if there was a woman walking around today with a sign about loving her gay son, she had to be one in a thousand. Or a million.

Just telling <u>me</u> was a big deal for Peter. And when Tammy's family found out about her, she had to leave her entire life behind.

I wondered if Harvey's words were making her uneasy. But when I glanced over, there were tears in her eyes...and she was beaming. As I was about to ask if she was all right, the crowd erupted into another cheer.

"WOO-HOO!" Tammy shouted along with the rest of them.

She looked back at me, her smile as bright as ever, and when she saw me turned her way, she reached for my hand and threaded her fingers through mine, her smile widening.

For a second, I thought I was imagining it. She seemed so casual about it, I wasn't even sure it was really happening. Until she turned back to the stage, and I screwed up the courage to look down.

There it was. Tammy and I were holding hands. Right in the middle of the street.

I didn't know what to do. No one else seemed to have noticed, but...did this mean something? Who did it mean?

My fingers twitched. Tammy must've thought I was squeezing her hand, because she squeezed back and smiled at me again.

Harvey finished his speech, and the crowd let out its biggest, wildest cheer of the day. I pulled my hand out of Tammy's to clap along before she could notice I was shaking. She glanced at me for a second, and now she looked a little uncertain.

"Sharon?" She had to lean in close so I could hear her. Very close. Close enough that she could've kissed me. Or I could've kissed her.

"Hey," she began. "I, ah..."

Why was I thinking this way? Did I want to kiss her?

I did. Oh, God, I did, I did, I did.

The crowd surged around us, thousands of people moving in every direction, laughing and pushing and shouting. I couldn't see Tammy in the throng, and suddenly, I realized just how lost I was. In every way there was to be lost.

I started to run.

"SHARON!" I heard her shout, but I didn't stop moving.

Running wasn't easy in that swarm of happy, cheering people. I had to duck under arms and over feet, darting around couples with their arms around each other's shoulders and between groups of men and women holding beer cans overhead. It was too loud for me to make out individual sounds, much less individual footsteps, so I had no way of knowing if Tammy was following me, but when I reached the sidewalk and felt a hand on my arm, I knew without having to look that it was her.

"Sharon, wait." She wasn't holding tightly—I could've pulled away if I'd tried—but I stopped, anyway. "I'm sorry."

"You're sorry?" All I felt in that moment was fear, but somehow, anger was what came out. "You—you think you can just <u>come</u> here and—"

"I— You're right. I'm sorry."

"You showed up out of nowhere, and now everything's different. You put on this huge act for everyone, saying whatever they want to hear—and I don't know where I fit, with you or with anyone else, and I can't—"

"What?" Tammy stared at me, her eyebrows crinkling. "What act?"

"I— I don't know—" People were turning to look at us. Maybe I was shouting. I couldn't tell. "I keep thinking all this stuff that doesn't make sense, except—except—"

"Except what?" Her face shifted, her lips parting. "What are you talking about?"

"How you <u>are</u>." I could barely get the words out. I was blushing. In seconds, I'd be crying, too. I had to get out of here, fast. "You're so— How you're so..."

She waited, but I couldn't find the words. My head was about to explode.

"Look." She reached out to touch my hand again, then pulled back. "I'm sorry if I scared you. Or if you aren't ready for this, or—or anything, but..."

I didn't wait to hear what was going to come after that. I turned around and started running all over again, darting through the crowd and pounding down the street as fast as I could, until her shouts after me faded into the distance.

Yours,
Sharon

Sunday, June 25, 1978

Hi, Sharon.

I wanted to say I'm sorry about today.

I moved my stuff down to the living room. I thought it'd be easier for you if I slept on the couch. I can't stop wondering if you're all right, though, so I thought I'd write to you.

I really, really hope you'll write back. You don't have to talk about anything. Just tell me if you're okay, and I promise not to bother you anymore.

I'm sliding this under your door now. I'll come back in fifteen minutes and check the hallway if you want to slide something back.

Yours,
Tammy

Tuesday, June 27, 1978

Dear Sharon,

Okay, well…it's been two days since we last talked. It can't be easy avoiding someone who lives in the same house as you, so I know you've got to be furious with me to be going to all that effort.

Your brother said he hasn't seen you much since you left Gay Freedom Day, either. I think he's still upset about that argument you two had. I told him you were only trying to help, but I'm not sure he believed me.

Anyway, I can take a hint. I won't write to you after this. I just wanted to say I'm sorry. If I could go back and undo it all, I would.

Yours,
Tammy

Dear Diary,

I talked to my brother tonight.

He got home earlier than usual—before eleven. I'd been waiting, lying on my bed in my dark room that feels impossibly huge with Tammy gone, until I heard his footsteps trudge up the stairs. I went on waiting while he rummaged around in the bathroom, brushed his teeth, went into his room, and shut the door.

For two days, I've hardly spoken to anyone, but after I read Tammy's letter this afternoon, I knew that had to change. For the past two mornings, I've watched from my upstairs window as she left the house, tossing her short hair as she twisted her key to lock the door behind her, and wondering yet again if I'd made a mistake.

But I still can't talk to her. If we were face-to-face, I wouldn't even be able to think.

My brother, though…I can always talk to him.

I stepped silently into the hall. Mom was in her room, and Tammy was downstairs. As far as I knew they were both asleep, but either way, I didn't want them hearing. I knocked as softly as I could.

From inside Peter's room came a soft groan. A minute later, the door swung open. He didn't say anything. Didn't even raise his eyes to look at me. Just turned around and flopped back onto his narrow bed.

He was still dressed in the polo shirt and jeans he'd worn to work, with something I couldn't see clearly sticking out of his back pocket. He stunk of smoke, and his eyes were red. He must've been at a bar. I waved my hand in front of my nose and shut the door behind me, carefully turning the knob so the latch wouldn't make a sound.

I stepped over to the portable turntable he'd jammed into the corner. There was a record already on it—Queen, <u>A Night at the Opera</u>.

That wouldn't work. You can't have a conversation with Queen playing. I lifted it off, found an old Elton John album in the stack next to the wall, and dropped it onto the table, turning the volume on low.

"Hi," I whispered after the first song started. "Do you think Mom can hear us over this?"

"Mom's asleep." Peter hadn't moved. He was lying on his back with his arm cast over his eyes. "Which is also how I'd like to be. You know who's asleep downstairs, too, but I guess you don't care about that."

"Not really."

"Please don't lie to me, sister dear."

I sighed. "You talked to her."

"We live in the same house. We talk all the time. You used to talk to us, too."

I sighed again. "Where'd you go tonight? Out with Dean?"

"Sure you want to know?" He lowered his arm and wiggled his eyebrows.

"You already told me way more than I wanted to hear about that guy from camp. I had to listen to the story about how you snuck into the counselors' cabin during the marshmallow roast at least twenty times."

Peter tilted his head with a serene smile. "I'll always think of Curtis whenever I bite into a s'more."

"What, you're into <u>him</u> again?"

"No, merely relishing a brief moment of nostalgia. I'm very much into Dean now." His smile widened. "What do you think of him?"

"Why do you care?"

"I don't. I'm being polite." He smirked. "Anyway...come on, what do you think?"

"I don't know. He seems okay, I guess. He seriously goes to Stanford?"

"Yeah. He's a political science major. His family lives in Bakersfield, but he's spending the summer in the city so he can work on Prop 6."

"Huh. Is he a nerd?"

"Probably, but he's a cute nerd. I'm not sure how much he likes me, though."

"He came running across a whole crowd to make out with you. I'd say he likes you."

Peter's grin widened, and he stood up, stretching. His elbow knocked into the window, and the frame clattered. He winced and rubbed his arm. "Eh. He might be flirting just to flirt."

"Making out in the middle of the street is 'flirting'?"

"Sometimes. And on that subject, may I ask why I very clearly saw you holding hands with a certain blond lesbian from Orange County to whom you're currently not speaking during Harvey's speech on Sunday?"

I was so stunned I couldn't even blush.

He <u>saw</u> us?

"Look, it didn't mean anything." I was stumbling over the words, scrambling to come up with some explanation. "It was an accident."

"Uh-huh." Peter crossed his arms over his chest. He was enjoying this. (In other news, my brother is a horrible person.) "Which is it? Was it an accident, or did it not mean anything?"

"Both! I mean, I had no intention of doing it. It just...happened."

"Sure. So you pulled your hand away?"

"Yes. Of course."

When I shut my eyes, I could see exactly how Tammy looked when she turned toward me that day. Her smile was so clear in my memory, it was as though we were back in that spot right now.

I'd been feeling too many different things to sort them all out when I stood next to her in the crowd that day, but now that it was just me and Peter—the memory of being in that place, with her hand in mine...

It felt right. It shouldn't, but it did.

"Shar?" Peter's voice dropped lower. "Are you crying?"

I turned to face the wall. I hadn't cried in front of my brother since fifth grade, but suddenly I couldn't stop. "No."

"Is she the reason you broke up with Kevin?"

"I—I don't know." My face was a wet mess. All I could do was hide behind my hands. "When I was with him, I didn't feel the slightest bit gay."

"Ew." Peter wrinkled up his nose. "I didn't need to know that."

"I can't be gay. That's what I'm saying. I never thought I was. I was positive I was straight, until..."

"Until a certain cute blond girl came along."

I shoved him with my shoulder. He shoved me back, gently.

"I'm sorry I said what I did." I couldn't bring myself to meet his eyes. "You were right. If you want to be with Dean, or, I guess, with anyone, it's none of my business how you do it."

"Yeah, well, I'm not so sure myself anymore." He reached around behind him and pulled something out of his back pocket. A magazine. "Look."

He bent down to face the floor, rubbing the back of his neck. The magazine was one of the local weeklies. The lead article was about the Giants' odds of making the playoffs. I frowned at him, confused.

"It's toward the back," he said.

I flipped to the end and worked my way forward. I'd turned five pages when I finally saw it.

The headline said CITY HOMOSEXUAL PARTY DRAWS BIGGEST CROWD YET. At the bottom of the page were two black-and-white pictures. Both were covered with crudely shaped penises and testicles drawn onto the page with a ballpoint pen.

One photo showed Harvey Milk riding in a convertible. The other was of Peter and Dean kissing in the middle of the crowd. In the far corner of that picture, slightly out of focus, was a short-haired blond girl I immediately recognized, even facing away from the camera. Her arm was out to her side, and there was a hand intertwined with hers. The photo cut off without showing any more than that, but there was no question that it was Tammy and me.

"Oh, my God," I whispered.

Peter yanked the magazine out of my grip. Then he started ripping it, tearing the paper into strips, tearing the strips into confetti.

"Where _were_ you tonight?" I asked him, my voice starting to shake. "Your eyes are all red."

He ripped off another strip of paper, then another. "I was finishing my delivery route, and I ran into Gary Knopp. Or, well, he ran into me."

I shuddered. "Was he alone?"

"He's never alone. Had two other guys with him. Stupider than he is, if you can imagine that."

I could imagine it easily. I tightened my hand into a fist. "What did they do to you?"

Peter rolled his eyes. "Said some shit. It's no big deal. I didn't know what brought it on at first, but as they were leaving, they threw that in my face."

I stared down at the magazine scraps on the floor. Then I grabbed the biggest shred and crumpled it in my fist. I grabbed the next-biggest piece after that, then the third-biggest, crumpling them all. It wasn't as satisfying as I'd expected. "Do you think they'll come back?"

"It doesn't matter. I don't care about Gary Knopp. I want to know who else's seen this."

Oh. Oh, <u>shit</u>. "You mean..."

"That crappy little paper has boxes all over the city." Peter gave up on ripping and threw himself back onto the bed. "It's only a matter of time before Mom sees. For all I know, someone's already shown her."

I shook my head, my heart pounding. "We'd know. She wouldn't keep that quiet."

"What do you think she'll do?"

I had no idea what Mom would do if she saw a photo of Peter kissing a guy. I freaked when <u>I</u> saw him do it, and I already knew he was gay.

What if Mom recognized Tammy in the photo, too? What if she figured out that was my hand entwined with hers?

"Fuck," I muttered.

"I'd been thinking of telling her, too." Peter shook his head without lifting his arm from his face. "Can you believe that shit? I was talking to Dean about it last week. He came out to his parents last year, and they didn't kick him out. It's a good thing he had a scholarship for college, though, because his dad refused to pay tuition anymore. Without that, he'd never have risked telling them."

"I thought you didn't want Mom to ever find out."

"I didn't. I don't, but..." He lowered his arm and met my eyes. "I hate all this lying."

I sunk onto the mattress by his feet. "Me, too."

"I was thinking about moving in with Dean." He picked at a stray thread on his quilt. Our grandmother made it before we were born. Dad's mother. "I could get a job down there. To help with rent."

"In Palo Alto?" I don't know which part of what he was saying stunned me the most. He was thinking about telling Mom? About moving away? "What about going to State in the fall?"

"There's not much point. Mom can barely afford it, anyway, and it's four years to get a degree—that's another four years of lies, and if she finds out, I'll have to leave no matter what."

"Oh, God." I can't lose my brother. I <u>can't</u>. I've already lost Dad.

And if Mom found out that was me in the photo...what if I lost her, too?

Can Peter take that kind of risk? Could I?

"Anyway..." He smiled darkly, stirring the scraps of paper on the floor around with his foot. "You really think you're one of us?"

I winced. "I don't even know how to find out. At school the closest the teachers got to saying anything about sex was when they told us to ask our mothers how to use maxi pads."

Peter winced, too. "Once Father Murphy told us if we ever felt like jerking off, we should pray to Jesus to make it go away."

"Oh, my gosh, are you serious?"

He laughed harder than before. "Thanks for saying, 'Oh, my gosh.' That's the most you've sounded like my actual sister in weeks. When you said 'fuck' before, I almost lost it."

I laughed so hard I started hiccuping. We were risking being too loud, though, so I hiccuped into a pillow, waving my arm so Peter would know to be quiet, too.

"Anyway, if you have the option..." His voice turned serious again. "If you <u>can</u> be straight, I mean. I'd think about it, if I were you."

My laughter faded. "What?"

"Well, you said you were scared...and maybe that's good." He shrugged. "If I'd been more scared, that picture wouldn't have wound up in there."

"I thought you—?"

He frowned, and I could tell he was about to interrupt me when there was a knock on the door.

We both froze.

Was it Mom? Did she hear us? <u>What</u> did she hear?

"Peter?" Tammy's voice was barely above a whisper. "Are you awake?"

The record was still playing. She knew he was here.

I could see Peter doing the same mental calculation as he stood up and brushed off his jeans. I tried to signal him to wait so I could hide or something—not that there was anywhere to hide in this tight space—but he was already at the door.

"Hey," he whispered, holding the door open just enough to peer out, blocking her view of me. He's a good brother. "What's up?"

"I can't sleep. Could I borrow that book you were telling me about?"

"Yeah, one sec." He stepped back, trying to close the door while he reached for the stack of books behind him, but Tammy stepped forward at the same moment. She saw me over his shoulder.

"Oh." She stepped back quickly, but it was too late. "Sorry, Sharon. I thought you were in your room."

"I couldn't sleep, either."

All three of us fell silent. I looked straight at Tammy, and she looked back at me. Peter glanced from me to her and back again.

"You know what?" He took a breath, then nodded, as if he'd made a quick decision. "I'm going to the bathroom."

"Wait..." I began, but he was already gone.

"I'm sorry." Tammy reached both hands behind her neck, as though to gather her hair into a ponytail, but then I guess she realized her hair was too short for that and turned the movement into an awkward shoulder stretch. "I didn't mean to interrupt. I really thought you were asleep. I should be, too. You know how sometimes you lie there staring at the ceiling for hours because, I don't know, you're thinking too much, and you know you should be sleeping, but there's absolutely nothing you can do to make your body go along with that idea? It's the worst, don't you think?"

She was babbling. It was kind of adorable.

"Right?" she said, when I didn't answer. "You get what I'm saying?"

"I get it." I nodded, studying her.

She was dressed in a plain white T-shirt and threadbare blue sweatpants she'd gotten at a thrift store during one of our trips to Valencia Street. Her skin was still Southern California bronze, and her blue eyes were perfectly wide and round and locked on me. She was stammering a little, as though she wanted to fill the silence, her lips opening and closing and shifting around as she let out little ums and ahs, and I wanted to kiss her. I wanted to kiss her badly.

More than I'd ever wanted to kiss Midge, or Kevin, or anyone.

More than I'd ever known it was possible to want something.

"Anyway, sorry, I'll leave you alone." She whispered the words so quietly I wouldn't have heard her over the music if I hadn't been watching every movement of her lips. She turned back toward the door, nearly tripping as she spun around.

"Wait," I said.

Tammy froze, her hand on the knob.

I stared at her—the rigid line of her tense shoulders, the hesitant set of her jaw, the freshly shorn hair curling past her ears—and that was when I knew it was true. Everything I've been afraid of.

People like Anita Bryant and Senator Briggs, and Tammy's aunt, too—they hate me. They could come after me, the same way they've come after so many others.

And Mom. Oh, God. What about Mom?

"Sharon?" Tammy asked, half-turning back to me. "Are you okay?"

I was crying by then. Tears dripped down my cheeks in a sloppy mess, right in front of Tammy.

"I, um… You probably want me to go." She looked down and drew in a sharp breath. "I'm sorry I bothered you. I'll, ah, I'll see you…"

She reached for the doorknob. It took her three tries to pull it open and step through.

I wanted to tell her to wait. I wanted to tell her to stay. I wanted to beg her to stay there with me.

But she was already sliding the door shut silently behind her.

Yours,
Sharon

Tuesday, June 27, 1978

Dear Sharon,

Hey, so. I just wanted to say I'm sorry, again.

It's obvious I screwed up your life by coming here. Besides, it's past time I found somewhere else to live. You and your family have been so generous to me, and I need to stop taking advantage of that.

You probably won't read this until tomorrow, if you read it at all. I'm sticking it under your door now, but it's been more than an hour since you left your brother's room and you're probably asleep. I'll try to be out of the house before you wake up.

I'm so, so sorry, Sharon.

Yours,
Tammy

Tuesday, June 27, 1978

Dear Tammy,

Oh, my gosh, no, please don't leave! I'm sorry I've been so horrible lately, but I don't want you to go.

I'm going to sneak downstairs and leave this for you after you're already asleep so you'll find it as soon as you wake up. Seriously, please, I can't stand the idea of you living anywhere but here.

I just... I don't know. I need to think more. I'm sorry.

Yours,
Sharon

P.S. I was awake when you slid that letter under my door. I wanted to get up and let you in, but I was afraid I'd fall apart and embarrass us both all over again.

Wednesday, June 28, 1978

Dear Sharon,
    All right, but…could we talk soon? Please?

Yours,
Tammy

Wednesday, June 28, 1978

Dear Diary,

I don't think I've ever felt this lost.

My dreams last night were horrible. I was running from a crowd of people, all of them seconds away from catching me. I couldn't turn around to see their faces. All I knew was that I had to keep running, faster, faster, faster...until I stumbled and felt long, thick fingers dig into my shoulder. I turned slowly, fear pulsing through my entire body, and when I finally saw them, they were laughing at me.

Tammy's aunt. Sister Catherine. Gary Knopp and the boys from school. My mother. Hundreds of others, too—faces I recognized and faces I didn't, all of them dissolving into an angry, laughing darkness, pinning me to the ground.

When I woke up, it took me twenty minutes to stop shaking.

I don't want Tammy to move out. That's the only thing I know for sure. My mind's been too muddy to think about anything else.

I got lucky, though—my letter back to her was short and probably incoherent, but it worked. There was a short note from her under my door when I woke up this morning, and when I went downstairs she'd already left for work, but her stuff was still stacked up neatly next to our plaid sofa.

I went to the O'Sullivans', tried to pretend everything was normal for Chris and Penny's benefit, and spent the next few hours wandering around the city. When it finally got dark, I started walking up to North Beach. There was a show tonight, and shows are the one place where I <u>never</u> have to think.

It was a long walk, but I didn't care. Once I was in the thick of the crowd, I knew I'd made the right choice. All I had to do was shut my eyes and let the screaming fill my head.

A band I'd never heard of was on the stage, and they were having technical problems. Feedback whines filled the room, and the crowd was getting more raucous than usual. The last thing I'd seen before I shut my eyes was the lead singer flipping off the audience, a bunch of people in the crowd flipping him off in return, and one of the other band guys trying to smash his guitar on an amp and stopping because the singer punched him in the face. The whole room was a sea of anger.

It was exactly what I needed.

Until a sudden force jostled me from the left. I stumbled to the side, my eyes flying open. Fists were already flying just a few feet from me, so I didn't wait to see what would happen. I spun around and charged toward the bar.

I'd already had one screwdriver—the bartenders only bother checking your ID if you're a man—but I needed another drink. Anything that would make it harder to think.

I wove through the crowd, dodging the guys surging in to watch the fight, and reached the bar quickly. I spotted a free stool and lunged for it, sliding my hand over the sticky plastic-covered countertop to wave at the bartender. I was reaching into the pocket of my worn leather jacket for a five-dollar bill when I saw them.

They were around the corner of the bar, only a yard or so away.

Evelyn was standing with Midge Spelling at her side, and on her other side...was Tammy.

I pushed back from the bar so fast, the legs of my stool scraped across the floor. It was so loud in that room I was sure no one would hear, but Tammy's head swiveled my way.

"Sharon?"

Her voice was incredulous, and as soon as the word was out of her mouth she clapped a hand over it, her eyes widening in a silent apology. It was too late.

"Hey, Sharon!" Evelyn waved while Midge silently lifted her cigarette in my direction. "Join us!"

"I, um." I stepped backward, stumbling. Suddenly, it hurt to breathe. "I've got to...go."

I tried to act normal, but before I knew what was happening I was angling my way through the crowd elbows-first, ignoring sharp voices in my ears and shoves against my back, and the guy who shouted, "FUCK YOU!" as I pushed past. I shut it all out until I'd forced my way past every obstacle and the front door was swinging closed behind me.

I focused on breathing, since I didn't have the strength for anything else. I barely had the strength for that, as it turned out, and I had to bend forward, my hands on my knees.

Two men on their way into the club leaned down and said something to me. I tried to wave them off, but they lingered. They were asking if I was okay, but they weren't asking in a particularly friendly way.

"She's fine," a voice said above me. Tammy's voice—I could hear the smile in it. She was charming them, the way she charms everyone. "I've got her. You can go on in."

The men shuffled away. I wanted to stand up, act normal, but I couldn't lift my head.

"It's okay." Tammy's hand dropped lightly to my shoulder. The feel of her touching me, the sound of her saying my name, nearly made me choke. "Just breathe."

I wanted to tell her I couldn't, that that was the problem, but my throat swallowed the words.

"She all right?" The new voice was husky with cigarettes and something thicker. Midge Spelling was out here, too. As if I hadn't been humiliated enough already.

"I don't know." Tammy kneeled and looked up at my sweaty, probably purple face. "Sharon? Can you stand up? I'll get us a cab."

Hell no. If I had to share a back seat with Tammy, I'd never breathe again.

"Uh," Midge said above us, "no offense, but I think you're making her worse."

Tammy pulled away. With her out of my space, my eyes fell closed, and I managed to gasp in a breath of air.

"Do you think she needs to go to the emergency room or something?" Tammy asked. I twisted up to look at them out of the corner of my eye. Midge was wearing a man's button-down shirt with a pleated skirt that was about two feet shorter than the kilt I wear to school, with black boots laced up to her knees.

"Nah, I've seen this before." Midge exhaled slowly. Of course, she was smoking right next to me while I could barely breathe. "I'll stay. You go back inside."

"But—"

"Trust me. She'll be better off."

Tammy's feet shifted on the sidewalk as she considered what to do.

Listen to Midge, I silently begged her. Go away, Tammy. I can't function when you're this close.

"Well…" Tammy touched my shoulder again. I flinched. "All right.

Sharon, I'll wait by the bar. Come find me when you're feeling better, okay?"

Somehow, I bobbed my head, bending back down toward the pavement. When I heard her shuffle away, I finally managed to take in a little more air.

"She's gone," Midge said a moment later, blowing out a stream of smoke above me. "You can get up now."

Did she think I'd been <u>faking</u> it? I twisted my head back up as Midge popped her cigarette into her mouth again.

I flattened my hands against the greasy wall behind me, slowly pressing my upper body into a slightly less horizontal position. I didn't know if it was Tammy's absence or Midge's judgment that had changed things, but she was right—I <u>could</u> get up. My chest kept heaving, though.

Midge didn't look at me as I staggered to my feet. She was gazing coolly at the line of traffic rolling down the dark street in front of us, her free hand tapping out a quick rhythm on her hip, her skirt swinging with each movement.

"It's okay, you know." Midge exhaled a long stream of smoke. "I don't think she knows you're mad at her. Assuming you're trying to keep that a secret."

"I'm not <u>mad</u> at her." I sighed. Those were more words than I'd thought I'd be able to string together. "It's...complicated."

"It always is." Midge laughed, then popped the cigarette back into her mouth and inhaled sharply. "Anytime you run out in the street because you see a girl talking to somebody else, there's gonna be a story behind it."

"That isn't what happened at all."

"Okay. Well, either way, she came after you. That's what you wanted, right?"

"Not at all."

Midge laughed again. "Okay."

I groaned. "I'm fine now. You can go smoke inside."

She shrugged. "If you want. I wouldn't recommend hanging out here by yourself looking like you're about to pass out, though. Some of the guys here can be complete jackasses."

My chest was getting heavy again. I stopped to catch a breath.

"Hey, take it easy." Midge dropped her cigarette and ground it out with the heel of her boot, then stood directly across from me, meeting my eyes. "Deep breaths. You're okay."

I watched her, my eyes never wavering from her face. A moment later, I could breathe normally again. "Thanks."

"No worries. I had a friend once who used to freak out the same way you do. Did you drink more than usual?"

I'd only had the one drink, but that <u>was</u> more than usual. I drank it kind of fast, too. "Yeah."

"That'll do it. So, are you and the blond having girlfriend troubles, or what?"

"She's not my girlfriend. I..." I sighed again. Maybe it was time I said it out loud to someone who wasn't my brother. "I don't even know if I'm gay."

Midge nodded, no trace of surprise on her face. "I had a friend like that, too. Turned out she was bi."

I stared at her. Was she joking? "What?"

"Bisexual." She didn't laugh. "You've never heard of it?"

I was about to shake my head, but...I <u>had</u> heard of it. It just never occurred to me that it was something <u>I</u> could be.

"It's for people who are into men <u>and</u> women." Midge fished in the pocket of her button-down and pulled out another cigarette. "Want one?"

"No thanks."

"Okay." She popped the cigarette into her mouth and lit it while

I waited to see if she'd say more. "Lots of people are bi. David Bowie even is."

I blinked, stunned. "Wait, really?"

"Look, it's none of my business who you're into. Maybe you're totally straight. I sure as shit have no clue. All I know is, I saw you with that chick just now, and..." Midge jammed her thumb over her shoulder toward the door. "You were both acting as if you were awfully into each other."

A million different memories started boiling together in my head, all at the same time.

Going parking with Kevin. Watching Midge dance in that tiny skirt. Tammy, breathing softly in her sleep on my bedroom floor. Holding hands while Harvey Milk's voice rang in our ears.

The way I always felt when I unfolded a new letter from her. As though there could never be anything better in the world than hearing what she had to say.

"I should get back inside." Midge exhaled a long stream of smoke. I wondered if this was something she did every now and then. Stand outside clubs, smoking and introducing teenagers to mind-blowing concepts. "A decent band's actually about to start a set. You coming?"

I shook my head.

It was time I stopped shutting this out. I needed to think. Really think.

"That's cool. Anyway, don't bother listening to me, because I don't know shit. Except for one thing." Midge dropped her second cigarette to the sidewalk and crushed it with her boot. "There's no point worrying so hard you can't breathe. Life's short, and you've got to make sure there's time to live it."

Yours,
Sharon

Wednesday, June 28, 1978

Dear Sharon,

Are you okay? I think you're awake—your door's closed and your light's on—but I didn't want to bother you by knocking. Midge said you decided to take the bus home on your own. I'm glad you made it back safe.

I'm sorry. I know I shouldn't have followed you outside tonight, but I could tell you were upset. I thought it was all my fault. Now, though, I'm wondering if you might've been upset about something else, too.

I'm sliding this under your door now. I'll come back in ten minutes and then again ten minutes after that if you want to slide something back to me. If you don't, that's okay. If there's anything you do want to talk about, though, our pledge still stands.

Anyway...just wanted you to know I'm thinking about you.

Yours,
Tammy

Wednesday, June 28, 1978

Dear Tammy,

Okay. Since you asked...

Tammy, I feel so stupid.

There's so much I don't understand. This all seems to come easily to everyone else, but I've been so mixed up.

My whole life, I never fit. Not at school, not at church, not in this city. Or at least this neighborhood.

That changed the first time I went to a punk show. It changed more when I went to the bookstore. Then <u>you</u> showed up, and everything changed all over again, a hundred times over. Do you know what I mean?

Wait, listen to me. What am I saying? You <u>can't</u> know what I mean. You fit everywhere without trying.

I'm so glad you're here, Tammy. Please don't think you messed anything up for me. I wish you could stay forever.

Also... Midge told me something tonight, and I've been thinking, and...maybe she's right. Maybe I just need to live my life.

Sorry, I'm not making sense.

Write back if you're awake.

Yours,
Sharon

Wednesday, June 28, 1978

Dear Sharon,

You make total sense. And of course I'm awake. Getting letters from you is way more exciting than sleeping. It's like in the old days, except instead of waiting for the mailman, I can just come up the stairs to see if there's a folded piece of notebook paper waiting for me.

Anyway, I <u>do</u> know what you mean. I never fit anywhere either until I got here. I could pretend I belonged—I guess I've gotten good at that—but it's not the same as really finding a place. I know that now.

But I should probably stop writing before I say something I regret later.

Have a good night, Sharon.

Yours,
Tammy

Wednesday, June 28, 1978

Dear Tammy,

I don't think we should worry about saying things we regret. We made a pledge, and pledges are serious business.

Besides, there are some things I want to say now that I might finally be starting to figure things out.

What Midge said tonight made something shift inside my head. It's as though I've been trying to solve a puzzle for months, maybe years, but I was missing a piece the whole time, and tonight I might have found it. It's scary to think about what it could mean, but it's still a huge relief to have it worked out.

It would be good to talk about it all. Especially with you. Since a lot of it's about you.

Not tonight, though. We'd have to whisper, and that's not what I want. Could we meet after work tomorrow? There's a coffee shop on Felton where we shouldn't see anyone we know.

What do you think?

Yours,
Sharon

P.S. I see what you meant. Writing that down wasn't easy, pledge or no pledge.

Wednesday, June 28, 1978

Dear Sharon,

<u>Yes.</u> Tomorrow after work. I switched my shift with Peter so I could go to SFAI tomorrow and work in the darkroom, but I should be done by the time you're finished babysitting. I'll come meet you at the coffee shop right away.

And as much as I hate to say it, we should probably stop writing now. You have to be at the O'Sullivans' early, and running after toddlers is hard on no sleep.

Yours,
Tammy

P.S. Given the pledge and all, I'll admit—I'm already counting down the hours.

Dear Diary,

I spent most of today in gleeful anticipation. It feels like a million years ago now.

I was distracted all through babysitting. Penny kept having to shout to get my attention. When Mr. O'Sullivan finally got home, a few minutes earlier than usual, I hugged the kids goodbye and sped out the door.

I wanted to run home and change so I could beat Tammy to the coffee shop. I knew what I wanted to say to her, but it'd be easier if I was sitting down when she arrived. I needed time to breathe, or I'd get flustered and blush and probably forget everything I'd practiced in my head.

My hands trembled, heavy with a mix of eagerness and nerves, as I pushed open our front door. I expected Mom to be home alone, since Peter was working Tammy's usual shift, but I'd barely cracked open the front door before I heard a voice floating out from the living room.

At first I thought Mom was watching TV, but it was too early for <u>The Waltons</u>. Besides, the voice was extremely familiar.

"Ah, that must be your daughter now," the voice said. My breath caught. "Sharon, how lovely to meet you at last!"

A middle-aged woman with perfectly teased brown hair was sitting on the couch next to my mother, holding a lipstick-stained coffee mug and smiling up at me.

I stepped inside fast and locked the door behind me, pressing my back against it and fervently praying for Tammy not to come home.

I'd never seen Aunt Mandy before, but I was as certain it was her as I had been the morning Tammy first showed up at my door. Some people are impossible to mistake.

I had to get rid of her, and fast. If Tammy saw her, she'd be terrified.

But she was probably already at the coffee shop. Right? Please, God, let Tammy be at the coffee shop.

Except—what if she wanted to change clothes first, too? Besides, what was her aunt doing here, talking to my mother?

Wait. Wait. Oh, God.

What if Aunt Mandy already told Mom?

Oh, God, oh, God, oh God…

"Sharon, dear, you look as though you've seen a ghost." Aunt Mandy set her mug on the coffee table next to a Tupperware dish and stood, smoothing out her spotless blue dress. Mom didn't get up, but she was beaming, looking way too cheerful for someone sitting next to one of the worst human beings on the planet.

No—no, that was a good thing. If Mom was smiling, Tammy's aunt must not have told her anything significant. Yet.

Aunt Mandy held out her hand, beckoning to me, her smile wide and brittle. "I was just visiting with your mother. Come, sit with us and have a treat."

"Tammy's aunt was kind enough to bring over some delicious homemade cookies." Mom brushed crumbs off her fingers and reached for the Tupperware dish. "I told her we'd thought Tammy didn't have any other family, but she says the two of you have spoken before?"

"I, ah…"

I was trapped.

There was nothing I could say to both of them together. If Peter were here, or Tammy, they'd know how to handle this. They'd have some smooth lie ready to go, but I was too terrified to speak.

No. I couldn't think that way. Aunt Mandy could do a lot more damage to Peter and Tammy than she could to me. I had to be the one to fix this, somehow.

"I was telling your mother how much we've appreciated your positive influence on my niece." Aunt Mandy's smile was thick and saccharine. "You're such a sweet Christian girl, and we know how much you wanted to help your pen pal. Unfortunately I fear her situation is, well…beyond the help of lay people such as ourselves."

Mom's smile faded as she turned to Aunt Mandy. "The poor girl. You think the situation's that bad?"

Mom wouldn't call Tammy a "poor girl" if she knew the truth. She wouldn't act sympathetic—just outraged. Aunt Mandy couldn't have told her the specifics of Tammy's "situation"…yet.

"It may well be." Aunt Mandy made a face as though she'd just bit down on a plump homosexual lemon and turned back to me. "That's why it's very important that I speak with Tammy. Your mother said you'd know where to find her. I already went by the market where she works, but a young man—I assume he was your brother—was there alone."

"Yes, I wasn't sure what Tammy's plans were for today." Mom tilted her head at me. "Will she be coming to the house soon? She'll be so happy to see her aunt."

"Of course she will." Aunt Mandy didn't let me get a word in. Not that I had any idea what I could've possibly said. "In any case,

Sharon, just let me know what Tammy's up to. I told your mother I was sure you'd want to help. A good girl like you would never hesitate to tell an adult what she needs to know."

The threat in her words made me swallow tightly. I had to think of some sort of lie. Anything at all. "Um, she's, er—Tammy is..."

A key turned in the lock behind me.

"Ah, that must be her now. Never mind, Sharon." Aunt Mandy walked swiftly toward the door, trying to pass me, but I didn't budge. She paused, waiting for me to step aside, meeting my eyes with a challenge in her own.

I didn't look away. Maybe I couldn't fix this with words, but at the very least I could physically put myself between Tammy and the person who wanted to hurt her.

The door opened a crack. I turned, ready to tell her to run, but it was my brother who peered through the gap, his mouth quirked in confusion. There was no sign of Tammy with him. He pushed the door open the rest of the way, until he was face-to-face with Aunt Mandy.

"Oh, you must be Sharon's brother." Her fake-sweet voice rang out behind me. I didn't turn to look, but I could hear her smiling that sick smile again. "I spotted you at the store. What a strapping young man you are."

Peter turned back to me, his eyes saucer-wide.

We were wasting time. Tammy could get here any second. I stepped forward, trying to slip out the door behind Peter so I could catch her before she came in, but he didn't move.

"Sharon?" Mom asked behind me, sounding confused. "Are you going out again?"

"My name is Mrs. Dale, Peter," Aunt Mandy said pleasantly. "We spoke on the phone once. Your sister is being very resistant to helping your poor friend Tammy, but I'm sure you'll be more reasonable. After all, I've heard so much about you."

I stopped moving.

She wouldn't tell Mom about Peter. Would she?

Of course she would. She had no reason not to.

Peter's face had gone white as he registered the threat.

"Mom." I turned around. I couldn't stand there, paralyzed, any longer. "Don't believe anything she tells you. She isn't here because she wants to help, she's only—"

"I'm gay, Mom."

My brother's voice sliced through the room.

Mom froze on the sofa, her lips parted half an inch, her eyes unblinking. Even Aunt Mandy looked stunned.

"I'm sorry, if—" Peter swallowed. I turned back to face him, trying to support him with silent, steady eyes, but he was looking straight at Mom, a pleading expression on his face. "I'm really sorry if that upsets you, but it's who I am. Tammy is, too—that's why she had to leave home. Her aunt's probably here to drag her back for electroshock therapy or something. So...now I guess you know everything we've been so scared to say all along."

A quiet moment passed. Mom hadn't moved.

Peter glanced my way. He nodded, a small movement, but enough for me to see.

This was my chance. Peter was wrong—Mom didn't know everything. She didn't know about me.

I could tell her. I should tell her. Telling her meant I'd never have to lie again.

But I hadn't even told Tammy yet. I still wasn't sure I understood it all myself.

Aunt Mandy jumped in to fill the silence.

"Peter." Her smile had gone thin. "You're a very confused boy, and I feel a great deal of pity for you, but I do hope you understand you've just broken your mother's heart."

I wanted to kick her, but Peter didn't even seem to hear. He was focused solely on Mom, his eyes watery.

Aunt Mandy lifted a sleek brown canvas purse onto her shoulder. "Mrs. Hawkins, this should be a family conversation. I'll pray for your son to find guidance through our Holy Lord and Savior. Now, I'll see myself out. It was a pleasure meeting you."

She was going to look for Tammy. What would she do when she found her? Drag her kicking and screaming back to Orange County to face her family's wrath? Or was she only here because Tammy had proof that she and her husband were a pair of opportunistic thieves?

I wasn't waiting to find out.

I shoved past Aunt Mandy, ignoring her yelp of complaint, and tore through the door and down the front steps. She was quick to follow in my wake, moving with astonishing speed in her brown suede pumps.

"You're wise to leave, Sharon." Her breath was cool and steady over my shoulder, as though we weren't running at all. "No need to get involved in this messy situation with your brother. Let's find Tammy so we can get her the help she needs, and I'll be on my way."

I whipped around to face her. "Shut UP!"

Aunt Mandy stepped back, her eyes widening in surprise. She wasn't expecting me to shout at her. Neither was I.

"After what you just did?" I stood, my chest heaving. "You don't know me, or my brother. You couldn't care less if you've destroyed our family. All you care about is..."

But I couldn't muster the rest of what I wanted to say.

I wanted to tell her to stop pretending she'd come here to help anyone. She only cares about herself—that's all she's ever cared about. She thinks she's so important, that her church, her town, is her very own little kingdom.

But she's going to lose. And when that happens, she'll be left with <u>nothing</u>. Her, and all the others like her. They can keep trying to stop the world from changing, but nothing they do will make them matter in the end.

I wanted to shout the words loud enough for my entire block to hear. But my chest was heaving, and my voice couldn't squeeze through the anger in my throat.

Aunt Mandy's smile had faded a little, though. "Your brother is...confused."

I wanted to tell her Peter wasn't confused at all. He understood a lot more about the world than I did. And he knew a Hell of a lot more than her.

From the new tilt to her head and the thin line pressed between her lips, I wondered for a second if Tammy's aunt might actually be starting to realize just how badly she'd screwed things up for my brother. I wondered if she might even feel guilty for it. Before either of us could say any more, though, footsteps rang out on the sidewalk, then stopped abruptly.

I turned. Tammy was watching us from ten feet back, her mouth hanging open, her purse slung over her shoulder.

She spoke quietly, but clearly. "Hi, Aunt Mandy."

The strange expression on Mrs. Dale's face transformed instantly into her usual sickly smile. "Tammy! Good heavens, your hair is so...well, never mind. Your friend here was just about to bring me to you, but I'm delighted you found us instead."

"Don't bother lying." Tammy didn't smile back. Her lower lip was trembling.

I wanted to shout at Aunt Mandy to get away from us, to leave

Tammy alone. Yet when I opened my mouth, it was all I could do not to choke out a sob.

"You don't have to pretend for Sharon's benefit." Tammy lifted her chin. "She already knows the truth. Every bit of it."

"Then this should be easy." Aunt Mandy's smile didn't fade a smidgen. "Let's just get your things, and we'll go back home."

"Don't act like you care about me going back." Tammy reached into the purse on her shoulder, fumbling with the flap. Her eyes filled with tears, but her voice never lost its strength. "I know you don't want me screwing up your perfect fucking family portrait."

Aunt Mandy's smile finally faltered at sound of the word fuck-ing. "Young lady, I don't know what you—"

"Here. This is what you came for. The only one of my things that matters to you."

Tammy pulled a small, flat brown object from her purse and tossed it to the ground. Aunt Mandy's eyes lit up. She stepped forward, bending down to snatch it up in an instant.

The check register.

Tammy was right. Her aunt didn't come here for her at all.

Now my mother knew about Peter. She knew about Tammy, too. All for nothing.

"Is there some favor you're expecting in exchange for this?" Aunt Mandy's smile was slightly warmer than it had been before. It's possible she was genuinely happy.

"I'm not stupid enough to expect anything from you." Tammy crossed her arms. Her eyes shone with tears. "All I want is for you to leave me alone. You can consider that a parting gift."

"I see." The glee in her aunt's eyes didn't lessen. "Your parents will be disappointed you won't be coming back, but I suppose, if that's your choice…"

"It is."

"Well, it may turn out to be a blessing." Aunt Mandy's eyes glittered. "Your family should see that soon enough. If they haven't already."

"Go to Hell." Tammy balled both hands into fists.

"Such <u>language</u> you've learned in San Francisco." Aunt Mandy chuckled. "Well, I'll be on my way. Take care, girls."

We waited as she walked slowly, casually, away from us, her hurried movements from a short while ago replaced by a light spring in her step.

I understood the full depths of Tammy's hatred now.

I waited until her aunt had turned the corner and disappeared from sight before I turned back to Tammy. "Are you all right?"

She wiped the last of the tears off her face, her gaze focused on the spot where Mrs. Dale had disappeared. "I honestly don't know."

"I'm so sorry." I wanted to touch her somehow, but I didn't want to startle her. I settled for laying a few light fingers on her elbow. If she noticed, she didn't show it. "I tried to catch up to you before she could, but—"

Tammy let out a short laugh. "There was nothing you could've done to stop her when she was on a tear like that. We're lucky we got out alive."

"I guess." I rocked back on my heels and took my hand off her arm. I knew she was upset, but I couldn't help wishing she'd look at me. "Also, um. I should tell you. She came to the house first and talked to Mom. Peter got home, and your aunt was threatening him, and…he told Mom about him. And you."

Now Tammy did look my way. "What did your mom say?"

"Nothing. I came to find you before she'd answered. She seemed upset, though."

"Oh." Tammy turned back to the house. We were halfway down the block, but we could see the front steps, looking the same as ever.

There was no hint that a catastrophe had just happened inside. "Then I guess I'd better not go in."

"I mean…it's probably all right. She already said you could stay with us." But I could hear the uncertainty in my words. Mom had said that before she knew.

"I don't think so. But <u>you</u> should go in. You don't want to leave your brother alone right now."

Shit. I should've thought of that. "You're right."

"Take this with you." Tammy pulled a notebook out of her purse. It was bent, the spiral bindings coming uncurled. She opened it, ripped out a sheet of paper, and folded it in half. "I wrote it last week, but I chickened out before I could give it to you. This is what I would've said at the coffee shop today."

I took the paper. "Thank you. Tammy, I'm sorry, I…"

"Don't worry about it. Just go back in, please."

"What about you? Where will <u>you</u> go?"

She shrugged. "I don't know. You can call me at the store. Leave a message with Rosa and I'll get it tomorrow."

"What about until then? You can't walk around the city all night again."

"I'll figure something out. Don't worry."

I shifted on my feet. This felt too much like a goodbye, and I still had a lot I needed to say to her. "I'll come meet you at the store tomorrow."

"Don't. I'm not sure when I'll be around—it depends on a lot of things. Besides, your brother's going to need you."

She was right. Still— "I'm so sorry this happened, Tammy."

"Me, too." She let out a tiny choking sound. "God, I'm <u>so</u> sorry. I ruined everything for your family."

"You didn't. It's not that simple. Besides, none of this is your fault, not even a little bit."

She shook her head. "There's no point trying to figure this out now. Go. I'll see you later."

I wanted to touch her again. Instead I nodded and turned back toward home.

I told myself it was all right as I crossed the short distance up the block. I told myself I'd see her again. Soon.

But she was already out of sight when I climbed the steps and twisted the knob on the front door.

It was unlocked. The living room was quiet and empty. I stepped across it warily, as though I was walking into a war zone and had to keep alert for stray bullets.

"Mom?" I called. "Peter?"

My only answer was dishes rattling in the kitchen. I stepped through the door.

Mom was at the sink, twisting the faucet to run water over the breakfast plates. They were piled high, crusted with old syrup. I was supposed to have washed them this morning. Mom turned the water on full blast and shoved a plate under the tap.

"Mom?"

At first I didn't think she'd heard me, but a moment later she turned her head without meeting my eyes. "Hi, Sharon."

"Is Peter upstairs?"

She turned back to the dishes. "That girl can't stay here anymore. I don't want you seeing her again."

I swallowed. "Mom, she didn't do anything wrong, she—"

"You <u>lied</u> to me." She wouldn't look at me. "You might think I'm a fool, but I'm still your mother and <u>you're</u> still a child, and I will not allow you to carry on this way."

"I didn't—"

"That's <u>enough</u>. You're grounded for the rest of the summer. I'll pack up that girl's things and put them on the porch. She can come pick them up when we're not home, or if she doesn't, I'll throw them in the garbage, but she's not setting foot inside this house again. Don't go thinking you'll be calling her or writing to her, either. Whatever it is that's been happening to this family, it ends now."

I gulped, tears pricking at my eyes. "I'll pack her stuff. Peter can help me."

"I don't want you touching her things."

What did Mom think? That Tammy was contagious? "Okay. I'll just go upstairs then. Is Peter—?"

"Your brother's not here." Mom finally turned off the tap.

"What? Isn't he grounded, too?"

"No. He's gone."

"What?" I didn't understand.

Or...maybe I did.

"I told you. He's gone. He isn't coming back." Mom turned her back on me, wrapping her arms around herself, her fingertips turning white as she gripped her elbows. She let out a hiccup, then a sob. "He said...he asked me to tell you goodbye."

Yours,
Sharon

FALL, 1978

Friday, September 22, 1978

Dear Tammy,

Hi.

I'm writing this early in the morning, staring out my window at the fog. I couldn't sleep. I can't stop thinking.

It's been so long since I saw you. More than two months—gosh, it was June when you got here, and it was still June when your aunt showed up and everything went to Hell.

Please believe me, I tried to call you at the store the way we planned, but Mom wouldn't let me touch the phone for two days after you left. She unplugged both extensions, took the phones into her room, and hid them. She made me call in sick to the O'Sullivans, too, even though it meant Mr. O'Sullivan couldn't go to work. When she finally let me go back to babysitting she made me swear on Jesus's name I wouldn't use the phone while I was there, and, well... I did it, anyway. I didn't think Jesus would mind. But Rosa told me you'd quit, and you hadn't given them a number to reach you. She sounded sad about it, but I bet I sounded sadder.

I'm so sorry, Tammy. There were so many things I wanted to say to your aunt that day, but I couldn't do it. I wanted to stop what was happening, but I didn't know how. I was scared. So scared I was useless.

I've been permanently grounded since you left. I can only leave the house for babysitting and church, and school, too, now that it's started back up. Mom barely goes out, either, so we do a lot of avoiding each other. She spends most of the time in her room with the door shut. Even more than she used to.

I guess that's mostly what I've been doing, too. I miss hanging out at the bookstore. I miss going to clubs, too, but not as much as I thought I would. I've got my records—I still listen to <u>Horses</u> every night—but going to shows, losing myself in the anger there...I don't need that as much as I used to. I'm angry because I'm sick of everyone expecting me to want the same things they want, but I don't need to yell about that as much as I did before. Instead I'm thinking more about the things I <u>do</u> want, and how to make them happen.

I think about you every day, Tammy. Ever since I talked to Rosa, I've been desperate to know if you were still in the city, and if your aunt went looking for you again. And a lot of other things, too.

I know the answer to the first question, finally. My brother called yesterday while Mom was at a faculty meeting. He'd heard through the Castro grapevine that you're staying with Evelyn and her roommates at their house near Valencia. He couldn't get your phone number, but he found your address so I could write to you. He's a good brother.

I was so happy when I heard that you'd found a place. So, so, <u>so</u> happy. I'm glad you're with friends, but mostly I'm just glad you're okay.

Peter even heard you're going to be in some kind of art show soon. That's so awesome! Maybe I can sneak out to see it.

I can't help being angry you had to go hunting for somewhere to live, though, with no help from your family at all, even after they found out where you were. You're only seventeen, the same as me. As Mom tells me over and over, I'm legally a child, which means I'm her responsibility. Well, that makes you your parents' responsibility.

It's different for Peter. Where he lives is his choice, and things between him and our mother are...not good.

They still haven't seen each other, not since that day. He told me the rest of what happened, though.

As soon as your aunt and I left the house, Mom started crying. Peter went over to the couch and tried to reassure her, and at first he thought it was working, but then she started to scream. She shouted about how she hadn't raised Peter to be gay and it was our father's fault for walking out on us and...well, you get the idea.

So Peter left. He went up to his room, grabbed some clothes and some books, came back downstairs, and walked out the back door.

Mom didn't speak the whole time he was packing up. When he said goodbye she just sat on the couch, staring out the living-room window, as though if she ignored what was happening, my brother would magically start being straight.

He hasn't been back to the house since, but I've seen him a few times. He's come to visit me at my babysitting jobs, but it's hard for him to get away from work much, so mostly we talk when he calls the house. He always waits until he knows Mom will be out.

He's living with a bunch of guys on Polk Street. Dean invited him to move to Palo Alto, but he decided to stay in the city and take classes at CCSF instead. He's got a new job at a restaurant that pays a lot more than he used to get at Javi's, so he can cover his own rent and tuition.

Mom wrote him a letter a couple of weeks ago and asked me to mail it to him. She wants him to move back home. She offered to pay his tuition to State the way they'd planned, but she made it clear he'd have to live under her rules.

He wrote back and said no. He's making his own choices now.

I'm happy for him, but...I've lost him, Tammy. I always knew I would someday, but I wasn't ready for it to happen this fast. He'll always be my brother, but he isn't <u>mine</u> anymore.

But that doesn't bother me as much as I thought it would, either. When I see him now, he looks so <u>happy</u>. He's finally getting to be himself, even if he's doing it without me.

Anyway, I...

Okay, look. Tammy, I've got to admit, I'm kind of stalling.

I didn't sit down to write this letter because I wanted to give you an update on my family. I sat down to write because I wanted to tell you everything I didn't get to say that day.

I read the letter you gave me. It was incredible, Tammy. Still, though...you wrote that months ago. With everything that's happened, the way you feel might've changed. I totally understand if that's what happened.

But for me...the way I feel has only gotten stronger.

So, here goes. I'm going to write all this, straight through, without going back to cross anything out or erase it.

I think I'm bisexual.

And...it's like you said in your letter. I feel the same way you did. I want to share the world with you, too.

Wow. Okay. I wrote that down. Everything else should be easy from here, right?

No—this isn't easy at all. My hands are shaking so hard I can barely write. The idea of saying that was so scary, for so long.

I'm sorry if knowing this makes you feel awkward. I missed my chance back on Gay Freedom Day, and that's my own fault.

And you'd have every right to hate me after the way I completely failed to help when your aunt was here. Or maybe you're dating one of those cool women you live with now, and you'd have every right to do that, too.

I just needed you to know.

There's only one other thing I have to do, and then I'll make sure you get this letter. I can't mail it—there isn't time—but I've got a plan. The thing I have to do first is a big deal, a <u>really</u> big deal, but writing this gave me the courage I needed.

I'm so sorry. Even after we made our pledge, it took me this long to be truly, totally honest.

It took me longer to be honest with myself, too, but I'm trying to do better on that front as well. Starting right now.

Yours,
Sharon

Friday, September 22, 1978

Dear Diary,

This is going to be messy, since I'm writing on a bus. There's no way I'll have time to write about everything that's happened so far before we have to stop, but I need to get down what I can before I start to forget.

The first thing I did this morning, after I finished my letter to Tammy and slid it into my backpack, was go see my mother.

I knocked lightly on her bedroom door and hefted the backpack on my shoulder. Mom doesn't come out of her room much lately unless it's for work or church. I've started eating alone most nights, standing up in the kitchen. I've become an expert on stirring Rice-A-Roni.

I waited until I heard movement on the other side of the door. First came rustling sheets, and a minute later, soft footsteps. It was past seven on a school day, but when the door swung open Mom was still in her nightgown, her hair matted to her head. She's been sleeping later since Peter moved out. "What is it, Sharon?"

I waited to see if she'd notice I was already showered and dressed, and very much not in my Holy Angels uniform, but she just blinked wearily and waited for me to talk.

It's been hard for her. I know it has. But that doesn't make what she did okay.

"I have to tell you something." I bit my lower lip. I've started doing that lately. It was something Alex told us at the bookstore—that a tiny bit of pain could help her remember it was worth doing scary things. "Mom...I'm bisexual."

"No," she answered instantly. I was fighting to stay calm, not to let myself get overwhelmed by the rush of saying what I'd said, but I knew I needed to listen carefully to my mother's every word. "No. You aren't. You don't understand what that means, Sharon. I know you think you do, growing up in your generation and in this city, but that's because I haven't done a better job of showing you and your brother how the world works."

It was the most I'd heard her say in weeks. I got a strong impression she'd already had this speech prepared.

She knew.

How long? Did she know before I did?

I bit my lip again.

"You're wrong, Mom." I took a deep breath to steady myself. "We know how the world works, but that doesn't change who we are."

"Stop this." Mom took a deep breath of her own and turned away. "We'll be late for school. I'll drive us today, and then we'll both come straight home after the final bell so we can discuss this."

"I'm not going to school today." I swallowed, then squared my shoulders and lifted my chin. "Harvey Milk is debating Senator Briggs near L.A. and a group of us are driving down to hold a rally."

"You're doing no such thing." She spat the words.

"I'm sorry you're upset, but I'm leaving now." I took a step backward, then another.

"You are not." Mom followed me out into the hall, pulling her nightgown tighter around her as I moved toward the stairs. The cords in her neck were straining. "Your brother's a legal adult, and unfortunately that gives him the right to go where he pleases, but I forbid you to leave this house."

I started down the stairs.

"Sharon!"

"Goodbye, Mom." I was already halfway down. "I'll be back to-night."

I unlocked the front door and stepped outside, my teeth digging into my lip so hard I tasted blood.

I didn't look back until I'd shut the door. I waited on the stoop to see if she'd come after me, but I didn't hear anything. It was a still morning, and the house was dark and quiet.

I took another deep breath. In, out. One more. Then I turned around and started walking, my backpack heavy on my shoulders.

Crap, the bus is stopping. More later.

Yours,
Sharon

Friday, September 22, 1978

Dear Harvey,

I can't believe my life's turned into what it's become. Some mornings I wake up and lie in bed staring at the fire escape out past the window curtains and I think, over and over, I'm here.

My life has turned out so much better than I ever imagined it could, Harvey.

Yet…there's still something missing.

I guess there's no use dwelling on it. No one gets to have everything they've ever wanted.

I just wish I could see her, Harvey. One more time.

Shit, I've got to go. Evelyn's already up and yelling. If I make the bus late she'll probably toss me out a window before we hit Oakland.

See you this afternoon.

Peace & joy,
Tammy

P.S. Is it okay that I'm still writing to you? I know it's kind of strange now that I have real friends, but I still like to think of you listening to what I have to say.

Friday, September 22, 1978

Dear Diary,

We're crammed back onto the bus. The others are starting to doze off, so it's a good time to pick up from my last entry. There's still so much I need to get down on paper.

I left Mom with my heart pounding and went straight to the bus stop. I was in luck—one pulled up seconds later. My heart kept on pounding for the entire Muni ride north, but when I finally stepped off onto Valencia, I could hear horns honking and cable cars clanging, and I started to feel like myself again. A second later, when I heard my brother shouting, that sealed the deal.

"Sis! You're late!"

"Oh, my gosh!" I started to panic, looking at my watch as Peter ran toward me...until I realized he'd obviously just gotten there himself. There was no sign of the rented VW bus that was supposed to pick us up at the corner yet. I wasn't late at all. "Jerk."

"Did I fool you?" He grinned.

"Shut up." I elbowed him.

"Sorry. I wanted to see if I could get you to say 'Oh, my gosh' again."

I hugged him. He hugged me back.

I've missed my brother so, so, so much.

His hair's been getting longer since he got out from under the St. John's dress code, and today his curls hung down to frame his face. He's got a new wardrobe, too—a collection of flannel shirts and Levi's and Converse sneakers assembled from various thrift shops. I'd asked if he needed me to bring anything from home with me, and he'd said he wanted a few books, but no clothes. He's started over fresh.

I finally released him and reached into my backpack. "Your books are really heavy," I told him as I handed them over.

"Sorry. Thanks for being my pack mule."

"Don't mention it." I glanced around to make sure no one was listening, but Evelyn and Leonard and the others were milling around by the corner, talking and laughing. Everyone's been waiting for this day for a long, long time. "I, um... I told Mom."

Peter's eyes widened. "When?"

"This morning."

He whistled. "How'd she take it?"

"Not well, but I expected that."

He nodded slowly. "Good for you. I have faith she'll come around. Seriously, I do."

I nodded, too, biting my lip again.

"Also..." He lowered his voice, his eyes flicking up to a point over my left shoulder. "Guess who just got here."

Suddenly it was hard to breathe. I closed my eyes.

"Hey, Peter." Her voice was so familiar I might as well have heard it yesterday instead of months ago. Then her footsteps slowed behind me, and I heard her quick inhale. "Oh, my God."

It was something from a dream. Literally. I've had this dream.

"Oh, my God!" The footsteps came again, faster and closer. "Sharon? Is that you?"

I turned in time to see a whirl of short blond hair and denim as Tammy flung her arms around me.

Okay, I guess she didn't <u>completely</u> hate me.

I was scared to hug her as long as I did Peter, though, so I pulled back. Her smile faded a little, but her blue eyes stayed bright. Peter grinned and hugged her, too, then mumbled something about checking on Dean and disappeared.

"Sharon!" Tammy bounced in her sneakers. "I can't believe you're here!"

"I know!" I was probably grinning like a fool—she'd said my name, <u>twice</u>, and it sounded exactly as good as it always used to—but I tried to rein it in. I had the letter in my backpack, and I'd give it to her when I found the right time, but first I wanted to figure out if Tammy was just happy to see me or if there was any chance she might still be open to something bigger. "I'm <u>so</u> sorry. I've been grounded ever since you left. My mom wouldn't let me touch the phone, and then I didn't know how to reach you, and—"

"No, no, <u>I'm</u> so sorry." Tammy shook her head, her smile now totally evaporated. "I got you and your brother into so much trouble. I messed up your entire <u>life</u>."

"Are you kidding? My life was so much better when you were in it." I couldn't keep going or I'd say too much. "Did your aunt ever come back?"

"Not a chance. Once she had what she wanted, she was done with me." Tammy laughed. "All for the better. Evelyn helped me get enrolled at Mission High, and I'm working three nights a week at the bookstore. I'm their first paid employee. Lisa thinks I might be able to get a scholarship to SFAI next year. It's a completely different universe from my old life."

I beamed. I was jealous of her freedom, but more than that, I was thrilled for her. "That's amazing. I mean, I'd heard you were living with Evelyn and the others, and I'm glad you're going to school and everything. Also I was wondering if, um—"

"Everybody!" Evelyn shouted from the corner. An ancient pale blue Volkswagen bus was trundling up to the curb, spewing exhaust behind it. Lisa was at the wheel, holding a cigarette out the window and twisting around to say something to Alex in the seat beside her. "Get in fast, it's gonna be a tight squeeze and we're running late!"

I turned back to Tammy and forced a laugh. Casual. I had to act casual today. "Guess we'd better..."

She laughed, too, but hers didn't seem any more natural than mine. It was the first time I could remember us ever being awkward around each other. "Guess so."

We were the last ones onto the bus, which turned out to be even less roomy than it looked. Behind Lisa and Alex were two wide bench seats, each of them already jammed with people sitting half on top of each other. Evelyn and Becky greeted me warmly, but there was no space for us in their middle row. Suitcases, boxes packed with brochures, rubber-banded campaign signs, and a big black trash bag stretched out over a wide rectangular frame were already stacked in the luggage section at the back, so we couldn't sit there, either.

Peter and Dean were wedged onto the three-seater back bench with two other guys. The only spot in the entire bus that wasn't occupied by people or stuff was the small patch of floor directly in front of them.

I glanced at Tammy. She shrugged. We stuffed ourselves into the space, carefully folding our legs and arms between the guys' shins and resting our backs against the seat in front of us. We had no choice but to squish against each other, shoulder-to-shoulder and hip-to-hip, and I was blushing from head-to-toe by the time we got into place.

"Hope we all remembered to brush our teeth this morning," Dean said brightly, stretching his arms out across the other three guys. The whole bus laughed.

"It'll be six hours of luxury," Tammy chirped, earning an even bigger laugh from the group. Laughter comes easily when you're as excited about what you're about to do as we were.

As soon as we hit the highway, I knew why Lisa got picked to drive. This should be a six-hour trip, but at the rate we've been speeding past the traffic on I-5, we'll be south of L.A. by lunch.

"Are you staying over?" Tammy asked me as Lisa whipped across two lanes to pass a tractor-trailer.

I shook my head, gripping the seat behind me. "I promised Mom I'd be back tonight. You're staying?"

"Yeah, we're crashing with a friend of Leonard's in Pasadena. There's another bus heading back Sunday. Lisa and Alex and some of the others have pieces in an art show tomorrow down there, and they got permission for me to show a piece, too. That's it right there." She pointed to the enormous trash-bag-wrapped rectangle.

My eyes bugged out. "It's huge! Is it a collage?"

"Yeah. Something new I've been working on. It started out as the same format I've always done, but Alex showed me how to use the enlargers in the darkroom, and I wound up doing it on a bigger scale. I'd show you, but there's no space to take it out in here."

"That sounds incredible. I wish I could come to the show." I wouldn't mind crashing overnight with Leonard's friend, either. Getting in a few extra hours in close quarters with Tammy.

"Bad idea, Shar." Peter bumped my ankle with his sneaker. "Mom might actually have a heart attack."

"Try to stay on your mom's good side as long as you can, Sharon," Alex called, twisting around from the front seat. "I need you in one piece so you can join the softball team in the spring."

"I'll probably still be grounded," I called back, but she laughed.

Slowly, the conversations in the bus got quieter and then died off, the others lost in thought or drifting off to sleep. I got out my diary and wrote that last entry. Then, south of Bakersfield, Lisa pulled over at a rest stop.

Everyone charged to the bathrooms while Tammy, Evelyn, and I hung back. Evelyn pulled a cigarette out of her purse and paused to light it.

"Hey, I didn't get to hug you yet." Evelyn grinned and gave me a side-hug. "How've you been holding up on your own in Dan White territory?"

I shrugged. I didn't want to bring everyone down by talking about how isolated I've been. "Okay, I guess."

"We've missed you at the bookstore."

"I'm sorry I haven't been able to volunteer. My mom will barely let me out of the house."

"I know how that goes. Believe me." Evelyn's lips spread in a sympathetic smile. "Thanks again for bringing Tammy to us, though. She's hand-sold more books in the past two months than I have in the past year. I told her if she wants to keep working a side gig while she's making her way in the art world, she's always welcome."

"Since it's not as if I've got a future working in the school system or anything," Tammy said. They both laughed, but I couldn't join in.

According to the <u>Chronicle</u>, the polling numbers for Prop 6 look worse than ever. It'll pass in November, and soon it'll be illegal for people like us to work at public schools. I guess I have to either leave the state or come up with a new career plan.

Of course, I could always keep quiet about who I am. But I'm not counting that as an option anymore.

"It'll be all right, Sharon," Evelyn said, her voice resolute. "We've lost every fight so far, but we'll win the war. That's why Harvey's doing these debates—to change as many hearts and minds as we can. Every time we go out into the community, we're showing the public that gay people are no different from them."

"Hearts and minds. Right."

"Anyway, I've got to pee or I'll explode. See you in a minute."

Evelyn paused before she took off, raising her eyebrows at Tammy. Tammy laughed, waving as Evelyn started up the hill toward the low white building.

I turned my back to the highway. If you could've shut out the sounds of the traffic rushing past, it would've been a beautiful spot. The hills ahead of us were dotted with green and brown. Gentle slopes rose to gentle peaks and dipped back down again.

"So, um..." Next to me, Tammy shifted on her feet. I met her gaze, then blushed and looked down at the grass. It was the first time we'd been alone since the day she'd left.

I could've given her the letter then and there. I had it with me, folded neatly into squares in my back pocket. But having her so close made me not want to wait for her to read it.

I thought again about what she'd said in her last letter. The line that had run through my head every day since. If not every hour.

I want to share that world with you.

I lifted my gaze to Tammy's face. She was smiling.

"I, um..." I blushed again and looked up at the hills. Maybe I should just say it. Maybe it could be that simple. "I came out to my mom this morning. Told her I..." I bit my lip again. "I'm bisexual."

"You did?" Tammy grabbed my elbow and cracked a wide smile. "Sharon, that's wonderful! Congratulations!"

She'd said my name again. "You really think so?"

"Of course! This is a big deal!"

"What if it turns out to be terrible? The way it did for you, and

Peter? Mom acted as if she was going to lock me in my room for the rest of my life."

"Well, she's the one who's wrong. What you did takes so much courage. I never had the nerve to come out, and it's not as if that made life any easier."

I hadn't thought of it that way. "You had the nerve to curse at your aunt, though."

"I did, didn't I?" She grinned. She was still squeezing my elbow. "So, bisexual, huh? You know, Becky's bi, too."

"Really? I thought most of that group was gay."

"They are. Becky doesn't say much about being bi, but I bet she'd talk to you if you wanted. She told me some lesbians don't trust bisexual women, but she thinks that's stupid and I do, too. I don't think any of our friends think that way."

"I hope they don't."

"Anyway..." Tammy's smile faded a little. "So did you, um...get back together with Kevin?"

"No. I see him at church sometimes, but he mostly ignores me now. I don't think there's any risk of us getting back together even if I wanted to. Which I don't."

It was the perfect opportunity to ask if she was seeing anyone. If I could find the words.

"I'm so sorry about what happened." Tammy spoke in a rush before I could try. "I'm shocked you're willing to see me after everything. I showed up at your house uninvited and caused a ton of problems, and now you had to tell your mom. And your brother... God, I can't imagine how it's been for him."

"None of that's your fault. Besides, my brother's doing great. And I wanted to tell her."

"It is my fault. I should've known my aunt would come after me. I'm the one who stole that stupid check register, and—"

"What your aunt did was <u>her</u> choice." I sighed. "Tammy, please, there's something I—"

"Back on the bus!" This time it was Alex who was shouting. The rest of the group was charging down the hill from the rest stop. "We're making good time, and we're not stopping again even if Anita Bryant and her army of straight angels try to pass us on 101!"

Tammy looked at me with quizzical eyes. I turned away.

She feels guilty. She feels <u>sorry</u> for me.

She has a perfect, happy life in the Mission, and I'm the same boring, sheltered girl I've always been down in District Eight. It would be selfish of me to interfere with all the great things that are happening for her by trying to drag her back into <u>my</u> messy world.

Tammy's moved on. I've got to do the same thing.

We climbed onto the bus in silence. As soon as we were crammed into our spots on the floor again, I shoved the letter into the bottom of my backpack, crumpling it up into a ball. Twenty minutes later, when Tammy's eyes drifted closed, I took my diary back out so I could write this down.

We're getting close now, though. People are starting to wake up, and Tammy's stirring, too. I'll try to write more later.

Yours,
Sharon

Friday, September 22, 1978

Dear Diary,

Oh, my God. Oh, my God. What a day this was.

It first got intense during the demonstration this afternoon.

"VOTE NO ON PROPOSITION 6!" I shouted, waving the sign over my head at the cars passing by. "SUPPORT HUMAN RIGHTS FOR ALL!"

Our group had packed the narrow sidewalk. Behind us stood the high-school gym where Harvey was getting ready to debate Senator Briggs, and across the street was a bored-looking photographer from the local paper. He'd snapped a few pictures of us before lowering his camera and lighting a cigarette.

Evelyn was annoyed that he was staying so far back, but I didn't mind. I knew getting covered in the press was part of changing hearts and minds, but if I was going to show up in a newspaper holding a sign that read DEFEAT THE ANTI-GAY REFERENDUM, I'd prefer that the picture be from far away.

A passing car honked its horn, but I couldn't tell which side the driver was on. I waved, anyway, then turned back before I could see him pass the opposite end of our block.

There was another crop of protestors there, and they had signs, too. HOMOSEXUALITY IS A THREAT TO THE SURVIVAL OF THE UNITED STATES and A YES VOTE ON PROP 6 IS A VOTE FOR THE SANCTITY OF THE AMERICAN FAMILY and other cheery slogans. The photographer had snapped plenty of pictures of them already.

"The debate starts in thirty minutes," Evelyn called from behind us. She'd been running back and forth all afternoon between our group of demonstrators and the makeshift campaign headquarters we'd set up by the bus. "Harvey wants everyone inside in fifteen."

"Got it," Tammy called back. She was standing next to me, holding a sign she'd made. It read WE ARE YOUR CHILDREN on one side, and on the other, she'd painted two overlapping blue-and-purple women symbols. "Is he coming out for the cameras?"

"No." Evelyn wound through the group toward us, passing out glass bottles of soda along the way. Behind us, people were starting to come up the walk toward the gym. Regular people, here for the debate. I wondered if they were with us or against us. "He's in with the students. A dozen stayed after school to talk to him in the library, and the music teacher, too."

I wondered if I'd have the nerve to stay after school and meet Harvey Milk in the library. Not that it mattered, since my school would never let him inside in the first place.

I do hope I'd have the nerve, though.

"Well, if he's not coming, we have to do something to get the press's attention," Tammy muttered. "The story's going to be all about the other side."

I saw what she meant. The photographer had crossed to the opposite end of the lawn again, and now he was snapping photos of a scowling middle-aged woman in a blue floral dress, holding a sign that said MY CHILDREN HAVE THE RIGHT TO GROW UP IN A DECENT COMMUNITY! YES ON 6!

Next to the photographer, another man was leaning in to talk to the woman, scribbling on a notepad. We couldn't hear them from this distance, but I'm sure she was giving that reporter lots of quotes about decency, and how we didn't know anything about it. He hadn't come over to talk to our side yet.

"I have an idea," I said as the photographer glanced up, looking around for his next shot. I bit my bottom lip and waved to get his attention. When I caught his eye, I took Tammy's hand.

She drew in a quick, sharp breath, but she caught on fast. She threaded her fingers through mine as the photographer bounded toward us, the reporter close behind him.

The lens zoomed in, and I clung to Tammy's hand that much tighter, lifting my sign so it would be easy to read. If these pictures showed up in any of the San Francisco papers, I didn't want to think about what my mom would say, let alone the nuns at school, but I ordered myself to let go of the fear.

Tammy squeezed my hand. I squeezed back—and that was when I realized I didn't have to be afraid. It had gotten to be a habit, but it was one I could break. Especially with her beside me.

I lifted my chin boldly and looked straight at the camera. I squeezed her hand again, and it felt glorious.

The photographer snapped away, his lens focused right on Tammy and me, as Lisa stepped forward and smoothly introduced herself to the reporter. He asked her why we were demonstrating and she recited the talking points against Prop 6 with poise and precision, telling him about human rights and the First Amendment and how Briggs's initiative would cost thousands of taxpayer dollars that should be spent on textbooks and school supplies instead.

I tried to make sure my face looked serious for the photos, as if I was thinking hard about the First Amendment, instead of being wholly absorbed in the sensation of holding Tammy's hand.

When the photographer finally moved on to get some shots of

Leonard and Dean, I exhaled. I thought I'd be relieved, but to my surprise, I was exhilarated.

"Well done, you two." Alex grinned. "Way to play to the press."

"That was brilliant, Sharon." Tammy beamed at me. She hadn't let go of my hand. "You're a genius. Did you see that lady's face when the reporter walked away from her? She probably—"

When Tammy pointed back to the other group of protestors, her smile faded. She jerked her hand away from mine so hard it hurt.

"That's—" Tammy stammered, her breath coming fast. "It's Carolyn."

"What?"

Then I saw her, too.

A girl about our age was walking through the group of pro-Prop 6 demonstrators. She had long red hair styled in soft Farrah Fawcett-Majors curls, and she was wearing a yellow wrap dress that probably cost more than our VW bus. She couldn't have looked more different from Tammy and me in our protest T-shirts and jeans.

"What's she doing here?" I whispered. Suddenly, the distance between their group and ours didn't seem so wide.

"No idea. But there's no chance she's here alone."

Tammy was right. A new group of people was filing in among the protestors down the lawn. A mix of teenagers and adults, all dressed in Sunday school linen and lace, passing out pamphlets and brochures.

"There's Carolyn's mother," Tammy muttered. "And Mr. and Mrs. Murdoch from the church board, and... God, half my church is here. Oh, shit—that's my sister. And my other sister, and my nephew. There's Uncle Russell, and...oh, damn it, Sharon, that's my mom..."

It wasn't hard to pick them out of the group. Behind a tall, wide older man who carried himself as though he was by far the most important person here, there was a cluster of blond women, two of them holding babies. A little blond kid toddled along behind them.

And emerging from the back of the group was Aunt Mandy, strolling toward the school in a Chanel suit and heels, her lipstick painted in such a perfectly straight line it must've been gearing up to cut someone.

"They haven't seen us." I turned back to Tammy, but she'd already gone sheet-white. My heart was pounding fast, too, but I had to stay calm. This time, I had to help her. "Move to the back of the group. You can slip away to the bus once you're out of sight. They won't ever have to know you were here."

Tammy didn't move. She didn't even blink.

I turned back to the group. Aunt Mandy was striding as quickly as ever, but she'd veered off from her original course.

She was coming our way.

"Holy shit." Peter pushed through the others until he was at our side. "Isn't that your aunt, Tammy?"

"Is it?" Alex leaned in. "God, she looks worse than you said. I'm going to go get it, in case..." Alex disappeared before I could figure out what she was talking about.

"Come on." I stepped in front of Tammy, trying to block Aunt Mandy's view. "We've got to hide you—"

"Pardon me, sir." Aunt Mandy's simpering voice was just a few feet away, and the sound of it brought my fear racing back. She was talking to the reporter, but we might as well have been in my living room all over again, with Aunt Mandy pouring poison in my mother's ear.

If it was that hard for me to hear her voice, I could only guess how Tammy felt.

"I want to introduce myself," she was saying. "I'm Mrs. Amanda Dale, wife of the Reverend Russell Dale from New Way Baptist

Church in Ocean Valley. I wanted to let you know that my husband and I are available for interviews to offer up the Christian viewpoint on the militant homosexual element assembled here."

The reporter replied in a low voice I couldn't make out. Aunt Mandy clearly hadn't seen Tammy yet, but the distance between them was far too short, and Tammy's cheeks were pale.

Maybe she was in shock. Maybe I should push her to the back of the group.

I glanced at Peter, trying to silently ask his opinion, but before I could do anything Tammy darted past me. The reporter was still talking, but Aunt Mandy's eyes flicked over in our direction.

Just as the reporter turned to the photographer, Tammy stepped out into full view. Aunt Mandy's eyes widened, her lips narrowing.

The rest of our group went quiet. I didn't hear the pro-Prop 6 protesters making much noise, either. Until—

"Tammy?" The voice came across a distance, but the word was clear. Carolyn sounded as if she'd just seen someone climb out of a grave. "Is that you? What happened to your hair?"

Tammy glanced in Carolyn's direction, then looked away fast. Her gaze landed on the group of blond women, and I caught the moment she made eye contact with her mother for the first time.

Mrs. Larson held Tammy's gaze. She looked scared, disappointed, and remorseful, all at the same time. It wasn't all that different from the way my own mother looked at me this morning.

That woman at Gay Freedom Day, with the I LOVE MY GAY SON sign—could she possibly be real? Are there mothers like that? Or is that only a fairy tale kids like us want to believe?

"Tammy." Aunt Mandy abandoned the reporter—who as far as I could tell wasn't that interested in talking to her, anyway—and charged toward us, that sick smile sliding onto her face. She swept her gaze right past Peter and me, as though we were insects she didn't need to bother stepping on. "I hope you aren't here to cause trouble for your mother."

Tammy stared, her breath coming in heaves. Aunt Mandy glanced around, as though realizing for the first time that the rest of us could hear her, too.

"You know, your uncle and I never stopped praying for your salvation." Her smile widened. She and Tammy were the same height, but only because Aunt Mandy was wearing heels. "It may not be too late for you to accept God's love."

"What's going on?" The new voice sounded jarringly similar to Tammy's. It was her mother, hurrying up to stand beside Carolyn. The younger blond women—Tammy's sisters—were following behind her. "Tammy? You...you're here?"

"Mom." Tammy's voice was a tiny squeak. Her lip trembled, her eyes softening.

"You ran away. We didn't know— We didn't mean to— After what happened, we..."

Mrs. Larson trailed off, and Tammy shook her head. I don't think she could've spoken if she'd wanted to.

"I must say..." Aunt Mandy's voice rose up, sensing her advantage in Tammy's paralysis. "Your friends here, these avowed sinners—" she glanced at me again for the briefest of seconds, and my fists clenched at my sides "—they're weak. It's sad, really. They're selfish, focusing solely on pleasure, because they don't understand the sacrifices we Christians have made. But you know better, Tammy."

"Yeah, well, if you want, we can pray for your salvation next. If you think God'll listen to a bunch of avowed sinners, I mean."

Everyone froze. Peter turned toward me, slowly.

It took me a long moment to realize I'd said that out loud.

I bit my lip. They were all looking at me now.

Tammy. Her mom. Aunt Mandy. My friends behind me. The reporter and photographer were watching, too.

I lifted my chin.

"You're the one who's selfish." I locked my gaze on Aunt Mandy. Her smile twitched. "We're out here because we believe we have the right to fall in love. You're here because you hate people who are different from you. Who do you think God would agree with?"

"Young lady, don't you dare speak His holy name," Aunt Mandy hissed. "You're talking about things you don't understand—"

I cut her off.

"Your gay niece understands love a lot better than you ever have." I raised my voice for the whole group to hear as the reporter scribbled on his pad. The camera clicked, then clicked again. "You're nothing but a bully. You want to talk about sacrifice? How about all the people here who've been cast out by their families because of who they are? You think you're the one who's given something up?"

Aunt Mandy stared at me. For once, she seemed to be at a loss for words.

In the stunned silence, Alex tapped Tammy on the shoulder. She was carefully balancing a very large object in her arms. "Hey, I brought— Do you want…?"

Alex was holding a collage. An enormous one, at least three feet across. The background was a massive black-and-white photo, a shadowy image of neat cursive handwriting on thin black lines.

It was the check register, blown up twenty times its actual size. In the foreground, set against the photo, was a drawing of a woman with perfectly coiffed hair and immaculately straight red lipstick. Her head was tipped back with laughter, and she held a pitchfork in her hand. The drawing was outlined in thin, precise lines, leaving her image transparent, so the handwriting behind her came through.

The drawing was of Mrs. Amanda Dale. That would've been obvious even if she weren't standing right next to it, but now the whole crowd was looking back and forth between the collage and Aunt Mandy, making the connection.

The line at the top of the blown-up check register read New Way Protect Our Children Fund, and below it were handwritten entries showing payment after payment. Posh Hair Lounge and Ocean Valley Golf Club were right at the top. Half a dozen lines down were five payments to K-ROY Los Angeles.

Cut-out words were pasted across the image, too, the same way Tammy had used them in the collage on my bedroom wall. Another poem, sort of. I picked out SINNER and LIAR and GREED, but the one that appeared most was HYPOCRITE. It popped up in at least three different places. Running sideways up a pitchfork tine was another set of pasted-on words: THOU SHALT NOT STEAL.

"Thanks, Alex." Tammy took the collage from her and smiled at me. "And thank you, too."

Then she turned around and lifted the collage, waving to the pro-Prop 6 protesters hovering on their end of the school lawn.

"Hey!" Tammy shouted. "If you ever donated to the New Way Protect Our Children Fund, come see what your pastor and his wife have been doing with your money!"

For a second, I thought Aunt Mandy was going to snatch the collage out of Tammy's hand, but she didn't move. Maybe she already knew she'd lost.

Carolyn's mom was the first to approach us. At first I thought she was coming to yell at Tammy, but instead she peered forward, studying the collage.

"What's that?" Tammy's mother leaned forward, too.

"Your daughter's a very lost child..." Aunt Mandy said, but now Mr. and Mrs. Murdoch from their church were stepping forward, too.

"Could you tell me what this is all about, miss?" the reporter asked, coming up to me.

"Tammy's the one you need to talk to," I told him. "Here, I'll hold this."

Peter stepped up, too, and he and I each held one end of the collage so the church members could read it for themselves while Tammy told the reporter all about the check register, promising to send him the original copies she'd kept back in San Francisco. While they talked, Mr. Murdoch went up to Aunt Mandy and said something I couldn't understand. It was clear he was furious.

I couldn't believe it. Tammy might have actually <u>won</u>.

The reporter went over to Aunt Mandy and Mr. Murdoch, which was sure to be an interesting conversation. Tammy's mother and her sisters went over to join them, too. The other members of their church were studying the collage as Tammy came up beside me.

"Thank you." She smiled, but her eyes were full of tears.

"You're the one who made this happen." I smiled back at her.

"Not true. If you hadn't said what you did, I'd still be standing there like a rabbit in headlights."

She reached out to take my hand again, even though the camera wasn't on us anymore. I gazed down at our intertwined fingers.

Tammy must've seen the surprise on my face and pulled her hand away quickly. "Sorry. I shouldn't assume, I—"

I reached out and grabbed her hand again.

"All right, Sharon," Lisa said over my left shoulder, and laughter erupted behind us. I blushed redder than I'd ever blushed before.

"It's time to go in," Evelyn called. "Sit in the front row of the bleachers if you can. We can't let the other side get all the good seats!"

Everyone moved fast. Lisa gave me the keys to the bus, and Tammy and I gingerly carried the collage over. It took us a few minutes to delicately wrap it back up so it would be ready for her exhibit tomorrow, and when we closed the trunk door and turned around, we were the only ones left outside.

"I'm still shaking," I said, lowering myself onto the back bumper. "I can't believe how intense that got."

She held out her hand, showing me her goose bumps. "I can't believe we did that. I was so scared when I saw my mom watching."

"You were incredible. Now it's going to be in the paper and everything. The whole world will know about your aunt and uncle."

"I hope they print what you said, too." She grinned and leaned back next to me. "Especially the part about sacrifice. And the part about love."

"Right. Love."

I turned and met Tammy's eyes. She didn't look away.

I bit my lip. "I, um. There's something I want to give you, but it's in my backpack. In the bus. It's kind of crumpled up, but I hope you can still read it. Not right now, though. Maybe I can get it for you after the debate and you can read it on the ride home tomorrow."

She glanced behind us at the bus. "You've got to know I want to skip the entire debate and go get it right this second."

I laughed. "No, don't. We should get inside."

"Okay." She hadn't looked away from my face once. She hadn't stopped smiling, either. "If you say so."

"Yeah. I..." I kept looking back and forth, from her eyes to her lips.

It wasn't that I wanted to know how it felt to kiss a girl. It was that I wanted to know how it felt to kiss <u>her</u>.

"I..." I blushed again. "I, um..."

Her lips parted. "You what?"

"I...love you." Oh, God, I said it. I said it, and it felt better than anything else has ever felt. "I'm in love with you."

The smile that spread across her face felt even better. "I'm in love with you, too."

Then I kissed her. And I finally understand all those songs I didn't get before.

This is what people mean when they write songs about love.

This feeling. This perfect, overwhelming knowledge that everything is finally exactly right.

Yours,
Sharon

ELECTION NIGHT, 1978

Tuesday, November 7, 1978

Dear Harvey,

Can you believe it???

I can't! It doesn't feel real.

I'm back home now writing this, but I was at Sharon's when we got the news. It was the perfect place to be. Usually I hate having to sneak around, but tonight it was worth it. Being with her when something like this happens is worth a little deception.

"Channel Five hasn't said anything on Prop 6 yet." Peter's voice was hard to make out through the phone line, thanks to all the people talking in the room behind him. The fact that Sharon and I were both trying to listen from the same phone, huddled on the couch with the receiver jammed against our ears, didn't help, either.

"Switch to Channel Seven," Sharon told him. She'd refused to let us turn on the election coverage since I got there, partly because her mom was asleep upstairs and we had to be quiet, but probably also because she was nervous. It was easier to hear it secondhand from Peter than straight from the TV. "Don't bother with Eleven. Mom had it on earlier and they were only talking about the stupid governor's race."

While we sat squashed together in Sharon's living room, her brother, ironically, was at my house, with my roommates and some of his, too. When I'd left the Mission every house had a TV blaring. Every gay and bi person in the entire state of California was in front of a screen right now, collectively biting their nails to shreds.

Well, except Sharon and me. But being with her was better than being in front of a hundred screens.

"We only need to win San Francisco," I said. It's the same refrain Evelyn and Lisa keep repeating. I don't know if Sharon found it comforting—I didn't—but it was all we had to hold on to. Winning San Francisco would definitely be good, but we'd need the rest of the state to stop Briggs's initiative from becoming law.

Still, we'd done absolutely everything we could. The bookstore crew had gone on a dozen bus trips to knock on doors, and we'd folded so many pamphlets my paper cuts would probably never fully heal.

Sharon had managed to join us a few more times. Her mother had partially ungrounded her a month after we got back from the debate, but her new curfew was strict, so trips to our part of town were rare. Fortunately, we've gone back to writing each other letters every other day, and I've gotten good at sneaking in through a window off her kitchen.

But if things work out the way we hope, we might not have to do it much longer. Peter's coming over to their house for Thanksgiving, and he and Sharon are planning to just start talking about Dean and me during dinner, as though there's nothing strange about it. Even though she's been keeping my letters hidden, Sharon has a feeling her mom knows about us, and Peter and Dean, too, but they never talk about it. Sharon and Peter both think it's time to start. They don't think she wants to keep fighting. The whole family's had enough of that for three lifetimes.

Maybe someday it'll seem normal for all of us to talk about our lives. To live our lives. Maybe next Thanksgiving I can come over and have dinner with them, without having to hide the truth.

But even if her mom does try to stop us, she can't do it forever. We'll both be eighteen next year.

"If we can beat Prop 6 here, the rest of the state will follow when it's ready," I said when things had been quiet too long, even though we all knew I was only parroting Evelyn again.

"I want to beat Prop 6 <u>everywhere</u>," Sharon said.

"Don't we all." Peter paused through the phone. "Wait— wait, they're getting ready to say something."

"What?" Sharon said, way too loud.

"Shush!" I told her.

"Hey, everybody!" Peter called into the room behind him. "Shut up so we can hear!"

"Oh, my God." I couldn't handle the tension. "What are they saying? Tell us what they're—"

"They—wait— They're saying—" Peter choked on the words.

"WE <u>WON</u>!" someone shouted in the room behind him, loud enough for us to hear. I think it was Alex. "We fucking <u>won</u>!"

"<u>What?</u>" I couldn't believe it. "Peter, what did it say? We won San Francisco?"

"We won L.A.—we won <u>California</u>!" There were tears in his voice. "Prop 6 is <u>done</u>!"

I started laughing, from shock and from happiness. "Really!?"

"Hell <u>yeah</u>!" Sharon cried. I could hear whoops and cheers coming from the room behind Peter.

Oh, my God, oh, my God, this was <u>real</u>!

"Three to two against!" Peter shouted. "It's over!"

We did it, Harvey!!!

"Oh, my <u>God</u>!" I dropped the phone, leaped off the couch and started jumping up and down in the middle of the living room carpet. Sharon leaped up and started jumping, too.

"Oh, my gosh! Oh, my gosh!"

"We won, we won, we <u>won</u>!" I grabbed her and spun her in a circle, both of us being way too loud and neither of us caring. "I can't believe it. I can't believe it!"

"Me neither!" Her voice was giddily high. Shrieks were coming from the receiver where we'd dropped it on the couch, but we didn't bother to pick it up.

"God, remember all those nights when they beat us?" I wrapped my arms tight around her waist, speaking into her ear, trying to keep my voice soft even though I wanted to scream in triumph. "How it always seemed like the end of the world?"

She nodded fervently. "Now here we are!"

"I'm <u>so happy</u> right now."

I kissed her. I was smiling so big, my whole body filled with such joy. It was as if we were having our first kiss all over again, outside that high-school gym with Harvey waiting inside.

I pulled back just long enough to say, "I love you so much." Then I leaned down to kiss her again.

"I need to write you a letter," she said, the next time we broke apart. "As soon as you leave."

I laughed. "What are you going to put in a letter that you haven't already said tonight?"

"A million things. There's so much going through my head right now, and for the first time, it's all <u>good</u>."

I smiled. "Me, too."

"It's going to be all right, isn't it? Things are going to keep getting better."

"Yeah." I listened to the tinny cheers and whoops pouring from the phone. I shut my eyes and pictured our friends grinning and celebrating. All that love in one room.

When I opened them, I saw all the love in this room, right here, even though it was only Sharon and me.

"Yeah," I said again. "Yeah. I think they are."

Peace, love & hope,
Tammy

★ ★ ★ ★ ★

ACKNOWLEDGMENTS

"All the forces in the world are not so powerful as an idea whose time has come."

That's a translation of a Victor Hugo quote. Harvey Milk copied it out by hand and hung it on his office wall.

After a series of groundbreaking protests in the 1950s and 60s, including at New York's Stonewall Inn, as well as earlier demonstrations at Compton's Cafeteria in San Francisco, Cooper Do-nuts in Los Angeles, and other sites, the movement for lesbian, gay, bisexual, transgender, queer, and questioning equality was on the cusp of a breakthrough. The time had come. By the mid-70s, you could almost feel it in the air.

Or so I've heard. I was a teen of the 1990s, but the collective memory of the '70s hung heavy in my high-school days, from the fashion to the music to the language. But I was well beyond my teen years when I truly learned about this era and the history of the movement to which I owe so much. Harvey Milk and legions of other activists, including Sally Gearhart, Marsha P. Johnson, Frank Kameny, and countless others put their own lives on the line because they had faith that their work would lead to a better future for the generations that came after them.

I ended Sharon and Tammy's story on a high note, with the defeat of Proposition 6 in California—a major event in a time when ballot-box victories for the LGBT rights movement were virtually unheard of—but there were many, many ups and downs during this period, just like we're seeing today. Only weeks after the Prop 6 win, Harvey Milk was assassinated, along with San Francisco Mayor George Moscone. The killer was Dan White, who'd served alongside Milk on the Board of Supervisors. Although White confessed to the crimes and there was plenty of evidence that they were premeditated, he was ultimately convicted of voluntary manslaughter rather than first-degree murder. Riots and violent police raids on the Castro followed the announcement of the verdict.

For all the movement's successes, it was clear there remained a lot of work to do, and that's still the case today. Reports of hate crimes against the LGBT community are rising, with transgender women of color at a particularly high risk. Meanwhile, the Trump administration has banned transgender people from serving in the military, and dozens of states continue to allow people to be fired or lose their housing based on their sexual orientation or gender identity. For all the positive changes we've seen in the decades since Harvey Milk's death, we still have so much more to accomplish to ensure that LGBT people and other marginalized communities aren't subject to violence and discrimination.

The idea for *Music from Another World* came about as I reflected on this history, particularly in light of the activism we're seeing around us right now as a new and powerful generation fights back against a frighteningly emboldened conservative movement.

When I started this book, I turned first to researching the

activists working during the 1970s against odds that must have truly seemed impossible. I'm very grateful to the journalist Randy Shilts, whose biography of Harvey Milk, *The Mayor of Castro Street*, was one of my most helpful reference books as I was writing. Thanks also to activist Cleve Jones for his memoir, *When We Rise*, and to Lisa McGirr, the author of *Suburban Warriors*, a fascinating account of the conservative movement in Orange County, California.

Thanks, as well, to the readers of early drafts of *Music from Another World*, including Anna-Marie McLemore, Jennie Kendrick, and Nicole Overton. You helped to improve this book more than I can say. Thank you to my agent, Jim McCarthy, who's stood by me through queer story after queer story and offered amazing insights every time. Thank you to my editors, T.S. Ferguson and Lauren Smulski, and to Kate Studer, for helping to make this book so much better than its first iteration, and to Kathleen Oudit for designing another truly spectacular cover. And thank you to the rest of the team at HarperCollins who helped to put this book out into the world, including Laura Gianino, Bess Braswell, Connolly Bottum, Brittany Mitchell, John Oberholtzer, and Allison Draper.

Thank you to Patti Smith, whose music went totally over my head when I was in high school but still impressed itself upon me so deeply that when I needed to call on it to create these characters, it was right there. Thank you, too, to the classic rock station in my hometown, which provided me with a musical education that I never imagined would come in handy until I sat down to write this book.

And most of all, thank you, as always, to Julia, and to Darcy. For everything there is to be thankful for.